HAUNTED

By

Rebecca Guy

Also By Rebecca Guy:

Ruin
Shattered

For my ghosthunting pals, Sarah and Hannah, and for
all the avid ghosthunters out there.

Here's to finding out the truth!

Author note.

You may or may not know that Spookbuddy is based on the latest fad of ghost hunting equipment which form the guise of dolls and teddy bears. The actual teddy bear is called Boobuddy, and although Spookbuddy is loosely based on this bear, please bear in mind that I have never used Boobuddy when ghost hunting, and don't presume that he is anywhere near as unruly as Spookbuddy! I have, however, used Boobuddy's little brother which is basically an EMF meter, and a very cute one. (He also behaved exactly as he was supposed to, and didn't tell us to go home - bonus points for that.)

The way Spookbuddy performs in this book is in no way linked to the way the real Boobuddy performs, or how he would be used in a ghost hunting session. Spookbuddy is an entirely fictional character for the purpose of this book only. Any resemblance to the way the real Boobuddy performs is completely coincidental.

Finally, do I want my own Boobuddy to ghost hunt with? Hell Yes!

Rebecca Guy 2021

PROLOGUE

I wasn't there when my sister died. I was two miles away at St Mary's Catholic Primary School. We weren't a religious family, but this was a 'good' school, and so I was to learn about Jesus by day and get scoffed at each night when I told my parents what I had learned. I learned to avoid talking about religious stuff fast. I wasn't sure what I believed anyway.

I still remember the lesson I was in when my dad came to collect me. Something BAD had happened and I was to go home. I still remember Mrs Feeney's reaction.

Get your coat dear, we'll see you when you feel up to it.

I didn't understand. I felt FINE, and I loved school. I always felt UP TO IT. We had been making snowflakes out of coloured paper; I had to have help to attach the string because my fingers fumbled with the small hole. They were for the Christmas tree at home. My snowflakes hung on our tree for so long that they were discoloured and dusty before they were eventually thrown away. I remember that day too.

Thursday 25th June.

It was the 25th of June before mum finally let a neighbour, Mrs Grey, persuade her to take the tree down and move the presents. Mine were still there among Evie's, the bright wrapping paper hidden under a layer of dust. Mrs Grey put the tree and presents in the loft. I think they're still there.

Dad had disappeared by then. He had walked out in February of that year. He had donned his too-large suit and coat and left for work with a sad smile, as he always did.

He kissed my cheek and held onto my shoulders. 'See you later, Munchkin. Keep your chin up.' Just as he always did.

And I lift my chin and giggled before he squeezed me in a tight hug. As he always did. Our little ritual since Evie had GONE.

That morning he broke the ritual. As he squeezed, he murmured something in my ear and I frowned, puzzled as he picked up his laptop bag and left the house.

'Take care, Meredith.'

Take care of what?

Then he broke the ritual again. He didn't come home.

In fact, he never came home. I decided that he must have meant take care of mum, who wasn't doing so well. And so that's what I tried to do.

I say 'tried' because all mum did back then was sit on the couch and stare at a certain brick on the surround of the old electric fireplace. I brought her crisps and yoghurt to eat, orange juice to drink, but everything was left untouched. I asked her what she needed, and what was wrong. More than once I sobbed, draped over her knees as she sat, legs pressed together, eyes glazed. Eventually I gave up. It was as though I didn't exist.

It was as though SHE didn't exist.

I often examined that brick to see what secret powers it held that could keep mum so captivated. I never found out, and by the time she had broken free of its hold, she denied knowing anything about the brick, or its powers. I avoided looking at it after that, just in case it got me too.

I learned to fend for myself, thinking often of dad's last words. TAKE CARE. Maybe he meant to take care of me as mum was paralyzed by the brick. So I did.

I got myself up and dressed every morning. I made myself breakfast, I did my own packed lunch, and then I walked two miles to school every day and two miles home again. When the food ran low, I used money from mum's purse to get supplies from the corner shop. When the money ran low, I used the plastic money card that mum put into the machine. I knew the number. Mum had always picked me up when she used the CASH MACHINE at the back of The Co-op in case there were any BAD MEN around. As I grew bigger, she simply put an arm around me, drawing me close to the number pad. I always watched her punch the number in, and I corrected her every time she shouted at the machine.

'No mummy, you did it wrong, it's a six not a three.'

Some days, if there was no one else around, she let me punch the number in for her. I was only to press ten pounds each time she allowed me to do the machine. And so, thinking that must be the children's amount, that's what I got each time I went. I don't know why nobody stopped me. There were never masses of people around, but if there was someone waiting, I would join the line as mum had done, and take my turn when it came round.

Those ten pounds never ran out, although I was getting some out every day for SUPPLIES. Later I found that dad had been putting money into the account each month since he had WALKED OUT. I didn't know whether to love him or hate him for it.

I managed. Mrs Grey helped me with lots once she knew how bad the fireplace had hold of mum. She checked on me all the time, sometimes giving me a lift to school, sometimes helping to get the GROCERIES, and helping me to clean.

She tried to talk to mum often, but with NO JOY. She asked where dad had gone, and I told her he hadn't come back from work since 12th February. She helped a lot after that. The teachers at school were kind too, packing me food to take home because of my PROBLEMS. They thought it was a TERRIBLE SHAME for me and mum, and that things would pick up, they just had to help us through this AWFUL ORDEAL. It would all turn out okay in the end.

But nothing would turn out okay in the end.

I was just six years old when my sister Evie died, seven when the fireplace gave up its hold on mum, and people whispered that she had TURNED TO DRINK. Eight when dad's money finally stopped, and he was found swinging from the rafters of an old barn in Cornwall, and Nine when Evie came home.

I wasn't there when my sister died, but it was my fault she came back.

CHAPTER ONE

The air became thick and oppressive, and Meredith Knight held her breath as she clasped the hands of the people on either side of her. The camera panned around the table, taking in the strained faces of its four occupants.

'It's getting cold,' Helen said next to Meredith, 'Do you feel it?'

'Temperature has dropped three degrees.' said Steve Gittins, soundman, also in charge of the temperature and EMF meter at this sitting.

Meredith took a breath. The cold circled her legs under the table, coiling like snakes.

'Let's do it then. You know the drill, left index fingers on the glass, right hands on the table where the camera can see them.'

With serious faces, the four unlinked hands and placed their fingers lightly on the glass in the middle of the table in front of them. Helen was last, her nerves getting the better of her. She hadn't wanted to take part in this experiment, but the director had asserted his authority firmly—*do you want to work on this show or not?*

Meredith turned to smile and nod lightly at her. Helen met her eyes and with a small smile of her own placed a trembling finger to the glass. Meredith swallowed hard, pressure increasing around her. Steve had said no more, but she was sure the temperature must have lost a further couple of degrees.

'Are there any spirits here that wish to communicate with us?' she said. She waited a beat before continuing.

'Come forward, we're listening, we don't mean you any harm.'

The room was silent, only the whir of the camera as it panned in, the shuffle of cable as Matt traversed the tight dark space, training the camera on the glass, making sure to get everybody's hands in shot as he had been briefed.

'Spirits, if you're here, could you move the glass for us?'

'Temperature has dropped a further seven degrees, we're now at minus one,' Steve said.

Meredith glanced at Gwen Stanford, the programme's historian, sat opposite. In front of Gwen's calm face, her breath came in clouds and Meredith felt a trickle of excitement. Could this be it? Something real? This room was windowless and sealed, and although the old Manse was ancient and drafty, could this small space with all the team squashed inside really drop so cold in such a short space of time?

'We're here for you,' She said again, 'If a spirit has joined us, please could you use our energy to move the—'

Meredith cut off as the glass rocked. Just a fraction, but most definitely movement.

'Did you get that Matt?' Meredith said.

The cameraman nodded, aiming the camera at her face. 'I think so,' he whispered back, before panning the table again, closing the shot right in on the glass.

Meredith took a shaky breath. There was a spirit wishing to talk, apparently. Not having spoken to one before, and not wanting to lose this one, she nodded to Donald Gritt, the team's psychic medium.

'Do you want to lead?'

Donald closed his eyes, lifting his chin, and drawing his bushy white eyebrows together importantly. The table waited silently, the glass still.

'It's the girl,' he finally said, 'she's here, she wants to communicate with you Meredith. You lead.'

All eyes turned to Meredith, and she felt the camera train on her face. Heart hammering in her chest, her mind went instantly blank. She struggled to think of anything she was supposed to say.

Get a grip, Meredith, you're on camera. The girl wants to speak to you, so treat her like any other child. The only difference is that this one is dead. Just a minor detail, right?

'Okay.' she said, feeling a little calmer. 'Well, thank you for moving the glass, I know it must have taken enormous effort. I'll try to keep it simple. Please could you slide the glass to the left for yes, and right for no?'

The group demonstrated with the upturned glass, pushing it to the left and right before coming back to the centre of the table. The glass remained still, but these things took patience. No one moved. Meredith's heart raced. Should she address the spirit girl by name?

There's nothing to lose.

'Cara, sweetie? Is that you trying to come through to us?'

There was a period of silence where Meredith thought they had missed their chance, but then the glass tipped a little and plopped back down onto the wood. Meredith almost grinned and whooped for joy—until she remembered she was on camera.

'Thank you, Cara.' she said calmly, 'Do you understand the instructions? Left for yes, right for no?'

The glass slid slowly left and Meredith caught Donald's eye with a smile. He nodded back reassuringly as Gwen confirmed the yes out loud.

'You're doing really well, Cara, bring the glass back to the centre if you can please.'

The glass slid back, and Meredith gave herself an internal high five. Every finger on top of the glass rest lightly, Meredith had learnt to look for the whitening of the nail bed if anyone applied pressure. A subtle way of assessing if there was any foul play.

'Okay, Cara,' She said, gaining confidence, 'can you confirm for us that you are Cara Crawford, daughter of the former vicar Douglas Crawford?'

The glass slid a little and came to a stop.

'Yes.' Gwen said, for the sake of the camera.

'Fabulous,' Meredith said, struggling to keep her voice under control when all she really wanted to do was lap the table, arms in the air, giving high fives to the rest of the group. 'you're doing so well Cara. You lived here with you mother and father and four sisters? Is that right?'

There was a beat, and then the glass tipped and slid an inch to the left, before coming back to centre. Meredith nodded as Gwen confirmed.

Why have I never tried this before, this is amazing! A real live spirit—or should that be a dead spirit? Of course, it's much easier with a crew than on your own in your bedroom though, eh?

'What happened, Cara? Why can't you rest?' She said, excitement rising. This was easier than she thought.

The glass was still, and it took Meredith a moment to realise that the spirit couldn't answer with a yes or no. She tutted at her own mistake and tried again. Gwen smiled across the table.

'There was a fire wasn't there, Cara?' she asked, 'Your family was caught in the fire, is that right?'

The glass shot right with renewed energy and stopped. The silence stretched.

'No?' Gwen finally confirmed. She caught Meredith's eye with a look of confusion. It was certainly the story that Cara and her sisters had perished here in a fire in 1810 after an accident with a candle one winter evening. None of the sisters had survived. Their mother had been critically injured and left so scarred that she had become a recluse for the remainder of her life. Only their father had not been hurt. He had been at the church nearby, and by the time he had noticed the blaze the large building had been too far gone, as had his daughters. The manse had been left an empty shell for the following fifty years before being torn down and rebuilt in a sympathetic representation in 1865. Since then, as far back as 1890 until present day, there had been reports of paranormal activity and many previous investigators had tagged the presence as being that of young Cara.

'Cara, are you still here?' Meredith wanted to confirm before asking any more.

The glass moved vigorously left. Meredith nodded and looked to Gwen for instruction, but she only shrugged and looked bewildered.

'Let's ask her for more information,' Donald prompted. 'She's obviously keen for someone to know the truth.'

Meredith looked at him. The truth? And then she understood. If Cara and her sisters didn't die in the fire, then there was a discrepancy that history and other investigators had failed to grasp or listen to. Meredith's heart flipped and began to thud. Not only was she on the cusp of learning something that no one else knew about young Cara's fate, but she was apparently talking to an actual ghost, and communicating without the usual debilitating fear!

She looked back at the glass to speak to Cara, as though the little girl herself was trapped inside. She realised that it was silly, Cara could be anywhere in the room and she probably hadn't chosen to sit in a glass, but she didn't know where else to look.

'Cara, honey, are you saying that you didn't die in the fire?'

The glass tipped and slid left. Gwen confirmed the yes, now with a look of surprise that matched Meredith's own.

'Okay, but there *was* a fire. We know that from past records, and we know that they found the bodies of you and your sisters in the ash, is that correct?'

Movement. Confirmation. Yes.

Intrigued, Meredith continued quickly, eager to get to the truth of this poor girl's end. Goosebumps littered her arms, joining the tingling that ran up and down them. In a talk before filming, Donald had told her that this was Meredith's sign of a presence around her, or of a small psychic shift. Meredith had felt it before, a few times, but then she hadn't known what it was, and it hadn't gone so well.

'Right, thank you, Cara, you're doing really well. So, tell me, did you die in the fire?'

The glass sat unmoving, and Meredith felt a chill creep down her spine.

'Cara? Can—'

The glass juttered slowly right, knocking against the tabletop.

'So, the fire was after you died.' Meredith murmured with surprise, more to herself than the entity, but Cara responded by moving the glass, anyway. Yes.

Something is very wrong with this tale. Very wrong indeed.

She took in a breath. 'Cara, honey, if the fire broke out afterward, how did you die, and who the hell started the fire?'

There was silence, and then Meredith rolled her eyes, remembering the yes and no system again.

'Was there an accident, Cara?'

A slide right, confirmation, no accident. The room was so cold now Meredith felt she was sitting at the heart of the Arctic circle. She shuddered even in her padded jacket and wondered whether it was more the implication than the chill of the air. Helen was whimpering quietly beside her. Meredith grabbed her cold free hand in her own on the table.

'What happened Cara,' She said. 'Were you and your sisters hurt?'

Movement. Confirmation. Yes.

Meredith's breath caught in her throat. She had a feeling she knew why five-year-old Cara Crawford walked these halls in misery. She also had a feeling she knew why her father was also said to stalk the Manse's rooms, angry and menacing. History said that he was angry at himself for not being able to save his girls, but Meredith thought it was worse than that. A lot worse.

'Were you murdered, Cara? You and your sisters?'

The glass shook and toppled violently, before making a huge fast circle around the table, leaving its four energy hosts bewildered. This was a first for the team, at their very first location. A seemingly real, and incredibly strong, paranormal connection.

The glass came to a stop, but it shook and trembled under their fingers as though powered with an energy of its own. As adrenaline flooded through her, Meredith thought of all she had learned about how hard it was for a spirit to move something physical. This was a little girl who was desperate to have her story heard for sure.

'Thank you, Cara, we appreciate all you're doing.'

The glass trembled, and Meredith caught movement from the corner of her eye. Her stomach flipped. Then she realised it was Kevin Spalding –director extraordinaire with extraordinarily bad timing—his hand performing his 'wind it up' sign. Meredith rolled her eyes. Could he be any more annoying? She knew that he liked to run a tight ship, and to run on a precise schedule, but wrapping up now would be stupid. He would lose valuable, priceless footage for the show, and poor Cara wanted to talk. More than that, Meredith wanted to honour hearing her story.

Looking straight at Kevin, Meredith shook her head firmly, and pressed on. Surely, they were almost done now, anyway. Ten more minutes wouldn't hurt.

'Cara, can you tell us—'

The table suddenly tipped, two legs screeching across the floor as the other two lift into the air. The glass flew violently, smashing against the wall between Meredith and Helen in a shower of lethal sparkles. It missed Meredith's face by inches as she jumped up, pulling Helen out of the way by the neck of her jumper. The table crashed into their empty chairs.

'It's the father!' Donald hollered from his seat, where he

and Gwen were still sitting, unmoved, the table in front of them gone.

The lights flickered as Helen's high-pitched scream reverberated around the room. She sank to the floor, hands over her ears, knuckles white. Amid the chaos Meredith wondered how the hell she was supposed to get control of the situation, and then Donald shouted again, making her jump, and sending ice down her spine.

'The father! It's the father! What do you want with us, Crawford?' He cried.

Donald wailed, and then moaned, and then sank to the floor, his eyes rolling as he passed out. A horrified looking Gwen snapped her head to Kevin, who was now making his 'continue on' sign with no worry about schedule, but Meredith was worried, and now Gwen was screaming too.

'We need to stop shooting,' she shouted to Kevin, 'we're antagonising him. Someone will get hurt!'

An icy wind whipped by her, taking the breath from her mouth as she spoke, and a low roar filled the room.

Kevin was making rolling motions to Matt and Steve, who were forced to keep recording through the commotion. After all, this was what the show was about, trying to capture the paranormal. Meredith floundered, she had no idea what to do with this malevolent spirit, Donald was passed out on the floor, Gwen and Helen were both hysterical, Matt and Steve were busy recording, matching looks of shock on their faces. Busy recording her, looking like a very flustered and out-of-control parapsychologist, she thought, as Helen's screams reached a pitch so high that Meredith thought there just may be a large gathering of dogs outside the manse right now.

Flustered, she swung to Kevin for guidance, and he gestured at her wildly. His meaning was clear. Do something and do it now.

Feeling as though she were in a vortex, the storm swirled around Meredith. Wind, screams, shouts, and somehow the tinkling of glass as it still fell to the floor. Everything was moving in slow motion. Acting on instinct, Meredith grabbed the small silver cross hanging on a chain around her neck, and held it aloft, as high as it would go, as she turned in circles.

'Leave us alone, Mr Crawford!' She yelled. 'You can't hurt us and we're not afraid of you. I command you to leave us. We know what you've done, and we will expose your secret if you don't leave us alone this instant! Go from here, leave us, now!'

The room fell instantly silent. The wind stopped, the roar stopped, and Gwen stopped, passing out on top of Donald with a low moan. Even Helen was only whimpering, the strength of Meredith's shout quieting her into submission.

Meredith sank to the floor, putting a firm arm around the terrified twenty-one-year-old as the silence thundered around them. Her heart galloped as adrenaline coursed through her veins. She felt that she was in a dream, a nightmare that she would wake from at any moment… and then Kevin's voice piped up from the corner.

'Aaaaand cut. Well done ladies and gentlemen, with the footage we shot yesterday I think that's a wrap for Moweth Manor. And God knows it will be nice to get out of this blessed room and into bed, quite claustrophobic. I'll leave you folks to pack up and see you tomorrow at 10am sharp for a brief on the next location before we move on.'

CHAPTER TWO

Sat around the table in Kevin Spalding's hotel room—or should that be suite—things were a lot calmer than they had been the night before; although not getting to bed until 6am when a terrified Helen had finally calmed enough to leave her room was not doing much for Meredith's mood. She was tired and grouchy, and she knew she wouldn't be able to hold her tongue after a night of sitting on Kevin's reaction to last night's events. Poor Helen had sobbed and shook for hours. They may be a crew, and they may be making a television show, but they were all real people with real feelings, in an extreme and stressful situation.

Meredith picked at the skin on her forefinger as Kevin discussed the plans for the next location, Lynton Castle, as though last night hadn't happened. He laid out plans of the building on the table and went through the rooms it had been agreed they would use, outlining how they would rig them ready for the investigation tomorrow night.

Today would comprise going back to Moweth Manor, getting reactions from the crew back at the scene, and having a final chat with the Manor's occupants before they left. At 3pm they would travel to the tiny village of Lynton, two hours north, and throw their things into more hotel rooms before travelling to Lynton castle to meet the family, go over the schedule, and prepare for the following evening.

Gwen would follow up on the history to add to the knowledge she had already gained from books and the internet. Donald would complete a walk-through to see if he could pick up on energy in any particular rooms (much to Kevin's annoyance) while Helen and Meredith would be shown the rooms that they would conduct investigations in—regardless of anything extra Donald picked up. That information would be dismissed, as had been the incident at Moweth.

Steve and Matt would set up and check the equipment, placing cameras and microphones in specific places throughout the rooms to add to the handheld footage that Matt would capture. Meredith and Helen would go through the script detailing where they would be and when, and the activities they would perform in each location.

Meredith had thought it would be better to feel out each location and choose an activity or device to communicate accordingly, but when she pressed Kevin about it, he had shut her down. It was essential he know what they were doing at any given moment with approximate timings so they could start at 10pm and finish on schedule at 2am as smoothly as possible. It seemed forced, but after their first location going so well, it seemed the spirits weren't too bothered about his schedule.

Last night's investigation still made her skin tingle with fear and exhilaration. After only two nights in one of Scotland's most haunted locations, she'd already had her first 'communication' with a spirit and shouted loudly at subsequent spirit's angry father. It seemed a little unreal in the daylight this morning, so dream-like that she knew the only way she could believe it had happened would be to watch the show.

She frowned as something flapped in front of her face, bringing her focus back to Kevin's room and the meeting. The flapping thing was attached to Steve Gittins she thought with amusement—until she saw it was his hand. She reddened as she saw everyone looking at her.

'Woo hoo, earth to Meredith, come in Meredith.' Steve laughed as Meredith blinked. He jerked a thumb in her direction. 'It's okay everyone, I think she's faking, she's not dead. Merely asleep. We don't need the EMF and the Ouija just yet! She's alive!'

Meredith gave a sheepish smile as the chuckles rippled

around the table. The only person not looking amused was Mr Big Shot Spalding. He looked less than impressed.

'Meredith, so glad you could join us. Anything going on in there that I should know about, or is it just that you already know everything and need not listen? Maybe you're the real psychic in the room, or maybe you're just ignorant? Which is it to be?'

Donald swung his head to Kevin.

'I'm not sure that was—' He began, but Kevin raised a hand, cutting him off.

'Donald, I really don't want to get into a silly argument now. We're on a schedule. You know what I meant.'

Donald looked back down at the papers on the table, face red under his white beard.

'I have never faked anything in my life.' He muttered.

Kevin either didn't hear or didn't want to respond. He gathered up the papers, shuffling them into a rudimentary pile before looking back to Meredith.

'Well, now is the point that I normally summarise the meeting, make sure you all know where we go from here, but I think we have someone better qualified. Meredith, would you like to take us through the day's events please?'

Meredith felt herself redden again.

'What?'

Kevin pat a hand onto the papers with a smile that said he would happily push her into muck and rub her nose into it. Hard.

He looked at his watch.

'You have a minute to summarise. Go ahead, we need to be on the road in five.'

He looked at her with an air of calm that was infuriating. Tired, and not in the mood for games, she felt the anger surge through her before she had a chance to check it.

'That's not my job, it's yours,' She spat, 'And if I wasn't so tired and freaked out after last night's events maybe I would be able to focus!'

Kevin's eyebrows twitched, and a small smile crossed his thin lips.

'Tired and freaked out? We're making a ghost show, darling, what would you like me to do? Tell the little ghosties to tone down their scariness? Investigate in the daylight? I'm afraid the ghosties are usually asleep then. Tired is the name of the game, it's only eight weeks, if you can't cope you shouldn't have pushed for the job.'

Meredith huffed.

'I can cope with tired, what I can't cope with is the attitude of the person who is supposed to be watching over these shoots. You have a crew of people. Real people. And what we went through last night was just not normal—'

'Nope, it was *para*-normal!' Steve let out a hoot and stood, laughing loudly at his own joke. His long frizzy beard touched the top of the ghostbusters ghost trapped in the red circle on his t-shirt, giving it a ridiculous new hair style as its backside bobbed against the top of Steve's protruding gut. Even the ghost, with its new hair, and looking for all the world like it was riding a space hopper as it bounced, understood how inappropriate the comment had been. Its mouth sat aghast in a round 'o', eyebrows raised, hands out in horror.

Steve's laughter fell away as no one joined in with his mirth. Only Meredith and Kevin were looking at Steve, the others focused their gazes away from each other. Helen squirmed uncomfortably next to her.

'It wasn't normal,' Meredith repeated, looking back to Kevin as Steve sat down. 'It was an unusual situation. I wasn't prepared for that level of contact on our second investigation. The only person who could help was lying on the floor after telling me a violent entity was in the room. It scared me Kevin, I didn't know what to do with an angry spirit. I had no idea how to deal with the situation, and all you did was tell me to keep going.'

Kevin's eyes were hard, his mouth a firm line.

'Do you, or do you not, have a degree in

parapsychology?'

Meredith frowned, stumbling.

'That has nothing to do with it! I'd never *spoken* to a spirit in my life until last night. Nothing prepares you for that, and we all have to start somewhere. I needed support, I needed backup, and you did nothing!'

Kevin slapped his hands on the table, making Helen jump beside her.

'I'm not part of the show, Meredith, I can't be on camera telling you which way to go forward or how to handle a situation. Likewise, I'm hardly able to step in and say to a ghost – 'hey do you mind? We need to stop rolling while I give my presenter some advice.' The action was happening, I could do nothing. I'm not sure what the problem is anyway to be honest Meredith. You shouted at it, it left. It was hardly terrifying, was it? It didn't hurt anybody.'

'That's not the point. And for your information, some of us were hurt. The glass smashed right at the back of Helen and I for pities sake. Helen has a very real cut just behind her ear!'

Meredith was about to ask Helen to point out the plaster to him when Kevin stood, pushing in his chair, and picking up the paperwork. No one else moved. To Meredith, it seemed no one else was even breathing.

'So, what do you want to do, Meredith, sue the ghost? It's not my fault it got angry and threw a glass.'

Meredith stood, imitating Kevin's stance across the table. Minus the papers.

'It's not only the glass! The table tipped violently onto mine and Helen's chairs. If we had been sitting, our legs could have been badly bruised, it was lucky—'

'So, *what,* Meredith? Is this me you're coming at, or the ghost? Do you think the ghost has a vendetta against you? It was a ghost, it does what it does, I'm not in control. I'm here to record it for entertainment. That's all.'

Meredith fumed, her heart thundering in her ears.

'That's all? Both Donald and Gwen were passed out on the floor! Two of us had been hurt.' She flung a hand toward Helen, 'One of us was traumatised and your reaction was 'cut, thanks, I'm off to bed'? You didn't even check if we were okay? Any of us!'

'You're all fine. You're all sitting here now. Matt is the first aider for the team, if you need help go to him. I have things to do when I get back here. You lot get to go to bed, I am up prepping the day ahead. You forget that you were the one who forced the filming to carry on. I called time. You wanted to chat with the ghost. It's not my fault it blew up in your face, but it is my fortune that we got the activity we did. By that point I was already twelve minutes late getting back, thanks to you. I could do nothing more. You can look after each other, I have things to do. What was the point of me hanging around?'

'The point?' Meredith flung her hands in the air, narrowly missing smacking both Steve and Helen upside the head in an unprecedented double hit. 'The point, Mr Spalding, is that you are the boss. And being the boss means that you are not only in charge of making a hit show, but that whilst making the show you also take care of your team! Without us you're nothing. Without us, you have no show! That's the bloody point!'

Kevin smiled, but it was taut and strained.

'Oh, I'd have a show. With or without you, Meredith.' He looked around the room at each of them. 'With or without any of you. Do you see any of the others complaining?' He turned back to her. 'No, because they realise that this is just a job. A job they're getting paid for. A job where they knew they would be faced with the unusual, the frightening and the possibility of harm. That is what they signed up for. That is what you signed up for. And that is why you signed the disclaimer when you took the job.'

Meredith reeled.

'Disclaimer? I didn't sign any disclaimer. A disclaimer for

what?'

'You did. You all did. It was in the terms and conditions of employment. It was on the contract you signed, in black and white. If you didn't read it, that's your issue, not mine. Do not come up here shouting what I am and am not to do with my show. Yes, I need a cast. Do I need you? Absolutely not. There were a further hundred people out there, with far more experience, that wanted your job. I have all their contact details, right here on computer, I could replace you within the hour. You are not indispensable, Meredith. Do your job or get out and let me do mine!'

Meredith shook her head, still confused about the disclaimer.

'I didn't sign—'

'It was in the contract you signed.' He thundered, 'Do you understand, Meredith, or do I have to put you on a bus back to London?'

She shut her mouth and nodded lightly. Her veins pulsed with injustice, but she hadn't fought so hard for this job to leave after just two shoots. If the boss was going to be an asshole, then she would just have to deal with it. After all, like he said, it was only eight weeks.

'Good,' Kevin said, lowering his voice to normal. He looked around the room. 'Anyone else have anything to add?'

The murmurs around the table suggested not, and Meredith felt a little peeved that none of them had stuck up for her. Was this the way it was on all locational shoots?

'Okay, so now we have wasted a further fifteen minutes. Thank you for that Meredith, that's twenty-five minutes I should dock from your pay for your little ego trips. I will not be wasting any more time going over events for the day. Get your things. We leave for Moweth Manor right now.' He glanced at his watch, 'We'll meet there in precisely fifteen minutes. That will make it exactly 10.55am Don't be late.'

There were murmurs of agreement as he picked up his

bag and left the room. The others filed out slowly. No one said a word to Meredith, only Matt placed a hand on her back in silent communication as they left.

CHAPTER THREE

'You certainly know how to make life hard, Meredith.' Matt said as he drove. He turned to grin at her, one hand on the wheel of the SUV.

'Well, there's a fucking understatement,' Steve said from the back seat between mouthfuls of chicken sandwich and cheese crisps purchased from the petrol station a few miles back. 'Not only does she like to make her life hard, but she also likes to make ours difficult too. Christ, how I managed to get the boom mic in the wrong position all day when it was an inch from the person speaking is beyond me.'

Matt huffed a laugh.

'The mic was so low it was almost in shot! And to top you I got told how to work my camera and where I should stand for the best shots all morning.'

'I got told to speak up, even though I wasn't supposed to say anything.' Helen added.

Everyone laughed and Meredith turned to look at Steve and Helen in the back, their little stash of food between them. The Ghostbuster looked like he was being eaten by Steve's stomach folds, his hair already grown so long it completely covered his shocked face, only his hands stuck out from underneath. She smiled.

'I'm sorry guys, I guess I saw red. Anyway, I think I probably got the worst of it, I couldn't even breathe the right way.'

'That's what you get for poking the bear, Bangers.'

Meredith's mouth dropped open as Helen tittered.

'Bangers? What the hell?'

Steve chewed innocently; eyebrows raised.

'Bangers. You know like the firework? Cause that's

what you go off like when you get a bee in your bonnet. A bloody rocket.'

Meredith laughed along with Helen and Matt.

'Well, rocket would probably suffice. I thought you meant *bangers,* and I don't mean sausages!'

'Me too,' Matt said through a guffaw of laughter.

Steve swallowed and cocked his mouth as though they were mad.

'Why the hell would I call you bangers?' He grabbed at his own man boobs under his t-shirt, the ghostbuster ghost almost disappeared entirely. 'These are bigger than yours, baby. In fact, I may just start calling myself bangers.'

Meredith shook her head with a grin as Helen crumpled with laughter next to Steve. She turned to watch the dull landscape pass outside the window taking in the mountains and the scarce tops of towns and villages as they passed. Matt tapped the steering wheel along with the song on the radio as he concentrated on the road, and Helen and Steve bickered playfully in the back seat. It was a far cry from last night when Helen had been so scared that she had sobbed in Meredith's room until dawn had broken. Helen was quieter than Meredith, of that there was no question, but they were kindred spirits all the same. Both had come to this show for their own reasons, and she knew Helen wouldn't quit any more than Meredith would herself.

Helen and Steve dropped quiet, and Meredith turned to the back seats.

'How are you today, Helen? Feeling okay about the next investigation?'

Helen nodded, tucking her shoulder length mousy hair behind her ears shyly.

'I'm good,' she said meeting Meredith's gaze, 'And yeah, I'll be fine. I'm sorry about last night, I'm such a scaredy-cat. Thank you for letting me stay with you and letting me talk. I always feel okay in the day, it's the dark that gets me, but as Kevin said this morning, we can't do an investigation in the daytime can we?'

Meredith smiled.

'I don't think spirits care whether it's day or night, but I suppose for entertainment it's better to ghost hunt in the dark. Anyway, last night was no problem. I wouldn't have slept anyway; I was too wired. I meant what I said to Kevin, I was scared too, I had no idea what I was supposed to do. I always said to myself if anything happened that I couldn't handle, at least Donald is with us. He's used to this; he would be my go-to. And where was Donald when I needed him? Passed out on the bloody floor.'

Matt grinned as Meredith turned back to the front.

'It's always going to be that way, there's some law—' He clicked his fingers trying to recall.

'Sod's.' Steve said bluntly.

'What?'

'Sod's Law,' Steve and Meredith said together.

'Hey jinx,' Steve said making Meredith link little fingers and make a wish. Meredith had stopped that little ritual at around ten years old, but it seemed Steve was damned to eternal childhood. She rolled her eyes good naturedly as she turned back to the front.

She liked Steve, he was light-hearted, and although most of his jokes were bad, he did make the shoot more fun. He also had a caring side that had come out yesterday after Kevin had left, taking care of Helen and patching her up, while Matt and herself had seen to Gwen and Donald, who had both seemed shaken. Along with Helen, Donald also had a cut on his stomach from landing on a piece of the broken glass.

Meredith sighed and lay her head back against the headrest. Helen and Steve fell silent, and Matt kept his eyes on the road ahead. Some old nineties tune played on the radio, and the sun was starting to peep out from behind heavy clouds, lighting the dreary landscape, and making abstract pockets of dark on the mountains around them. Lynton was almost right at the top of the Cairngorms, just below Speybridge, which made their journey from just below Peebles around two and a half hours. The sat nav advised that they still had an hour and a half left and Meredith wondered if she would be able to grab some sleep. She closed her eyes, letting the rock of the car lull her.

* * * * *

The ghost chasing Meredith was green and very 'Slimer' like. It dipped and rose through the air as she bolted down the corridor screaming that she would tell it's secret if it didn't stop, right now! But Slimer wasn't like the angry ghost at the manse, he didn't seem to care if she told his secret—did he even have one?—She couldn't think.

He rushed toward her, roaring and falling silent in strange bursts, like he hadn't the breath to carry them on. He was almost on her when she fell with a scream. Slimer rose above her with a roar…

…and she lurched awake. Or at least she thought she was awake, but the ghost was still roaring. She frowned, confused, and glanced at the passing scenery out of the car window. And then the roar stopped.

'Steve wake you up?'

She swung to Matt, who jerked a thumb at the back where Steve snored again, long, and loud. Meredith looked round. Helen and Steve were both asleep. She would say soundly, but Steve was making enough noise to wake a hoard of pygmies over in Africa.

She looked back to Matt.

'That noise actually immersed itself in my dream. How long have we been out?'

'Only for the last fifty minutes together.'

She rubbed the sleep from her eyes and glanced at the sat nav. Thirty-five minutes to go. Steve pulled in another loud snore and she glanced back at him.

'God, Matt, I'm so sorry, you've been left alone for fifty minutes with the snore from hell.'

'Curse of the driver,' he said with a smile. 'I've travelled with Steve before. I knew it was coming eventually.'

'You worked with him on other shoots?'

'Quite a few times. Kevin tends to opt for the two of us if we're available.'

Meredith glanced at him.

'Kevin *chooses* you?'

'Yup.'

Meredith looked back out of the window.

'Well, to be honest, I don't know how you haven't jacked the job in. Or moved far, far, away. Or just hung yourself from a hotel window with a shoelace.'

Matt laughed.

'Well, I'm glad I never hung myself, Kevin is retiring after this show, there's a good chance I won't work with him again. I would have missed out on a possible fifty years of life!' He glanced at her with a grin, hazel eyes twinkling amusement under a mop of dark hair. 'and it's not been so bad. Once you're familiar with how he is and how he works, he's all right.'

'Once you know he's a thoughtless, feeling-less, moron?'

'But a clever and creative moron. I've learnt a lot from him.'

'I hope that doesn't include his lack of empathy.'

Matt chuckled.

'He's just doing his job, that's all.' He paused to turn down the heater. 'So, you have a degree in Parapsychology?'

Caught off guard at the sudden change of conversation, Meredith nodded at him as her heart accelerated.

'What does that involve?'

'Well, lots really, not just ghosts. Anything out of the ordinary, UFO's and stuff too. Metaphysics, all that kind of thing. It's interesting.'

'It is, I have to agree, Moweth has certainly been an eye

opener for me.'

Meredith found her interest piqued.

'Do you believe in ghosts, Matt?'

'No. Well, I suppose I *was* a non-believer. After last night I guess I'm on the fence.' He turned to look at her. 'What about you? Did you believe before you came here? I suppose being a parapsychologist you must have.'

Meredith swallowed and looked out of the window away from him. 'I'm not a parapsychologist, I just have a qualification. It doesn't mean I'm a different person, I just have a little more knowledge.' She said.

'Which earns you the title.'

Pursing her lips, she turned back to him with a shrug as he assessed her, narrowed eyes curious and inquisitive.

'If you say so. To answer your question... I... I'm not sure, although certain things have happened that made me ask the question. Above all, I love people's stories and I've always been curious to know if there is anything out there. You know, metaphysically. We can't be the only energy forms, can we? What if we don't leave? What if we stay on another plane after we go? What if we can still be with the people we love?'

Her thoughts drifted to her bedroom at home. The curtains. Billowing. Forming a shape. A small shape but distinct all the same. And the bear. That damn bear.

She shook her head, forcing the image out of her mind with a chill.

Matt glanced at her and then back to the road.

'What sort of things?'

Meredith looked to him, taking a moment to take in his straight nose and full lips. He was a good-looking guy. Not only that but he was forthright and honest, juxtaposed with kind and easy going, a combination she hadn't come across in many people.

'Things?' she said.

'You said certain things have happened. What sort of

things?'

Meredith forced out a small laugh. Why had she made that flippant remark?

Stupid, Meredith. Not only is he all of those things, he's sharp too.

'Oh, nothing really,' she said. 'Just small stuff, movement out of the corner of my eye, a feeling of being watched on the stairs, cliched stuff that's all. Nothing concrete.'

'So, you *do* believe?'

Meredith blew out her cheeks.

'Um, well, that's not so clear cut. There's a lot of evidence. I mean, a *ton* of evidence. The problem is that the evidence is as paper thin as the entities themselves. A dot of light on a photograph, a story from memory, when we all know memory is exceptionally suspect as evidence. There's nothing that has been recorded that has convinced me, and the problem with technology these days is that, although it's probably better able to pick up this stuff, it's also almost impossible to tell if something recorded recently has been faked or edited. It's a double-edged sword. The only way to know for sure is to experience it personally I suppose.'

'And that's why you're here?'

Meredith nodded. The shortened version anyway, minus the drunk mother and dead sister to gather respite from. Matt sniffed and took a slug of orange through a straw, from where it sat in the top central cup holder. He swallowed before adding:

'The only reason you're here?'

She glanced at him, a frown crossing her face.

'What do you mean?

He looked back at her with a smile.

'Well, Kevin said you pushed really hard for the position. I mean way above and beyond what you needed to. He isn't normally susceptible to badgering but something about you struck a chord with him. He told me he took a punt, his words, and he hoped you could manage. He had someone on standby until you had done the screen tests and fake runs. In fact, they were on standby until we came up here.'

Meredith felt her defences crawl up. Kevin had been discussing her with Matt? And he'd had someone on standby?

'He needn't have bothered,' she said, 'Everyone has to start somewhere, it doesn't mean they're useless.'

Matt swung his gaze back to the road, slowing for the bend ahead.

'No, of course not, I wasn't saying that at all. You've done great so far, and as much as you've felt you weren't in control at times, you've always come across in control on camera. That's what Kevin needs. A credible show with a credible presenter, not someone who flounders. Especially on a show such as this. You've impressed him, whether he shows it or not, and I'll tell you now, he usually doesn't, so don't expect a pat on the back. You won't get one.'

Meredith sat back in the seat with a sigh, the wall of defence crumbling again around her. Impressed Kevin? That was good to know, although she wasn't so sure how impressed he was with her after this morning's outburst.

'So?' Matt asked.

'So what?'

'My question. Bearing in mind how hard you pushed, how hard you're working, and how intensely you like to know how everything works, even though you've never presented a show before, is curiosity the only reason you're here?'

Meredith pushed a breath from between her lips. Her heart began to thud behind her ribs. She looked back out of the window to avoid Matt's gaze.

'Why would it be anything else?' She turned back to him. 'I think if you're interested in the paranormal then the obvious next step to learning about it is to seek it out. I pushed because it seemed like the perfect opportunity and these jobs don't come up often. I pushed because I had no experience, and I wanted the job. I pushed because I wanted it badly enough, and just because I pushed doesn't mean I have an ulterior motive, does it?'

Matt smiled.

'Nope. Just curiosity, I get it. And after the first two shoots? What do you think? I know the first night was quiet, but that was pretty intense stuff last night.'

Meredith turned back to the window and chewed on a nail. She still didn't know what to make of it. Part of her was ecstatic, the other part wondered how they could have fell on such amazing activity in just the first two shoots. How had a bunch of amateurs managed to have a full-blown conversation with a young girl, change some historical facts, and shoo away an angry murderous father. It seemed unreal now that it was over, and time had passed.

'Meredith?'

She shook her head.

'I don't know. I'm still undecided. There was a lot going on and I was in the middle of it, it's hard to make out objectively, it all seems a bit unreal sitting here now.'

Matt raised his eyebrows at the road.

'So, you don't believe it was real?'

'More like I *can't* believe it was real.'

As she spoke a realisation came into her head. It was recorded. Matt not only had the footage, but he also did a rudimentary edit each night, she supposed it was so that Kevin could check that they had enough footage for the episode. She swung her head back to him.

'Actually, maybe you could help me out with that. I'd like to have a look at the footage from last night if you can. Just so I can relive it, so I can be sure what happened. It was so much. It just seems like a dream now.'

Matt kept his eyes on the road, but his body tensed.

'Um… Ah, Meredith, you know, Kevin would kill me if I showed you any of it. He hates anybody seeing it until the show airs, just the minimal staff needed to edit, and the Kentwood Studio's production team. He likes the control and the air of secrecy.'

Meredith stared at him and he shrugged.

'I'm sorry, but I'm not joking when I say showing you could literally get me fired. He's very protective of it.'

Meredith nod her head at him, eyebrows raised.

Really?

'Okay.' She said, 'I appreciate that, and it's completely up to you. It doesn't matter. It was a lot to take in, that's all. I can't imagine we'll be lucky enough to experience anything like that again at this next place. It's rare to have such a perfect sitting.'

Matt sighed heavily.

'Meredith, I'm sorry. I just can't.'

Meredith nodded.

'Okay, that's fine,' she said, 'don't worry about it, really. I won't ask you again. I didn't mean to put you in an awkward position.'

He concentrated on the road as they lapsed into silence and she vaguely wondered if she had overstepped the mark.

The radio played quietly as the loud snores continued from the backseat.

CHAPTER FOUR

Lynton Castle was small as castles go, scalable only by its height. Seven stories and complete with a tower to the west. The tower was the only eighth story floor and boasted formidable views. Its ground floor comprised only three rooms; a large kitchen with dining at one end, a living room, and a sitting room which was used as a playroom for the children of the castle. Freddie, Asha, and Ollie.

The couple who owned the castle were in their mid-forties and seemed, to Meredith, like genuine people. When interviewed their stories corroborated so well that they often finished each other's sentences. The main paranormal trouble in the castle seemed to focus on the cellars, which used to be kitchens and servant areas. They were now closed off to keep the children upstairs after little Asha used to follow what they thought was an imaginary friend down there to play. When she was caught playing with the old boiler and receiving third-degree burns to her arms, the door had been locked and bolted securely.

'But this door is often found open?' Helen said, legs crossed, pen and pad in hand as she glanced up to Orla Stanton.

Orla nodded. Her wife, Stephanie, took her hand.

'The presence, the noises, we can live with. Most of the activity is downstairs, but obviously with Asha, it concerns us that the door can't seem to be made safe. The bolts are always slid across and padlocked, and the key we leave high above the door where none of the children can access it. Who or what opens that door I have no idea, but only last weekend Asha was found at the top of the steps saying her friend Elana was calling her down to play again.'

Meredith felt her interest fire. It was the sort of story that would get her blood pumping if she had watched it on TV or read it in a book. Tomorrow night, however, she was going to investigate it herself, and if the previous couple of nights were anything to go by, they would be in for a treat.

'Would it be okay to speak to Asha about her friend before the investigation?'

Orla shook her head frantically as Stephanie nod her head, yes. Meredith looked from one to the other as they caught each other's reaction.

Stephanie squeezed Orla's hand.

'Look, honey, if these guys can get to the bottom of this and convince Elana to move on it can only be good for us and Asha, can't it? But they're going to need all the facts.'

Meredith thought the chance of them getting the spirit to move on with their combined experience of almost nil was highly improbable, but she did want to get the story in full. Who knew, maybe they *could* exorcise the spirit, and she could write a book about ghost hunting with egomaniac men and Psychics prone to fainting, but still getting the job done— as only a woman can.

Orla was still shaking her head.

'No, I don't want Asha to speak of her. It may make Elana come up out of the cellars altogether. At least down there she's contained.'

'She's not contained, honey, she can come up and out whenever the hell she wants. The open door every morning gives that away, and Asha can go down whenever that door is open. This needs to stop.'

'I'm frightened, Steph.'

Stephanie placed an arm around Orla's shoulders and whispered something into her ear. Meredith felt she was intruding on a moment far too tender for a paranormal investigation interview. She coughed quietly and looked at the photographs of the family which lined the fireplace. The children, Asha aside, were theirs through surrogacy. Asha, the middle child, was the only one adopted, just four years ago, and it was obvious which one she was in the photographs. A pretty girl of black origin with tight curls on her head and large brown eyes. According to Stephanie, Asha was the only one to have a connection with the spirit of the house. The boys had only seen and heard what their parents had, which didn't amount to much.

Meredith stared at Asha's photograph as Stephanie coaxed Orla into a talk with the nine-year-old. An age which seemed far too grown up for imaginary friends, as the Stanton's liked to call it.

Eventually Stephanie got up and left the room before bringing into the room the girl from the picture.

Asha was tall for her age and had a quiet air of intelligence about her. Only the lollipop in her mouth belied her young age, or Meredith may have mistaken her for older than her years. Asha held herself upright and sat when she was told. After a brief introduction Stephanie and Orla left the room at Asha's insistence. As the door shut, Asha immediately slumped back in the seat, twirling the lollipop stick in her mouth.

There was a period of silence where the two women and the girl eyed each other, and then Asha took the lollipop out of her mouth, holding it aloft in her right hand.

'So, you want to know about Elana?'

The girl's voice was soft and pronounced, with a hint of plumb reserved only for English gentry. Meredith wondered where it had come from. Orla was very Irish and Stephanie very Scottish, but there wasn't a hint of either in Asha's voice, although she had been here since she was just five years old.

'If you want to tell us.' Meredith said, 'Are you happy to talk about her?'

Asha shrugged her slim shoulders.

'It doesn't bother me. It may bother her, though. Are you going down with her tonight?'

Meredith heard Helen swallow hard.

'Not tonight, 'she said, 'tomorrow.'

'Oh.' Asha hugged herself with a small smile, 'She'll like the company.'

Meredith smiled.

'She will?'

'Yes. She likes to scare people. It's been a long time since she had someone new to scare.'

The smile slipped from Meredith's face as she looked at the little girl sitting innocently before her, slouched back in the chair, legs crossed. The slight smile on Asha's face was starting to unnerve her.

'Right. Well, we don't frighten easily I'm afraid—'

'She does.' Asha said, pointing to Helen. 'Elana will go for her.'

'I... I'm not scared.' Helen said, sounding for all the world like she had been asked to scale the outside of London's Shard building, harness free.

'You are,' the girl said, full lips curving into a pretty smile which had the power to beguile and terrify at the same time.

Meredith frowned.

'Okay, Asha, that's enough, we're here to talk about Elana. Do you know who she was, or why she's still here?'

'She's Elana, and she likes it here, she enjoys having me as a friend. Orla thinks she's the scariest thing ever, which is funny really, because her dress sense is the scariest thing I've ever seen. I'd be more scared to look in my mirror if I were Orla. Actually, Elana sometimes pops up in mirrors too. I see her in my bathroom mirror all the time.'

Ignoring the comment about Orla's dress sense, which Meredith kind of had to agree with, she pressed on to the subject that they had come for.

'If she can appear in your mirror to talk to you, why does she need to open the door to the cellars. Does she often roam the house? Is Orla wrong to say she is contained down there, do you think?'

Asha put the lollipop back in her mouth and appeared to think. The girl seemed unfazed, taking her time as Meredith watched her. Slowly she took the lollipop back out.

'Elana isn't contained anywhere. She can come and go as she pleases. She just pleases to stay down in the cellars where she is buried. Plus, she likes to freak Orla out with the whole door thing. Thing is, they think the key is all safe and out of the way, but if I just climb onto the cupboard and lean across to the door, I can reach it easily. If I wanted to, I could let Elana out all by myself.'

'She was buried in the cellars?' Helen asked, sounding a little more like herself, which Meredith was pleased about. She was also pleased that Helen had avoided the whole getting the key thing. Given Asha's attitude, she wondered if at least some of this ghostly activity was down to a living and breathing little girl.

Asha nodded and went back to sucking on the lollipop.

'She's still down there,' she said.

Helen recoiled with a gasp next to her, and Meredith narrowed her eyes as Asha's grin arrived firmly back on her face.

This was getting them nowhere. Asha may or may not have seen and spoken with a ghost, but the more the girl said, the more Meredith felt that she was just trying to secure a reaction from them. This couldn't be documented as anything other than a young girl messing around. If they came across Elana in the investigation, then maybe they would have some useful information. If not, then Asha was probably just trying to scare her parents for reasons known only to her.

'Okay,' Meredith said, looking at Helen's notes, for effect rather than recollection, 'So we know that Elana likes to stay down in the cellar—'

'With her rotting corpse,' Asha interjected. Meredith glanced up at her.

'Elana likes to stay down the cellar,' she continued, 'but she isn't confined to it. She can unlock and open the cellar door, and she can roam around the house, especially using mirrors. She stays here because her body is possibly still in the cellar somewhere. Is that about it?'

'Her body *is* in the cellar. She showed me, ages ago, when I was six. That's why I have these.'

Asha pulled up her green cardigan sleeves in a last attempt to shock. The scars were there, albeit they were faint now. Three years of healing on a child. In another three, they would barely be seen at all. Meredith nodded, careful to keep her expression neutral.

'Yes, we heard you put your hands into the boiler.'

'Not in the boiler. Under the boiler. That's where she is. You can look tomorrow if you like. The boiler was disconnected and taken away, but you can see where it sat easily enough. The pipes have been boarded over. Elana is under there. I've lifted the boards, I've seen her.'

Meredith sighed, more than a little frustrated with the young girl who sat twiddling her lollipop with a grin.

'Right, I think we'll give that a miss. It's not corpses we're after tomorrow. Just ghosts. Thank you for that Asha I think we have everything we need.'

Helen drew a thick line under the few lines she had written as the girl replaced the lollipop back into its spiteful cave and sat upright, clearly unsure whether to stay or leave. Meredith nodded to her.

'You're free to go, thank you, Asha.'

The girl opened her mouth and shouted so loudly that both Helen and Meredith jumped.

'Muuuuummy, I'm done!'

The door opened and Orla flounced in so quickly Meredith wouldn't have been surprised to hear she had stood outside the room the whole time.

'Asha, darling, are you okay?'

Asha rose from the chair and flung herself straight into Orla's arms.

'Mummy, that was so frightening. I hope Elana doesn't

punish me. She hates me talking about her. She won't get me, will she, mummy? Will you make sure the door is locked tight tonight? Will you use the padlock?'

Orla took a distressed Asha from the room, leaving Helen and Meredith alone.

Meredith shut her mouth with a small snap.

'What the hell did you make of that?' Helen whispered as the door swung shut.

'Bullshit. All of it. This family has issues, not ghosts. If anything turns up tomorrow, I'll eat my own converse. Where the heck did Kevin dig this place up from?'

'Apparently it's in a 'ghosts of the Cairngorms' book. I don't know.'

'Well, they were obviously scraping the barrel with the book because I don't feel a thing here, do you?'

Helen shook her head. 'Not like at Moweth, that place was really creepy, this feels... homely.'

'I agree. There's nothing more we need to add here, let's go find the others. I think this will be a waste of a couple of days, but at least my ears will be saved from the pitch of your scream. Dogs will sleep well in Lynton. Heck, I may even sleep well in Lynton.'

Helen got up from the chair with a laugh, clutching her pad and pen.

'Thanks, I'd be hurt if I didn't know sarcasm was your default setting.'

Meredith grinned back at Helen, joining her laughter as they left the room.

Neither saw the photographs on the fireplace tip to face down, one by one, in careful succession. And both were out of earshot when the photograph of Asha fell to the floor, smashing into many jagged pieces.

CHAPTER FIVE

In the small but homely hotel room, Meredith sat on the edge of the bed and untied her converse pumps, pulling them off and dropping them onto the floor. It had been a long day with completion at Moweth, the drive, and the meeting at Lynton, and after a meal in the hotel's small dining room, Meredith had gone straight back to her room, where she had fallen asleep watching TV, and decided she should just be done with it and go to bed.

They were due to meet in the hotel lounge at 9am sharp, Kevin having organised a small corner to be sectioned off for their breakfast, to allow them to discuss the day's events, and go through the details for the evening at Lynton. Tomorrow morning, as much for the crew's sake as her own, she intended to be refreshed.

As she undressed the madness of the last few months, and the few days they had been on location, ran through her mind like a movie of someone else's life.

All of this was new to her – a fate like cacophony of her own problems, a freak email announcing the opportunity, and raw instinct to apply. Before this job she had never presented, never travelled, never been on camera, never been on a shoot; never been interested in the world of television. But after that email she had hounded Kentwood Production Studio for tips, spent a week shadowing different departments, googled presenting like a madwoman, memorised names of equipment and filming terms, and hounded Kevin for not one chance, but four, before he finally relented.

Matt was right, she had been dogged in her determination, and that desperation had blurted a lie she regretted about the parapsychology degree. In leu of presenting experience, she had embellished the side she knew inside out and pushed it. Kevin was the expert in television, but she was the expert in the paranormal. The perfect team she had said. Whether he believed it she would never know, his serious face never showed anything but disdain, but ultimately it had worked.

She was here.

She grinned as she pulled on her pyjama's and slipped under the cool duvet, her thoughts landing on the previous night and the tussle with Cara and her father. Exhilaration and terror coursed through her at the thought of anything on that scale happening again, but she knew that such instances were rare. They would be lucky to get a repeat performance.

One thing was for sure, there would be no activity at Lynton because she had never been to a castle that felt less haunted in her life. They would be in for a quiet couple of shoots over the next few days, she would put money on it.

She laughed in the quiet of the room and leaned to turn off the side light.

The outline of furniture came into focus as her eyes adjusted to the darkness, and the sound of a plane crossing the sky outside turned her face to the window. The curtains were open, as they always were. She never slept with them closed, not since the night after her fourteenth birthday, when she had been so terrified that she had wet her bed. Not only that, but she had lay in it, too scared to move, for three hours, until daylight.

Luckily, mum being an avid and committed drunk back then, had known nothing of the incident. She hadn't even registered the sheets blowing in the breeze on the line the next day when she had risen at 1pm and grabbed a bottle of tequila. Meredith had never been as embarrassed (or as scared) before or since.

To top it off, she hadn't known if she had wanted mum to notice—to tell her it would be okay, like when she was little, and she'd had a bad dream—or whether she was glad mum was so out of it she hadn't known a thing.

Finding something tangled in the curtains at night was a habit that had gone on for far too long ever since, a step up from the early years of only feeling watched and smelling Eve's perfume.

In the cosy silence of the hotel room Meredith turned onto her side, facing the window, staring at the plane's lights blinking far away in the sky.

Something has to be done, I only hope this is it.

Meredith swallowed hard. The older she got the more persistent and frequent the manifestations seemed to be, and though she was terrified of Eve's spirit, she also knew that fear was only a response to the unknown. Meredith's response to the fear was to study the paranormal, to find out what was happening to her, and what she could do about it.

She managed just seven months of the parapsychology degree before it had fallen through. Money was scarce, especially with an alcoholic mother spending all they had. It was simply too costly to continue, so she had dropped out and researched manically on her own. If she understood enough, then surely, she could dampen her fear enough to be able to communicate with Eve, instead of hiding under bedclothes or running from the room.

But it hadn't worked like that. Years later she understood volumes more about the spirit world, but that hadn't banished the fear of Eve herself. Meredith had been at her wits end when the advert had popped into her email, she knew it was a huge opportunity, one she couldn't miss. If she got comfortable communicating with other spirits, maybe that would diminish her fear of Eve. She got paid for the learning too, bonus.

There was one other reason she had pushed for the job and lied about the degree. Eve had only ever appeared at home, and home was also where her now recovering alcoholic mother was. After years of caring for mum, and fearing Eve's presence, the last reason was simple.

Respite.

On location in Scotland for eight weeks? No problem at all. Hunting and communicating with spirits with a team she could learn from? Perfect.

Just not Eve. Not yet.

But soon, I promise, when I know more of what I'm doing.

Meredith felt her heavy eyes close as she drift easily into a deep sleep.

* * * * *

JUNE—197 DAYS UNTIL DEATH

Evie's laughter rippled around the room, soft and flowery, just like she always smelled. She would never allow me on her bed, so I was lying on the furry cream rug on her bedroom floor, chin propped in my hands. The fur on the rug was itchy, and sometimes made me sneeze, but it was softer than her carpet where I had laid my books and pens ready for her.

'Oh Meredith, you're such a silly moo! Meredith Moo, that's what I'm calling you from now on.'

I turned the name over as I watched her float around the room, the warm sun shining on her through the window like a spotlight. She twirled the dress so high it almost showed her underwear as she spun.

I thought about telling her, but Evie wouldn't care. She was far too grown up to worry about things like that. One skirt that she had worn last summer had been so short that dad asked her to remove it and throw it out. It barely covered ALL SHE HAD. Evie had sulked. Taken it off. But she still had it.

I had found it in her wardrobe during hide and seek with dad last week, on the floor under a bag.

It was scrunched into a zillion creases, but it was definitely Evie's grown-up skirt. Her NAUGHTY skirt. My heart fluttered and I couldn't help myself. I took it out, game forgotten, glancing over at the bedroom door as I put it on over my jeans. The waistband slipped off my hips, so I had to hold it tight at the side. I looked in the mirror, stood up straighter, hoiked the skirt up shorter, but I still didn't look like Evie.

I opened the dresser draw to find Evie's favourite lip gloss, which I put on carefully and then sprayed a puff of perfume, just on the neck as Evie did. There, that was better. Now I just had to grow my hair darker and grow my waist. After that I spent ages pulling faces and poses, and talking in the mirror, pretending to be my sister. If I pretended enough, I could grow to be just like her.

Evie had been mad when she got home from school and found me wearing her perfume, but she soon calmed when I told her I had found her NAUGHTY skirt.

'The skirt is to be our secret, Meredith. Promise to never ever tell mum and dad and I won't bother about my perfume, but just this once. In future I will be so mad that you will have a heart attack and die from just my angry stare, have you got that?'

I promised and nod so hard that Evie had laughed and told me my head looked about to fall off. I had laughed too, and everything had been all right.

'Meredith Moo. Meredith Moo.'

It sounded sweet coming from Evie's lips. I decided I liked it, but the twirling was getting on my nerves.

'Evie, can we draw now? You said you'd draw with me.'

Evie stopped twirling and looked at me with a smile.

'Meredith Moo, I have to get myself ready to go to the skating rink. I don't have long.'

Long enough to twirl forever, I thought, but that may be a grownup thing too. Evie was sixteen after all, and I was only six. As Evie would often say—what did I know about being a grownup?

I pouted and rolled onto my back.

'Please,' I begged, watching her upside down. 'Evie, you promised. You promised!'

Evie loomed over me and flopped onto her bed; arms spread wide. I scrabbled to my feet, grabbing my pens, and putting them on the bed.

'Please.'

Evie rolled her eyes.

'Okay Meredith Moo, we'll draw. But not for long.' She picked up the pack of glitter gel pens she always liked to use. 'Where's the paper?'

I collected the two drawing pads from the floor, handing her my favourite to use, and she patted the bed, indicating for me to climb up.

My heart soared. Evie's bed was so much softer and comfier than mine. Evie's bed was like a princess bed. I lay my head down on her pillow and spread my arms as she was, my hand knocking her arm as I closed my eyes.

The softness. The flowery smell of her perfume. Lilies, she had told me once.

The bed moved, making me bump and bounce. The cardboard packet rattled as Evie grabbed a pen, and I heard the pages flutter in the book as she turned to a clean one. I lay on the softness, feeling like a princess, eyes closed, listening to the sounds of my sister. Listening to her last sigh of frustration.

'Come *on,* Moo, we don't have much time.'

* * * * *

We don't have much time.

Meredith woke to the darkness of the hotel room, the words reverberating around her head. They seemed to carry an urgency, but she didn't understand what they meant. It wasn't the first dream she'd had containing memories with Eve, although they were less frequent now. Usually, they left

Meredith feeling warm and nostalgic. This one, although there was nothing sinister about it, left her feeling on edge.

Sitting up in the darkness, she pushed the covers down to her waist, and rubbed her eyes. It was hot in this small room, too hot, and she needed to pee. She lift her wrist to activate the Fitbit on her arm and saw that it was 2.10am. Still a good few hours of sleep to grab yet, and that was good. She felt as though she hadn't slept for months.

Rolling back the duvet, she climbed out of bed, and padded to the en-suite bathroom with a yawn. She pulled the light switch, illuminating the stark white of the small room, used the toilet, and washed her hands in the small basin.

We don't have much time.

Meredith paused with a frown and looked at herself in the mirror, noting the worry in her eyes. She rubbed at the dark circles underneath with a forefinger.

It was just a dream. What are you so afraid of?

She knew she was being silly, rattled by something that hadn't even been eerie, but she couldn't shake the feeling of unease.

Eve isn't coming here, Meredith, Eve has never been anywhere but home.

Heart thudding behind her ribs, Meredith forced a smile at her reflection, and shook her head chastising herself.

Stop getting carried away with nonsense. Concentrate on the job, don't get pulled into the murk of home. This job is vital.

With a small sigh, she turned off the tap. There was a small thud from the bedroom.

Her breath caught, hair at the nape of her neck prickling as she paused to listen, but there was only the hum of the lights from the corridor outside the door. She let her body relax in the silence, blowing out a long breath. Then a smell reached her nostrils.

Flowery, familiar. Lilies.

Only a waft. And only faint. Gone so fast Meredith

wouldn't have been certain she had smelled anything at all if not for the goosebumps on her arms and the hammering in her chest.

No. I imagined it. It was auto-suggestion from the dream. That's all. There's no smell. No smell.

Tentatively she sniffed again, getting only the acrid fragrance of the products used to clean the bathroom. She breathed a heavy sigh of relief. No smell. Imagined. She leaned a shaky hand on the countertop.

She didn't need this. She had to focus, concentrate on the job, learn all she could, and stop bringing up crap from home. It would mess with her mind—heck, it was messing with her mind already. Her eyes flicked back to the mirror.

Get to bed, get some sleep. In the morning, this whole thing will seem ridiculous.

She left the bathroom, pulling the light cord too hard in her haste. It bounced back into the socket with a pronounced throng, small plastic handle bouncing off the wall tiles with a rhythmic tic.

In three strides she reached the bed and jumped in. No longer bothered about the warmth of the room, she pulled the covers over her head and lay listening to the silence, until she calmed enough to slip back into sleep.

She didn't notice her phone, lying face down on the floor where it had fallen from the small side table. Nor did she see the curtain ripple softly in the darkness.

CHAPTER SIX

The larger rolling mountains had disappeared as they approached the top end of the Cairngorms National park yesterday, and from the village of Lynton the lie of the land was as flat as it got, the mountain tops visible only in the distance. Lynton castle, however, was built on an outlying hill, a ten-minute drive from the village, and being raised up high, the tower had phenomenal views of the rolling, heather streaked mountains.

Meredith took in the awe-inspiring view, before moving to the other side of the tower. From this side you could see the whole village of Lynton nestled amongst woodland. One road in, one road out, leading to further villages in the distance before the larger town of Grantown-on-Spey sprawled into view, the river winding past to its south.

'Beautiful isn't it,' Stephanie said, pulling Meredith's attention back into the room. 'Both Orla and I like to come up here for quiet time. I come up here to read, Orla likes to reflect as she takes in the view. It's peaceful. There's no noise that travels from anywhere in the castle up here, and the views are stunning whatever the season.'

Meredith nodded back at Stephanie. 'You certainly don't get views like this in London.'

'That's for sure,' Helen added with a grin. 'I'm a city girl at heart, but I could take this for a few weeks. It is beautiful, almost healing.'

'It's solid, and solid is what I like to base my life's foundation on.'

Meredith frowned, 'How do you mean?'

Stephanie smiled back at her.

'You may have the buildings, the people, the government,

the majesty, but it is all man made. London is very egotistical. Its history is far reaching, but it has been rebuilt and restructured over and again. Lives have been ruined, wiped out in an instant.' she clicked her fingers. 'The plague and the Great Fire of London are two such examples of how things can go abruptly wrong when people get to close, too caught up in their lives, and forget that nature itself will provide, regardless of towers, power, and men. With the flip of a switch, it could all come crashing down. Modern life is so easily disrupted and disintegrated, and now so much more than ever. Everything teeters on a balance. It works, or it doesn't. When it doesn't, ninety-nine percent of people crash down with it, unable to cope. They flounder. Their base isn't solid. Their lives are in cyberspace. Here, however, you have mountains and scenery that have been here for billions of years. Changeable, for sure, but immovable. There is nothing to crumble around us here.'

'You still have technology here, though.' Helen said. 'Electricity, the Internet. Surely wherever you live, what crashes down affects us all.'

Stephanie waved a hand at her.

'Of course, to a degree. And the youngsters may flounder more than me, as I will flounder more than my ancestors. But we are rooted in the earth here.'

Meredith felt a twinge. Of what, she wasn't entirely sure. Knowing? Truth? Lives were certainly balanced on the edge of a die these days, especially the fast-paced lives of cities worldwide. Everybody precariously held up, ready to topple like a house of cards.

In that sense, the land here did seem solid. Reliable. Strong. The mountains, sentinels of the people. Gods.

Mountains were worshiped in some countries, weren't they?

She vaguely wondered if they had ever been worshiped in Scotland as she looked across the rolling landscape, lit by the autumn sun, the tops of the trees speckled with russet as their leaves swayed in the breeze.

'Meredith?'

Meredith swung to Helen, who stood in the small wooden doorway that was both entrance and exit to the tower. Stephanie was holding it open with a smile.

'Yes?'

'We're not on holiday, we need to see the rooms we'll be filming in! Duh.'

With one last look at the view, Meredith followed Helen out. The door was locked when the tower wasn't in use, and Stephanie held the large key up as she pulled the door shut and locked it behind them. They carried on to the bottom of the stone stairs where Stephanie produced another key and locked a further wooden door. Meredith thought this was excessive, but then, she didn't have children. Or unruly ghosts.

'Food for thought, eh?' Stephanie said as the lock turned over with a clunk.

'Very much so.' Meredith agreed.

Stephanie nodded and grabbed Meredith's arm. Hard, but not quite hard enough to hurt.

'Yes, I think you get it.' She said. 'And so, you understand why this presence upsets my balance.'

'It's not solid.' Meredith said, searching Stephanie's eyes. Stephanie needed no more, she nodded. Helen's eyes flit warily between the two women, unsure what was going on.

'We've never had a team investigate the presence here,' Stephanie said. 'I really hope you can do something about it or the castle, my ancestors' home for generations, will have to be sold. I can't carry on like this. Orla is a mess, Asha worries me, and I can't find anything to hold on to. There's nothing solid, nowhere safe for us and the children. I know I sound desperate, but I don't know what to do anymore. I feel the only safety is away from here, and that makes me feel... well...'

She let go of Meredith's arm with a sigh.

'I'm sorry,' she said, 'I just can't see a way out sometimes.' She closed her eyes briefly with a sigh.

The pressure and weight of the statement hung on the invisible grip of the lady's grasp, and Meredith suddenly felt a sadness wash over her. This family was real. Genuine people with genuine issues. How could the team help them? They were simply making a television show, they hardly had an ounce of ghost hunting experience between them, and as Kevin liked to remind them—'It's entertainment, sweetie, and that's all it is.'

Meredith felt her stomach turn over as Stephanie broke into a forced cheery smile and began leading the way to the bathroom where part of the investigation was to take place.

Of course, the other problem here was that Meredith wasn't completely sure that there was a spirit here at all, and if Asha was the problem, then Stephanie wouldn't appreciate the team figuring that out either.

* * * * *

In the small bathroom on the first floor, where Asha had seen the entity in the mirror, Matt and Steve were cheerily setting up the equipment for the evening. Helen scribbled notes on a neon pink pad as Stephanie talked them through what had happened, but even the retelling of the tales couldn't raise a hair on Meredith in this bright modern space.

The only thing Meredith worried about in here was fitting everyone in. She smothered a grin as she thought maybe they could put Kevin in the bath, out of the way. Maybe someone could accidentally flip on the shower while he was there.

She would even give it a go herself.

'Nothing has been moved or misplaced in here,' Stephanie said as Helen nodded back at her, 'It is purely the mirror interaction with Asha.'

'So, Asha communicates with Elana through the mirror?'

Meredith said.

Stephanie shook her head, catching her eye in the mirror. 'Not exactly. Asha describes it as going into her. She says she looks at her own reflection and somehow just… changes into her. Then she communicates. That's usually when Asha ends up at the cellar. I know it sounds ridiculous, but neither myself nor Orla have seen it, and the boys have experienced nothing at all. All I have to go on is her word. Asha's that is.'

Stephanie shrugged her shoulders as her face reddened, the embarrassment almost radiating off her. Meredith nodded and placed a hand on Stephanie's arm.

'It's not so ridiculous. There is a technique which uses the same process called transfiguring, or face morphing. It's basically the same thing. It's not unheard of.'

Stephanie's eyebrows shot up.

'It's real? She's telling the truth?'

Meredith thought about her answer.

'It's an actual process, and it's sometimes used. I'm not sure of its success for communication, or how much the change in features is due to the viewer's mindset, and what they expect to see. I've never seen it myself, but in theory, yes, it can happen.'

Stephanie fingered a silver cross that hung at her neck.

'Right, I wasn't sure… I mean, well, I suppose it doesn't matter now. Your team will get to the bottom of it tonight. Come on, I'll take you down to the living room.'

Meredith glanced at Helen as Stephanie left the room. Two things flit between them, unspoken.

How the heck was their team supposed to get to the bottom of it? And Did Stephanie's embarrassment indicate that she didn't believe Asha, confirming what they had suspected themselves?

Meredith held out a hand, motioning for Helen to follow Stephanie. And then she looked back at the mirror with a frown. Face morphing was a real process, but she had never heard of anyone physically taking on an appearance and then moving around as that entity. As far as her knowledge went face morphing and channelling were separate things, and unless Asha was a natural medium, how was she channelling and controlling how far Elana went by herself? How was she grounding? Asha didn't seem bothered by it, so she was obviously only possessed at will, and according to Stephanie, she had only done this a handful of times over the years.

As her thoughts ran Meredith became aware of a face alongside hers in the mirror. It hovered, staring. Her heart gave a little jump, and then she noticed it wasn't staring at all. Its eyes were crossed, mouth slack. And then the long hair, frizzy beard and double chin came into focus and she rolled her eyes.

Steve and Matt burst into laughter. And then Steve adopted a low, whispery growl.

'Did you find her in the mirror, Meredith?'

Meredith raised her eyebrows and flipped them both middle fingers.

'Funny.' She said.

She shook her head with a grin and left to follow Stephanie and Helen to the living room. Their laughter fading behind her.

The living room was as bright and homely as it had been yesterday, a roaring fire providing warmth, the three windows, two on the left, one ahead of the large oak door providing spectacular views. It was cosy. A room she could take to. She wondered again why Stephanie had brought them here. The remit had said the bathroom and cellars would be the focus of the investigation, but when they had arrived this morning both Stephanie and Orla had been adamant that the living room be included tonight too.

Kevin had agonised over having an extra room to work into his schedule. Huffing and puffing, and letting the women know that he wasn't at all pleased with a late change of plan. He now sat in a chair by the fire, shuffling papers and writing with a frown.

On the larger couch, Orla sat with Gwen going through the history of the castle, working through any significant events or information that may be linked to the unlawful burial of a small child in the cellars.

Meredith fleetingly thought it was strange that Stephanie wasn't speaking to Gwen about the castle's history. After all, it belonged to her ancestors, being in her family for well over two hundred years. Orla had her own heritage over in Ireland. Stephanie had explained that Orla felt too uneasy showing the bathroom and cellars to them, so she had taken on Gwen instead.

Stephanie stopped at the fireplace and turned toward them. Her eyes flit to Orla, and then Kevin, and back to Orla in succession. Finally, she met Meredith's.

'I suppose you're wondering why we want you to investigate in here.'

Helen gave a nod, poised with her pen and pad. Meredith smiled; she looked like an eager schoolgirl interviewing for an assignment about puppies.

'It would be extremely useful,' Kevin grumbled from his chair. No smiles there. He didn't even bother to look up.

Meredith gave an apologetic shrug, and Stephanie waved a hand, dismissing it.

'This room, like all the others, bathroom and cellar aside, had no activity until recently. Last month Freddie was adamant he left his tablet in here. We searched high and low, but it didn't come to light. A few days later I went up to the tower to read and there it was. In the middle of the floor, plain as day. You remember we always keep the tower locked, top and bottom doors. Those stone stairs are precarious enough for adults. The children would be sure to have an accident. They're only allowed up when we're in there.'

'Right,' Helen said, scribbling on the neon pad.

'So how did the tablet get up there?' Meredith said.

Stephanie looked at her.

'I don't know. The children denied it of course, and with the tower locked and the keys up high with the cellar key it wouldn't be easy for them to play a prank.'

Meredith thought of Asha and her confession that she could climb up and get the key to the cellar easily. Freddie was the eldest of the three, surely that meant he could get up there too, even if youngest Ollie couldn't. Two out of three could probably play a prank.

'I also thought either myself or Orla could have forgotten to lock the doors, but it's not likely. We're both vigilant, for the children's sake. Even if I could forgive myself for forgetting to lock one door, I would surely have locked the other. Two doors, two keys, and we'd forget both? I just can't see it, I just can't.'

Stephanie rubbed a hand over her face.

'It's okay, darling,' Orla piped up from the couch, 'There was no harm done, the tablet was okay. If you forgot to lock the doors, it's fine. We just can't forget next time. Don't start blaming yourself again.'

Meredith glanced over to Orla, who was gazing at Stephanie with a sad smile. Stephanie may blame herself, Meredith thought, but Orla sure doesn't, even though Stephanie said that both of them used the tower at least twice a week. Meredith frowned, she had thought Stephanie was the strong one, but the power seemed to have shifted here. It was strange. But then most folk were strange when you got down to it.

Stephanie nodded and smiled at Orla, blowing her a light kiss before continuing.

'Anyway, after the tablet episode a couple more things have gone missing, some found, some not. And a few things have been moved. Nothing that made us think anything other than we were all going doolally, but then yesterday... yesterday chilled me to the core.'

Stephanie hugged her shoulders with opposite hands and

shuddered. Meredith waited until she had composed herself enough to talk.

'What happened?' she said.

Stephanie swallowed, adam's apple bobbing. 'It was after you were here, obviously, or we would have asked you to investigate this room in the first place.' She glanced at Kevin who continued to write with no acknowledgment.

'Anyway,' she continued, 'I want to ask you something first. Did you see anything wrong with the photographs on the fireplace?'

Meredith glanced to them, all in a row across the top, as they had been yesterday.

'No, they were as they are now. I remember because I was looking at them as we waited.'

She turned to Helen, who nod in agreement.

'I was looking at them too, they were just like that.'

Stephanie seemed to pale, and her fingers found their way back to the cross around her neck.

'Right, and Orla and I both saw them there as we were speaking to you too.'

Helen and Meredith waited as Stephanie tugged at the cross harder.

'I came back in here straight after letting you out, to tidy the chairs and take out the mugs, and every one of those photographs was turned to face down.'

Meredith looked at the little ledge and frowned.

'Surely the top isn't wide enough, they would have fell.'

Stephanie sighed.

'It's wide enough, if you place them down very carefully, and make sure they're pushed right back to the wall. The bigger ones need to be slightly offset. But that's by the by, the fact is it can't be done with any speed, it needs precision, and patience to get the right angle.'

Helen began to speak, but Orla cut her off.

'We tested them yesterday, after we put them back up.'

Helen turned to her.

'You tested them?'

'The photographs,' Orla said, 'Like you said, the ledge didn't seem wide enough.'

Helen shot a look of confusion at Meredith.

'But you could see that it was, they were there in front of you. Face down.'

'We wanted to check that it wasn't… supernatural, you know.'

Meredith gave her that. She had read many incidents of things balanced in impossible locations, or the item itself sitting in strange positions, only to fall when someone went to investigate.

'So, do you think it was supernatural?' she said, 'You said that it was possible for them to be placed in that position by hand.'

'Yes,' Stephanie said, 'We managed it, but like I said, it took a good few minutes between us. The thing is, there wasn't a few minutes for it to happen. They were normal when you were in here. No one touched them, you were the last ones to leave, we were right behind you. I came straight back in here to tidy. I guess what I'm trying to say is that the children wouldn't have the time or dexterity to complete such a feat. So, who else could it have been? Orla and I were at the door with you.'

Meredith saw the problem but wasn't convinced that Asha couldn't have completed the feat single-handedly. She would have liked to get the children in here and give it a go, make it a game, just to see if they could. But they were staying with a friend in the village for the next two nights, so that was out of the question.

'The thing that chilled me most though,' Stephanie continued, 'chilled us both in fact, was that the smaller picture of Asha. The *only* picture of Asha. Had dropped to the floor and smashed.'

No, not the only picture of Asha, Meredith thought, the only picture of her alone. That would have freaked her parents out. In fact, it clearly had. The point is that Asha would have known. She was intelligent enough to have orchestrated this for the response that it had got. In fact, she would have revelled in it, and the attention that she would have been showered with afterward.

Helen sniffed and scribbled on the pad.

'Okay,' she said, 'So the photographs were all face down in a line, except the one of Asha, which was smashed on the floor.'

'That's right.' Stephanie said, her neck now going an angry pink where the necklace chain was being pulled and scrubbed against the skin.

'If one was smashed, it had obviously fallen. So why do you think…'

Meredith knew where Helen was headed and commended her silently for following through with a question that she would have found hard at the last location, leaving the tough stuff, as she called it, to Meredith. She was learning fast, and Meredith was enjoying working with her. Unfortunately, Orla also sensed the vein of the question and didn't appreciate Helen's forthrightness. She rose and strode to Stephanie, who placed an arm at her back. Meredith noticed that Orla's fashion sense wasn't any better than yesterday. Another dress, just as shapeless, just as vile a pattern, with a long cream shapeless cardigan. Pink fluffy slippers completed the look.

How on earth did Stephanie, in her comfortable but stylish jeans and shirt, not tell her she looked terrible? That was love, she supposed, and love was blind. Never a truer statement.

'It's obvious, isn't it?' Orla snapped, 'The photograph was the only one of Asha. Asha said that the ghost would punish her for talking to you about her. She was so frightened last night she had to sleep with me. It's a sign. A signal from Elana that she is out to get her. Asha believes that things are going to get worse here now.'

Stephanie pulled Orla in tighter.

'Ssshhh, honey, it's not their fault.'

'It *is* their fault, they wanted to speak to Asha, I told you we shouldn't have let her. Look what's happened now!'

'Honey, after this investigation there may be no more ghost, and Asha isn't around. It will be all right, they're here to help us.'

Or to make a stupid TV show, Meredith thought. Help certainly wouldn't be in Kevin's remit. She glanced over to him, legs crossed in the chair, papers on his lap, balding head shining in the light. He hadn't looked up at this exchange, but Meredith thought she saw a small smile on his face. He really couldn't care less about these people and wasn't bothered if they knew it.

The trouble was, how was Meredith supposed to help them with a script and a camera in her face. Kevin would scrutinise her every move now that she had rocked the boat, and she suddenly regretted not keeping her mouth shut.

Twenty minutes later, after a tea break allowing time for Stephanie to calm and console Orla, Helen, Meredith, and Stephanie stood outside their final location—the cellars in the old kitchen. Running down the back of the castle, the kitchen was long, but not quite narrow enough to be called a galley, with a small dining area at one end, and the cellar door placed centrally in the far wall. The cupboards and large range cooker blended with the walls, which could only be described as dirty white. In stark contrast to the modern bathroom, this room didn't appear to have been decorated for many years. Old pipes ran down the walls, painted white to blend in, and the old servant bells were still attached to the wall at the entrance.

'They've not been used for some time now.' Stephanie said catching Meredith's gaze, 'They were disconnected when my nanna lived here. She was very suspicious of servants, so she ran this place all by herself. There have been no servants here since. It's not like the place is huge now, is it?'

Meredith thought she had enough trouble keeping on top of the cleaning in her mother's three bed semi back in London. She wouldn't like to be cleaning this place every week. And yet, they did a good job. Everywhere they had been today was spotless. The kitchen was old and faded, but still very much clean.

'The cellars were kitchens for the first few hundred years, and since then mainly wine and meat storage, and the butchering of animal carcases after hunting. Now we only use them for storage.'

Matt and Steve squeezed past the trio with the last of the equipment to install. Stephanie reached for the key above the door to let them down, light illuminating the space from a switch just inside the door.

A blast of icy air found its way around her legs, causing Meredith to shudder. There was a strange smell too. Faint, not enough to curl your nose up at, but certainly a tinge of something off, something rotten.

Talk of butchering animals, and Asha saying that Elana's body was down there... your imagination needs keeping in check, Meredith.

'Phew-wy, could do with a glade plug-in down here,' Steve said as he disappeared down the stairs behind Matt.

Maybe not, she thought.

For the first time in this castle, Meredith had found a spot that she didn't like to be. She had never liked cellars and standing in this kitchen watching Steve disappear down those stairs was giving her chills. Literally.

'Right, shall we go down?' Stephanie said.

'I suppose we have to,' Meredith mumbled.

CHAPTER SEVEN

JUNE—181 DAYS UNTIL DEATH

'Shall we go down?'

Evie wiggled her eyebrows and shot me a smile over her shoulder. It was one I didn't like. It wasn't one of her nice smiles—it was one of her pretend ones. Her lips were too tight, pulled back too much.

'Or are you too scared, Meredith moo?'

I stood up straighter and lift my chin. I had grandpa's carved stick that he used to walk with before he went to heaven. Apparently, he didn't need it up there, he could walk just fine, so we got to keep it as a REMINDER. It didn't feel good using the stick, dad would be mad if he found that we had taken it from the corner by the front door. It was not to be touched, and absolutely not to be moved. Under any circumstances.

I wondered if secretly grandpa may come back one day and that was where he had asked for it to be kept so that he could find it. I wanted grandpa back, so I had no reason to move it, but Evie said I needed something to help me in the dark. She said it would be okay as she handed it to me.

'I'm not scared, there's nothing down there. Mum said.'

'Mum and dad are too old now. They can't see the bad man like we can.'

Evie was staring at the wooden door a few paces in front of us. I swallowed hard as I looked at it. Evie nod her head, looked down at me and then smiled. A much nicer one this time, it made my tummy feel better about doing this. Evie wouldn't do anything to hurt me, this was just a stupid dare, and I would get to use her perfume for dinner tomorrow.

'But anyway, I'm sure mum's right, there's probably nothing down there.' Evie said quickly as she placed a hand at my back and shuffled me toward the cellar door.

I moved slowly, the stick giving a little thunk at my side each time I brought it to the floor, walking like grandpa did. I think I may have got a funny limp in my foot like him too when I used it.

'Come on Moo, walk properly. You're such a funny thing.'

My limp was there to stay until I reached the door.

'Right. Listen closely if you don't want to come face to face with the bad man—and you *don't*. I'll turn the light on, you go down to the bottom of the stairs and sit. I'll turn the light off. All you have to do is sit there in the dark for five minutes. If you can do it, you can have ONE spray of my perfume tomorrow. Okay?'

I swallowed hard again as I nod my head up and down. My throat seemed smaller now. Grandpa was little, was I turning into him? Would I go to heaven if I turned into him? I frowned as I listened to Evie.

'This is the really important bit. On the shelves in front of you, way up high, is a clown. It looks like a doll, but it isn't, it's where the bad man lives. You'll know he's there because his eyes glow and they will make you want to look at them. That's his power. Don't look. Ever. And if you do, look away quickly. Never look at the clown's eyes and count to three, even in your head. That allows the bad man to come out, and if that happens Meredith Moo, then I'm not sure I'll be able to save you. Have you got it?'

'Got it. Don't look at the clown, and don't count to three.'

'*Even* in your head.'

'Got it.'

'Good.'

Evie smiled, but it was her pretend one again and then she opened the door and turned on the light.

The concrete stairs led away in front of me, and I could see the boxes of STUFF on the shelves against the back wall. My eyes travelled up until they glimpsed the clown Evie was talking about. His eyes weren't glowing now, they were covered with cracked blue paint. His peach face had flaking rosy cheeks and a wide red smile. A shock of orange hair stuck up from his head. He didn't look so scary, he just looked old.

He had been dad's clown. From when he was a BOY, and if dad had been a BOY, then this clown must be ready to fall apart, because dad was really old. Once Evie had even called him ANCIENT. I had to ask her what that meant, and she said he was as old as the dinosaurs. I was impressed with that. How many people have a dad who has seen dinosaurs?

I felt a foot push at my shins.

'Get a move on Moo, you're just wasting time. Mum will be home soon, and if you don't do it, you can't wear my perfume.'

I put the cane on the step first as grandpa used to do and shuffled my feet down beside it. A grunt left my mouth like grandpa too. If I turned into him would the bad man get me? Evie said adults couldn't see him anymore, so maybe not. That was good.

As my feet touched the bottom step of the staircase Evie shouted from the doorway.

'Time starts now, good luck Moo.'

The lights went off and the door shut with a reverberating bang that made me jump. I tried to force my eyes to see, but everything was black, so I opened them as wide as they would go, but it made no difference.

Shuffling my feet against the step to see if I was in the right place, I sat down to wait.

I forced my eyes wide again but still couldn't see, and I suddenly knew why. Grandpa had glasses. And if I was grandpa now, I would need them too, but I didn't have any.

I huffed a breath, thinking hard about what I could do.

I'd heard mum say to Evie that she would get eye STRAIN if she looked at the telly for too long. She told Evie she would need glasses if she wasn't careful, and then she told her to take a break and stretch her eye MUSCLES every ten minutes. Mum showed Evie some funny faces to make, crossing her eyes and looking up and down, and then told her to look at things all around the room.

I tried some exercises as I sat waiting. I looked up and down, tried to cross my eyes but I could barely see my finger to follow it as Evie had shown me. I shut and opened them, squeezing them tight three times and then opened them properly.

It was working!

I could see more now than I had before. I could see the outline of the shelves and the bulky shape of the bags and boxes on the floor. I couldn't make out things farther away like I could in my room at night, but mum had been right. Now I just had to look at things around the room. Which was hard because I couldn't see much.

I widened my eyes, stretching my forehead up and my mouth down. I looked hard. Trying to find things too see, and then I saw them.

The eyes.

Glowing, just as Evie had said. They didn't look blue anymore. Now they were a weird green. No green I had ever coloured with had been that sort of green.

I frowned, and then I remembered what Evie had said. The bad man was in there!

My heart jumped and I looked down at my feet, just about seeing the white laces of my pumps. Yes, my eyes were starting to work again now.

What an odd shade of green though. I thought I would look in my colours upstairs when Evie let me out. I would need to remember it though. It would be okay if I didn't count to three, right?

Taking a chance, I glanced up. The eyes were still glowing. I tried to focus on the green, but my mind was playing tricks. It started to count without me.

One ... Two ...

Look at the laces! the laces! I made my eyes go down.

Stupid mind. Why had it done that? I hadn't got to three though, so that was okay. But how would the bad man know? I thought maybe I needed to tell him, just in case.

'I didn't get to three, you can't come out.'

That was better, my heart had slowed down again now too. I would have to remember the green now, I really didn't want to see the bad man. I had never seen him, but Evie had seen him. She said he was DANGEROUS. Mum always said not to be scared of things I didn't know properly, but the bad man scared me. He scared me bad.

There was a scrape to my right. I swung my head toward the noise and my heart knocked at my chest again.

I couldn't see anything, it was black. I swallowed hard. Had the bad man left the clown anyway?

A small noise left my throat, and I tucked my legs into my chest as I stared at the spot where the noise had come from. After a while I looked back to the clown. His eyes were still glowing. Did that mean the bad man was still inside? I huffed through my nose and kicked myself for not asking Evie what happened when the bad man came out.

SCRAAAPE.

I turned my head to the sound, seeing nothing in the black around me. I stared into the dark, feeling the cold wrap itself around my arms. When had it got so cold?

SCRAAAPE.

Nearer this time.

I wanted to call Evie, but I didn't want her to know that I was scared. Plus, I wanted to wear her perfume really bad. If I sat real still, would he leave me alone? would he even know that I was here?

A hundred spiders seemed to run through my hair as the

noise came again. Shuffling. Scraping. It was walking toward me. The bad man was walking toward me. My body shook as I whimpered and pulled my legs in tighter. My head falling onto my knees, eyes shut tight.

I would remember all of the colours in my box and try to remember if I had one near to the green of the clown's eyes.

SCRAAAPE.

Close now.

My hands closed around the cane, fingers gripping so tight I hoped they wouldn't snap off. And then it spoke. A low whispering growl.

'Mer-e-dith.'

I let out a yell. He knew my name? It was the bad man, and he knew my name!

Terror flooded my body. I jumped to my feet and scrambled up the stairs as fast as I could, all signs of grandpa's shuffle gone.

There was a nasty growling laugh behind me as I banged on the door with all my strength.

'Evie, Evie! Let me out, it's the bad man. Evie! Please let me out!'

Tears were streaming down my face, and I couldn't get my breath through Grandpa's throat.

'Evie, you have to let me out! PLEASE! PLEASE, LET ME—'

Then something touched my back. I screamed. Every part of my body shaking with terror and I knew I had only one option to save myself.

I swung my body around so that I had my back to the door. I caught a glimpse of a shadowy figure just in front of me before I closed my eyes and swung grandpa's cane with all my might.

It landed against something hard with a thunk. Blind terror forced the cane back and down over and over to push the thing away from me. I was only half aware that the bad man's growl had turned into a high-pitched shout.

'Ow, get off me. Meredith! Stop, it's just me!'

Propelled forward down the steps as the thing retreated, I raised the cane high, intent on finishing it off and destroying the bad man forever. My hands were slippery with sweat, my heart jumping hard as I brought the cane down through the air with a neat swoosh.

The door to the cellar opened, and the area was flooded with light.

'What the hell is going on down here?'

I saw too late that it was Evie stood before me. The cane hit, striking her left shoulder and the shelving behind as she dropped to the floor with a howl.

The jolt from the shelf hurt my arms and there was a loud snap as I was thrown backward to sit on my backside with a thump. The breath knocked from my body with a gasp.

I saw Mum run down the stairs to Evie, who was holding her shoulder and sobbing with pain. I saw her swing her head to me.

'What on earth do you think you're doing Meredith! Eve is hurt, she's hurt!'

I couldn't get my breath to answer as I looked at Evie terrified. Evie, not the bad man. It had been Evie.

I was a little hurt that she would frighten me so much, but mostly, I was upset that I had hurt her. I had hit Evie with grandpa's cane.

Mum's face was in front of mine. Scrunched into an angry ball. She took my shoulders and shook me so hard that I thought my head would come loose.

'What the hell were you thinking, Meredith? What have you done?'

I felt a sharp slap to the left side of my head. It stung worse than a thousand bee stings, and I started to cry as mum helped Evie up the stairs, and out of the cellar.

Through my tears, I looked up at the clown on the shelf. It's eyes no longer glowed. The bad man was gone.

I sobbed with relief.

CHAPTER EIGHT

The rest of the crew went back to the hotel after the briefing at Lynton Castle, but Meredith was still unsettled after the cellars.

Declining the pre-paid hotel lunch, she decided to find a cafe in the village alone. She ambled down the quiet street, breathing the frigid air, enjoying the scenery and the fresh nip on her cheeks as she passed grey stone houses with pitched windows and one with a small round tower to the side. At the end of the street, she found what she was looking for.

Carla's Cafe.

It was empty aside from an elderly gentleman and the black and white collie who lay at his heels. The dog hardly looked her way. The man tipped his head without a smile as he scrutinised her approach to the counter, and order of a sandwich and coffee, with wary interest.

The lad behind the counter told her he'd bring it over when it was ready, so Meredith chose a seat by the window, looking out over the street, her thoughts drifting to the cellars as she waited.

The room at the bottom of the stairs had been ordinary. A larger space than the one at home, but still full of the same junk that wasn't used anymore, boxed and bagged up until it found somewhere else to go. This wasn't the only room down here. Stephanie referred to the second room as the boiler room, off to the left through a small door. Meredith was vaguely surprised that it didn't have a lock.

The smell had hung around, Stephanie admitted it had smelled bad for some time, and could probably do with a deep clean after all the years of bloodshed. As they didn't use it, and the smell never filtered through to the kitchen, they hadn't bothered.

The rooms were equal in size and looks. Both with off white dirty walls and dirty concrete floor. Both lit by a single bulb hung in the centre of the ceiling, casting the edges in shadows. The only difference was that this room was empty. A rudimentary channel ran down the centre of the floor and back toward a small hole in the outside wall. This room was colder, and Stephanie pointed out the small air vents carved into the top of the wall where the land fell away outside, allowing fresh air into the room.

'The channel was to drain the blood. The vents to curb the smell, I suppose.' Stephanie had said. Meredith had shivered as Stephanie added that the meat her ancestors brought back had been carved and hung in here, the kitchen had been in the first room. After the tour she had shown them grainy black and white pictures of the men at work, and carcases which hung on giant hooks from the ceiling. Helen had turned down her mouth in distaste, and although Meredith understood that this was how they had fed the family, she felt bile rise from her stomach.

The boiler had been in this second carving room, just inside the doorway to the left. Stephanie had shown them the circle of board, under which they found no child's body, but the disconnected pipework from the boiler that ran underneath the concrete floor. Even Stephanie could offer no explanation as to why the pipework didn't simply run across the floor or up the walls of the cellar. There would have been no reason other than aesthetics to dig down into foundations, but apparently it had been important enough to do.

The first room, at the bottom of the stairs was used for storage now, this second not at all after the boiler incident. Meredith thought she would never have used the second anyway. The smell was worse, and although nothing else about Lynton felt haunted, something about this room made her want to run.

Far away.

'There ye go lass, one filter coffee and one cheese and onion sandwich. There anything else I can get you?'

Meredith looked up at the young man with a forced smile.

'No, that's great. Thank you.'

He smiled and left. Her stomach rumbled as she looked at the sandwich. Thick white bread with crusty edges, a handful of homemade crisps, and a small salad at the side. She took only one polite sip of coffee before demolishing the sandwich and its sides, which tasted as delicious as they looked. This was a place to come again, she thought.

Stomach full, she ordered another coffee and sat looking out onto the street. The time alone was doing her good. No questions as to why she was quiet, why she had been eager to leave, why she had snapped at Steve as he had quipped about the animals that had been butchered, and the smell that lingered. She was alone to sit with her thoughts, and although they ran, she found herself feeling calm.

A buzzing against her leg drew her attention to her phone. She pulled it from her coat pocket, supposing that with such a small crew one person was missed even after a short time. The smile left her lips as she checked the screen.

Mum.

The word lit the screen like a beacon, and her stomach dropped. Running a hand over her mouth, she chewed her lower lip as she stared at the screen, the feeling of peace leaving as quickly as it had arrived.

Thanks mum. Even from London you manage to upset the equilibrium. Congratulations.

Mindful of the noise in this quiet café she pressed the end key with only a small feeling of guilt. They hadn't left on good terms, and the call would end in an argument she didn't need right now.

The phone rang again as Meredith pushed the chair under the table and said goodbye. In the street, she swiped the end icon again and took a breath of cool air, catching sight of the mountains, just visible in the distance from this end of the street.

Sentinels. Solid and dependable Stephanie had said.

Everything her mother had never been.

You should call her, though.

The familiar guilt reared its head and Meredith reined it back.

I'll call her when I get back, just a few more minutes of peace, please.

Meredith continued back down the street to the quaint village hotel, feeling peace descend over her again as she wandered through the pretty surroundings. It was so much quieter than London here…

…Except for the damn phone!

Meredith snatched the phone from her pocket and felt another stab of guilt as her finger hovered over the end key.

What if something has happened?

She swiped to answer with a sigh.

'Mum?'

'Meredith! Thank God. I thought something had happened.'

Meredith raised her eyebrows in mild surprise.

'Happened… to me?'

'Yes, to you Meredith, who the hell else am I talking to?'

Meredith paused, a little off kilter.

'Meredith?'

'Yeah mum, I'm just confused. I…'

'Confused? You're confused? I'm the one sitting waiting for my daughter to come home. It's been two days Meredith, where the hell are you? And what makes you think I don't need to be informed of your whereabouts.'

Meredith closed her eyes and took a breath.

'Mum, I haven't been away for two days, it's been five. I'm in Scotland for—'

'Scotland? What are you doing in Scotland you stupid girl? Why would you leave me here alone? How could you

Meredith? You know I'm a dependant!'

Meredith dropped to a bench over the road from the front of the hotel and ran a hand over her face. She ignored the name calling and the need for her mother to lean on the words they used at her meetings to ensnare guilt. She counted to five silently before answering.

'I'm working in Scotland, mum. As I told you many times. I'll be up here for eight weeks.'

She braced herself for the onslaught, holding the phone down in her lap in readiness.

'Eight weeks?! Eight weeks? How could you? I don't understand, Meredith, how can you even think of leaving me alone for that long? It's negligence. I'm not safe. Do you hear me? I'm not safe!'

Meredith rolled her eyes and placed the phone back to her ear.

'Mum, I told you about this six months ago. I told you week after week and the very second before I left. You knew. I couldn't have said anymore. And as I told you back then, Mrs Grey will be popping in each day to check—'

'Mrs Grey? Who the hell is Mrs Grey? I won't let her in, it's not safe to let in people I don't know. Mrs Grey?'

Meredith frowned, a trace of something not right in mum's voice awakening her unease.

'The neighbour, mum. She's been living next door to you since you and dad moved in thirty years ago.'

'That's not Mrs Grey, you idiot, that's Mrs Green. She's already been. She's a meddling witch.'

Meredith's nerves twitched as she realised what was wrong. The untrained ear may not have captured the faint slur as each 'Mrs' became a 'mssss's'.

Her heart began to thump.

'It's Mrs Grey, and she's not a meddling witch, she wants to look after you.'

'She poured my cranberry juice away. Just now. She took it all, Meredith. Poured it down the fucking sink.'

Meredith felt her stomach turn over. Mrs Grey had poured away drink?

Maybe there was a misunderstanding...

There's no misunderstanding, listen to her! Anger and confusion are normal, slur is not.

Meredith swallowed hard, warm tears filling her eyes. It had taken so much effort, and so much heartache to get mum dry last time, she had sworn this would never happen again. She put her head into her free hand and took a frustrated breath. Why?

You left her, that's why.

So I'm not allowed eight weeks? I'm doing the best I can. I've done the best I can. It was only eight weeks to try to deal with my own issues. Give me a break!

She felt anger flare as mum's indignance punctuated the silence.

'Are you listening, Meredith? She took it FUCKING ALL. Next time she comes round here I'll—'

'You'll what?' she shot back. 'She took the bottle because you're drunk, mum, and it wasn't cranberry juice. It was probably gin.'

'It was CRANBERRY JUICE! And I'm THIRSTY Meredith. THIRSTY!'

Meredith recoiled as mum screamed down the phone. Words punched and hard edged. There was no speaking to her in this condition. No point.

'There's a tap. Drink water mum. Water.'

'I'm not drinking that SHIT! Water? Pah!'

'If you're thirsty you'll drink it. Mum, listen I have work to—'

Meredith cut off as sobs now floated down the phone. Gut wrenching, full bodied sobs. She looked skyward and muttered a curse.

'What's the matter now?'

A sniffle came down the phone.

'I don't understand. Meredith, how can you be so

mean?'

'Mean?'

'Go off for a holiday and leave your poor old mum to fend for herself. Eight years! How could you? I could be dead when you come home.'

Mum dissolved into loud sobs again, and Meredith sighed, fighting the temptation to put the phone down, and ring again when the alcohol had worn off. The anger was starting to boil in her stomach, and she knew she had to hold it back. Her mum wouldn't remember this conversation in a few hours anyway, just as she hadn't remembered any conversation beforehand, obviously.

'Eight weeks. And I'm not on holiday. I'm working. You won't be dead.'

The sobs subsided a little, and there was another sniff.

'Working? You got a job?'

Mum's hysterics diminished as suddenly as they began, and Meredith decided to leave out the fact that she'd had a job since she was thirteen as someone needed to bring money into the house.

'Yes, I got a job, mum, but it's only working away for a while, and then I'll be home.'

'In Scotland.'

'Yes, in Scotland, for eight weeks. Seven now, as one of them has gone already.'

More's the pity, she thought, but left that comment silent.

'What are you doing up there? Why can't you work in London like everybody else?'

The insinuations were starting to creep back into mums' tone and the hackles began to rise on Meredith's neck.

'I'm filming, and the location is Scotland. I don't get to choose where, the director does that.'

Instantly mum was interested again.

'Director. You're making a film?'

'No, a TV series.'

'Ooohh, Well, look at you. A big fancy film star, eh?

What's the film about?'

'Series. We're recording a paranormal show where we —'

'Ghosts? Pah! I should have known!'

Meredith could almost see the look of distaste on her mother's face. The same one she had seen many times over the years. At least, since Eve had started showing up anyway.

'Yes,' she said quietly, 'ghosts.'

Her mother practically roared, and there was a bang in the background that she thought was possibly something being thrown, that was now broken or very bent.

'For God's sake, Meredith, when will you let this go? This paranormal SHIT is driving me to the brink. It's your fault I took to the drink, and can you blame me? Whatever you think you see, or saw, isn't real. Whatever you hope to get out of bringing me down with you, it won't work. You're a selfish little bitch Meredith, do you hear me? A selfish BITCH. Why do I have to be reminded every damn day of the daughter I lost by the one that's living? It's enough that you still exist! Why do you rub my face in it and wonder why I need a fucking DRINK? Why do you think I need to continue to suffer? I don't—'

Meredith pressed the end button and wiped the stray tear from her cheek. Christ, if her mother thought she was mean maybe she ought to look in the mirror and see exactly where that streak had come from.

Before mum had a chance to call back Meredith dialled Mrs Grey.

'Hello?'

'Hey, Mrs Grey,' Meredith said, trying to keep her voice bright and airy, 'It's Meredith. I just thought I'd see if you were okay. I take it mum's been drinking. She just called ranting and raving, saying that you took a bottle off her. She's in a foul mood and it everyone's fault but her own, obviously.'

Mrs Grey sighed and Meredith felt guilty that she didn't

have anyone else who could help with her mother. The lady had to be well into her sixties, and although she was spritely and still very active, she must have better things to be doing. She certainly didn't need to be abused each day by the drunk that lived next door.

'Oh Meredith, I'm so sorry, I was going to ring you later. I wasn't sure whether you would be busy with filming or whatever. I'm sorry, I don't understand exactly what it is you have to do up there.'

'No, it's fine, don't worry.'

'But yes, I was going to call you and tell you she had a bottle of Gin. I have absolutely no idea where she got it from. She hasn't been out at all, and she's had no visitors that I've seen. It may just be that she had some hiding places that she forgot about and hit the jackpot while looking.'

Meredith closed her eyes.

'I'm so sorry, so you had a mess to contend with too?' she said.

'Just a small one, don't worry.'

A small one? Meredith knew her mum didn't do small mess. Especially when she was on a desperate hunt for hidden alcohol.

Where the hell did she hide that bottle?

Meredith had turned the place upside down and poured everything she found down the sink months ago. As part of her therapy, and to kickstart her withdrawal from the demon for the fourth time, mum had helped. Energised, and ready to start a new chapter in her life—this time for certain.

There had been a lot. Hidden in all sorts of obscure places, including the laundry basket, loft, knicker drawer, and shed. By the afternoon mum had been ready to kill for a drink, and energised, happy mum had turned into an emotional lunatic. She raged and ranted, moaned, and whinged, cried and screamed. And she stayed that way for hours upon hours, until she finally levelled at miserable and distant. Meredith had been exhausted and had vowed never to let her mum go back to drinking. Ever. They would get through this and start over. Both of them.

That had been seven months ago, and to her knowledge her mum had only slipped three times. Once she had snuck to the shop, the call of alcohol more than the pull of agoraphobia. The other twice she had found bottles hidden in places they hadn't been found initially. All three times she had got to her mum before she had emptied the bottles down her neck. This time she hadn't been there to stop her, to help her.

Guilt washed over Meredith. If her mum relapsed over these eight weeks, it would be her fault.

Dependant. The word rebounded in her head.

Yes, she is dependent. And yes, you did leave her for eight weeks in the care of a neighbour to chase ghosts through Scotland on a personal vendetta.

Guilty as charged.

Heat flushed her cheeks.

'Meredith? Are you still there?'

She shook the thoughts away as Mrs Grey's voice punctured her thoughts.

'Sorry,' She said, 'I'm still here. Um, how much of the bottle did she drink? She was furious that you took it away, so there must have been some left in there, right?'

'I'm afraid not. The bottle had gone by the time I got there, but she was hanging onto it for dear life. She was upset that I took it, yes.'

Meredith felt her heart sink. A whole bottle of Gin? In a matter of hours probably.

'That explains the ranting and raving then. Thank you so much for this, you're doing amazing. I just… maybe I need to come back. I don't know what I'll do if she relapses again. Those first few days are like a black hole of torture, I can't live through that again.'

'No, Meredith, listen to me. Last time we spoke you said you were enjoying the job, and I'm glad to help, Nancy has been a neighbour and good friend of mine for over thirty years. It pains me to see her go down this road and I want her to get better as much as you do, but you need the break. You've taken care of her alone for too many years and you must remember; she may be your mother, but she is not your responsibility. She is a grown woman, making her own choices—through grief, I know that—but if you can't help her, you are absolutely free, and completely within your rights to walk away. You've done more than enough. You are a grown woman with your own life too.'

'I could never do that. I feel like this is all my fault. Eve died and then I made it worse by just being there. She told me as much. '

'Alcohol-fuelled rants. She doesn't mean it.'

Meredith smiled but said nothing. Mrs Grey was kind, but she didn't know the extent of her mother's hatred. Drunk or stone cold sober she had told Meredith many times that she had made things worse for her. That the drink was to block her and her talk of Eve out. She had also added that it was Meredith's fault that her father had walked out, and her fault that he had hung himself.

Meredith had enough sense of self to know that none of these things were her fault, and that the issue wasn't hers. But she only had one mother, and she was her only family now. They had to stick together—left to her own devices Meredith wasn't certain how long her mother would last.

'Believe me, Meredith, she didn't mean it.' Mrs Grey said on the phone.

'I know.'

'Oh, there's someone at the door. I must go, but don't worry about your mum and me. I want the best for her, and if that means getting a bit of abuse, I'll take it. Enjoy the time away working, she'll still be here when you get home.'

'Thank you, I'm so grateful, you don't know how much.'

Mrs Grey chuckled.

'We both know Nancy is a big pain in the ass again right

now, but we'll get her through it. You get to work, Moo, enjoy the time without the responsibility. If anything happens again, I'll call you. Goodbye, now.'

'Bye.'

Meredith frowned, phone still at her ear.

Moo?

Only Eve had ever called her moo. Even mum and dad had never picked that one up, it had been their special thing. A sister thing.

A shudder ran through her as she ended the call and looked back to the hotel. Matt was outside smoking a cigarette. He raised a hand in greeting, and she returned the gesture with a smile, the unease fading a little.

There was no way Mrs Grey knew Eve's pet name. She must have imagined it, there was no other explanation.

CHAPTER NINE

'Cut. Cut, cut, cut.'

Kevin waved his hands in the air, a stern frown cut a line between his eyes.

'No, this isn't working. It's not enough.'

Meredith glanced at Matt, who shook his head at her. She wasn't sure if it was a 'keep quiet', or a 'Kevin's an ass' shake, so she dropped her gaze.

'We have just forty minutes left of filming and tonight has been a washout. The walkthrough revealed nothing. The experiments have produced nothing. Even the EMF isn't playing ball. This series is going nowhere if I don't get some action.'

Meredith rolled her eyes at the bath. The action wasn't in their hands, what he was now going to throw his toys out of the pram for was nothing to do with the crew, and everything to do with a non-haunted castle. A castle he bloody chose. Donald spoke up and Meredith wanted to clap at his speech.

'We've had a lot of action at the last place, to be believable don't we need to just go with it? Spirits don't work to schedule, and each haunting is different. Not every episode needs to be an explosion of activity surely, we're not making an action series.'

'No, we're not making an action series, we're making a paranormal series. Which means, Donald, that we need paranormal things to happen. Where's the entertainment here? What's happening? Nothing. One hour of nothing for fans of the paranormal is just not good enough. There's no show. Are we keeping you up, Helen?'

Meredith glanced across the bathroom at Helen, who

was trying to conceal a large yawn, and failing. Bad timing, she thought with a grin as she looked back down at the bath.

'No, sir.'

Kevin's beady eyes bored into Helen's as she squirmed beside Gwen.

'Glad to hear it. So, what's the plan?'

Helen's mouth dropped open a little as she gawped at him.

'The plan?' she squeaked.

'Yes. I'm sick and tired of trying to remember what gadget does what and what experiment does what. How do you think we should go forward?'

Meredith frowned and brought her gaze up to Kevin. A smug smile sat on his lips; eyebrows raised to Helen.

What was this little tete-te-tete all about? He had been okay today, bearable, and now here he was being a complete dickhead again. She glanced to Steve as he interjected, coming to Helen's defence.

'Well, we've tried the—'

Kevin swung to him, keeping the smile locked in place.

'Yes, Steve, but I'm not asking you. I'm asking her.'

He jabbed his pen in Helen's direction as Steve gave a quick nod.

'Yes, boss.'

Meredith exchanged a look with Steve, and then looked back to Helen, who looked like she had eaten too much beetroot.

'Well?' Kevin said, 'nothing? I thought so. Maybe you could keep yourself awake enough to learn—'

'We could use the Ouija board.' Helen said, cutting him off.

Kevin paused. 'What?'

'I said, we could use the Ouija to see if we could contact the girl. Asha.' Helen reddened further and spluttered. 'Sorry Elana, not Asha, she's the…um…'

Helen trailed off as Kevin stared at her hard. His body

almost rigid under the bright bathroom lights.

'I'm sorry.' She said quietly.

'Sorry? You're sorry? Miss Hartford that's the best idea we've had all night. Of course, we have the Ouija Board! Matt, go find it, we have half an hour. We'll shoot in the living room. Equipment downstairs everybody.' Kevin clapped his hands, 'I said now, people.'

Meredith grinned at Helen as he strode out of the room. She grinned back, and then Steve gave her a hearty pat on the back as he grabbed the mic and followed behind.

'Nice one, Heathen.'

Helen reddened further as the others left the room one by one and filed down the hallway to the stairs, Helen and Meredith bringing up the rear.

'Heathen?' Meredith said.

Helen shrugged and wrinkled her nose. 'It's my new nickname. I'm too scared to ask why.'

'I know why,' Meredith said with a laugh.

Helen turned to her, mousy waves bobbing at her shoulders, eyes puzzled.

'You do?'

'Yep.' Meredith began to whisper-chant a song she had learned way back at school. 'Helen and Steve, Sitting in a tree, K.I.S—'

'Are you kidding me?' Helen gasped cutting her off.

Meredith let out a low laugh.

'He's single. He likes you.'

'He does not like me.'

'Ah Helen, he so does. Even his t-shirt has been pointing your way all day.'

Steve's repertoire for the day included jeans and a green t-shirt emblazoned with the quip 'I'm ghost-hunting with her' on both the front and the back. An arrow pointed to his right, where he had kept Helen most of the day. Meredith peered around Donald's back as Steve reached the stairs. His arrow now pointing straight to Matt. She nudged Helen to take a look.

'Well, that's my theory out the window. Does he have a pet name for Matt too?'

'Yeah, Matilda. Guess I'm out of luck, hey?'

Helen wrinkled her nose and looked at her with sad eyes. Meredith couldn't keep her giggles in, and then Helen laughed too as they descended the stairs after the others.

Behind them, the bathroom light flickered, brightened, and then went out, plunging the room into darkness.

The living room was warm and cosy. The photographs all in a line on top of the fireplace where a roaring fire burned in the grate. Orla was staying in town with the children, only Stephanie was here tonight. She had made herself scarce during their living and bathroom investigation, but now she brought in mugs of tea as they set up chairs around the small coffee table where the Ouija board now sat looking ominous.

Kevin huffed and shooed her away with a flap of his hand.

'Yes. Yes, thank you. I'm not sure we have time for chats around mugs of tea, we're on a schedule.'

Stephanie raised her eyebrows as the rest of the group thanked her graciously and took sips from their mugs to make a point.

'Thank you, it is appreciated.' Meredith said, catching Stephanie's arm as she passed to leave the room.

Stephanie smiled, and lowered her voice to a whisper.

'I don't mind, as long as you get to the bottom of this nonsense.' She raised her voice again so that Kevin could hear. 'I'll be in the kitchen if you need anything else.'

Meredith gave her a reassuring smile. She didn't like to say that they had found nothing at all so far. Squat.

'Places then, please. Let's get this rolling.'

Matt set up the camera as they busied themselves getting comfortable around the small coffee table ready to start.

'Do you want to lead this one Donald?' Meredith asked.

'I'll be honest, I don't really get a lot of feeling in here. The girl hasn't come forward at all yet. I'll concentrate on calling her, you lead the investigation.'

'Okay, no problem.'

She assessed him as he closed his eyes, wondering if he was really psychic, after all. Kevin didn't seem impressed so far. But then, he probably wouldn't be impressed if the spirits decided to show themselves and perform a jig on the table.

Maybe time would tell. His online reputation was certainly solid, she knew that. But really, was there any point to a psychic who wasn't going to contribute? He was the one supposedly able to call spirits forward and communicate, but instead he always seemed to be sitting quietly... or keeling over with a moan.

She took a sip of her tea and placed the cup on the table in front of her.

There was an almighty huff from behind her.

'Cup in shot, Meredith. Tell me, are we filming a ghost show, or a chat show?'

Matt leaned in to take her cup.

'Well, hopefully we'll be chatting to a ghost.' He said, placing it on the fireplace out of shot.

Laughter rippled around the table and Meredith grinned at Gwen, who was wearing a rare smile. Kevin, however, wasn't smiling.

'We *will* be chatting to a ghost, but I guarantee it won't want tea.'

Meredith's smile slipped. That was pressure right there. If this spirit, or indeed any spirit, didn't come through there would be trouble in the real world, that was for certain. She sighed as Kevin nodded to Matt and Steve.

'Ready?'

'Yes boss.'

'Oh, for crying out loud...' he began again.

Meredith was in eyeline with Steve, it didn't escape her attention that Kevin now stood to his right. She felt a flutter of giggles start to rise from her belly. Steve's 'I'm ghost hunting with her' slogan was pointing straight to Kevin as he now had a hissy fit about the lighting. Apparently, there was no dimmer, so they would perform this investigation by Matt's camera light, and the small amount of flickering light from the fire.

'We'll never see the letters,' Gwen said.

'Of course you will. Christ is this investigation doomed by the incapacity of the crew? I need action, and you need glasses.'

Gwen glanced down at the glasses bouncing around her neck on string and obviously decided he may be right. She put them on carefully.

'Right, is everybody ready?'

There was a murmur of agreement and Kevin started the countdown to roll. A flutter of apprehension rippled through Meredith's gut at the thought of the last seance.

That was the glass test, though. This is different.

But Meredith couldn't convince herself. She took a breath as Kevin counted three, two, one, with his fingers, and then they were recording.

The planchette began to move almost immediately, taking the group by surprise. Donald sat frowning as the wooden pointer circled aimlessly around the board.

'Donald? Do you have any idea who's trying to come through?' Helen asked, taking the words from Meredith's mouth.

He closed his eyes, keeping his finger on the spinning planchette as it finally came to a stop in the centre of the board.

'The girl.' He said. 'The girl is here.'

Well, a name would be good, Meredith thought, we're on TV here.

'Elana?' She prompted.

'Yes. Yes, that's the one. Elana is here. She wants to

talk to us.'

The camera was panned to Donald, brow creased with apparent effort, and Meredith couldn't help rolling her eyes.

No shit sherlock, I wondered what this thing was spinning for. Christ, I could have told him that with no psychic ability.

She straightened her face into presenter mode as the camera panned back out.

'Okay, Elana—'

She cut off as the planchette moved to a letter and stopped.

'Helen, make sure you get all this down.' She whispered.

Helen picked up the pen in front of her and opened the day-glow book. She had been apprehensive to join in this seance after the last session, Kevin had been three quarters of the way to boiling by the time Donald had suggested that they would need someone to note the letters if the spirit said anything complex.

Helen had readily agreed, setting her things before her as Kevin relaxed back to a simmer.

The planchette swung from letter to letter, each time it paused the group said the letter aloud, and Helen wrote it down.

The first few words were easy, simply no, no, no followed by go, go, go. Then it stopped.

'What does that mean?' Gwen said slipping her glasses down to peer at Meredith.

'No and go?'

The planchette started to slide again.

A.W.A.I.Y.

'Ah,' Gwen slipped her glasses back up her nose with her free hand. 'No, go away.'

Meredith said nothing. The planchette stilled and sat, waiting in the centre of the board. She blinked. Something about this seemed unreal. The room was warm and cosy, a fire crackled in the fireplace. Sure, the fire cast shadows which danced across the walls of the plush room, but even they couldn't muster an air of spookiness.

There was just no atmosphere in here.

Meredith looked to Kevin, he stared back at her expectantly. She cleared her throat.

'Go away? Do you want us to go away Elana?'

The planchette shivered under their fingers but made no move.

'Elana,' Meredith said again, 'Are we welcome here?'

The planchette moved to 'No' in the top left-hand corner of the board.

'No,' Gwen said.

Right, Meredith thought, but you're not kicking up too much of a fuss. Is that a good thing? She is only a child talking to a group of adults after all.

'So, we need to leave, Elana?'

The planchette slid to the Yes but went no further.

Meredith could only think of one reason that this all felt so weird.

'Donald, how is Elana feeling to you? Can she not muster much energy? This all seems very polite and trivial after what we know about her.'

Donald shook his head. His face had lost a little colour in the glow of the fire.

'No, indeed, she's very powerful. I can feel the force of her, she's hard to keep hold of.'

He made a strangled moaning, as though he was pulling something extremely heavy up a set of stairs. Meredith frowned.

Here we go again. Is this his trick? Is he going to moan and faint at each sitting?

She glanced at Kevin, who was looking at his watch, and decided to concentrate on Elana. Maybe poking her a little would shake things up. Kevin wasn't looking too impressed right now.

'Elana, if you're so powerful, why do I not feel as though

I need to leave? I don't believe you have any power to make me.'

There was a sharp intake of breath from Donald and the planchette shivered before sliding violently around the board.

G.E.T pause O.U.T.

Repeated over and over. The only pauses coming between each of the two words. Meredith continued to push.

'I think you're weak, and I think you prey on little Asha because she's weak too. You don't scare me.'

A.S.H.A. The planchette spelled.

'What about Asha?' Meredith said.

A.S.H.A.

Meredith huffed a laugh. 'Asha isn't here.'

A.S.H.A. The planchette paused and spun on the board before taking a new turn back to the original message.

G.E.T. – O.U.T.

'We're not going anywhere Elana. How about you answer some questions for us? What do you want with Asha?'

As the planchette hurried to each letter Meredith scanned the room. Helen was writing busily in the book, keeping her eyes cast down. Donald sat with his eyes closed, face pale. Gwen and Steve were watching pensively, following the pointer around the board, and calling each letter as it came. Matt's camera was trained on her, watching. Everyone was silent.

A.N.S.E.R. the board spelled out.

'Yes, please answer the—' Meredith cut off as the planchette continued.

M.E.

She looked up, catching Gwen's eye, and frowned.

'Answer me?' Gwen said.

Meredith shrugged. 'Answer what?'

G.E.T – O.U.T.

Gwen let out a small breath. 'But you didn't ask anything, Elana,' she said, looking to Meredith who gave an equally puzzled stare back.

A.N.S.E.R.

Meredith was careful not to roll her eyes. This was so cliched it could have been any hammer horror film seance.

'Well, just ask the question, Elana.'

I – K.N.O.W.

The planchette was moving quickly again now, and Donald gave another moan.

C.E.L.L.A.R.

'The cellar? That's interesting Elana, why would you mention the cellar?'

C.E.L.L.A.R.

C.E.L.L.A.R.

'Elana, what—' Meredith broke off as the planchette continued to spin wildly around the board, spitting the same letters up over and over.

C.E.L.L.A.R.

C.E.L.L.A.R.

This is ridiculous.

'Elana.' She said firmly, 'Enough! Just tell us what you mean.'

C.E.L.L.A.R.

C.E.L.L.A.R.

With a shake of her head she looked to Kevin, who motioned for her to keep going. Meredith thought this would be the most boring episode they had shot. The spirit apparently comes through with no other signs of a haunting at all. No cold, no breeze, no static, no *feeling*. Period. If she didn't know better, she would think someone was playing her for a fool right now. And still the planchette ran on, stating the same word over and over.

Donald groaned, and Meredith felt something inside her snap.

'Elana, this is ridiculous! Either tell us the reason you want us to go, or you go! I'm getting fed up with this now.'

C.E.L.L.A.R.

Meredith threw a frustrated look at Kevin, and finally at Donald.

'Donald. How in the heck do we stop this? Can you help us?'

He gave another moan and shook his head.

Right, well she knew how to stop it anyway.

'On three, I want everyone to take their hands off the planchette. This is getting us nowhere. Everyone understand?'

Gwen nodded. Donald moaned.

'Donald? Do you understand?' She said a little sharper than she had intended. Still the planchette spun on.

Donald met her eye at last and gave a pained look as he nod his head.

'Good. Three, two, one, let go.'

All three of the seance participants let go of the planchette which suddenly fell still. Inanimate.

Meredith gave a sigh of relief.

'Right. I think that may be all we get out of Elana unless she wants to show up for more tomorrow.'

Donald was wiping a sheen of sweat off his forehead, and Gwen took off her glasses.

Helen shut the book with a thud as Kevin signalled to Matt to stop recording. 'What on earth was that all about? It was just weird,' she said.

'It's obvious, heathen,' Steve said, he put on a low spooky voice, 'she doesn't want us to go into the cellar, mwahhh hah haaaahhhh.'

Helen wrinkled her nose at him with a grin.

'That's for sure,' Meredith said, 'that must be the most frustrating conversation I've had in my life, and I've had a few clangers!'

'Well, I don't think we're getting anything more from her tonight.' Gwen said. 'Are there any other phenomena here? Anything on the static readings?'

Matt shook his head. 'Nothing EMF either,' he said.

'We could do with some different equipment, something new to try out here. How does she manifest with no change in the energy of the air around us? It's strange.' Meredith said.

Matt shrugged. 'I think there are some more bits we can try in the car. Maybe tomorrow we can set them up in the cellars.'

Kevin huffed and slapped his pen on his own paper pad.

'Yes, I think so. Tonight was a wash out, I can't have this happen again tomorrow, folks.'

Donald coughed once and moaned, pulling Meredith's attention to him.

'She's still here,' He said, not sounding quite himself, 'She wants… um...'

Now the air finally seemed to change. There was no direct change in temperature, it was more an oppressive sensation, and the EMF meter finally went off.

'Get rolling.' Kevin said urgently, and Matt instantly took back to the camera.

Meredith wasn't sure how this would go, or what they were to do so she took to Donald.

'What does she want, Donald?'

Donald's face changed. He looked at Meredith, cocking his head to one side with a slow smile that sent goosebumps up and down her arms. She shuddered involuntarily.

'Donald?'

He grinned at her now. She couldn't explain what was happening with his face, but his features didn't seem right. One glance at Helen, who sat rigid, eyes wide and mouth slack, told her that she saw the same.

Meredith fought to keep some professionalism now that terror was starting to envelope her very core.

'D…Donald?' she said, swallowing hard.

'Hello, Meredith.' He said.

The voice sent ice up her spine. It wasn't Donald's voice. It possessed his tone but more of a sweet, childlike voice overrode his usual gruffness. His gaze was firmly locked on hers. She would have sworn afterward that he didn't blink through the whole episode.

'I said hello, Meredith.'

'Hello,' she replied, 'I… I take it I'm speaking…' She stumbled over her words and Donald laughed. In fact, that was wrong. He giggled. A sound Meredith had never heard Donald make. Ever.

'Elana, of course. Who else?'

The hair at the base of her neck prickled. The fire flickered, sending shadows skittering over the room as the air pressed around her.

'What do you…'

Donald gave another slow smile.

'You don't like the cellar, do you Meredith?'

Donald's tone was mocking. He giggled again and a flutter of fear circled Meredith's abdomen as she shook her head.

'I don't understand.' It was all she could manage.

'But I do, Meredith.' Donald said, bringing his hand to his mouth and giving a coy giggle. 'I understand. I *know*.'

Meredith swallowed hard.

'You know what?'

'I know about the cellar, Meredith Moo.'

Icy fingers crawled down her spine and Meredith began to shake as Donald continued, his voice now high-pitched and singsong.

'I know what you di-id.'

Meredith's heart skipped, and she struggled to breathe as she stared at Donald's innocent smile and cold, clever eyes. Donald's, but not his at all. This wasn't happening. It couldn't be. No one knew what had happened. Donald grinned, and then broke into a sudden loud shout.

'Don't go down there, Meredith! Don't look into his eyes!'

The team's shouts and screams reverberated behind her

as Meredith fled the room. She spun out of the back door, and ran onto the lawn where she eventually stopped, gasping, hands on her knees. Her stomach cramped hard, and she heaved, losing what little she had eaten today on the back lawn with a ferociousness that she thought may bring her stomach up and out with it.

CHAPTER TEN

JULY—162 DAYS UNTIL DEATH

'You're an absolute superstar, Moo!' Evie yelled from her room next door. I grinned, pleased with myself, as I reached for the glitter pens on top of the cupboard in my own room.

My fingers caught them with the tips, pushing them further away. My tongue flicked between my lips as I stood on tiptoe and reached again.

From Evie's room, music started to play. Jerusalem. The song she always played from the last night of the proms collection cd she had received for her birthday last month. It was a song we sang in school assembly, and one that mum hated.

I didn't understand. It was just a song, and the people singing on the cd sounded like me and my friends singing in school. Maybe a little better. A CHOIR Evie told me. It sounded nice.

I had seen it once, sang by CHOIR people, on TV one Sunday morning. The people rounded their mouths into perfect 'O's, their chins lifted high. Evie had found it hysterical that I had lifted my chin and formed my own 'O' as I joined them from the living room.

Then mum had come in from the kitchen, wiping her hands on a kitchen towel as she flicked the 'tripe' off the screen, and replaced it with the NEWS. A man, who looked like he never laughed, told us of many BAD THINGS happening as he shuffled papers on his desk.

Evie and I had gone to play outside after that.

Now I grasped my hand around the pens, and formed my

mouth into an 'O', as I quietly sang the words.

'…Bow of burning gold…'

Evie lifted her voice next door, joining in with vigour. I grinned as I pad to her room with the pens. Downstairs, the kitchen door shut with a reverberating bang.

I glanced to the stairs as I went into Evie's room without knocking. I grimaced as I realised my mistake, but Evie was away in the world of the song, one hand to her chest, eyes closed.

'…till we have built Jer-oo-salem…'

I threw the pens onto the floor and joined in loudly. My own hand went to my chest as I closed my eyes to FEEL the music as Evie did.

'…in England's green and pleasant land.'

I lingered after the song had finished, feeling enormously proud as the trumpets and piano played the last few notes. My eyes flying open only when something soft and furry hit my face.

'Moo, if you're not on stage, I'll eat my shoe. You're sooooo dramatic.'

I giggled as she flicked the cd player back to ten. The number of Jerusalem. The band started up again. There was a bang and mum shouted up from downstairs. Something I wasn't allowed to do. It was rude to shout through walls, but mum OWNED the house and so could DO AS SHE PLEASED.

'For God's sake, Eve,' She yelled. 'Turn off that bloody song!'

Mum sounded mad, but I thought she was wicked to blame God. She wanted it turned off more for her sake than His, I knew. Would God hear and punish her? I frowned as Evie grinned at me and turned the volume a bit higher. My eyes widened and she put a finger to her lips.

She grabbed the pad of paper and flopped onto the floor by the pens. My hands over my mouth I sat next to her.

'Are we ready for today's lesson Moo?'

I crossed my legs and folded my arms across my chest as we had to do at school to show that we were LISTENING and READY TO LEARN. My back was straight, chin up, as I nod my head.

Evie grinned and grabbed the glitter pens.

'Today we learn about horses.'

I slumped, my back rolling forward, stomach crunched.

'But Evie…' I moaned. Evie put a hand up to my face.

'Now, don't be silly. Nature is an important subject.' She picked up the plush brown bear that had hit me in the face a few minutes ago, sitting it upright against the leg of the bed. 'You can help me Egor, you know all about horses, don't you?'

Evie put a hand to the back of the bears head, and it nodded like it was alive.

'Yes Eve, I do.' It said in a gravelly voice that came from Evie's mouth.

My eyes widened as Evie took her hand away, Egor sat back against the bed leg watching. I watched him carefully, just in case his eyes glowed green. And then I remembered.

'Ooh, ooh, Evie…'

'Hands for questions, please.'

My hand flew into the air, as high as it would go, I was barely keeping my BACKSIDE on the floor I jigged so much.

'Yes, Meredith?' Evie said importantly. She pointed at me with the end of a pink glittery pen.

'I just remembered, I wanted to find the green of the clown's eyes from the cellar. Have I got a pen that—'

Evie gave me a sharp stare.

'You saw the clown's eyes?' She said cutting me off.

I nod my head hard.

'Yes. Yes. I wanted to find the green—'

Evie cut my words off again.

'You looked into the green of his eyes? Did you count?'

I shook my head this time, blonde hair flailing around my

face and sticking to my lip. I pulled it away with my fingers.

'I didn't count. But I did look. I wanted to find the green.'

'There is no green on God's earth that looks like the bad man's lair Meredith. You shouldn't have looked. That's why you were so mad when I came to rescue you from the cellar, it all makes sense now.'

Evie was looking thoughtful, but I wasn't interested. She had said there wasn't a green like it on earth, and yet, the glittery green pen in the packet on the bed looked like it to me.

'Evie,' I said pointing to the packet, 'I think—'

But Evie was on a roll now. Her lips had gone loose, and her words wobbled and wobbled out of her mouth.

'Meredith, I knew there was something up. I knew you couldn't have broken grandpa's stick over my shoulder like that. It was the bad man. You looked too long. Meredith you must have counted to three. Even in your head. It was him, you're not strong enough, it had to be him! He broke the cane and broke my collar bone!'

I jiggled on my crossed legs, looking at the packet of pens.

'But the green, Evie,' I pointed again, but Evie wasn't listening.

'Oh God, Meredith, do you know what this means?'

Her voice had raised, and I stopped jiggling to look at her. I shook my head.

'What?' I said.

Evie looked at me. Her faced seemed too white and too pinched.

'Meredith you're probably possessed now.'

'What?'

'Possessed. It means that the bad man may have passed into you. That's how you swung the cane so hard.'

I wrinkled my nose and thought. No one else appeared to be in my head, and surely, I would have noticed if a big bad man was in there.

'No. He's not here Evie.'

'He must be. You must be possessed.'

I shook my head again. There was only me in my head I was sure of it.

Evie's pinched cheeks were getting colour now. An angry red was spreading across them, like two splotches of paint.

'Meredith! You broke my god damned collar bone!'

I inhaled a sharp breath at God being used as a scape goat again. This time he was damned. Or maybe it was me that was damned. My heart thumped behind my ribs.

'Right,' Evie said, 'I know how to protect you. And I know how to get him out. Egor will help us, won't you Egor?'

She reached down and grasped the brown bear. Her hand circling the back of its waist. Egor said nothing this time.

Sitting the bear between her knees, she pat the bed in front of her, where I was supposed to sit. I climbed up and sat READY TO LEARN quietly. My heart hammered. I still just wanted to know whether the green would draw the same as the eyes, but I knew Evie would want me to keep quiet. She seemed to be ON A MISSION.

She narrowed her eyes at me, and my belly skipped over.

'Right, hold this, I need to get some things,' She said, throwing Egor at me and jumping off the bed.

I held his soft fur in my left hand and reached for the green pen with my right. The pad, my new sketch pad, was open to a clean page, and as Evie scrambled around, I took the lid off the pen and scribbled on it. The green was bright, maybe too bright, I couldn't remember now. It had been over a month ago. I cursed to myself, leaving God out of the equation, as I tried to think.

And then Evie put the things she had gathered onto the bed with a soft plunk.

'Okay, this should do it.'

She explained what everything was for. Perfume, because the man hated girly things, a hairclip, same reason. A torch so that Evie could see if the man was in my throat, a 'blackjack' sweet (that looked old), because the man hated sweets, a dark blue cape because the man couldn't cross through blue, and a mirror to reflect him into something not dangerous when he left my mouth. This would be Egor.

I grumbled. 'Evie, I hate blackjacks.'

'You want the man to live inside you forever? You must do this Meredith. You have no choice.'

'I can't feel him anyway.'

'Maybe not, but you hurt me. Who knows, next time you could hurt mum or dad. Remember you broke the cane, and my bone Meredith. How did you do that?'

I wanted to say that she had scared me, terrified me to the point that I thought she was the man. I wanted to beat him. I wanted to kill him. It was lucky I hadn't killed her! I knew she didn't want an answer though.

Evie pulled me forward and draped the cloak around my shoulders, she pulled the front edges together covering my arms.

'Don't move them Moo or he could get back into you when he leaves. This is a special cape. It blocks him and keeps him out.'

I blinked up at her, keeping as still as I could as she arranged the hairclip at the side of my head. I felt the small pings as some of the hairs pulled out. I balled my hands into fists and kept silent. My left ankle began to itch. I tried to ignore it, but the more I did, the more it needed scratching.

I begged and pleaded with God that he make it go away, just for a while as Evie got the bad man out, but it seemed God was having his penance at hearing his name said to often in this house—and never for good reasons.

I wondered if God listened at all, and if I couldn't see him, how did I know he was even there? Maybe he was on holiday. God never left a note, and he never answered. How would I know?

The itching got worse until I could bare it no more. I snatched a hand from under the cape and scratched, the pleasure overriding Evie's shouts as she sprayed the perfume into the air where I had been seconds ago.

'Moo! Jesus, what a waste! Sit up and keep your hands under the cape. This is important.'

I sat up, saying sorry to God and now Jesus too in my head. Evie sprayed the perfume at my chest. The flowery scent tickling my nose, making me want to sneeze.

'Right,' Evie said. I think we're all done. Now let me see if I can see the bad man. Open wide.'

I opened my mouth and Evie held the torch at its entrance shining the light inside with a frown.

'Hmm.'

'Cag oo ee in?' I said.

Evie pulled the light back.

'What?'

I swallowed, tasting lilies.

'I said can you see him?'

'Well, I think I got a glimpse, but you keep messing around, Moo. Stay still and quiet and do as I ask. Open wide.'

I opened my mouth again and the light reappeared at its entrance.

Evie's eyebrows suddenly jumped, and her eyes widened.

'I can see him,' she whispered, 'He's definitely in there. Stay still.'

My heart pattered and I felt a bit sick. How had the man been in there all this time and I hadn't known? How had he got in without me knowing? Had I breathed him in?

My mouth started to shake with the effort of holding it open.

'Ee-ee.' I said.

'Shhh.' Evie was back to her frown. Then the light

flicked off with a snap.

'Right,' Evie said as I shut my aching mouth. 'He's near. So, I need you to eat the blackjack but in a special way. I need you to listen Meredith because this is very important. Are you listening?'

My stomach swirled with butterflies. I nodded my head as Evie unwrapped the sweet.

'Put it in your mouth only when I say. Then chew twenty times and swallow. How many times?'

'Twenty,' I said.

'Good,' Evie held the sweet in front of my face. I knew the harsh aniseed taste well, and I hated it.

Twenty times. Just chew twenty times and swallow.

'Ready?'

I swallowed, my throat already wanting to push the sweet out before it had got there, but I said yes.

'Open wide,' she said and popped the sweet in.

I gagged, my tongue falling forward.

'Chew Meredith!' Evie yelled as she grabbed the mirror, facing it so that it reflected both me and Egor the bear. I chewed. My eyes watered as I tried to keep the sweet in and I gagged again. Count. I needed to count to take my mind off this taste.

In my head I counted each time my teeth came down on the sweet until I had reached twenty, and then I swallowed. My eyes had made tears course down my cheeks and the sweet, still too big to swallow, seemed to get stuck. I coughed, head falling forward.

'That's it! Keep with it Moo, he's coming out that's why it feels bad! Swallow, push it into his lair!'

Through my blurry tears Evie seemed wild with excitement. I coughed and choked, the sweet hurting my throat as it made its way slowly down, scraping the sides painfully as it went.

Finally, the pain slid into my chest bones and the coughing stopped. I gasped some breaths and looked at Evie. She sat stock still on the bed, mouth open. The mirror sat in her lap, still reflecting both me and the bear.

'Oh. My. God. Meredith, you did it!'

My heart jumped with joy, although I didn't recall feeling the man come out.

'The bad man is out?'

'Yep. He's in the bear. Egor is no longer to be trusted, but at least you're safe Moo.'

She gathered me in a hug, and I squeezed her back, my chest hurting from the sweet and the cough. Or maybe it was from the bad man I supposed.

Evie pushed me back and gathered the bear up in two fingers. She strode across to the wardrobe, opened the door, and threw him inside. I saw him hit the rear and bounce forward as the door shut. Then she sat back on the bed.

'I'm in complete awe, Moo. I don't know how you did it, that was so brave.'

I was starting to get a little scared now. The bad man had been in me and I hadn't known. What if he could get out of Egor? What if he hadn't gone into Egor at all, but gone into Evie instead? I told Evie my concerns.

'I saw him, Moo. With my own eyes. He went into the bear. It worked. I'll prove it to you.'

Evie picked up the pad and a black pen and began to draw. Fast and smooth she drew a black mass of scribble with arms and legs. It didn't matter that Evie had scribbled a drawing. It was the man. I knew it. My heart knew it.

'That's him. There, see?' Evie said, as mum's voice called us down for dinner.

I wanted to cry but Evie didn't like tears. I knew she would banish me from her room for the rest of the day if I started to BAWL. And I knew she wouldn't like mum and dad asking questions. I pulled in a juddery breath and looked at the page as Evie got up to leave the room.

A tear fell with a plop onto the bad man, spreading the black down. Giving the bad man three arms instead of two.

And surely that would be worse. Fear bubbled in my belly as Evie's laughter floated out of the room with her.

'I was just joking! I was messing around, silly Moo, it's just a drawing. There's no need to cry like a baby.'

CHAPTER ELEVEN

Meredith was sullen all the way back to the hotel, despite Steve and Matt's attempts at humour. Helen was quiet too. No one dared to bring up the elephant in the car—what the hell did Meredith do? and why had it sent her running from the room to throw up on the back lawn of the castle?

Kevin wasn't complaining. He had been pleased with the way the night had ended. A bit of action in an evening of almost nothing had felt like some consolation, apparently.

Back at the hotel she went straight to her room, locked the door, and threw herself face down on the bed. She hadn't wanted to show it, but she was still shaking from the ordeal with Donald—or Elana—whichever was the truth.

The more she filmed with Donald the more she distrusted the way he worked. He said nothing, never got involved, but both times had apparently been so overcome by what he had encountered from the other side that he had fainted on the first shoot, and now been possessed at the second.

Meredith sighed and pushed herself up onto her arms, running her hands over her face.

What was wrong with this situation? She had enough knowledge to know that ghost hunting was seldom this easy, or this rewarding. Both occasions had thrown up relatively rare and strong phenomena. At Moweth the scene had been set, the manor had certainly not felt right, it had a cold oppressive air, and the presence of something otherworldly had seemed in place, however the strength of the presence had caught her by surprise.

At Lynton, however, the castle had seemed homely. No air of anything untoward. Meredith and Helen had both said that they would be quite happy to spend the night alone there.

And yet… the presence there had been so strong it had managed to take over Donald, using him as a means of communication when Meredith put a stop to the Ouija board.

Really? Twice?

And why the hell was it that whenever she tried to prove to herself that she was not going insane, that Evie's spirit was with her, and that she may be able to communicate with her and lay her to rest, did something have to throw suspicion in the mix?

Was this real, or not?

Meredith felt the frustration like an itch that had to be scratched. She needed more. Real conclusive evidence that this wasn't just the workings of an overactive imagination as her mother and the therapist had implied—*It's the trauma, she can't let go. And no wonder with what happened.*

Donald had said it. The one thing that no one else could have known. Heck, if she was being honest with herself, Donald's features hadn't even looked like his. They had taken on a more youthful, childlike quality, she would have sworn it in court.

It should be enough. It should be real, convincing evidence. You spoke to a spirit; you know you can deal with Eve. How much more do you need?

What were the chances though? What if she hadn't? What if Donald was just great at faking? What if he had found out the information from somewhere else?

She groaned, face planting into the cover beneath her, as there was a knock at the door. She pushed herself back up onto her elbows with a grunt.

Ignore it, someone has the wrong room.

At this time in the morning? Could be Mr Ego Spalding himself. Maybe he's come to see how you are?

She went to the door and opened it a crack.

Matt stood on the other side, two bars of Cadbury dairy milk in his hand. Meredith blinked.

'Figured you could maybe use some company and a pick

me up.'

She frowned. 'Is that chocolate?'

He shrugged with a grin. 'Hey, it's all I could get at this time of the morning. Hooray for vending machines.'

She laughed, touched that he cared enough to be here, let alone to go out of his way to bring a gift.

'I don't know what to say.' She said.

He smiled, his aura calm, eyes kind.

'Caught you off guard, huh? Listen, you can tell me to get lost if you don't want company, the chocolate is yours either way. It's been a strange night, make yourself a drink and take the time to wind down before you sleep, eh?'

He held the chocolate toward her, and she stalled. The lack of pressure, his natural warmth, and obvious care made her want to invite him in; but she was wary that he had only come for the story. A story she wasn't willing to go over tonight, with anyone.

'Meredith, your face!' He said with a chuckle, 'I want to cheer you up, that's all. You seemed so downbeat in the car. I promise I'm not here to ask what happened. Just chocolate and a chat with a friend if you need it. What do you say?'

Meredith let a smile crawl onto her lips.

'You realise it's two-thirty in the morning?'

He glanced down the hotel corridor, at something she couldn't see, before turning back to her.

'Are you tired?'

She shook her head. 'Not at all.'

'So…?'

He held the chocolate aloft and she finally gave with a grin.

'Why not.'

She opened the door wider for him to step inside, and he passed her in a whiff of aftershave and cigarettes. He waited next to her as she shut the door, and handed her the bar of chocolate, before following her into the room.

'I'll make us a drink,' he said, 'sit yourself down, what do you fancy?'

'Tea. Milk, one sugar. Thank you.' She said sitting on the bottom of the bed to watch him as he pulled the twin teacups from next to the kettle. 'You didn't have to do this you know.' She said.

He huffed a laugh.

'I know. Listen, there's a lot of shit that goes down on shoots, and there's a lot of shit people bring with them. It can be lonely when a team has been thrown together and placed into a pressure cooker, it can feel like there's no one to talk to, that's all. I don't like people to feel that way, especially when something happens like tonight.'

The kettle boiled, and he made the drinks, handing her a cup.

'Thanks,' she said. 'Sounds like you've been there.'

'Oh, yeah, lots. It's not nice, but it is part of the deal unfortunately.'

He sat on the chair opposite the bed, under the room's tiny window. Close enough for her to notice the flecks of green in his warm hazel eyes, and the hint of colour in his cheeks. Close enough to reach out and take his hands if she wanted to...

She shook the thought away, clenching her own hands into fists to chase away the tingle in her fingers.

It's the care that got you, no need to get carried away.

'So, do you take it upon yourself to take care of all the waifs and strays that are lonely or need a chat?' She said, grinning as he creased his brow and wrinkled his nose.

'Not all of them, just the ones I like.' He grinned back at her, 'So, how are you feeling, are you okay?' he said taking a piece of chocolate and popping it into his mouth.

Her smile died away, and she looked to the bedclothes, tracing the pattern with a finger to avoid his gaze.

'Yeah, I'm good. The whole thing just caught me off guard, that's all. What Donald said just... well... it just resonated, and I was already wound up. You know?'

She looked back up to him and he nodded, taking a sip from his cup as she popped a square of chocolate in her mouth, letting the velvety smooth richness melt on her tongue.

'Yeah.' He said, 'And it's late, and we're all tired. I must admit though, the whole scene had me spooked from behind the camera. It was an unbelievable bit of footage to end with. I felt for you, I really did. Kevin was praising the whole crew for pulling it together just before he left.'

Meredith shook her head and rolled her eyes.

'He's an idiot. These things don't pull together, Matt. We've been lucky to get what we've had so far, 'ghosts' do not perform on command.'

'No, I remembered what you said in the car about the amount of activity at Moweth. I told him we'd been lucky. He said it was nothing to do with luck.'

'And everything to do with his authority.'

'of course.' He smiled. 'Seriously though, I know he's hard work Meredith, but it's only because he cares about the shows he produces. This isn't a show he chose to make; he was kind of forced into it, he's had to go into this blind. He's nervous that's all. It's his last ever show. He wants results.'

Meredith put her cup down, shook her blonde hair free of its ponytail and worked her fingers through the knots, scalp tingling from the tightness of the band.

'That's what bothers me.' She said.

'That he has no knowledge?'

'No, how badly he wants results...'

She trailed off, sipping from her cup as Matt stared at her.

A frown finally furrowed his forehead.

'What exactly are you saying, Meredith?' He said slowly.

She shook her head as she met his eyes.

'I'm not sure,' she said. 'I guess I'm not sure of anything. All I know is that there shouldn't be this much activity. I mean there can be, it's not unheard of, but still, it all seems a little excessive and… and… dramatic.'

Matt took a sip from his cup as he assessed her.

'Especially from a bunch of amateurs like us.' She continued, 'I barely know what I'm doing in practice. A degree is one thing, leading a ghost hunt is quite another. Gwen is a historian. Helen is barely out of university, studying business for heaven's sake. You and Steve have experience in production, not ghosts. As does Kevin. Only Donald has experience working with the paranormal in his day-to-day life. This should be a walk in the park for him, but he offers barely anything of value at each sitting. Even his moans seem cliched. And tonight? An actual possession?'

She stopped, blowing out a breath. What was she trying to say? And how much should she trust Matt with what she feared was about to come out? This was her issue. Matt had no reason to be bothered if it was fake or not.

She looked back at the pattern on the bedclothes, and then Matt sighed. She looked up to see him nod his head.

'Yeah, okay. I know. And even though I don't know much about ghost hunts, I have to admit it all seems a little farfetched to me too.'

A strange sensation flood Meredith's stomach. Half appalled that things may be being staged for effect, and she would get no real answers after all, the other half excited to be part of some sort of scandal.

'Who do you think it is?'

Matt raised his eyebrows.

'Who what?'

He looked blank and Meredith realised he had missed the point entirely. She felt herself blush, kicking herself that she assumed he had been on the same page when he clearly had no idea what she was talking about.

'It doesn't matter. The only way I could clear this up in my head once and for all is to see the footage, and I know that's out of the question. So, I guess I just have to roll with it until the shoot comes to an end.'

Matt looked down into his cup.

'You know I can't do that.'

'But why?'

Matt brought his surprised eyes to hers.

'Why can't I show you? I told you before, Kevin would fry my ass. He hates anyone to see pre-edited material.'

Meredith finished her drink and Matt took the cup from her, placing both empty cups by the kettle.

'Thanks,' she said, 'I know that, but why?'

'I don't know, Meredith, but it's nothing to do with this shoot. He's always been like it.'

'So, people have asked to see footage before?'

'Not often, but on occasion.'

'And he's always said no.'

'Yes.'

''And it's a no big enough to fry your ass over? Have you ever wondered what he's trying to hide?'

'I'm the one shooting, I know all of the details caught by the camera. How can he be hiding what he doesn't know is on film?'

'Hmm.' Meredith took another square of chocolate, appalled to see she had demolished most of the bar.

Matt watched her, elbow on his knee, chin on his fist.

'What is all this about, Meredith? What do you think you're going to see? Does this have anything to do with what happened tonight?'

'I don't know. I actually have no idea.' Meredith held her hands out. 'I just... I feel that for a first-time amateur crew, on location, considering it's just the first couple of investigations with the team, we struck very lucky with the amount of activity. That's all. Despite what happened tonight.'

He narrowed his eyes, finally finding her wavelength.

'So, you're looking for strings, is that it?'

Meredith cocked her head, knowing he was on the right

track but not wanting him to think she had thought of it first.

'Strings?'

'You know, strings, fishing wire and the like? Rigged experiments. Foul play?'

'Oh!' She forced her eyes wide in surprise, hoping she sounded convincing. Lying had never been her forte. 'Actually, rigged experiments hadn't occurred to me. I just wanted to check to see how I felt about what had happened. It seems a lot, but is it really? Sometimes we blow things out of proportion, especially in abnormal situations. You think Kevin is rigging the experiments?'

Matt laughed. His shoulders relaxing.

'No, I actually don't. But it has crossed my mind that you might as you've been so keen to see. Look, Kevin is no stranger to producing on location but as for ghosts? He has no idea. I can't imagine he would know where to start rigging a set for paranormal activity.'

'As far as you know.'

'Well, yes, as far as I know, of course. Why is this so important to you?'

Meredith took the last square of chocolate and popped it into her mouth. Her head was already woozy, tiredness was starting to creep over her. She clasped her hands on top of her head.

'I want to believe. I want to investigate something real. It's a passion, you know. I just feel it's too much, but I've never been in this situation before either. I don't know.' She shrugged and smiled at him. 'I'm probably just crazy.'

He grinned, shaking his head at her, back to his easy-going self. She was glad. She didn't want to upset him, he'd been so kind, and all she'd given him in return was a grilling.

He wanted a friendly chat, Meredith, do you have to be so dogged?

She felt a twinge of guilt.

'I'm sorry, Matt, I didn't mean to bring the footage up again. I've just had a weird night. Things seem too good to be true, and yeah maybe I think there could be trickery involved and that pisses me off, but in truth, Donald had the last laugh tonight. Donald or Elana anyway. It did hit a nerve, and there is no way anyone could have known what was being referred to. So how could he say what he said with such conviction and it coincidentally mean something?'

She sighed, leaning forward to rest her elbows on her knees, mirroring Matt sat in front of her. He reached out and put a warm hand over hers in silent consolation.

The urge to curl her hand around his, linking their fingers sent her stomach spinning. She was utterly drawn to his calm honesty like a bee drawn to nectar.

Heat in her cheeks she shook the thought away as her heart bumped.

She looked at him, but realised she had no idea what to say. She couldn't tell him what had happened. Telling someone here, someone she barely knew, would be ludicrous. And to what end? It made no difference to the outcome.

He squeezed her fingers, his gaze intense, and she thought he was going to ask for the story he had promised not to dig for, but then he took his hand away, pursed his lips and ran a hand through his dark hair with a sigh.

'Okay, can I be honest?'

'Of course.'

'I think there's a whole lot more to this story,' Matt began. Meredith began to object, and Matt held up a hand to stop her. 'I know you won't say and that's fine. Let's just see how tomorrow night in the cellar goes, okay? If there is another mass of activity, then maybe we'll have a look at the raw footage.'

Meredith's heart leapt as she inhaled a sharp breath.

'But,' he said, stopping her with a hand before she could speak, 'It will have to be after a shoot, when everyone has gone to bed. An hour or so after, I can't chance anyone being up and guessing what we're up to. It's more than my jobs worth.'

Meredith was nodding like the forever nodding dog that used to sit on the dashboard of the car.

'Okay. That's fine. Thank you so much, I can't tell you how grateful I am. If you change your mind at any point, I won't be offended, this is your call, Matt. Are you sure?'

Matt smiled and rose from the chair with a stretch, his arms above his head.

'Yeah, I'm sure. We just need to be discreet.'

Meredith felt a rush of warmth, and without thinking she pushed off the bed and threw her arms around him; surprising herself with the level of emotion hanging on the fact that she needed to find out the truth, surprising herself with the level of desire at being this close to someone she didn't really know, and cursing the tears that sprang to her eyes.

'Thank you so, so, much. I can be discreet. I won't let you down.'

He closed his arms around her with a surprised laugh.

'All right, settle down.' He said as she gripped him fiercely.

'I'm sorry. I just can't thank you enough. What made you change your mind?' She asked into the neck of his jumper.

He gently pulled her away and they stood facing each other. Strangers only a few weeks ago.

'This,' he said, gesturing to her as she brushed a tear from her cheek, 'Meredith, I don't know what this is, and I know you won't say, but if you need to see the footage so badly that it causes a reaction so strong, for whatever reason, then we'll do it.'

His kindness only made her cry more, and she wiped at her tears as he watched with concern. What was wrong with her? she hardly ever cried. At anything. He reached out and touched her arm giving it a gentle squeeze.

'Are you okay?'

'I'm fine, really.' She brushed the remaining tears from

her face as he assessed her. 'I promise.' She said.

He nodded, stuffing his hands into his pockets.

'Whatever this is, keep your chin up. You know where I am.' He said.

She smiled back at him.

'Thanks for everything, Matt, and thanks for the chocolate and the chat. I didn't realise how much I needed it.'

'Anytime.'

He led the way to the door, and she smiled as he opened it, raised a hand, and said goodnight, before striding off down the corridor. Meredith watched him for a beat, thinking that Matt Corrigan had to be the most caring human being she had ever met.

Shame he won't be back after the ear bending you've just given him.

She shut the door with a sigh and made her way to bed.

CHAPTER TWELVE

Meredith woke to the smell of flowers. No, not flowers. Perfume.

Lilies.

She rolled onto her side and looked to the window where the open curtains revealed a grey morning forming outside.

The grey morning of the evening of the cellar investigation.

Her stomach knot into a tight wad of nerves at the thought, and on top of that, the flowery smell seemed to be getting stronger. Getting into her head. Squeezing the knot so that she thought she may just vomit with the sickly familiarity of it.

Swallowing down the feeling she threw back the bedclothes, there would be no more sleep to snatch right now. She could lie here worrying about what would happen later, or she could do something about it.

Swinging her legs out of the bed and rubbing her hands over her face she checked her watch. 6.35am, which meant she'd had just under three hours sleep.

Fantastic.

Grouchy was just the right mood for handling Kevin this morning. Fortunately, she had a habit that would put her in a better frame of mind. A habit that had helped her every time mum had refused help, or said something hurtful, or blamed, or embarrassed her, like the time she had slept through Meredith's high school awards ceremony, snoring loudly, and falling off her chair, causing a commotion in the large hall.

Run.

Every time Meredith wanted to hit out, or felt frustrated, or had a problem to work through she would run. As fast as she could, until the fever passed, and she could think clearly. She hadn't had much time or inclination to run since this job had started. Late nights and busy days meant she was either tired or wired. But she found she needed to run now.

Down the road, just before the cafe, was a path that led to the base of a hill that lay on the village's south side. She would head that way this morning and go as far and fast as she could to get out of this mood.

After throwing on leggings and splashing water on her face, she went down to reception, tying her hair into a ponytail as she pushed open the door.

The chill air pressed around her, and she shivered. No coat this morning though, she would be warm within minutes. After a quick stretch, she jogged down the road, letting her limbs work out the knots and tightness of sleep, and feeling her muscles start to warm and loosen as her legs and arms pumped. At the track she let go, running faster, breath pumping, wet mist batting at her face. She passed no one, saw no one. Her breath clouded and disappeared behind her, feet slapping the dirt below. Her breaths were full, chest rising and falling with regularity as her heart thud behind her ribs.

Damn Kevin. Damn technology. Damn television ratings. Damn haunted houses. Damn ghosts. Damn drunk parents. Damn accidents. Damn dead sisters. And most of all damn dead sisters that come back.

At the hill she turned to race up the path, each damning statement coming with the thud of her next footfall. She damned everything she could think of until there was nothing else to damn. When her mind was clear, empty, and calm, she noticed the hill around her. The mist, the trees, the grass under her feet.

She slowed to a jog, enjoying the buzz in her legs and arms, the tingle of exertion. Reaching a plateau just above the roofline of the houses in the small village below, she stopped, gasping ragged breaths, hands on her hips. There wasn't much to see up here today, but she didn't mind, she hadn't come here for the view.

When her breath settled, she completed a few stretches, enjoying the opportunity for solitude and contemplation.

And then a form in the distance caught her eye.

Lynton Castle. Sat on its own hill, top half poking through the mist, bottom greyed out. Like it was a ghost itself, unreal and not solid at all.

Meredith sighed and stared at the imposing brick-built structure, odd little windows seemingly spread randomly around the walls, single tower at the corner of the west side. Stephanie and Orla were nice people, accommodating. The couple had seemed genuine, and very worried for Asha, if not frightened by Elana, but the whole place seemed as harmless inside as it looked from this hill.

But that isn't quite true, is it?

She swallowed. The castle did have a homely atmosphere, and she still felt that she would be happy to stay there. But it had seemed to change last night the instant that Donald had changed. The room had felt charged. Cold and electric…

… Or had that just been the fear that she had felt as he had seemed to morph into a small girl and repeat things he couldn't possibly have known? Her mind pulled forward images of Donald's face, the tone of his sing-song voice, the words he had said, and her heart began to pump. Had it been real, or was Donald just an incredibly good actor with a nugget of information that he knew would scare her?

Even so, the question remained—why would he do it? What did he stand to gain? Was he that bothered about his reputation that he would fake a possession at each sitting?

Meredith huffed a breath. She put her hands on her waist and shook out her legs and feet, trying to push away some of the cold creeping into her bones. As she turned her hips in large slow circles, she felt a pressing responsibility to find out the truth, for herself as much as the family.

If this was a real haunting, even if she could do nothing about it, at least Stephanie and Orla could decide what to do to keep Asha safe and progress onto real paranormal experts. And for her part, if Elana was a real entity Meredith would be glad to leave her behind, just in case she spilled the rest of the truth to the room – but at least she would know the truth. On the other hand, if there was trickery involved then she wanted to expose it, to allow Stephanie and Orla to feel safe in their home again.

The problem with fraud was that both Meredith and Helen had been convinced Asha was behind the haunting— so where did Donald and his possession fit into that equation?

Meredith's teeth tugged at her lip as she assessed the staunch grey building. She certainly wasn't looking forward to the cellar investigation tonight, but she knew she had to throw herself into it with conviction. Stephanie needed the truth to save her family home, and although Meredith didn't have any responsibility to conclude things for her, she felt a connection, and a need to provide her with answers. Tomorrow, however, the crew moved on. This would be her last chance to find out the truth or leave both herself and the Stanton family no further ahead.

Meredith shuddered. Damp, cold, and with stiffening joints, she decided to get back before she froze to death on the hill. She turned away from the castle and found the small track she had come up.

Well, at least if she died on the hill, she could stop this insane hunt for the dead and see for herself. She had an idea she would come back and haunt Kevin Spalding, give him something more to record. Then she thought she'd go home and show her mum just what a ghost looked like, and just how real they were.

* * * * *

Meredith was halfway down, finally calm and relaxed, and

enjoying the fresh air when her phone rang. She had felt pumped and ready for the briefing with the crew following a nice hot cup of coffee and a bite to eat in the hotel restaurant. Now, as she looked at the phone, her heart plummeted. She had heard nothing from her mum in above a week, and now twice in as many days?

Please, please, please don't let her have found any more bottles.

'Hey mum,' she said, answering the call quickly to get it over with.

'Meredith.'

Meredith paused on the path, shocked by the harsh whisper of her name. She blinked. The whisper came again.

'Meredith? Are you there?'

'Yes, I'm here. Mum, why are you whispering?' she found herself whispering back.

There was a strange whimper on the end of the phone.

'You need to come home, now.'

Meredith swallowed and closed her eyes.

'Mum, I can't come home, I'm in Scotland. You know that. I told you yesterday, remember?'

The whimper again, and then a whisper. Muffled, like mum had her mouth too close to the speaker.

'You need to come home, please Meredith. I'm frightened. There's someone in the house.'

Meredith felt her heart flip as her mouth dropped open.

'What do you mean there's someone in the house?'

'What do you think I mean? There's someone in this god-forsaken house.'

Meredith felt the breath leave her. Someone had broken into the house, and she was all the way up here? Did they know she was away? What were they still doing there at this time in the morning?

'Right, well mum, if you're sure then you should be calling the police right now. Where are you?'

'Bedroom.'

'And they're downstairs?'

'I don't know where they are,' mum hissed, 'I haven't looked. I'm not going to seek them out and offer a bloody beverage, am I?'

Meredith raised her eyebrows.

Keep cool, just keep cool until we know what's going on.

'Okay, but you must have an idea. You said there was someone there, so you must have heard them, right? Can you hear them?'

Mum let out a huff of breath and suddenly the whisper was gone.

'No, I can't hear them. I'm not you, I don't *hear* things. This is not some of your spooky shit. This is a person. A person in the god-damned house!'

Meredith grit her teeth and closed her eyes saying sorry to God out of an ingrained habit. She still wasn't sure she believed in God, and she knew it was probably stupid, but you could never be too careful.

Confused, Meredith pulled in a breath of cool, clean air.

'Mum, that makes no sense, if—'

'They've been in the bedroom.'

Meredith stopped short, unsure what to say.

'Ah, not so cocky now, are we young lady. Yes, Meredith, in the bedroom. While I was asleep. So, you need to get your little backside home and help me out. I'm scared.'

Mum's voice rose several octaves until she was practically screeching. Meredith held her free hand out at the air in front of her. A calming gesture to her mother, who was over eight hundred miles away and had no idea it was being performed.

'Mum. Calm down, it's okay. Listen carefully. I'm going to put down the phone and call Mrs Grey to come and check the house with you.'

She looked at her watch and grimaced. It was only just after half past seven in the morning.

'I need you to call the police and sit tight until they come, or Mrs Grey arrives, right? What have they taken? Did you check the rest of the house?'

'Do not tell me to calm down, and do NOT put the phone down on me. I'm frightened—'

'Yes mum, I know.' Meredith said, cutting her off, 'That's why I'm going to call Mrs Grey, but I can't do that with you on the phone, and neither can you call the police with me on the phone. I will call you straight back afterward, I promise.'

'Meredith, I am not calling the police. I'm not sure they'll be doing anything about a bunch of blessed flowers.'

'Flowers?'

'They left flowers. On the dresser. I've checked the house. That's it.'

Meredith ran a hand over her face. Had she been drinking again after all? The tell-tale slur didn't seem to be in her voice this morning though. Why were things never straightforward where mum was concerned?

But why would someone break into the house and leave flowers? Just flowers.

Then her heart leapt into her chest and sat there pounding heavily.

'Meredith? Are you listening to me?'

'Yes, mum. Just flowers? Are… are you sure?' she said, almost more breathless than she had been when running up the hill.

'I know what a flower is Meredith, of course I'm bloody sure! There are flowers. On the dresser. Put there while I was asleep. You don't think that's something I should be worried about? Someone is in the house!'

Meredith grimaced. If there was someone in the house, she needn't have bothered starting the conversation whispering. From the way she was shouting now, *they* were fully aware of the fact that *she* was aware that they were there. For the moment Meredith let it slip, she needed a more important answer first.

'What type of flowers?' she almost whispered.

'For Fuck's sake Meredith. What does it matter? And why are you whispering? I can hardly hear you, silly girl!'

'It might matter. It might be important, mum, please, what type of flowers?' She said.

The strong smell of Lilies from this morning filled her nostrils again. The perfume. Eve's perfume. Her stomach rolled over and she gagged. From the other end of the phone came her mother's answer.

'Lilies, Meredith. There was a bunch of fucking lilies on the dressing table…'

Meredith heard no more. The phone slipped from her hands and the ground seemed to shift beneath her feet. She found herself on her hands and knees on the path, retching onto the grass in huge gulping dry heaves.

CHAPTER THIRTEEN

Matt was huddled against the wall outside the hotel door as Meredith approached. Cigarette in one hand, large duffel coat zipped under his chin. He pulled his free hand out of his pocket in a wave as she came nearer.

'You're out early.' He called.

Glad she had taken the time to pull herself together after calling Mrs Grey to sort her mother out… again, Meredith smiled, and realised that Matt was as easy to smile at as he was to talk to. He said he had been a cameraman with the production company for seven years and had worked with Kevin Spalding for most of them.

She wondered if that made him an idiot.

You didn't think so last night.

'Been for a run.' She said, relaxing as she walked toward him.

He raised his eyebrows as he finished the cigarette, stubbing it out in the bin provided.

'I didn't know you ran,' he said, blowing smoke.

'I don't, not really, only when I have things to think through.'

He studied her.

'So, have you thought them through?'

'I have.'

He gave a small nod and waited. She smiled but offered no more. Finally, he huffed out a breath.

'Okay, well, I hope you feel better than last night.'

Sorry to keep him out of the loop, but not willing to let him in just yet either, she grinned and placed a hand on his padded arm.

'I do. I'm sorry I can't tell you more, but I do feel lots

better, and you played a big part in that last night. Thank goodness for you and the chocolate, I was a mess.'

She rolled her eyes as Matt smiled.

'Not too much, all things considered.'

Meredith cocked a lip at him, and he laughed.

'Okay, yeah, a fair mess. I'll give you that. You want to get breakfast, it's after eight?'

She nodded and he moved to the hotel door, holding it wide as she passed through ahead of him. The smell of breakfast filtered through the reception area. Coffee, toast, bacon, sausages. Her mouth watered as her stomach gave a loud rumble.

'Hungry?' Matt said from behind making her laugh.

'Starving. Running is hungry work you know, much more so than holding up the building with a cigarette.'

She threw a look back at him as he winced.

'Helps me think,' he said with a shrug. 'I had actually given up for a few months just before the shoot. I found a pack at the bottom of my kit. Lethal I know. I should have thrown them away.'

'So how did you think during those few months of freedom?'

'Yeah, yeah, all right. I know, you don't have to tell me. When this lot is over and I'm home, I'll get back on it.'

She grinned. 'I'm not judging. But if you need tips on thinking, I have a better way. Healthier too. Maybe you should join me tomorrow?'

'You mean with more chocolate?' He asked, feigning innocence.

Meredith stopped short, and he bumped gently into her arm as she turned to look at him. A few butterflies let go in her stomach and she squashed them fast.

'No Matt, you idiot. Chocolate certainly doesn't help clear thinking; it makes you fat. Also, why I need to run this morning.'

'I'll bring grapes next time,' he said. Meredith raised an

eyebrow and he laughed knocking her shoulder with his arm playfully before motioning the restaurant and walking on ahead. 'Come on I'm starving.'

As he led the way, Meredith vaguely wondered how her mum and Mrs Grey were getting on, and why they hadn't rung back yet. What was going on back home? If there really had been someone in the house Meredith hoped they had called the police, just flowers or not. How long had it been since she had called?

She glanced at her watch.

Give them chance, Meredith. It's only been fifteen minutes. Not enough time for them both to be murdered and the bodies concealed yet.

'...he say?'

Meredith realised she had missed everything that Matt had just said.

'What?'

'Doesn't matter.' Matt said, stopping to look over his shoulder at her 'Listen. Your way may be healthier, but it certainly doesn't clear up the whole issue in one go, huh?'

Meredith sighed stopping next to him.

'Well, this issue is a little too big. Small chunks at a time, I'll get there.'

'That bad huh?' Matt said, moving aside as a young couple made their way past to the doors of the dining room ahead.

Meredith nodded. She couldn't tell him, but she also knew now that he wouldn't ask either and she appreciated it. It took the pressure off.

He placed a hand at the small of her back.

'I'd give your way a try happily Meredith, but something tells me you need the space to work things through. I'd just get in the way, so I'll stick to my unhealthy way for now.'

Meredith gave him a small smile, half sad that he wouldn't be joining her, half relieved because he was right.

He steered her to the dining room doors, holding one

open, as she passed through.

'I'm up for the odd late-night chocolate-grape rendezvous though if you are.' He said.

Meredith thought she would like nothing more. She opened her mouth to reply as a bald headed, suit wearing, bull charged through the twin door, using his shoulder for force.

'Not on my watch.' Kevin said, letting the door swing shut before glancing at the two of them. 'Breakfast. Now. We need an earlier meet, something's come up. Matt, you know how I feel about romance on set. It doesn't work. Keep it until after the shoot, eh? There's a good lad.'

Kevin gave Matt's shoulder a hefty pat before stalking off to find their breakfast table. Meredith caught Matt's surprised stare as he watched Kevin, mouth open. She smothered a smile and tutted quietly as she turned to him.

'No romancing the presenters, Matt, There's a good lad.' She said with a wink.

She pat his shoulder in imitation of Kevin and made her way to the table with a grin leaving Matt to bring up the rear.

* * * * *

Coffee was divine. Breakfast was even better. And now this brief was turning out to be the severe pain to the pleasure/ pain theory.

Kevin was irate and irritable. Nothing to do with the shoot or any of the crew he said, although it was them that he took it out on. Without a jot of remorse. Before any briefing took place, he made it clear exactly what was expected of them today. What they were to do and not do. Expressly. Without deviation.

Meredith was not to run out of a set again. She had done it once. That was entertainment. Twice and her ass would not make it within half inch of a seat on the bus back to London after his boot had been in contact with it.

Donald was to stop making that ridiculous face when a

spirit was coming through, it was off-putting, and probably as much so for the ghost.

Gwen was to stop messing around with her damn glasses or he would stick them so far up her ass she would wear them from the inside.

Steve was to stop with the heinous jokes and the pranks. They were as funny as sticking your head in a nest full of angry wasps.

Matt was to stop thinking he was Brad-damn-Pitt and do his job. Flexing his muscles wouldn't hold the camera steady or keep his attention on the action.

Helen was to speak up, or he would get her a fucking megaphone and strap it to her mouth with parcel tape.

The whole scenario had been so surreal that, if he hadn't been so angry, Meredith may have actually laughed. She could have added some of those metaphors to him about being such a pompous ass too. Why should he get away without a roasting?

She pushed the end of her pen into her chin as she watched him, listening to the brief for this evening harder than usual, because she really didn't fancy putting a foot wrong with Kevin in such a foul mood.

His cheeks were flushed a deep red, his chin jutting over the collar and top button of his shirt as his jowls wobbled and shook with the force of his instructions. She watched his frown lines deepen as he assigned tasks and went over room details and roles with precision, but, she noticed, he barely looked any of them in the eye as he spoke.

Despite this the group sat riveted, all eyes on him as though it were the most engaging speech he had ever given, all of them tense, and afraid of his wrath at a wrong move.

No one rolled any eyes, Steve's jokes stayed confined to the domain of his head, no one spoke unless spoken to.

This morning's meeting was very much a dictatorship. Meredith wondered what had happened to put Kevin in such an awful mood. They had all felt it at breakfast, and the chat between the group had steadily declined since then to the silence that now remained.

I hope his mood lifts before this evening, or this may be the quietest ghost hunt on record.

Maybe that wouldn't be a bad thing all things considered. Especially as it was the cellar tonight.

Meredith's heart began to pump. Thoughts of the cellars leading to thoughts of the cellar at home, Evie being hurt, the bad man, and Egor's possession. She shuddered as she thought of Egor's furry face. So innocent until given a new role, and that role had been keeper of the bad man, guardian of Evil.

Even as an adult, a well-adjusted and smart adult, Meredith thought, she still couldn't rid herself of that damn bear. He was still stuffed in a box in the cellar at home. It still made her feel sick to think of him down there, even after all these years.

Even so, she couldn't get rid of him… just in case. It had always been easier to keep Egor after Eve's confession. Hadn't it?

Meredith sighed and chastised herself.

Ridiculous Meredith. When you get home, get rid of the bear. It is not possessed. Eve made the whole thing up as a childish game. It's not her fault that she died before she had a chance to reassure you that she was really only joking. Stupid how he still has such a hold over you, it's just a teddy bear. Just Egor.

And Egor had been a teddy bear that had been well loved before the bad man had arrived.

It was time for Egor to go to a new home. Time for Meredith to move on.

'Right, is everybody clear on the instructions for tonight?'

Meredith pulled her attention back into the room and nod her head at Kevin, who was now wiping sweat from his brow. There was a rumble of agreement from around the table, and Kevin dismissed them all with a flick of his hand as he strode to the door.

'We're out in thirty minutes,' He said, as the door swung shut behind him.

The collective exhale around the room released the tension, which had increased to such a force that Meredith thought she could physically feel it pressing against her skin. Weight seemed to physically lift from her shoulders as Kevin left the room. She sat back in her chair, as Steve stretched his arms above his head next to her.

'Well, I think that was the most effective meeting yet,' Donald said, after a small silence. 'Kevin Spalding has some serious people skills.'

Meredith grinned at him. Donald was rarely one to speak up, or out, against anyone, but this small bit of sarcasm was going a long way to breaking the last of the atmosphere. Steve finished the job.

'People skills?' Steve cut in, his lip cocked in disbelief, 'Old Kev should be in the business of teaching the skill of how to push glasses so far up someone's ass that they wear them from the inside. There's a skill he could get an Oscar for.'

It was Donald that started the chain of laughter. Looking to Steve with a weary sigh, that turned to a slow silent shaking of his shoulders. Gwen, who had looked startled and reddened at the reiteration of her punishment, regained her composure, and also began to laugh. Meredith's grin widened as Helen began to titter, hand over her mouth, and then Matt, openly laughing, caused Steve to guffaw too. Finally, Meredith joined in and suddenly the bleak day started to look better.

'Well,' Gwen said, as the laughter died down, 'I think we should make a move, I'd rather chase a ghost around a cellar on scripted cue, than find out just how that particular skill is performed.'

CHAPTER FOURTEEN

The wind roared around the old brickwork with a groan and a whine, and Meredith looked up from the sheets of paper in her hand as her hair lift in a small breeze.

'Have to watch that tonight,' she said to Helen, who was standing next to her taking notes in the same fluorescent pad, now a green page instead of pink.

'Hmm?'

'The wind. My hair just lift in a cold breeze. Imagine that down here at midnight. Not only would I completely crack up with fear, but it would be totally misconstrued.'

'I'm down for that,' Helen said with a grin. At least Meredith thought it was a grin, in the dull light in this half of the cellar she supposed it could have been a grimace. The whites of Helen's teeth were all she could define properly in the light.

'You're down for me cracking up in fear?'

'Nah, misconstrued activity. It gives Kevin what he needs with a completely plausible explanation. Which means that I don't crack up in fear, because I know it's just the wind. Perfect.'

Meredith grinned as she sank to her knees next to the old boiler fittings. She ran a hand over the boards that covered the pipework.

'I suppose that's one way of looking at it.'

'You want to lift them again to check?' Helen said. She sounded much like Meredith felt. Like she would rather shovel a ton of shit with a teaspoon than lift the boards.

'No, they should be good. We looked yesterday anyway. Nothing but pipes under there.'

Well, at least, I hope that's all. Bones could be a

problem.

Meredith gave an involuntary shudder.

She pursed her lips as another gusting whine battered the building. The light from the dull bulb swung, pendulating the space with synchronized light and darkness. Taunting, teasing.

She heard Helen swallow hard above her.

'Just the wind,' she muttered, 'just the wind.'

Meredith felt the hairs lift at the base of her neck as she looked up at her. She stood and gave a final glance around the eerie space.

'Yep, just the wind. We're in for a good scaring from the elements tonight I reckon.'

'Let's just keep that in mind, eh? Shall we go back up?'

'Yeah, I think we have all of the info we need from down here. The only thing we haven't checked is whether the damn door creaks.'

Helen grinned, or grimaced, again.

'It'll have a job. I came down to bring the extra mics for Steve earlier and we couldn't even shut it. Wouldn't budge. Definitely no creaking.'

She scribbled on the jotter and Meredith thought she could be noting the fact, but more probably she was hiding her expression. She also wondered just what else Helen and Steve had done in the basement. The tension between the two of them was obvious. Kevin had the wrong man, calling Matt Brad Pitt. Steve was the one he wanted to watch.

She smiled at the top of Helen's head and looked toward the door.

Hadn't it been shut when they had come down yesterday?

She frowned, as Helen finally looked up.

'What?' she asked.

'I'm just wondering why the door is so stuck open today when it was completely shut yesterday wasn't it?'

Helen looked to the door with an identical frown.

'I can't remember now, but yeah, I think you may be right.'

'We'll ask Stephanie or Orla when we get back upstairs, they may know what's happened. Better to write it off now than find something out in the dead of night.'

Meredith's hair shifted again, and a whine circled the room. It was the wind, of that there was no doubt, but at this moment Meredith could quite easily be persuaded that something else was down here with them. Goosebumps littered her arms under her jumper and ice ran down her spine.

'Do you feel that?' Helen whispered, almost making her jump out of her skin.

Meredith nodded.

'Yeah, I think I do. Let's get out of here before I really don't want to return later. It's creepy down here as it is, without the damn wind whining around.'

'I feel more watched. Sort of like—

'No,' Meredith cut Helen off. 'No, it's just the wind, nothing more. We'll be good tonight.'

She wondered just how calm she sounded, but Helen gave a nod as Meredith swung to the doorway and fought every urge to resist bolting for the opening, and the safety of the kitchen above.

It took a moment for her to register the thing that stood in the doorway. Dark, small, and still. Watching them quietly.

Her heart seemed to notch up twenty gears in one go, making her catch her breath with a small 'oooww'.

Helen, who had seen the figure in the doorway at the same moment appeared to be on an exhale. She screeched as Meredith closed her eyes.

Oh God, I need to get out of here, I need to get out of here.

She pulled in long breaths, trying to calm herself, as the fear escalated inside her.

I need to get OUT OF HERE. I NEED TO GET OUT

OF HERE. I NEED...

Helen's sudden giggles brought her fear under the uneasy control of confusion.

What the hell is so funny?

'Oh my god,' Helen said, the relief in her tone evident. 'That is so ridiculous. What the hell are we like? Tonight is going to be a complete wash out if we're scared of some wind and a damn toy.'

Toy?

Meredith opened one eye to see Helen in a squat on the floor. When she rose, what she had in her hands was enough to send Meredith's composure packing and hitting the road, never to return.

Helen held the brown bear in front of her, her hands under its armpits as she wiggled it back and forth with a laugh.

The bear wobbled innocently but horror rose in Meredith's gut, a horror so wrenching that for a moment she couldn't speak, and Helen and the bear seemed to move in slow motion.

800 miles from home, in Helen's arms, down in Lynton's cellar was the teddy bear from Meredith's childhood. Keeper of all evil.

Egor.

It seemed Egor and the bad man had come to join the fun.

Meredith screamed.

CHAPTER FIFTEEN

SEPTEMBER—149 DAYS UNTIL DEATH

I'm sat on the sofa, curled in the yellow SICK BLANKET.
My head hurts bad, and mum says I have a FEVER. She
puts a cooled cloth on my forehead every hour, on the hour.
Not for me, for her, so that she remembers, and my
temperature doesn't spiral OUT OF CONTROL.

All I know is that I feel prickly, everything aches where I
lean, needles are pushed into my skin each time I move, and
the cloth seems to be burning my head within seconds. I lift
it, letting the cool air caress my wet skin, but mum notices.
She puts the now warm cloth back on my hot skin with a tut
and a small shake of her head. I don't know what that
means, but I'm almost sure that it's nothing to do with
NAUGHTINESS, and that's good, because I'm not sure I
could listen to her ROARING today.

I watch mum through aching half-closed eyes, spraying
the teak table with Pledge furniture polish and scrubbing with
a yellow duster. The smell, and her frantic activity seem to
make my head hurt harder, so I turn toward the back of the
settee, away from her. But now it's worse. Egor sits at the
other end of the settee, down by my feet, where mum placed
him to KEEP ME COMPANY and to help me to GET
BETTER.

He makes me feel worse, not better.

From this position I can see him, and now I can't decide
which is better for my head, Egor or mum.

Mum says I should go to sleep and get better for dad's
MEETING later, but now I can't. Egor is watching me. He
hasn't moved, but I know he's only teasing because mum is

around. If she leaves the room, he will come for me.

I'm scared to sleep. Scared to close my eyes. What if the BAD MAN crawls back into my mouth when I'm sleeping? Evie says sometimes my mouth falls all the way open, especially when I snore, and DROOL comes out onto my pillow.

My head hurts and my eyes close, eyelids too hot over my eyeballs.

When I open them again mum is gone. I lie for a moment, and then I hear a small dry cackle from the end of the blanket. My eyes stretch painfully wide, and my heart starts to bang, as I catch sight of movement down by my feet.

I lift my aching neck to look, though I already know what it is.

Crawling in slow jerky movements up the blanket, one fluffy paw at a time, is Egor. I yelp and flick my leg, kicking with all of my energy to push him off, but he merely flops down with the blanket and falls onto his face.

What if he has claws?

I start to whimper.

'Mum?'

A wisp of air runs through the room, making me turn toward the window as the heavy velvet curtain blows inward. The window is open.

Did mum go out of the window?

Panic makes my tummy swish and I feel like I need to be sick.

'Mum! Mummy, where are you?'

She doesn't answer. A whine starts in my head and my body aches and drags as I try to pull myself up onto my arms. My heart is POUNDING, and my head is too hot. Boiling.

I grope for the cloth.

Once, going on holiday to Cornwall, Dad had said that the car engine had got too hot. He'd had to pull over and cool it down or it would EXPLODE. I wondered if my head would do the same.

I pat my head with the now cooled cloth.

At my knees Egor rises and shakes his furry head before looking at me.

I don't know if teddy bears can grin, but he certainly seems to be.

Then he is on the move again, crawling toward me in his steady, slow gait.

'MUM!'

I shoot bolt upright on the settee and suddenly Egor is back in his spot down by my feet, quietly watching, as though he has never moved, and mum is back, as though she wasn't gone at all.

She jerks at my yell, her mouth a round 'o' like a cheerio. Her finger is still pushing on the polish trigger. Pledge swoops in a wide upward arc, its white stream emitting a sharp *pssstt*.

'Bloody hell, Meredith!' She says. The spray of polish stops as mum's face whips toward me, eyes wide. 'You scared the bloody life out of me!'

A transformers cartoon plays on the TV, but the music from the new radio in the kitchen drowns out the sound. I don't care. I'm not watching anyway. I'm more pleased to see mum than I have ever been in my life.

'Mum? Mum! Mum!'

'What Meredith? God, do you have to be so dramatic?'

Mum sits back on her heels and wipes a wrist across her brow which is beading with sweat. She looks mad, but not full on mad, weary mad. I can't help it, I grin at her like a LOON, I still can't believe she's here. My heart is still thumping like it's trying to get out of my chest.

Mum heaves one of her big sighs before looking at me, some of the mad gone from her face now.

'Meredith, please. I need to get the place cleaned before the meal tonight.' She looks at me with drooped shoulders and wipes a hand across her upper lip. 'I have to clean, cook, host, serve, and wait, while your father sits on his backside and tries to talk Mr Dutton into a deal. You know how hard that is? Hard. But do you know what? If the deal pulls off, we will finally be able to get the new drapes I want, and maybe we can go out to eat one evening. Won't that be fun? I want to sit and chat Meredith, but I have to work. If you won't say what it is then you just have to wait.'

I stare at her, my eyes burning behind my lids. She doubles as I look at her, one to the left by the coffee table, one to the right in an identical pose with an identical table. I bring my warm hands up to my eyes and scrub. When I open them again there is only one mum. She heaves a bigger sigh.

'Fine. God, Meredith, why you chose today to be ill, I'll never bloody know.' She mutters, 'Why can't I ever get an easy break, just a small one? Why is everything so god-damned hard?'

I blink my burning eyes, swallowing as I send up a small prayer of condolences to God for mums' blasphemy again, and she's back to double mum. I shift my focus from one to the other. One is real, one isn't. Which is which?

She leans over the table again, now concentrating on just one part. Double mum scrubs just as hard. I frown.

'Won't it come off?'

Mum bangs the duster down on the table and turns to me.

'Won't what come off, Meredith? For God's sake stop talking in riddles you're driving me insane. Why can't you just go to sleep like any normal sick child?'

I want to tell her I'm too scared of Egor, but I know she isn't in a LISTENING MOOD. She's too busy, and that means silliness will get me nowhere. I press on with the table instead.

'Not tired. Won't the pattern come off, on the table?'

Mum blinks at me.

'Why in the hell would I want the pattern off the table?'

I shrug and rest my head back down onto the arm of the chair.

'You're rubbing so hard.'

Mum was mad now, the side of her mouth twitched as she turned, standing over me, hands on her hips, the bottle of pledge angled out from her hip like a deformed tin limb. I scratch at a tingly leg, roasting hot, and yet freezing cold. I kept my attention on the itch to save looking mum in the eye. She started anyway.

'I'm rubbing so hard, Meredith,' She said, almost as though her teeth were glued together and she couldn't move them, 'because of the shit you and Eve put all over it. It won't come off. Nothing comes off where you girls have been. Anywhere. It's like you delight in sticking STUFF all over everything, just like you seem to delight in PISSING ME OFF! Stop that infernal scratching Meredith!'

'Sorry,' I whisper keeping my eyes averted, I know mum wants me to leave her alone, but Egor scares me more than her anger right now. 'Mum? I don't like Egor, he watches me. I can sleep, but not with Egor there. He's scaring me.'

Mum says nothing, but in a stride, she grabs Egor by one leg. He swings upside down as she leaves the room, and I hear her stomp into the kitchen. Within seconds she's back.

'Better?' She says. She feels my head and syringes strawberry Calpol into my mouth, before replacing the cloth with a cooled version.

I nod my head. I do feel better, it would take him an age to crawl from the kitchen surely.

At my side, the curtain blew up in a breeze. The window. Would he be able to crawl in the window?

'Could you shut the window?' I say.

Mum heaves a sigh, shuts the window with a bang, and turns back to me.

'Is everything okay now Meredith, because I REALLY need to clean, and I would REALLY like you to sleep now.'

I check. My heart is resting easy, and my tummy no

longer swirls.

'Yes, I think I can sleep now.'

I catch mum's quick nod just as I close my eyes.

'Good,' She says, 'I'll be in the hall. If you die of heat exhaustion now the window is shut, don't blame me.'

My mouth curls into a smile. Heat exhaustion is far better than dying at the hands of Egor and the bad man, and with mum in the hall between me and Egor, there was no way he could get to me either.

Sated, I slip into a fretful sleep.

CHAPTER SIXTEEN

'Hey, hey, hey! What's all the racket?' Steve exclaimed as he clomped down the cellar stairs two at a time. He was closely followed by Kevin, who clipped quickly behind with a look on his face that said he was more furious than anxious. But then, that was his default look, wasn't it?

Meredith's scream died off as Kevin moved an arm in front of Steve, pushing him roughly aside as he stepped forward.

'What the hell is going on down here?'

Meredith's heart was doing a quick jig behind her ribs, and all air seemed to have been pulled from her lungs. She looked at him, opening her mouth but nothing coming out. Kevin folded his arms across his chest, puffing it forward to make him look bigger. To intimidate Meredith supposed, although he was pint sized next to Steve, just behind him.

'I said, what in God's name is going on down here?'

Meredith closed her eyes, trying to catch her breath, while apologising to God out of ingrained habit.

Her eyes fell on Egor, hanging from Helen's hand by one brown paw. Her heart thumped. Helen's face could only be described as amused shock, eyes wide as she stared at Meredith.

Great, there'll be questions later.

'I don't want answers on a postcard, Meredith. I want them now!'

Meredith pulled her gaze back to Kevin's small angry eyes. She could tell him nothing but the truth—hopefully, he would see the funny side, even if she didn't.

'Erm, well, nothing.' She said, 'It was nothing. Just scared by the bear. The bear scared me.' She flicked a hand to the doorway Kevin and Steve were now blocking. 'In the doorway. There.'

She turned to point at the bear. Helen held it up, dangling it before her where Kevin could see. Nerves swirled in Meredith's stomach at its sight, and she let out a small titter, hand fluttering shakily to her mouth.

Get a grip Meredith, please.

Kevin glanced at the bear, and then back to her.

'Scared by a teddy bear?'

Meredith swallowed hard as she nod her head. Kevin was looking less than amused, in fact he looked furious. His mouth a hard line, no trace of humour on his face.

'Are we, or are we not, supposed to be professionals?' He said, 'You were supposed to be doing a walk around, noting things for tonight, nothing more, nothing less. I have two very distressed lady's upstairs who think the bloody ghost has done something to two of my crew, and you're down here screaming at a *teddy bear*?'

'Er, not teddy—' Steve began, his mouth pulled back into a tentative grin as he waved a hand and tried to step forward, but Kevin blocked the opening into the room keeping Steve behind him.

'What *is* the hope for tonight?' Kevin continued, oblivious to Steve who dropped his hand to his side as his words were cut off. 'What are the chances of my presenter not running off up the lawn again? What are the chances of her keeping cool and doing her bloody JOB? What are the chances if she gets scared—in daylight—by a bloody teddy bear?'

Kevin's face became redder in the low light of the bulb, and spittle stuck to his lower lip, as he clenched and unclenched his hands at his sides. In daylight Meredith thought she may see steam making its way from his ears.

She thought maybe he didn't want to hear that it was dark down here, daylight up there or not. Annoyed, and a little embarrassed at the insinuations, she wanted to defend herself, but her throat was dry, her head empty of words, and under Kevin's glare she found herself starting to shake.

'I… I wasn't, I mean I didn't… it was…'

Helen jumped to her defence.

'It wasn't like that, Mr Spalding, it was dark, eerie, we were doing our job. The bear just caught us off guard sitting there illuminated in the doorway. We didn't remember seeing it there before, that's all. It scared me too.'

Meredith nodded gratefully.

'Yes, exactly. That's all it was. Nothing to worry about, now.'

Kevin gave a low chuckle and ran a hand over his balding head.

'Nothing to worry about? Did you hear what I said? I have two hysterical ladies upstairs. What am I supposed to do with them whilst you two are pratting around with a teddy bear down here? I suggest you wrap this up ASAP, get upstairs and tend to these ladies. I do not have time for games.'

Steve cleared his throat for attention as Kevin snatched the offending bear from Helen's hands.

'Woah! Be careful, it's not—'

'I'll put this back upstairs out of the way, shall I?' Kevin continued, turning on a heel toward the stairs.

Steve lunged at Kevin, grabbed the bear from his hands, and held it to his chest like a baby—although the baby would have been smothered if it had been there for too long.

Kevin stood stock still, spine rigid, and Steve looked at him, mouth wide.

'You can't! Er, no. I'll deal with it, sir. I mean… it's not just a teddy bear.'

Kevin didn't move and Meredith watched Steve with horrified fascination. Did he know about Egor after all? Was he aware of the bad man inside him?

A hush descended over the basement and from upstairs a low wailing was coming from either Stephanie or Orla. Probably Orla, Meredith thought. Matt's calming tones filtered among the wails.

'I don't care if it's the bloody green giant.' Kevin spat. 'Get that thing disposed of before tonight. If I find out that you had anything to do with this Mr Gittins, prank or otherwise, you will be deeply sorry.' Kevin swung a look to Meredith, over his shoulder, 'and you? Get upstairs and deal with those two. Matt has a job to do, and it doesn't involve counselling.'

Kevin stalked up the stairs and out of sight. The air in the basement suddenly felt less oppressive and the room gained a couple of inches in height as collective relieved breaths were let out by its three occupants.

Steve blew out his lips and entered their room through the doorway.

'Sorry about that, ladies,' he said with a roll of his eyes.

'I don't know what you're apologising for,' Helen said, 'It's hardly your fault.'

Steve gave Helen a lopsided grin, and suddenly Meredith had had enough.

'It appears it is. He was obviously the one that placed the bear there to scare us, and now we're in a whole heap of shit and have to deal with Mr Psycho all evening again.' She threw her hands into the air as Helen and Steve turned to her. 'Thanks Steve. Can't you keep the bloody pranks out of the way of the show?'

'No, No.' Steve said, one hand holding the bear to his waist like a toddler, the other palm out toward her. 'Meredith you've got the wrong idea. It wasn't a prank, and I was apologising because I don't like the way he spoke to you, that's all. And I'm also sorry you got in trouble for something that I should have shown to you all earlier at the meeting. I just didn't get chance, but if I had we probably wouldn't be here now, because you'd have known what it was. It's not a simple teddy bear.'

Meredith's heart seemed to leap up into her throat, cutting off her air.

'If it's not a simple teddy bear, what is it?' Helen said.

Steve put a hand under the bear's backside and leaned it back against his chest, facing the girls. Meredith kept her gaze on the floor, wondering if its eyes would glow green in the low light.

'This is Spookbuddy,' Steve said, 'Say hi, Spookbuddy, these are your ghost hunting friends for the next few weeks.'

Meredith looked up with a frown to see Steve waving Spookbuddy's—Egor's—furry paw at them.

Helen giggled.

'Hi Spookbuddy, pleased to meet you.' She said waggling her fingers back at the bear.

Meredith said nothing. She kept her hands firmly planted in opposite armpits as she waited for Steve to explain. Except that explaining didn't seem to be on his agenda right now.

'Well, one is a little quiet, but isn't this one a beauty?' Steve said in a squeaky voice, placing the hand to the back of the bear's neck and turning its face a little toward his own.

'Spookbuddy, that's a little forward for your first meeting, dude.' He said down into the bear's face. 'She is cute though, huh?'

Helen giggled again and Meredith rolled her eyes.

'Look guys, as cute as this is, we have an angry director upstairs who wants me to go and console two hysterical ladies. What is the deal with the bear, and where the hell did it come from?'

Steve snapped his head back to Meredith, surprise lifting his features, as though he had forgotten she was in the room.

'Oh, yeah. Right.' He said, 'So, Spookbuddy is an interactive ghost hunting device. He has tech inside him to take the stats of the room, temperature, EMF, etc. He's a trigger object too, he can tell if he's moved, and—get this girls—he talks!'

'Talks?'

'Hell, yeah, baby! He'll tell you stats, when it gets colder, warmer, when there's spirit energy around. He'll even talk to the spirits themselves. He'll call them for us. How cool is that?'

'Cool.' Helen said.

'Hmm.' Meredith said, eyeing the bear which still looked too much like Egor. She took a breath and held a shaky hand out toward it. Steve thrust it at her, almost forcing another scream from her lips.

She took it tentatively, with a loud swallow, and forced herself to look into its eyes. Not green. Dark, a tiny light bulb just visible behind each one. She blinked, feeling the equipment inside the soft bear.

Like Egor after his surgery.

But this bear had a backpack with something else inside.

Heart starting to slow she turned the bear around checking it over.

Cream ears—Egor's had been brown. Dark paws—Egor's had been pale. Red backpack—Egor had never had a backpack. Soft silky fur. New. Egor was old and tired, and felt more greasy than soft from all his cuddles from two young girls—before the bad man that was. There had been no cuddles since.

Meredith turned the bear back to the front, to face her. Brown eyes. Not green.

It's okay, see? It's just Spookbuddy. An interactive ghost hunting bear. Not Egor. Definitely not Egor.

Meredith smiled.

'Cool huh?' Steve said.

Meredith pushed out her lips with a nod.

'Well, novel anyway.'

'I thought so, reckon we'll be the first to use him in a TV show—which is the only reason Kevin agreed to order it. Expensive teddy bear, man!'

'If Kevin knew about it then what was all the fuss about?' Helen said.

Steve pursed his lips.

'Like I said, I should have told you all in the meeting

earlier, but he was busy doing his Hitler act. I only got it this morning. Collected it myself from the local post office where I'd arranged to have it delivered. Kevin has no idea it's arrived yet.'

Helen nodded, and Meredith grinned.

'Good job, Steve. Why the hell didn't you say anything to him just?'

'I tried. He was on a psycho roll. I'll tell him later. We could use it tonight if he agrees.'

Meredith looked back to Spookbuddy with a nod.

'Yeah, I think that would add an interesting touch to the investigation. Something different, anyway. What do you say Spookbuddy?'

She wiggled him in front of her, hands around his waist. A loud beep emitted from the bear's body and the white fur on its chest began to glow. Not only glow, but glow green.

Green. It's a trick! Don't count to three!

Meredith thrust the bear back to Steve with a low growl that seemed to come from the pit of her stomach.

He took it, fiddled with the backpack, and the light went off.

Meredith gasped air, hand to her chest as Steve stared at her, mouth open. If she had looked to the side, she had a feeling Helen would be giving her just the same look.

'My, are we jumpy tonight.' Steve finally said with a chuckle, 'You just turned him on Meredith, that's all. He was taking room stats. Chill out.'

Meredith blew out a breath and tried to calm her shakes.

'Sorry guys,' She said, huffing a laugh that she hoped didn't sound as fake as it felt. 'Bit of a teddy bear phobia. Childhood incident. I'll get over it. Spookbuddy's cool.'

'What kid is scared of a teddy bear?' Steve laughed.

'This one.' Meredith said as she made her way to the bottom of the stairs. Light was what she needed now. Just to get out of the damn cellar and into some natural light. It seemed the wailing upstairs had stopped, but she'd still check, not to appease Kevin, just to get out of this room.

'So, Steve. Chief prankster,' she said, not looking back as she climbed the stairs, 'With that knowledge, please don't place him in a dark doorway like that again. I don't think my heart could take it.'

'He wasn't in the doorway,' Steve said, 'I left him in the box at the foot of the stairs with the other stuff.'

But Meredith didn't hear, she stepped out of the basement and into the normality of the moody daylight which filtered into the kitchen.

CHAPTER SEVENTEEN

Meredith had hoped to get away from Lynton Castle for a few hours before the evening's vigil, but Stephanie and Orla had offered to provide dinner for the crew as a thank you for all their hard work, and for getting rid of Elana tonight.

Meredith hadn't the heart to tell them they probably wouldn't be going that far, and especially if Asha was behind the incidents. Getting rid of Elana was one thing, getting rid of Asha, or even exposing her, would lead to its own problems. So, Lynton was highly likely to stay just as it was after the investigation had been completed and the crew had moved on.

Two tables and the little coffee table had been pulled together in the living room to make room for the group to eat with the family. Chairs had been pushed back, but with no real need. The room was large enough to accommodate either way.

Asha sat opposite Meredith, and not by chance, she had insisted, which had caught Meredith off guard. They were sat at the far end of the oddball table construction, Meredith next to Helen, Asha next to Steve, who was talking loudly to Donald at the other end of the table. Stephanie, Orla, and the boys were sat at the opposite end, as far away from Asha as they could be. Orla had been opposed but Stephanie had gently told her to hush, Asha was hardly sitting on the other side of the moon, she was mere feet away. Orla spent the rest of the meal with a face like she was chewing a wasp, luckily after dinner she would drive the children into the village to stay with a friend for the night. A fact Meredith had welcomed with vigour.

It would take the untrustworthy variable out of the evening, Asha, and remove the moody variable at the same time, Orla.

Two birds; one stone, she thought, tucking into the tender lamb steak as she listened to the conversation around the living room. Cutlery scraped and clinked on plates, and the warmth of the food and the fire comforted her a little. She was quiet, she knew that, and hoped that it didn't cause too much undue concern amongst the crew. It would have been nice to have a few hours away, to settle herself after her jitters this afternoon, to get her head around Spookbuddy and the fact that she would have to work with him whether he looked like Egor or not, but a place as comfortable as this, with food as good, she wouldn't have found. For that she was grateful.

'Scared?'

Meredith looked up into Asha's large brown eyes, a small smile winding its way onto the young girls' lips.

Meredith swallowed and shook her head, holding Asha's gaze.

'Why would I be scared? I've done hundreds of these vigils, Asha, and seen more than enough ghosts.'

'Not like Elana.'

Meredith sighed, holding her knife and fork static above her plate.

'Yes, just like Elana, some probably worse.'

Asha smiled innocently.

'I don't think so.'

'Why is that? What makes you think Elana is so special?'

Asha shrugged. She placed a small piece of lamb in her mouth, chewing as she considered Meredith.

'She scared you yesterday when you ran out and threw up on my lawn.'

Meredith faltered mid chew, narrowing her eyes at the girl before her. Asha's mouth curled as she hesitated, and Meredith saw dark amusement behind the girl's innocent stare and wide eyes.

Oh, wow. Asha really thinks she has one over on me, which is not only not very childlike, but also unnerving. Can a nine-year-old be this conniving? Not only that, but enjoy it too?

'Nope, you have it wrong, Asha,' she said, keeping her expression neutral. 'Elana didn't scare me, I was... I was sick. I just couldn't remember where the toilet was, that's all. I'm sorry I threw up on your *parent's* lawn, but I'm better now.'

'I'm glad you feel better.' Asha said, a grin playing on her lips.

'Thank you. I do.'

Asha nodded and placed more meat into her mouth, placing one elbow on the table where she could twiddle her tight curls with the finger of her free hand.

'Well, that's good, because Elana told me to tell you to beware tonight. She's coming for you.'

'Really.'

Asha bobbed her head in a nod, sneaking a glance at Stephanie down at the other end of the table.

Yes, you just make sure your mother doesn't see what a conniving little shit you are.

'She's coming for her too.' Asha said, looking to Meredith but pointing her fork toward Helen, who was thankfully deep in conversation with Gwen.

Meredith raised an eyebrow and anger welled in her stomach. She'd had enough of the girl's insinuations, the manipulative attempts to scare her, and the feeble attempts to wind her up.

'No, Asha. She's not.' She hissed, 'And do you know why she's not?'

Asha shook her head, free hand back to twiddling her curls, fork poised empty in mid-air.

'Because the spirit world doesn't work that way. She could no more 'get me' than I could contain her in one of the famous 'Ghostbusters' traps.'

Asha looked down at her plate with a half-concealed grin that Meredith would like to wipe from her face.

'If you say so.' She mumbled with a smile.

'I know so.' Meredith said, smiling back. Underneath the smile her teeth and jaw were clenched tight.

'Uh-huh.'

Meredith felt her anger spike, she was about to say something she probably shouldn't, when she noticed Steve looking their way. She caught his eye, eager to change the conversation.

'Good grub.' He said, motioning his plate, which was empty, he reclined back in the chair with his hands clasped over his large belly, a satisfied smile on his face.

Meredith nod her head as she finished the last bit of smooth buttery potato. It would have been beautiful if not for the bitter company.

'The best roast dinner I've had in a long time.' She said, placing the knife and fork together at one side.

'What did you think, Asha?' Steve said.

Asha shrugged. She still had half a plateful of various vegetables and a small piece of lamb that she was absently sliding around the plate. Meredith smothered a grin.

Not so vocal now someone else is in on the conversation. Interesting.

'I guess that means you're enjoying it.' Steve continued. 'So, little lady, where are you off to tonight?'

'Just a friend's house.' Asha put her fork down and looked intently at Steve. 'I'd rather be here, but Orla says I need to be out of the way. Elana is *my* friend. I don't know why I have to leave. I'm the only one who can control her, but they don't get that so…' she shrugged her little shoulders, 'You guys just have to deal with her, don't you?'

Meredith grinned at Steve. 'Asha says Elana will be the worst we've ever dealt with, she's different to other spirits apparently.'

Asha flicked Meredith a look so dark she was sure it

was meant to kill, as Steve gave a good-natured frown.

'Really? I thought all spirits were made of the same stuff. I would have thought little Cara's father the other night was about as angry as it got. How did we handle him now?'

'We told him to butt out, and he did.'

Steve chuckled. 'Yeah, angry old Mr Crawford didn't scare us, and I'm sure Elana won't be a match for him. We'll manage just fine.'

Asha looked to her plate with a huff that Steve misjudged.

'Hey, you don't need to worry, little lady. With any luck we'll have told her to pack her bags tonight. By the time you get back, she'll be on her way back to Oz.'

'Oh, she sure will,' Meredith said, 'and once a paranormal investigation team has set a spirit free there is no coming back, so Elana will *never* return, don't worry about that.'

It was a large exaggeration of the truth, but Meredith was enjoying the tables being turned, and she wondered just what Asha would make of not being able to bring Elana home with her after tonight. She placed a hand over one of Asha's pretending to be concerned.

'Did you hear, Asha? She can never return, so everything will go back to normal, just as it should be.'

Asha snatched her hand from under Meredith's.

'Oh, won't that be wonderful, honey?' Stephanie gushed from the far end of the table, a large smile on her face.

Meredith wanted the floor to eat her up as she realised the rest of the table had fallen silent and were looking their way.

'Yes, mummy.' Asha mumbled into her plate. The quick look she flashed Meredith contained the same volatile anger she had seen before.

'It'll be so nice to get back to normal family life,' Stephanie continued. 'to not have the worry of Elana and the cellar, and the—'

'May I leave the table, mummy?' Asha cut in, her voice pleasant, but loud and firm.

'What? No, Asha we—'

'Yes, darling, of course you may.' Orla interjected with a wave of dismissal at Stephanie. 'Go and pack a bag we'll be leaving soon, and you have nothing ready. Say goodbye to Meredith.'

Meredith raised her eyebrows as Asha stepped around the end of the table and grabbed her shoulders bringing her in for a quick, stiff hug.

'Have a good evening. Don't say I didn't warn you.' Asha whispered into her ear.

Meredith blinked. Shocked at the threat.

Asha didn't wait for a response, she turned and stalked out of the room without a backward glance, slamming the door shut behind her.

'Asha!' Stephanie yelled.

'Leave her,' Orla said, turning to Stephanie, 'She's upset. She'll come round.'

CHAPTER EIGHTEEN

The man outside the small corner shop was drawing attention, he knew that, but it would take patience before he could enter the store to get what he needed. First, he had to let the answers come forward. These things couldn't be rushed.

He bowed his head, large woolen hood falling further forward to conceal his face. He fingered the rosary beads in his pocket.

An elbow hit his side and there was raucous laughter as the group of teenagers passed him.

'Nice cloak.' One of them sneered, possibly the one whose elbow had caught him.

'Yeah, if you're living in the sixteenth century,' another quipped.

'Or you're just a flasher.' A smaller boy said. No more than ten years old, if he'd had to put an age on him.

'Are you a fucking perv?' the first boy said again, waiting for the man's response. The man simply smiled, pulling the cloaks hood to conceal his face further. It wouldn't do to be recognised. These boys would get their karma in other ways, for now he wasn't going to give them the joy of a rise. He had bigger business to attend.

'I like boys,' he said.

The boys scrabbled, all limbs and loud laughter as they moved as a group past the shop door.

'Told you,' the first boy shouted over his shoulder, 'fucking perv.'

Then he let go, running down the path, his clan behind him, their feet slapping the pavement under their hoots and howls.

The man waited as the quiet returned. A blonde lady gave him a wide berth before entering the shop, and then God answered, and he knew exactly what he needed to get to complete his work.

Ignoring glances from other shoppers, the man entered. Slowly and methodically, he worked his way around the shop, filling a basket with the things God had filled his mind with like a mental shopping list.

At the counter, he bagged his items, paid the nervous cashier, thanked her, and left.

CHAPTER NINETEEN

The phone rang out and clicked to answer phone three times before Meredith gave up and shoved it back into her pocket with a sigh.

Pulling her coat around her against the buffeting cold, she stared out across the lawn, her eyes following the lie of the land, which dropped away from the small village and rose up to the mountains. The sky was grey and heavy, the air damp, and she thought there may well be rain to accompany the blustery wind soon. The tops of the mountains were gone, disappearing into the cloud above.

A very real dark and stormy night for our tussle with Elana.

She huffed a small laugh, breath clouding briefly in the cold murk before being whipped away into the ether by the wind. It felt like years ago that the crew had left for Scotland, although they had only been here for the best part of a week. And yet, even with all that had happened so far, and what she had expected—which was a world away from this—she had managed to keep her head above water and was beginning to feel comfortable in her role.

Pushing her cold hands down into her pockets her thoughts turned to Asha and her part in Elana's haunting. The child may act like a brat, but the more she thought about it, the more she was unsure that she could have anything to do with it.

How does a real little girl come through a Ouija board and spill secrets that no one could have known? Asha had also warned of Elana coming for them tonight—but Asha was to be out in the village again. How could she be controlling ghostly activity if she wasn't even here? Unless she had an accomplice…

Meredith wrinkled her nose with a frown.

Really? I think you're getting a bit carried away now Meredith, the girl is just nine years old!

And yet something niggled about the child's behaviour.

Asha the innocent? Or Asha the deceitful?

Well, we'll soon see the nature of what is going on here tonight, and whether Asha's little prediction comes true. I'll just have to be extra vigilant that's all.

With a sigh, Meredith pulled the phone from her pocket again, and tried the number twice more with no response. She stared at the phone, willing it to ring, and knowing there was nothing she could do either way. When her fingers were frozen from the wind, she placed it back into her pocket.

Ring back if you're not dead mum—or just come through the Ouija board later if you like. Just get in contact so I can stop worrying about an intruder and some damn lilies.

She tugged her lip between thumb and forefinger. This was one of mum's games, she would probably leave Meredith hanging for a few days until she was going out of her mind with worry and guilt.

It was always about the guilt. It had happened when Meredith had first gone to work in the local newsagents (*I can't be here by myself Meredith, you can't leave me, I'm ill*). It had happened when she had signed up at university to start her degree, even though the course had been on-line with day release and exams which amounted to just ten days per term. (*How could you leave me alone Meredith? I need you here, I'm a dependant*). It had happened again now she was here (*I'm ill, Meredith, I could drink myself to death, and it will be all your fault),* although at the time she said that—two months before Meredith left for Scotland —she hadn't touched a drop for months.

But now she is drinking again… finding bottles that I'm sure were never in the house.

Meredith frowned. Mum had been in a good place when she left, other than the moaning at her going, but Meredith hadn't honestly thought that she would touch a drop of drink again after the horrific come down last time. She had thought it empty threats. She had only asked Mrs Grey to keep her company as a friend, and to make sure she was okay alone. She hadn't thought it would amount to this.

There's something else though, isn't there? If mum is so agoraphobic that she never leaves the house, how has she gone out to buy more drink?

Maybe she isn't as agoraphobic as you think, maybe all of this is a ploy to make you pay for Evie. Maybe she'll make you pay for the rest of your life. I think that may just be it, Meredith.

She felt a stab of unease run through her chest. Was she seriously considering that her mum would be malicious enough to start drinking again simply to spoil this opportunity for her?

Well, would she?

There were only two things Meredith had ever taken it upon herself to do. Her Parapsychology degree, and this job opportunity, and her mum had not only moaned and complained but had managed to make her life worse through both, by going to the extreme and getting herself in a mess while she couldn't be there. The degree had been a pain, but Meredith had been away for just hours at a time until she had dropped out. This time she was away for a full eight weeks, and Meredith knew that mum could do a lot of damage with time like that.

Would she kill herself—for revenge?

The unease grew in her stomach.

Should I just quit and go home? I have my doubts that this show is real anyway, it wouldn't matter, and I could get to mum before any major damage is done.

The familiar twinge of guilt sat heavily in her chest, but this time a small stab of anger also found its way forward.

And what do you get Meredith? You get to live with your mum until you're old and grey before you get to have a life?

Mrs Grey's words rang in her ears—She's a grown woman, not your responsibility, you can walk away.

Meredith swiped a long strand of hair from her face and tucked it behind her ear.

No, I can't walk away. But I'll be damned if I walk away from this job. It's just eight weeks. Not a lifetime. I need to be able to be able to deal with this Eve stuff, it's not too much to ask, is it?

Meredith blew out a breath. She was driving herself insane.

'Mind if I join you?'

She turned to see Matt, pulling a cigarette from the pack in his hands. She smiled and shook her head.

'I could do with the break.' She said.

Matt stopped, lighter halfway to his mouth.

'A break? You've been out here ages.' He said, cigarette bobbing between his lips.

'Yes, that's just the point, a break from the chatter in my head.'

'Careful,' he said, blowing smoke with a grin, 'you sound a little unstable.'

Meredith chuckled. Her mouth felt tight, like it had been far too long since she had laughed. She couldn't be bothered to correct herself, and she had a feeling he would understand anyway.

'Could do with a run, huh?' he said, proving her right.

She wrinkled her nose, falling serious as she nodded at him.

'Well, I'd say go,' he said, 'but I think Kevin may have something to say about you running off into the hills an hour before his shoot.'

'I'd tell him I was never coming back.'

Matt gave an easy laugh. 'It's an attractive proposition

after his mood the last day or so.'

'Yeah, it is. But I like tracking down ghosts, and this place feels off, doesn't it?'

Matt stared off toward the village as he inhaled smoke.

'Off how?' He said, giving her a sideways look before blowing the smoke away from her. The gusty wind blew it straight back, not that she minded too much. Smoke was one thing she was used to sitting in with her mother, smoke she could take over alcoholism any day.

'Off like... I don't know, it kind of feels heavy in there today.'

Matt raised his eyebrows at her, drawing down his mouth, and she knew that he didn't feel it.

'Heavy, like oppressive.' She continued. 'Maybe it's just this weather, or Kevin, I don't know, I just feel on edge today.'

Matt finally nod his head.

'Yeah, I get you. It's probably all of that stuff piled together. The weather, and Kevin, and the commotion with the bear, and Asha.'

'Asha?' Meredith said turning to him with a frown.

Matt took a last drag of his cigarette before throwing it down and crushing it with the sole of his trainer. He stuffed both hands into his pockets, pushing down so that his arms hugged close into his body, his shoulders hunched, bringing his neck and ears into the collar.

'Yeah, I saw what she was doing at dinner.'

Meredith felt her heart jump. Matt glanced at her and continued.

'Goading I believe the term is. I couldn't hear what she was saying, but I saw the look on her face. She was really trying to wind you up.' He paused and Meredith turned to him. 'Looked like she was doing just that too, until Steve joined in.'

Meredith huffed a sigh and turned back to the hills ahead, shuffling down into her own coat for the little warmth that was left as the cold wind buffeted past them.

'Goading is one word. I'd come straight out and say that she was being a little shit, actually.'

Matt grimaced.

'What was she saying?'

'Just the usual Elana's going to scare us to death crap. She knew that I'd thrown up last night.'

Matt's brow furrowed.

'Elana?'

'Asha.'

He shrugged. 'She could have heard Orla and Stephanie talking, they're bound to have discussed what went on. Orla will want to have known the details of the investigation probably.'

Meredith nodded.

'Yes, perfectly plausible, I get that. But the look on her face, and the way she used it. I know she could have come across the information, but even so, to use it in such a way still shocked me.'

'She's a little old for her age that way,' Matt agreed.

'Yes,' Meredith nodded. 'And clever. And manipulative. And condescending. And good at pretence. And prone to liking her way.'

Matt huffed out a laugh.

'All right Meredith, what are you getting at?'

'Well, I just wonder, you know? How far this kid will go to get attention. She's the only one adopted, the two boys were surrogates. Do they treat her differently? Even in minuscule ways?'

Matt held her gaze but said nothing, so she continued.

'I just wonder how much of this Elana stuff is true and how much is made up. I mean if you think about it, she could fake quite a lot if she wanted to.'

Matt blinked.

'You think she's faking?'

Meredith sighed, the emphasis on faking and the raised

eyebrows spoke volumes.

'I'm not sure, of course, just a feeling I guess.'

She cocked the side of her mouth into a mirthless grin, knowing she shouldn't have said anything, but not able to take it back.

'Meredith,' Matt started carefully, 'I understand that she has a way about her, and that she is kind of scarily intelligent for a nine-year-old kid. But to be faking a haunting for all this time? I mean, what the hell would she get out of it?'

Meredith shrugged, keeping her gaze on the mountains which were disappearing further as the cloud thickened.

'I don't know. Maybe she wants them to leave the castle, maybe she just wants the attention on her, like I said.'

'But that is some accusation...' He stopped and ran a hand through his hair before pulling the packet of cigarettes back out and putting another between his lips. 'Man, you are suspicious, Meredith! First Kev, now Asha, it'll be me next.'

He chuckled but not so much as to pull up her defences. She knew he was only making light of a serious situation.

'I know, and I know what you must be thinking, but let me tell you the reasons why before you judge.'

Matt lit his cigarette and gave her a nod.

'Shoot.' He said.

'Okay, so she was quite nasty about Orla when she wasn't in the room, when Helen and I were interviewing her. She laughed at her choice of clothing, and the way she went on, hardly playing the loving daughter. When I asked her about the cellar incident, which was supposed to have been so traumatic, she almost gloated over her scars. She told us that Elana's bones are in the cellar, and that Stephanie and Orla think they contain her, but they don't. The funny thing is that she didn't say that Elana came out of her own accord in so many words, she admitted that she could reach the key to the door by climbing on the cupboards—and hinted that she did so on a regular basis.'

Matt watched her quietly.

'She said she opened the cellar herself?'

Meredith nod her head, although she wasn't a hundred percent now that she had heard exactly those words.

'She opened the cellar for Elana to go in and out. I also believe that she could have tipped the photographs and broken the one of herself yesterday too.'

'But Stephanie said that there had been no one else in the room.'

Meredith huffed a breath, shuddering a little and wishing she had brought a bigger coat out tonight.

'Asha is hardly going to announce the fact, is she?'

Matt shrugged.

'I suppose not. And while I agree that some of this stands, there is just one little thing that doesn't make any sense—at all.'

Meredith frowned.

'What?'

'The Ouija last night, and the message...'

Matt let the intention hang and Meredith felt her momentum falter. He was right.

She slowly nod her head.

'Yeah, well, I suppose that is fairly hard to explain away.'

'There is no way a living nine-year-old girl who is down in the village a mile or so away can control a Ouija planchette. The other thing is, even if she could, is there any way that she could have known a secret so big that it sent you running outside?'

Meredith bit her lip.

'Well, no. Absolutely not.'

Matt nod his head.

'Listen, Meredith, I know you had a scare, and I know Asha is a pain in the ass, but let's not get carried away. Even if we were the Scooby Doo gang we're only here tonight anyway. Tomorrow we move on, so why get entangled in this? Let's just use the equipment, call some ghosts, if Elana does have big plans, then Kevin gets his footage. And really, that's all this is about, isn't it?'

Meredith sighed and nodded. She only wished she felt the same. He could put this aside, she wanted to help, but he was right, she had no control over the outcome either way.

Matt pulled a hand out of his pocket to rub her arm.

'Okay?'

Meredith nodded and cast her gaze down at the floor as Matt glanced at his watch absently. A sign that he was uncomfortable, at least in Meredith's book anyway.

'Yeah, you're right. She's just so…'

'Annoying, I know, but it doesn't make her Houdini of the ghost world now does it?'

Meredith grinned, unable to help herself.

'I guess not.'

'Tell you what,' Matt said, stubbing out the cigarette. 'We'll keep an eye out for your wires and… things. If there's foul play maybe we'll mention it to Stephanie, and they can take it from there with Asha themselves. Right?'

Meredith felt a little of her tension release. Yes, that did sound like a good, logical idea. And probably the only thing she could do about the situation, after all.

'Yeah, okay. Thanks Matt.'

'For what?'

'Just listening… and not saying what's really going through your head.'

Matt looked at her with an amused smile as the first spots of rain hit the ground around them.

'And what is really going through my head?' He said.

'That I'm some messed up, paranoid, suspicious lunatic.'

Matt laughed out loud and put an arm around her shoulders pulling her close for a quick squeeze, that left Meredith wishing he had held her a little longer.

'Nope, what I was thinking is that we only have fifteen minutes before Kevin starts. If we're not there, well…' He cut off, making sawing motions across his neck, before looking up at the tumultuous grey clouds. 'Looks like we're about to get wet, too. Come on, we should get inside.'

CHAPTER TWENTY

Rain streaked the kitchen window, the steady splatter of water from the overflowing gutter barely decipherable over the fast and thunderous downpour that roared outside. Wet would have been an understatement, Meredith thought, as the small group waited at the top of the stairs for their cue to enter the cellars.

A few shots had already been filmed in the kitchen, and living room, where Gwen had revealed some more history, and given some more of the background of Elana and the castle.

Elana's part had taken mere seconds. There was no history of any small children buried in the cellar, and no history of anyone called Elana associated with the castle. She was an enigma.

Or a figment of a small girl's imagination anyway.

Meredith wrinkled her nose. It made no odds for filming. There was a ghost called Elana, she had come through on the Ouija board and sent the presenter out to vomit on the lawn. That was all Kevin needed or wanted.

Meredith made a vow that she wouldn't be running outside tonight in this weather.

She chewed on her lip as she thought of the timetable for tonight. A sit and wait vigil with the equipment, a test of the Ghost Box, possibly Spookbuddy. Stephanie and Orla had already been interviewed to reveal the location of Elana's body, under the boiler boarding.

They had been horrified when they had learned of this information, Meredith had been horrified that Kevin had told them, but after overhearing Helen talking to Steve, he had decided that it was just too much information to miss out on for the show.

There would be a lifting of the boards where Elana's body was supposed to be, for entertainment purposes. Meredith and Helen both knew there was nothing but pipes under them, and she had never been so glad she had checked anything in her life. To have been asked to lift the boards for the first time on camera she may just have passed out in fear. Now she was more bothered about looking suitably terrified.

Which is why we shouldn't be forcing the show. I'm not an actress, and neither is Helen. Kevin should have kept the information to himself.

Helen's urgent fist poked into her back from behind.

'Meredith, go!' she whispered.

Go?

She frowned, and then Kevin's voice boomed up from below.

'Cut, cut, cut!

The cellar door flew inward, and Kevin rose before Meredith, sending her stepping back into Helen.

'For the love of God and a half decent crew, do I have to repeat myself over and over about the simplest of things? Action means action. It means that you open the door and descend the stairs into the cellar so that we can start. Does anyone have a problem understanding what I have said three times now?'

He held his hand up in front of Meredith's face, thumb holding little finger into his palm, three fingers raised in the air like a W.

There was a scattering of mumbled no's from around her, but Meredith was all that Kevin was interested in. His hard gaze held hers, obviously blaming her as the perpetrator, as she was first in line.

Well, he'd be right. Take it and carry on Meredith, and for crying out loud will you please learn to pay attention.

Meredith dropped her gaze to the floor.

'Sorry, I had trouble hearing you over the rain.'

There was a moment of stony silence where the incredulity of what she had said settled around them. Meredith closed her eyes.

As if you'd never hear his booming voice.

And yet, she realised that she hadn't. Not because of the rain, but for her own mindless chatter. Again.

Focus Meredith. From now on that will be your middle name or you will be fired and back home to mum before the week is out, which achieves nothing at all, and puts you back where you don't want to be. Just focus.

Kevin released a stale coffee filled sigh in front of her. She looked up to see the light bouncing off his thinning head as he ran a hand over his face.

'Listen very carefully. I am about to go back downstairs, and in approximately thirty seconds I will shout 'Action'. Even if you only think you hear it, open the door, and come down. Please?'

His jaw worked as Meredith nod her head. She presumed that the others were doing the same behind her. No one made a sound.

'Let's get this evening started, I do not wish to be here until sunrise.'

He turned on a heel and stomped downstairs, the door swinging shut behind him.

Meredith hardly breathed as she waited, but this time he came through loud and clear from below. Meredith put on her ghost hunting presenter head and descended the stairs by torch light, the others tagging behind.

* * * * *

A damp cold enveloped them as they stood in an energy circle, Meredith had one hand in Helen's, the other in Gwen's. Their respective hands were linked to Donald's to form a small circle. The EDI meter was at the centre of them, two motion sensor cat balls had been placed just outside the circle, one by the infamous no-longer-there boiler, the other in the doorway.

Another EMF meter sat just outside the circle to detect electromagnetic changes, and Steve had loaded the Ghost box audio filtering software onto the laptop and set it in the corner of the room so that spirits could speak via digital message if they so desired.

The circle fell quiet, drawing energy forward until Kevin gave the nod to go ahead. Meredith took a breath and began.

'Hello spirits—Elana—Could you give us a sign if you are with us and wish to communicate with us.'

There was nothing, no movement, motion, or flicker of equipment. The sound of the wind and rain thundered from above, and the breeze that Helen and Meredith had felt earlier returned to the room.

'Just the wind.' Meredith said as her hair lifted. 'Helen and I experienced this earlier.'

There were quiet nods from around the circle. No one spoke. Meredith tried again.

'Are there any spirits here that wish to communicate? We don't mean you any harm. Elana? Are you here with us this evening? Please can you make a noise? Touch one of us? Set off one of the cat balls around the room?'

There was no response.

Meredith tried again, each time waiting for something. A sound, A flicker of light from the EDI or EMF meter. A flicker of life from the Ghost box. But all was silent.

She glanced to Helen, who raised her eyebrows.

'Okay,' Meredith said, 'How about we each call out around the circle. We can see if there is a response to any particular one of us.'

Gwen gave a nod and went first, then Donald, Helen, and finally Meredith again. They were silent after each call out, waiting for responses that never came. Meredith glanced back to Helen with pursed lips, trying to make her intent clear.

So much for Elana's big showstopper.

Helen gave a small shrug, as Gwen called out again.

Meredith shivered in the cool air, but the temperature meter remained steady between 62 and 64 Fahrenheit. There were no unnatural drops or rises, no flashing lights from any of the equipment, no unusual noises or sounds. Nothing.

She felt a little deflated. She had expected a fight with Elana, or Asha, but there was no activity at all.

Which probably means that Kevin isn't rigging things either?

At the thought of Kevin, Meredith waited for Matt, who was circling them, to train the camera off her before glancing to him as they waited for a response to Gwen.

He caught her eye and waved his hand in a 'rolling' motion, urging her to move on, to get some activity. Meredith decided to press for Elana.

'Is Elana here with us? Elana, you spoke to us last night in the living room. Come forward if you are here. Give us a sign. Move the balls, make the lights flash. Move over the equipment to set it off.'

Nothing. Meredith felt herself getting impatient as Helen took over.

'Elana? Can you make a sound for us, show us that you're here? Please, we'd love to speak to you again.'

There was silence and Meredith could feel the irritability radiating off Kevin.

Come on Meredith, think. What can you do?

And that was when Donald began to moan.

Meredith had a hard time not rolling her eyes. It seemed he had taken over the lack of action himself. A flutter of fear circled her stomach after the last time Donald had channelled Elana, and again, she wondered if he did know anything. Could he have found out about her past?

With the right tools she supposed he could have.

Right, Meredith, go with it. If he comes out with the

crap from yesterday just carry on. He obviously did a little research of his own. Don't freak out, just take it.

She pulled in a long breath.

'Donald?' She said.

Donald brought his head up slowly meeting the gaze of Gwen, then slowly turning to Helen. When his eyes met Meredith's, he looked up from under his eyelashes, playing coy. A smile slowly crossed his lips.

'Not Donald.' He said.

CHAPTER TWENTY ONE

If it hadn't been such a serious moment, and at least some sort of action, Meredith may have laughed out loud at the look the aging psychic was giving her right now.

Not Donald? Well, that's not rocket science. As if Donald would give a look like that to anyone!

Meredith nodded.

'I guessed so,' she said, and tried to keep a grin from forming on her lips now that Matt had the camera trained back on her. 'Is it Elana?'

'Get out of here, Meredith. Go home.' Donald said flashing a wide grin and showing a row of perfect white teeth.

Meredith tried not to sigh.

Come on Donald, have you not got anything more? At least make it entertaining.

'Right,' Meredith said, 'So you are Elana.'

It was a statement, not a question. Meredith was certain where this line of questioning would go, and just what would come of it. A flicker of apprehension passed through her. She squashed it fast.

'Bye.' Donald said.

Meredith blinked.

'Bye?'

Donald gave a couple of small fast shakes of his head before blinking rapidly. He looked confused as he tried to pull his hand from Gwen's.

'No,' Meredith said, 'Don't break the circle. Not now that we have her.'

'But she said goodbye,' Gwen said looking perplexed, but holding firm to Donald's hand. 'Are you okay Donald?'

Donald turned to her and gave a curt nod. He looked pale, but surely, he should be used to all this possession business by now. What the heck made Elana different?

'I'm okay, lets proceed,' He said with a voice that managed to be both firm and shaky at the same time.

There was an impatient sigh from the corner and Meredith knew that Kevin also thought it was a mighty fine idea that they proceed. And as quickly as possible.

'Okay, Elana, I don't believe that was goodbye—'

A brisk wind lifted her hair and trailed around her legs.

'Anyone feel that?'

There was a murmuring of agreement.

'The wind did blow through here, remember,' Helen said in a low voice.

'Yes,' Meredith agreed, 'and if we all feel it, then it's most likely just that.'

The breeze died away, and all felt silent.

Meredith frowned.

'Donald, was it Elana that came through?'

'Oh yes, for sure. The entity felt the same as yesterday. All consuming, and quite frightening.'

'Frightening?'

Donald gave a nod.

'She's strong, as I said yesterday.'

Meredith nodded back. Whether Donald was playing a game or not, now wasn't the time to go into it.

'Elana? Are you still here?' Helen called out.

There was no response and Meredith felt anger stab in her gut.

If Elana had just been with Donald, and she was apparently so strong and out to get her, then where the hell was she?

Kevin huffed from the corner and Meredith felt the pressure snap her patience.

'Elana, I think this is Bullshit. I don't think you're strong enough to 'get' anyone. You're just a little girl with a big attitude—'

The cat ball in the doorway strobed its colour around the room, and Meredith looked to the doorway.

Kevin wasn't in reach and Steve and Matt were too far away at the other end of the cellar now.

Right. Here we go. You want to make this personal? Let's have a face off Elana, you and me.

'Thank you, Elana,' Gwen said, 'Could you do that again for us?'

It was usual custom. Meredith had taught the practice to Gwen herself, Gwen having no ghost hunting experience, but now she found she had no patience for the normal niceties and respectful spirit talk.

'Of course she can.' She said. 'That's about all she can do.'

The wind picked up again, colder this time, and the EDI flickered in the centre of the circle. Upstairs in the kitchen one of the old, disconnected servant bells rang.

'Yep, seen it a million times Elana, you're not so special.'

Opposite Meredith, Donald's face flashed a flicker of worry.

'Meredith—' He started, but she cut him off.

'No, Donald. If she can take possession of you so easily, then why can't she just tell me her goddamn problem? Huh? How about that Elana? You can't just go from possessing someone and spewing vile secrets, to making a puny cat ball and EDI meter flash. It's pathetic. Really. You want to get me? Show me what you've got.'

A breeze snaked back around her legs. Upstairs there was a loud bang, and the clang of the bell again. All heads turned to the doorway and Meredith caught the broad smile on Kevin's face as he jotted something in a notebook. An unrealistic surge of anger made her want to knock the book from his hands. Oh, now he was bloody happy? Well Meredith was seething.

'Is Stephanie upstairs?' Gwen said, her wide eyes

scouring the circle.

'The whole family is in the village tonight, there isn't anyone up there now,' Helen said.

Meredith boiled over.

'So what? Are you going to get us from up there in the kitchen? I'm so scared Elana. We're all terrified.'

'Meredith—' Donald began, his voice a mixture of worry and warning.

He looked pale again, his brow creased in large furrows. Gwen also looked nervous, although she was holding her tongue for now, while Helen squeezed her hand so hard Meredith could feel the tremors running through it.

Meredith could detect the change in the air, the static charge, even before the EDI confirmed it with a flicker of blue lights. The calm energy of the circle became anxious. Alert. And the temperature was now hovering around 60 Fahrenheit.

Four degrees? Really?

Meredith huffed a laugh.

Come on Elana,' she shouted now, 'Show us what you've got. Tell me the problem. Why are you here? What do you want with Asha? What do you want with me?'

Meredith realised that she was losing control but the tension in the air now was undeniable. Strong.

Cat ball one went off again and the EDI flickered at full capacity. The temperature dropped further and finally Meredith shivered. She looked to Donald and saw his breath cloud before him.

Good, this was good. This was exactly as it should be. Elana only had to give a bit more and they would surely have enough. It wasn't like they needed much activity after last night. All the drama had been hinged on the Ouija, and Kevin certainly wouldn't be taking that scene out, she knew.

The cat ball went off at the other side of the room, the strobe of colour bouncing off the ceiling and walls in the darkness.

'If you set off the balls any more Elana, we'll be able to start up some music and have a party.'

There was a small, polite chuckle from around the circle. It broke the tension and she prepared for another dig at Elana. As she opened her mouth there was a bang and a scratch from the corner, and then Meredith saw the cat ball hurtling toward her face.

She wouldn't have had time to move before it hit, but the ball stopped in mid-air, just short of the end of her nose, it's lights still flashing as it spun.

Meredith's breath caught in her throat, and her heart thumped noisily in her chest.

Poltergeist activity. Asha couldn't fake this, no one could. It simultaneously unnerved her and left her in awe.

The ball seemed to hang for hours, although it could only have been seconds before it fell to the floor at her feet with a reverberating bang and stopped flashing. Although, the bang wasn't the ball Meredith realised. It was the cellar door, the immovable cellar door, slamming with all the force of a hurricane.

For the first time tonight, she was lost for words, and it seemed the rest of the crew were too. No one said a word, and then the ball began to roll. It completed a circle and came to rest at Meredith's feet before being hurled from the floor, straight over Gwen's shoulder, and hitting the corner of the room with a thwack.

The ball dropped, straight onto the open laptop with a thud and Steve gave a yell.

'Aw, anywhere but the screen, man!'

Matt had the camera trained on Steve as he stooped over the small computer, but he turned to face Meredith, the shock on his face evident.

'Did you get it?' she mouthed to him.

He nodded quickly, flit his gaze to Kevin, and back to the camera and Steve sitting in the corner almost cradling the Ghost box like a baby.

It made Meredith think of Spookbuddy, who had been excluded from this investigation at the last minute. Excluded from all investigations until Kevin had checked him over and found out exactly what he did.

Steve made a noise. A kind of guttural moaning.

'Shit,' he said.

The group waited, the tension almost palpable between them, but Steve just sat staring at the screen his mouth hanging in a small 'O' surrounded by beard.

'What is it, Steve?' Helen said. Her voice wavered and ice travelled down Meredith's spine.

Meredith would have said that there wasn't anything in the world that would make Steve Gittins look like that. He was the joker, and even with everything that had gone on before this he hadn't been fazed. He was the ultimate unshockable man.

Or so you thought.

'Shit,' he repeated, eyes still on the screen. 'I forgot the fucking sound. The machine was on, but I forgot to turn up the fucking sound.'

He looked to the group, eyes wide, and then he turned back to the screen which lit his face in a green hue.

'Fuck!' He said.

And Meredith broke the energy circle and moved toward him.

CHAPTER TWENTY TWO

SEPTEMBER—122 DAYS UNTIL DEATH

'Fuck!' Evie hissed as the needle went right through the material and into the flesh of her finger. My eyes went as wide as saucers at Evie's BAD WORD, but a giggle came from my mouth at the same time.

'Fuck.' I tried quietly, eyeing myself in the mirror. I turned my head from side to side testing the velvet hat from every angle. It was too big, and the floppy rim drooped almost over my eyes. I lifted my chin so that I could see my concealed face and tipped the hat back.

Evie looked up at me with a scowl.

'Get the hat off, Moo, and get out of my room.'

Pushing my lips out in a pout, I pulled the hat from my head and placed it on the dressing table, taking care not to snag it as Evie always told me.

I waited for her to tell me to leave again, but she was having trouble with the needle, and for the moment it seemed I was forgotten.

I waited by the dressing table quietly, watching the drip of blood from her finger spread onto the material of the skirt.

Uh-oh, that would make Evie mad. My eyes went wide again as I wondered whether to tell her.

No, better not. If I made a sound now Evie would remember that I wasn't supposed to be here. I held my breath just to be sure that she wouldn't hear me. I held onto my breath so hard that my chest felt it would pop, but it still didn't work.

Evie's head flicked up and she scrunched her eyes at me again.

I scrunched mine back as I looked at her. Her eyes were dark. Well, not her eyes exactly but the skin around them, like she had been smudging too much of the funny black pencil crayon under them.

I wondered if this was the NEW THING. All of Evie's friends would look like this when they came round to go out. I vowed to try it with my crayon. Maybe in a different colour though, black was too creepy. GOTH mum liked to call it. I didn't want to be GOTH, whatever that was, I would choose purple, or red... maybe even pink.

Thinking of the crayons had taken my mind off Evie who was now throwing the skirt aside with a huff.

'Meredith. What is your problem? I said get out.'

She shoved a pointed finger to the door, and I fidgeted by the mirror.

I didn't want to go. Sundays were too quiet. Today Evie had been in for a change, and although there had been some shouting between mum and Evie about the skirt, mostly it had been fun.

Now it was becoming not fun.

Evie's scrunched eyes became wide, stern, and she shoved her hand at the door again.

'I said GET OUT.'

'But Evie, I'll be quiet, I promise. Don't make me go play by myself again, it's booorrrrring.'

I whined. I knew Evie hated whining, but I couldn't help it. The noise came from my mouth almost before I put it there.

'Pleeaaseee Eeeviee. I can help yooou.'

Now Evie stood, the thread falling from her lap and rolling onto the floor. She stood with her fists clenched, hunched over like a bear.

'I said GET. OUT. OF. MY. ROOM!'

Her cheeks flushed red highlighting the paleness of her skin. Her lips, usually so plump and shiny with lipstick were bare, red, and chapped.

'NOW!' Evie almost roared, making me jump. My bottom lip wobbled, and my eyes started to fill with tears.

Evie took a stride toward me and I finally ran. I ducked under her arm and tried to jump onto her bed, but she caught me just above the elbow.

The pull on my arm pulled me off balance, and mid jump my body swung to face her, before falling back onto the side of her bed.

The frame under the mattress caught my skin and I yelled. The pain scraped down my back like fingernails. The tears finally came as Evie grabbed my arm and dragged me forward. I couldn't find my feet quick enough as she pushed me, and I fell toward the door.

I clenched my whole body tight, waiting for the impact but then the door wasn't there, and I hit something hard and bony. Two things, actually.

I opened my eyes to the blurry outline of mum, who stepped over me and into Evie's room.

I watched her grab Evie and shake her by the shoulders, shrieking into her face. I watched because I couldn't move. I felt frozen to the spot with fear and shock. I had never seen mum LOSE HER TEMPER like this before.

I couldn't even tell if she was shrieking about me or something else. She didn't look back at me.

Then dad was there, his hands at my shoulders taking me to the one place I didn't want to go. My room.

'I'm okay. I don't want to go in there on my own. Don't make me daddy.'

'It'll be okay, princess,' he said, 'there, there, it will soon be over. Mummy has had a real bad day that's all. It'll be okay.'

He pushed me into my room and shut the door behind him leaving me alone to listen to the argument coming from the next room.

I stared at the door for a while and then moved to the wall to listen.

'I am sick to death of the BLOODY fights in this house.' Mum was screeching, her voice so high it didn't sound like her own. Evie's was equally high as she yelled back.

'I didn't do anything. She won't leave me alone!'

My tummy did a flip, and I felt the tears blur my vision again.

'I couldn't care LESS about either one of you, have you finished sewing the skirt yet?'

'I haven't had—'

'What Eve?' mum raged, I stepped back from the wall with a blink, 'What haven't you had? Time? Inclination? What the FUCK haven't you had?'

'I told you I couldn't do it.' Eve's now muffled voice said.

'You cut the bloody slits in it, and I'm supposed to have to sew them up to make you look decent? I told you how. Do you need lessons in listening or application? Tell me. Because this should have been done hours ago! HOURS a-goddamn-go.'

'I can wear—'

'You'll sew the bloody skirt Eve, and you'll bloody wear it. I will not have you walking about like some SLUT ON HEAT. Who do you think you are? It's disgraceful!'

'I'm not, you don't care anyway. You wouldn't care if I were DEAD!' Evie's voice hitched in the scream and I knew that she would be crying.

I made a note to ask mum what a SLUT ON HEAT was when she had calmed down, and that's when I heard the slap, and dad's voice joined the shouting.

I moved back from the wall. It was too loud there now, and I couldn't really hear what was being said anyway. Everyone was being rude, talking all over each other, their voices rising.

It was like a shouting contest, and I didn't want to find out who won. My stomach swirled and I clenched my shaking hands into fists.

'Stop it.' I said, but my voice only came out as a whisper. I whispered at the stupid wall while the storm raged next door.

'Stop it.' I tried again. 'Stop it. Stop it. Stop it. STOP IT. STOP IT!'

My voice was loud now, almost a scream as mum called dad a NAUGHTY WORD and there was a bang from the room and a screech from Evie. My heart banged along with the noise. Scuffles, scrapes, a few bangs on the wall, and then Evie was screaming too.

My whole body shook, and I thought I might be sick. I didn't want to hear anymore. Too afraid to go outside and stop them, too afraid to listen, I did the only thing that I knew would keep me safe. I scrambled into bed, pulling the covers over my head, and pushing my hands into my ears.

My heart thumped, I couldn't breathe, and tears flowed freely from my eyes, and still, I could hear the shouts and screams from next door.

I had a vision that they would all be dead when the screams stopped but I was just too afraid to go outside and stop them.

Fingers firmly in my ears, shaking in a cool sweat, I recited the Lord's Prayer loudly. Concentrating on the words. Making sure I got them right and in the right order.

Over, and over, and over again.

My teacher would be proud of me tomorrow, even if they were all dead.

CHAPTER TWENTY THREE

The high-pitched whine that came from the small computer on the worktop in front of Steve thrummed like the blades of a helicopter. There were sounds that came and went through the thrum. Sounds like a voice. A girl's voice.

The crew had picked out words between them, but no concrete message had come from it, leaving the whole group baffled.

Donald squinted at the screen, as though it would help him hear better.

'Did that say something, something, dead? I couldn't make it all out, but one word sounded like dead to me.'

'I can't really make *anything* out.' Helen said, and Meredith had to agree. Nothing that was concrete anyway. It seemed to be a voice, but what it was saying was anyone's guess.

'It could do with some context.' She said.

'We'll never get context, who was it speaking to? It's like an old tape reel recorded over too many times. We can hear the odd words but who knows whether the conversation is flowing behind the muffled bits.' Gwen said.

'That's not usually how they work,' Meredith replied, 'the spirits respond to what we're saying, they don't just converse in the background like a cocktail party.'

Helen giggled, but Steve held a hand out to the group.

'Ah, I think I have it,' He said.

'What was said?'

Steve shook his head, no.

'Bear with me, I think this could work.'

He tapped at the screen again and the room fell silent other than the odd slurp of tea. Everyone watched Steve until he turned and spoke again. This time his question was directed at Matt. One hand stroked his long beard in thought.

'Do we have the time?' He said.

Kevin huffed a sigh from his perch against the worktop. His arms were folded across his chest, his mouth a thin, straight line.

'Not much of it, if we could hurry up that would be fantastic.' He said.

Steve didn't so much as bat an eyelid at the obvious sarcasm.

'Nah, I mean time on the camera.' He said tapping at the screen on the small computer. 'I mean if we can get the footage to match up with the time on here, we could try to run them simultaneously. What do you reckon Matt?'

Matt was nodding as he played with the button on the back of the camera.

'Yeah, the camera was rolling all the way through. When are we at?'

'Eleven fifty... four, the first speech comes through.'

Steve tapped the worktop aside the screen, thick fingers working rhythmically from baby finger to forefinger in sequence. The noise reminded Meredith of the drumming rain.

'Okay, got it.' Matt said.

Meredith moved forward, breath catching as she watched. Could this work? Was there anything in it?

On the small digital screen, the camera trained on Meredith and Helen. Donald and Gwen's hands held onto theirs in shot. It was Helen who spoke.

'Elana? Are you still there?'

Matt clicked the screen to still it.

'Ready?' he said to Steve who was watching with his eyebrows raised, 'We'll need to click together to run properly.'

'Ready,' Steve said, 'Go on three. One. Two. Three.'

They pressed their respective screens together to run the

playback and there was an immediate voice on the computer. It sounded like a tinny 'no', but Meredith could have been wrong as the thrumming whine of the frequency continued.

The camera panned around the four of them in the circle, all of their faces serious and focused on the silence around them. Meredith would be the only one who knew she had been annoyed at that moment. Her face showed nothing of the inner irritability she had been feeling. And then she spoke.

'Elana, I think this is Bullshit. I don't think you're strong enough to even try to 'get' anyone. You're just a little girl with a big attitude—'

On the screen the cat ball lit up sending colour around the room in a whirling motion. If she had just been watching the screen, she would have thought it had been a good response, but with the Ghost box playing in time too, there had been interference as the cat ball strobed.

The tinny voice came from the speakers, this time clearer, definitely a word—who? Boo?—and followed by what sounded like feminine laughter.

The sound sent chills down Meredith's spine. Was Elana laughing at her? Something bugged her and she tried to think further but the footage continued as Gwen thanked Elana for her participation and asked if she could do it again.

'Of course she can. That's about all she can do.' Meredith heard herself say and almost gasped at how the retort had come across.

'We're close to the mark here, Meredith,' Kevin said gruffly. 'I don't care how much it worked you are not to get so cocky again. It not only looks bad on film it also loses you empathy with the viewers. You lose the viewers; we lose the show.'

'Ssshhhh!' Steve said, turning to look at them. 'I don't want to have to wind back and pair up again.'

There was static and a whine from the small computer again, and Kevin dropped silent, as did the rest of them.

'What the hell was that?' Donald said.

'Something...' Helen added, a strange look crossed her face.

'Something that was most definitely a word.' Matt said, leaning in towards the equipment. His face now inches from Meredith and Helen's as the whole group tried to contort themselves into the closest space to listen to what was now merely frequency again.

But yes, Meredith agreed, it had sounded like a word, quite a long familiar word. She frowned.

'We need to hear that again,' she said. 'In fact, we could do with transcribing the whole thing so that anything we don't get straight away may become legible as the conversation flows.'

'But if we don't hear the word, what do we write?' Gwen said.

'We'll just put down the various things we each think it may be, and then we can see if there is a correlation afterward.'

Kevin huffed and pushed himself off the worktop.

'That sounds like time consuming work and won't add anything at all to the show. This is all well and good folks, but we're all going to be extra tired tomorrow as it is, we completed the Ghost box scene anyway, and we're at Stanmore Lodge tomorrow. Any information that evolves from that voice is irrelevant. Pack up and get back to the hotel. I have a multitude of things to complete yet before the morning comes.'

Meredith nodded.

'The acoustics in here aren't great anyway, they're distorting the sound—'

She was about to ask if they could go over it at the hotel, but Kevin had taken it that the case was closed.

'Helen, give Stephanie a call and tell her we're all done. The rest of you, grab equipment while Matt and Steve dismantle and pack up what's left. Let's be getting on our way.'

He checked his watch and made for the back door, picking up his briefcase as he went.

Helen walked into the hall to call Stephanie as Steve shut down the Ghost box and went into the cellar to get the sound equipment. Gwen and Donald picked up the nearest things, Spookbuddy being one of them, and made their way to the door.

'Car, Matt.' Donald said as he opened the door. Matt fumbled for the key in his pocket and pressed the fob, as an engine started up outside and faded off into the distance with a crunch of gravel.

Nice of you to help, Kev, old boy.

And then Meredith noticed that she and Matt were alone.

Convenient.

'Matt? Just quickly, I have an idea. What say we meet in my room and go over things there when we get back?'

Matt stopped rolling a cable long enough to look at her surprised.

'You want to continue? Kevin's right, Meredith, there's nothing this can contribute anyway. If Kevin says leave it, then maybe we just leave it.'

'I don't think I want to leave it.'

Meredith cut off as Donald came inside and continued as his footfalls disappeared down into the cellar.

'Please?'

Matt wound cable slowly and methodically before turning back to Meredith with a sigh.

'I get the feeling there's a lot you don't want to leave. You scrutinize and analyse everything!'

Meredith felt a little stab of hurt at his comment, but the fact was, she had to listen to the recording, however mad she appeared.

'I know it seems that way, but this is important, Matt, please.'

Matt placed the cable alongside the camera bag on the

side and looked at her.

'Well, as Kevin already agreed this piece of footage, I suppose. But only if I'm awake long enough. Do you have coffee?'

'Tea and coffee, and I'm sure the hotel reception will give us more.'

Matt nodded at her.

'Why is this so important when we all need to rest? I have to drive to Stanmore tomorrow. I'm going to be shattered Meredith.'

'I do appreciate it Matt, really. And Stanmore is a mere seven miles from here…'

She let the statement hang as Matt pulled his lips under his teeth, mashing them together. Then he seemed to soften, she almost felt him giving in.

'And that's the only reason I'm agreeing to this. If we had the drive we had last time, I'd say no. But as Stanmore is so close, then okay. But… I still don't see what the big deal is. Oh, and let's do this in my room, I have extra equipment in there should we need it.'

Meredith nodded as Helen came back into the kitchen. She almost rolled her eyes in frustration. Was there nowhere that you could talk in private for just five minutes?

'Stephanie's on her way, is all the stuff in?'

Donald appeared at the cellar door, shuffling a couple of large bags beside him, one in each hand. 'Just a couple more things. Steve is nearly done I think, just tracing the final wire now.'

'Okay.'

Helen smiled and started down the steps as Donald left by the back door.

Meredith turned back to Matt before anyone else could interrupt. He was still waiting for an answer, but his gaze was soft, accepting.

'Well? Why the need for this? What is so important?' he said, turning his hands palm up to the ceiling.

'I think that last time... I think I heard my name, Matt. I think Elana *spoke my name*, through the Ghost box.'

CHAPTER TWENTY FOUR

Back in Matt's room Meredith checked the clock—2.55am.
Their morning brief wasn't scheduled until 11am so they
would have plenty of time for sleep if they could get this done
as soon as possible. Matt set up the camera next to the Ghost
box on the small table in the hotel room and turned them both
on, finding both recordings where they had been left at the
castle.

'Right,' Matt said through a yawn, 'See that small button
in the corner of the screen? Tap on it, and I'll press the
camera at the same time. Ready?'

Meredith nod her head, yes.

'No!' She said, hand shooting out to grab his arm 'no,
wait. We could do with winding back a bit more, just to
Donald and his very light possession.'

Matt stared at her.

'But Steve already got the time as eleven fifty-four. That
was the first time she—it—spoke. Why would we need to go
back further?'

'I just want to make sure from the beginning that she
was with us. I mean, there may have been something that
was coming through on here too if she was using Donald at
that point.'

Matt's eyebrows were raised as he looked at her
incredulous, and she sighed pulling her hands back to tie her
ponytail tighter.

'No, Matt, not for that reason...' She averted her gaze
from his, but he saw through her anyway, she could tell.
'Well, maybe a little. But mostly I just want to be sure we
catch everything. This is obviously personal remember?'

Matt shook his head and rolled his eyes as he rewound

the footage, Meredith watched closely over his shoulder until Donald looked from person to person like a demented chicken, and then bowed his head quickly.

'There!' She said, 'Stop it there!'

Matt stopped the rewind and then tapped the play button. Donald brought his head up slowly and looked at each person in turn, finishing with Meredith, and giving a slow smile.

'Not Donald.' He said on the screen.

Matt tapped the screen to pause.

'Okay, we're at eleven forty-three.'

Meredith looked back to the small computer and tapped at the screen. Where the hell was the rewind?

She almost jumped out of her own skin when there were three stern knocks at the door.

Meredith and Matt looked at each other, the shock etched on his face would match the look on hers she was certain.

'Fuck!' Matt whispered. 'What do we do?'

Meredith licked the lips of her dry mouth and gave a little shake of her head as there was another series of knocks.

'We won't move all of this equipment in time.'

Matt was still frozen to the spot. He looked pale, and she knew how serious this would be if it were Kevin. Meredith felt her heart jump for Matt.

'Go, Matt, just keep the door close to the catch, say you're… you're naked or something.'

Matt simply nod his head and turned for the door. He had no sooner unlocked the catch and started to pull it when it was flung inward. Matt yelled as he stepped back, and Meredith cringed in the corner. There was no possible way that this could turn out well now.

'Well, hey there guys, we've come to crash the party. Seems you were right, Heathen, these pair are on it!'

Meredith stood at the sight of Steve placing her back to the equipment on the table, although she knew her slight frame wouldn't hide much of it anyway.

Matt glanced back at her, his eyes showing a mixture of relief and guardedness. He swallowed hard.

'Steve?'

Helen came through the door and shut it behind her, pulling it from Matt's hand.

'Me too,' she said, her mouth in a half-embarrassed grin crossed with a grimace.

Helen put a hand up in salute and met Meredith's eye before lowering her gaze to her jumper and jeans.

'Oh dear, seems we didn't time it quite right. They're still fully clothed.' Steve said, his voice too loud in the quiet of the room. He grinned beneath his beard as he looked from Meredith to Matt and back again waggling his eyebrows.

Matt caught Meredith's eye.

'Have we missed something?' He said.

Steve and Helen turned to him.

'No, but we obviously have, or you're just not quick enough getting on with it.'

Meredith felt herself start to colour as Steve's meaning and subsequent intention suddenly clicked in her mind. Matt was obviously slower; tiredness, Meredith thought, he was usually sharp as a tack.

'Well, I mean, we started but Meredith said to go from the beginning, so it's taking longer that's all.' He said.

Steve's eyes widened, he filled his cheeks with air, pushing them out before blowing a loud rasping out of his mouth and laughing loudly.

Helen also began to giggle, putting a hand to her mouth, and as shocked and embarrassed as she was at their insinuation Meredith found herself laughing too, a giggle at first, but laughter is infectious, and she soon found herself laughing long and loud.

Only Matt was unaware of what was so funny, which made it funnier still.

'What?' He said, hands in the air, 'What's so bloody funny?'

They laughed harder. Steve laying down on Matt's perfectly made bed, a hand on his chest, and Helen holding onto the wall for support. Meredith wiped actual tears from her eyes as she bent forward from the sideboard, her stomach and cheeks aching, but unable to stop.

Finally, she composed herself enough to look at Matt, who was standing back against the door with his arms folded, Amusement in his eyes, but not a hint of humour on his straight face as he watched them.

He opened his mouth to say something to her and she was off again. She couldn't help it. Helen finally calmed, placing a hand on Meredith's arm, and releasing a final giggle.

Steve sat up wiping his eyes and released a large exhale which came out as an 'aaaahhhhh.'

Helen sniffed. Meredith gave a last low chuckle, and Steve shook his head, and still Matt watched them from the door quietly.

'Okay,' he said, when they had finally quietened, 'I'm glad that was so amusing… want to let me in on the joke?'

Helen started to giggle again, and Meredith felt her lips quiver, and a grin starting to pull them apart.

'They thought we were… we were,' she said, unable to finish as the giggles filled her chest and throat. 'And you said… you said…'

She trailed off as the laughter snorted down through her nose. Matt looked perplexed as Steve set off into loud laughter again, too.

'You said it was taking longer because Meredith said to start at the beginning.' Helen said dissolving into giggles.

'What? Well, that's right, I was talking about… oh man,' he said, shaking his head. 'I think I just got it.'

He put both hands over his face, shoulders shaking as he began to laugh, groaning at the same time. When he dragged his hands away from his face, he was crimson. He caught Meredith's eye and shook his head slowly.

She giggled back at him with a roll of her eyes.

'So,' Steve said, through the last trickles of laughter, 'I've said it before, and I'll say it again. Did we miss the show?'

'No, no, no,' Matt said. 'Absolutely not. There was no show. What I would like to know is why you're here, and where the hell you came up with that from anyway?'

Meredith frowned and looked to Steve and Helen. She wouldn't mind knowing the answer to that herself.

'Helen heard you discussing coming up here together after the shoot at the castle.'

Meredith's mouth dropped open as she swung to Helen. Helen put her hands out in front of her.

'I only mentioned it to Steve.' She said. 'He ran with it and wanted to come and bust you out. He said it would be funny to see your faces. I'm so sorry.'

'Don't tell me everyone knows, please,' said Matt, a look of worry on his face.

'No, of course not. I only told Steve.'

Meredith felt a stab of worry herself. She and Matt had already been chastised for a relationship they didn't have. It could be more than both of their jobs worth if Kevin found out about a little rendezvous in Matt's room after the shoot. Never mind that they were messing with footage and that Kevin may not approve of that either.

'How can you be sure that no one else overheard?' She said, 'That conversation with Matt was supposed to be private, but it obviously wasn't as private as I thought.'

'I'm sorry,' Helen said quietly. She dropped her gaze, chewing on her lip.

Meredith smiled as she touched Helen's arm bringing her gaze back up to her.

'I appreciate the apology, and it really doesn't matter anyway, as long as you're sure no one else overheard what you said. It's important.'

Matt was nodding at her too, and Steve looked at Helen with his lips pursed. His eyes were amused, however.

Meredith looked from one to the other of them.

'No. We were alone.' Helen murmured, a small smile crawling across her lips.

'Definitely alone.' Steve added with a nod.

Meredith felt a smile tug at her mouth.

'Oh, well Matt, it seems that maybe we should be storming Steve's room instead. The result may have been much more to the one Steve and Helen were expecting from us.'

Matt cocked a lip with a frown.

'No way. Steve?'

'Yes way,' Steve said, putting an arm around Helen's shoulders.

Helen coloured.

'Not that result. We haven't… you know.'

Meredith laughed.

'I really don't need to know more. Congratulations you two.'

'Yeah,' Matt said with a laugh. 'On a more serious note, though, keep it to yourselves. Kevin tore a strip off me yesterday morning for 'fooling around' with Meredith on set. Says he wants to keep it professional. And we're not even fooling around!'

Helen nodded.

'Yeah, we will.' Steve said, 'Man I thought you guys had hooked up too, we were going to come have a foursome!'

'Eeww,' Helen and Meredith said together.

'So, what the hell *are* you doing in here then?'

Matt looked at Meredith, who looked at Matt, keeping her back to the not-very-well-hidden equipment. His eyes told the same story as her feelings.

Tell them or not? Can they keep a secret?

Steve and Helen were both looking at them for answers, and other than admit that they were seeing each other too, which they had just denied, there seemed no other option but the truth.

Meredith shrugged at Matt, and he pursed his lips.

'Come on,' Steve said, sitting back on the bed with a frown, 'what's the big secret? Tell uncle Steve.'

'It *is* a big secret, and we need it keeping that way,' Meredith said.

Steve looked to her, his eyebrows raised, and then to Matt, who nodded agreement.

'I don't know whether Kevin would be spitting or not, but I really don't intend to find out.'

'So, what is it?' Helen asked.

'We were completing what wasn't completed at the castle,' Matt said, 'With the Ghost box and the footage.'

'Ooookaaaay,' Steve said, looking at them as though they had just crawled from the nearest swamp.

'I wanted to,' Meredith said, 'The last bit we watched at the castle, where the pitch went crazy? I think the word was my name.'

Helen's mouth dropped open, and then she frowned and pointed a finger into the air.

'You know, thinking about it now...'

Meredith nodded.

'Yeah, I'm pretty sure it was. I wanted to check, but I also wanted to do what we were going to, transcribe it and see if there was anything come through that was important.'

'Important how?' Steve said wrinkling his nose.

'Well, if Elana said my name, then I want to know what message she had for me, she wouldn't say it for no reason, surely.'

'I suppose that could be interesting,' Steve said. He scooted forward on the bed and circled his arms around Helen's waist. 'How can the dream team help?'

Meredith looked to Matt, she had thought that they would leave them to it, but four heads were better than one when trying to figure out ghost speech was involved. He shrugged.

'Up to you,' He said with a small smile.

Meredith smiled at Steve and Helen.

'Okay,' she said, 'That would be good. Steve and Matt, you can operate the machines and Helen and I can write it all down between us.'

'Who's going to suss out if Donald is faking?' Matt said with a grin.

'That's my job, as the expert,' Meredith said flicking her middle finger at him. Matt laughed, and Meredith grinned at him.

'What's this?' Steve said.

'Meredith has a thing about faked activity. She thinks Donald is a little too forward with his possessions.'

Helen grimaced. 'I have thought he seemed a little fake at times, but not knowing mediums I just presumed that was normal.'

'It is normal,' Meredith said, 'It's just that he seems to drop a spirit out whenever it's quiet like a joker with a good fart. Too perfectly timed that's all.'

Matt and Steve laughed as Helen nodded with a grin and rolled her sleeves up, glancing at her wrist.

'Come on then,' she said, 'it's nearly 3.15am.'

CHAPTER TWENTY FIVE

The man heard the ebb and flow of the television in the front room. The woman was distracted but he waited a further five minutes before moving from the cellar. The ritual that had become routine over the last few days was risky, but necessary.

Cracking open the door, he listened. Hearing nothing but the TV he left the cellar and climbed the stairs silently. It was God's work that the woman never noticed him, that she sat with the television and a bottle until the early hours of each morning. God's work that he was completing, but his choice that the room be cleansed of some of its impurity before he could do his job properly. Not entirely of course, that wasn't possible, but he could make it better.

He looked around the room. It was a mess, and that was to be expected. The woman was a mess. Before he entered, he crossed himself three times and muttered a prayer.

God would understand, he was on God's mission after all. But he would ask for forgiveness anyway, and flagellation would follow when his work with the woman was done. As it always was when he had finished.

He would be in God's grace. He would do anything to make sure that this was so. Always.

His eyes travelled round the room. Clothes were strewn across the floor, the dressing table was cluttered with old make up, tubs, and small bottles which spilled over onto the carpet. Joining them were bigger bottles. Bottles now empty of the devil's juice. He saw the grime that covered the window, and pinched his mouth in distaste, but the worst was the bed. Unmade and dirty. It seemed the woman had menstruated at some point and not bothered to clean the sheets. The blood crusty and brown.

The man shuddered. Water spilled from the vase of flowers, but the open bottle in his other hand held onto its contents. He scrunched his toes in his shoes lifting them off the floor as much as possible, glad of the barrier between his feet and the filth. On other occasions he hadn't been so lucky. He had had to work barefoot.

He crossed himself again, muttering forgiveness and thanks that he was still holy, still pure.

The woman was a mess, a disgrace, a manifestation of the devil himself. He was acutely aware that he stood in the devil's abode, and his body tingled with revulsion.

Shutting off from the chaos around him, the man walked to the dressing table, and placed the flowers down before the mirror, knocking the clutter away with the base of the glass vase gently. Then he placed the bottle next to it, reaching into his pocket to locate three small pills that he dropped into the neck with a satisfying plop.

He rearranged the flowers, allowing their beauty to lean into all areas of the room, before stepping nearer and inhaling gently.

Ah yes, the perfect, clean, pure, smell of Lilies. There was nothing better. Nothing more cleansing.

He clasped his hands at his chest, careful not to touch anything of the woman's. He had no intention of inheriting her dirty, sinful, disease. She was an unholy woman. She had completed the devil's work, drank the devil's juice. She would need to be disposed of indefinitely in time. In God's time, though. Not his.

The man curled his lip in disgust and caught sight of himself in the mirror.

His clear blue eyes shone, and he smiled, thanking the Lord for his grace and pureness of heart, crossing himself three times again, as he confirmed that he knew the work to be done.

It was work he would detach from, and he would make

sure that the woman's skin would never touch his. To touch her with any part of him would mean that he too would be defiled. He would be careful and diligent, as he always was.

This had been done before and he could do it again.

Looking at his reflection he pulled the long woollen cloak further around his body. Lifting his head, he pulled the loose hood closer around his face, concealing his features in shadow. The woman was not allowed to see him. It was imperative. It was God's wish.

And now God's wish was to be upheld.

The woman would be made clean. Or die.

It was not the man's decision to make which way she went.

He closed his eyes and muttered the words aloud.

'With your divine guidance and instruction, I complete your work with diligence, joy, and love. You are the master, and I your willing slave. So is my duty in life. Thank you, father.'

The man crossed himself again and opened his eyes. In the mirror, he noted the new steel behind them, the new strength in his stance. God always made it so, and now, he would go back down to the cellar to wait for the instruction for work to begin.

He turned and left the room almost silently. Clicking the door shut behind him and heading for the stairs.

CHAPTER TWENTY SIX

Sitting along the tiny table, the men at either end with the machines, the girls in the middle with a pen and paper, the footage and Ghost box played together as Donald's head came up.

'Not Donald.' He said with a slow smile. The rest of the group in the cellar were fixed on him as he looked at Meredith.

'I guessed so,' Meredith said, the camera now trained on her.

Steve sniggered.

'That was so accommodating for the little spirit girl, Meredith,' He said.

Meredith smiled, flicking her eyes at him. 'Shhh.' She said, 'anything on the box?'

Steve shook his head, no.

'Is it Elana?' Meredith said on screen.

'Get out of here, Meredith. Go home.' Donald answered.

Her stomach turned over at his smile, bile rising in her throat as she watched the scene play out.

'Right,' Meredith said on screen, 'so you are Elana.'

Steve snickered again, and Matt grinned.

'Shhh,' Meredith put a finger to her lips, her eyes straining for anything out of place, for any evidence that Donald wasn't really possessed. At the moment she couldn't find one.

'Bye,' Donald said. His voice higher pitched than usual.

She heard herself repeat 'Bye?' and then Donald blinked, looking genuinely confused. Either he was an incredibly good actor, or he had been possessed. A sheen of sweat lined his pale face which was unusual in the cold of the cellar.

Hmm, so okay, there isn't anything that suggests foul play here.

'Anything from the box yet?' She said.

'Nada.' Steve confirmed.

Meredith turned back to the screen.

'I'm okay, lets proceed,' Donald was saying, looking, and sounding, like he wasn't ready to proceed at all. Meredith felt a stab of remorse at how she had dismissed him down in the cellar. She should have been more considerate. She bit on her lip as she watched, squirming as she saw herself getting angry with Elana.

'Man, I don't know why I was so tetchy.' She muttered.

'Period due?' Steve said with a sly smile.

'No!' Meredith said, as Helen kicked at him, 'Wow, Steve.'

'Just ruling it out,' He said.

'I think it was just all this 'she's going to get me' stuff building up, especially after yesterday and the Ouija, and then the anticipation going nowhere.'

'Yeah, it has been strange,' Matt said reaching to rub a hand on her shoulder, his eyes still on the screen.

'Elana? Are you still there? Helen called out as the camera focused on her.

Next to Meredith in Matt's room, Helen shifted, and Steve pulled at his beard.

'Eleven fifty-three,' he mumbled, 'In just about a minute Meredith will kick off at the poor little spirit girl, Elana, who doesn't stand a chance.'

Helen and Matt laughed quietly, and Steve flashed her a grin.

'Ha, ha.' She said.

On the screen Meredith was getting annoyed.

'Elana, I think this is Bullshit. I don't think you're strong enough to even try to 'get' anyone. You're just a little girl with a big attitude—'

The cat ball strobed flashing green, red, and blue over

their faces. Luckily, it had just been in shot. No foul play there.

On the Ghost box the interference changed, and that first word again followed by eerie feminine laughter. Laughter that sent ice down Meredith's spine for the second time.

She heard herself swallow, the sound rushing past her ears.

'Sounds like who, or boo, you, two, maybe cue? Something like that.' Steve said, eyes narrowed in concentration. The others agreed and Helen wrote down the time on tape, what Meredith had said, and the possible replies in fast scrawl on the paper.

On screen Gwen asked if she could do it again and Meredith visibly lost her patience. It was slightly embarrassing to watch, and Kevin had been right—it wasn't very professional.

'That's about all she can do.' She said on screen. Her own and Helen's hair visibly moving in the breeze that had encompassed them. What was new here was a flicker of white in the bottom left corner as the servant's bell rang in the distance.

What was that? An orb? Something small and out of shape, and very white. Were any of us wearing white?

Meredith was about to ask if anyone else had seen the strange object when the Ghost box took the thought right out of her head.

Meredith.

Meredith's heart seemed to shoot up into her throat, thudding wildly.

'Stop.' Matt said, 'Back up, I need to hear that again.'

Steve stopped the screen and took the sound back a minute before restarting playback. There were a few moments of thrumming static, and then it came again.

Meredith.

Meredith shuddered as Steve pressed stop. Helen's hand came up to her mouth as she turned to her.

'I think you're right,' she said.

Steve pursed his lips.

'I reckon you're right too. That was a definite Meredith to me. In full. Matt?'

Meredith swallowed hard. It was ridiculous really, there was nothing Elana had ever done or said outside of the castle, there was no reason for her to follow Meredith here, so there was nothing to fear. And yet, just the thin, tinny voice flowing from the speakers was almost enough to send her running for the hills.

The hair on the back of her neck prickled as Matt nodded.

'We're all in agreement then?' Helen said, pen poised above the A4 sheet. 'The voice said Meredith.'

Meredith's heart took up a steady gallop. This wasn't just ghost hunting, this was personal. She gave a nod and the men made muffles of admission as Helen transcribed.

'Right, so at the moment, to no particular questions, we have an unknown word, and then 'Meredith'.'

Only Meredith seemed to be affected. She felt physically sick as the times were set back in sync and the footage played again.

Why the hell did you get so annoyed? Utterly stupid, you should have kept it professional, you made it personal, and now Elana is getting personal too. You know how dangerous this stuff can be, don't mess with it!

She saw herself losing control on screen and closed her eyes but listening to the barrage she had given to Elana was just as punishing.

Steve whistled through his teeth, as Matt sucked in a breath.

'Fuck,' Steve said, 'I'd say old Pops Spalding had a point. This is harsh!'

He sat back, cracking his knuckles, before leaning forward again.

'Meredith, what were you thinking?' Matt said quietly.

Meredith opened her eyes and shook her head as Helen scribbled the words furiously next to her. Damning her speech to words as well as pictures, the evidence clear for all to see, hear, or watch.

'I have no idea. Really.' She said, glancing to the footage of her angrily responding to Donald.

'Why can't she just tell me her goddamn problem? Huh? How about that Elana? You can't just go from possessing someone and spewing vile secrets, and then making a puny cat ball and EDI meter flash. It's pathetic. Really. You want to get me? Show me what you've got.'

They were so fixated on the spectacle in front of them that they almost missed it, it was Helen who shouted out, almost dropping the pen as she jumped up.

'Wait! Stop!' She yelled. 'Stop the playback.'

Matt stopped the footage as Steve gawped at her, slower on the reflexes.

'Steve!'

Steve tapped the screen, and everything went silent.

Helen stood with one hand on her heart.

'Did anyone hear that? The voice! A couple of times, on the box, as Meredith was shouting.'

The others looked blankly at her, but Steve rewound the box sound back. They listened for changes in the frequency, and sure enough the voice came through.

'Sounds like low, blow, below, throw,' Steve said.

'No?' Matt offered.

Helen scribbled the alternatives down.

'Any advances, Meredith?' Matt said.

She shook her head. 'Nope, any of those could be right.'

Steve played on and within a couple of seconds came the next word.

'Her, whirr, myrrh, the, burr? Man, that could be anything.'

Matt nodded at Steve. 'Carry on,' he said, 'see if there is any more.'

The next few seconds played out static and Steve rubbed at his beard.

'I think we're going too far now, let's back up and get together again.'

The footage started after Meredith's speech, for which she thanked God, and was right in time for a loud bang and the tinkle of the servant's bell.

Again, Meredith saw a flash of white in the bottom left.

Must be an orb. I'll just keep a look out for now, too quick for a dust speck. Mind you, it's a large orb.

As she was pondering the orb the footage played on with no real activity from the box. She cringed through the speech where she had said that they were terrified of Elana getting them from up in the kitchen, and put her head down into her hands, not wanting to see as the action played out.

*What the hell **were** you thinking?*

Come on Elana,' she shouted on screen, 'Show us what you've got. Tell me the problem. Why are you here Elana? What do you want with Asha? What do you want with me?'

The tinny voice appeared again, and the footage was stopped. They were getting into a good rhythm now, and it was going fast.

'Roof, poof, aloof, strewth… something of that nature?' Matt said.

'Agreed,' Steve said, as Helen jotted it all down.

Meredith wondered how she wrote so fast and still had legible writing.

The rest of the footage played through and Meredith found herself transfixed. Donald's breath clouded before him on screen, just as she remembered.

Bed, led, head, or said, came through the Ghost box, and the balls went off, strobing around the room, as Meredith told Elana they could have a party. That alone was pretty cool to watch, but the cat ball flying to Meredith's face was something else. It was a shame that Matt didn't catch the ball's take off, but the suspension and spin in mid-air, combined with the drop to the floor which coincided with the bang of the cellar door, was enough.

Helen gasped. Her eyes wide.

'That has to be the footage of the night,' she said.

The Ghost box agreed with another word—possibly moan, or tome.

Steve nodded slowly with a puzzled frown at the suggestions, and Meredith noted another small white orb on the right of the screen.

They watched the ball roll around the circle and then fly across the room to hit the wall. At that point Steve had run over to the Ghost box and seen the shift in frequency that they hadn't heard. Now that frequency formed a voice.

'Speller?' Steve offered.

'Cellar!' Helen almost shouted.

Makes sense.

There were no other takers for this word.

Then the camera footage shifted, and Meredith knew that was where Matt had stopped shooting the circle and started to shoot the Ghost box discovery scene. Which had all been half assed and fake. That bit, she wasn't happy with, but Kevin had insisted it would make good viewing, so in it went.

The Ghost box recording finished with no further noise and Steve turned it off.

'Well, it didn't catch too much after all did it? seven words in the whole forty-five minutes? Pitiful.'

Matt laughed, 'Hey don't you start on Elana, too. She had enough from Meredith.'

'It's most definitely Bangers, I told you,' Steve said.

Helen laughed and Meredith rolled her eyes with a grin.

'Eight words to be exact,' Helen said. She read out the words, and then read out the entire transcript to see if there was any correlation with what Meredith had been saying.

Finding no real match, they took to making different experimental sentences with the words they had. Steve took the lead with one he laughed at so long and loud they had no choice but to join in.

Who, Meredith? Blow her, Strewth!

'Oh man, that's perfect for you Meredith. So, so perfect. I think that's the one.'

'Could be 'no, her aloof'?' Helen added.

'You, Meredith, blow the roof!' Matt said, making them all laugh again.

Meredith's phone began to buzz in her pocket. She frowned as she took it out.

Mum. At 3.50am?

Her laughter trailed off as a lead weight seemed to drop into her stomach.

'Guys I really have to take this, it's my mum.'

They barely heard her as they continued to put things together. Matt raised a hand in acknowledgment as she went into the bathroom and locked the door.

The phone shook in her hand as Meredith pulled in a breath and swiped the screen to answer.

'Hi, mum.'

She tried to sound bright and breezy, but it was lost on her mother, the line was quiet. Meredith wondered if she had caught the call in time. She looked to the screen, which said that she was connected, and placed the phone back to her ear.

'Mum?' she said with a frown.

There was more silence to answer her, and Meredith wondered whether to put the phone down as she listened to the laughter of the others in the bedroom.

'Mum? Are you there?'

Meredith heaved a sigh and sat a while longer with the silence.

'Okay, mum, I'm going. Call me back when you want to talk.'

There was an immediate rustling and a scrape on the line

and Meredith frowned.

'Mum?'

She pushed the phone into her ear straining to hear the sound. The rustle came again, and Meredith felt her heart jump. What if this was the man who had broken in and left Lilies?

Maybe he came back to kill her. Maybe he'll leave more lilies which will have died by the time I get home, just like mum.

The shakes intensified as she tried to control the frantic beat of her heart.

No, don't be ridiculous Meredith, things like that only happen on the TV.

'Mum?' She whispered.

What if it isn't mum?

Of course, it is! There is no man, Meredith. Mum is drunk again, that's all it is.

Meredith felt her shoulders drop a little. It was probably exactly that.

'Mum! If you don't answer I'm going to—'

'Shhh, Meredith. For crying out loud, just be quiet.'

'Mum, what the hell are you playing at? Do you know what time it is?'

'Late. He's here, Meredith. He's back. Just be quiet.'

Meredith's stomach flipped over, and she wiped sweat from her upper lip.

'Who's back?' she said, already knowing the answer.

'The man,' Mum whispered.

'For heaven's sake mum, did you call the police?'

There was a scuffling and crackling on the line, then silence.

'Mum?'

'Ah, false alarm. It's fine, it was the cat.'

'The cat?'

'Yes, next doors. Go to bed Meredith, get some sleep. Do you know what time it is? I can't stay up chatting all night, I'm exhausted.'

And then the line went dead, leaving Meredith reeling.

'Mum? Mum!' Meredith looked at the phone and saw the line had disconnected.

She pressed redial and sat until the answer machine kicked in over and over again. Finally, she had to admit defeat.

She ran a hand over her face, heart still thumping hard behind her ribs.

Fuck! What the heck am I supposed to believe, now?

She shoved the phone back into her pocket and thumped the heel of her hand on the basin in frustration. She couldn't call Mrs Grey at this time in a morning, so this would just have to wait a few hours. There was simply nothing else she could do.

Blowing a long breath and pushing the loose strands of hair back off her face, she waited until her heart calmed, and unlocked the door. Pushing it open, she entered the bedroom which was now eerily quiet. Matt, Helen, and Steve had their backs to her, hunched over the sideboard.

'Why so quiet?' she said with a forced smile.

All three faces were grave as they looked to her.

'We think we figured the sentence out.' Matt said.

'And?'

'It's not quite as funny as the made-up suggestions were, put it that way.'

'Fabulous, hit me with it.'

Helen turned to pick up the paper and held it in front of her chest. The statement was written across the middle in large capitals:

You, Meredith, know the truth.
    dead bones cellar.

CHAPTER TWENTY SEVEN

'It doesn't make any sense.' Helen said, pushing her hair back off her face with one hand.

Steve yawned, shaking his head. 'Sure doesn't.' He said. 'How the hell would you know the truth, Meredith? Dead bones in the cellar kinda makes sense, but how would you know what happened? Or does it mean for you to find out the truth?'

Meredith frowned at the paper in front of her, the words swam before her eyes. Her stomach swirled with the thought of what was going on at home. Was it the cat, or was there a man? And who the hell was this man, anyway? Was he in her mothers' drunk fuelled imagination as she thought he probably was?

Could she take the chance that he wasn't? And what could she do about it from here anyway?

She placed the paper on the sideboard with a sigh and rubbed a hand over her eyes.

'We don't need to find any bones or any truth,' Matt said, placing a hand on Meredith's shoulder with a squeeze, 'we're done with Lynton. We can let Stephanie know what we've found out and they can decide what to do with the information, if anything.'

Meredith nodded absently, but the note did pull her. It was her that Elana had been speaking to, did that mean she wanted her to look for bones? Did she need to know the truth? Or was Elana trying to say she knew already?

She picked the paper up again, reading through it a few more times, trying to see if there was any other explanation, any other way it could be interpreted, but she couldn't focus. Her mind drifted to her mum. At 7am she would try to ring

Mrs Grey, and hope that she got a reply, or she may just go out of her mind.

She pulled out her phone, the display said 4.15am. Nearly three hours to go.

'Come on then guys,' She heard Matt say behind her, 'It's after 4am. We have a meeting at 11am and I don't fancy being half asleep after the way Kevin has been the last few days. We can discuss this in the car on the way to Stanmore tomorrow.'

'Good idea,' Steve said through another yawn.

Meredith heard the bed creak as he rose. She wasn't sure that she wanted to spend the next three hours alone in a hotel room that had smelt like Lilies last night, when mum may be in trouble.

I wonder if the lilies smell was a sort of psychic way of warning me that mum isn't lying, or drunk.

She turned from the note, mustered a smile, and raised a hand in goodnight as Helen and Steve left together with a wave.

'Thanks for your help, guys,' she said.

'No problem,' Helen said. 'We'll see if we can solve what's going on tomorrow with fresher eyes. Don't worry about it, Meredith, I know you must feel responsible somehow, especially as Elana named you.'

Meredith shook her head with a smile that she hoped looked less fake than it felt.

'I won't. As Matt says, the most we can do is call Stephanie anyway.'

Steve nodded, said goodnight, and ushered Helen out before him, a hand at her back before closing the door. Meredith felt a stab of envy.

Would they spend the night together?

She wished she could go with them. She would even opt for sleeping on the floor at the moment.

She turned from the door and saw Matt watching her. His arms were folded across his chest, a slight frown on his face, and she realised she hadn't made a move to leave.

'I'm sorry, Matt. I'm going now. Thank you—'

'What's going on, Meredith?' he said.

Meredith's mouth dropped mid-sentence. She was completely taken aback.

'Going on?' She said.

Matt nodded.

'Listen, I'm not stupid. You were all for looking at the footage and figuring this out until you took the call. Now you just look… I don't know… distracted, worried? It was a strange time for a call.'

Meredith wondered just how badly she didn't want to be alone. If she told him, was there a chance he would let her sleep on the floor here?

He moved to the bed, sitting on the edge, patting the space next to him with a yawn. He looked tired, and she probably looked the same. Suddenly, she felt guilty for keeping him up.

'It's nothing, really,' she said. 'The call was just mum having a bit of trouble with something. I'm just annoyed that I'm here and can't do anything to help. The message is playing on my mind too. That's all.'

'Really?' He stifled another yawn as she nod her head at him. 'You're sure there's nothing you want to talk about?'

She shook her head. Warmth spread through her as she looked at him, completely shattered, and yet willing to stay up and talk things through if she needed to.

'No. It's fine, really. I do appreciate your concern though.'

Matt looked down at his hands and pursed his lips before looking up to her.

'The morning you went for a run you said it was something to do with your mum, didn't you?'

Meredith frowned. Had she said that? She couldn't remember, but if he did then maybe so.

'I worry too much, that's all.' she said with a half-smile.

Matt chewed on his lower lip, waiting for her to continue, but she found she couldn't. If she started, she'd be here until noon, and he needed to sleep, dark circles were drawing themselves under his usually bright eyes.

No, she wouldn't do this tonight. Maybe not at all. In a few weeks they would part ways and never see each other again, anyway.

She swallowed hard as a raw pang of disappointment tugged at her heart.

'Okay,' he said finally, 'You don't want to share, I get it. But I am here if you ever need to. I have more chocolate if you need it too. Just not this morning though, eh?'

She huffed a laugh of genuine gratefulness.

'Thank you, Matt. I do appreciate it. And all that you did tonight with the footage too, I know that you didn't want to.'

He shrugged, keeping his eyes on hers.

'It's not a problem, and it won't be a problem when you need to look at the other footage either.'

He smiled and she grinned back.

'Thank you, you're an angel, really.'

Matt stood with a nod and Meredith stepped in to hug him, holding him a little longer than she had intended. Intertwined feelings of both not wanting to be alone and enjoying the feel of his arms around her a little more than she wanted to let on. Eventually, she pulled away with regret.

'I'll see myself out.' She said.

'You sure you're okay being alone? You can take the bed here if you like, I'll just sleep in the chair. You do look a little shaken if I'm being honest.'

She swallowed her honest answer, hoping it didn't show.

'Thanks Matt, but I'll be okay. Really.'

Matt nodded with a yawn and Meredith left the room, looking back with a quick wave as the door shut behind her.

He will never know that that was the hardest room I have ever had to leave in my life, she thought, as she made her way to her own room just down the corridor, dread creeping up her spine.

CHAPTER TWENTY EIGHT

SEPTEMBER—96 DAYS UNTIL DEATH

The light rippled across Evie's laughing face. Red, green, yellow, blue. Pulsing in rhythm with the music which beat loudly over the field. I held onto Evie's hand tight, my eyes as wide as they would stretch and my knees knocking together in time with my thumping heart. All around me the sounds of screams, laughter and shouts joined the music filling every space in my brain until I felt dizzy.

I wanted to put my hands over my ears, but Evie would call me a baby, and she had been told to bring me, so I pretended not to be bothered.

We stood at the side of a ride called the Waltzers with Evie's friends, Sammy, Jo, and a boy that was as tall and thin as a lamp post—Rizla. I didn't think Rizla was a proper name for a boy, but Evie had said that's what it was, so I supposed it must be. Maybe his mum had a DISEASE like mine did.

As I contemplated him Evie laughed again, flowery and light, and hid her face behind her free hand. Rizla leaned in to shout in my ear.

'Want to go on the Waltzers, cupcake?'

I stared at him. He had seemed to bend right from the middle and fold down like a crane. I blinked.

'Well? What do you say?'

He grasped my arm and turned me to the ride beside us. The cars were twisting and turning but they were only going in a circle. It didn't look too bad.

Evie rolled her eyes at him. 'Don't be ridiculous, she's not big enough. She'll be scared.'

Rizla kept his eyes on me. Blue eyes, rimmed with red,

221

dark circles underneath. His face reminded me of a rat. Pinched and small.

'Ah, she'll be all right, won't you, cupcake? It's not even a scary one!'

Evie shook her head as I nod mine.

I didn't want to look like a baby in front of her friends, and she had already said that I would ruin her night being here, so I thought I would give this little ride a try. The cars did seem to spin quite fast, but it wasn't a ROLLER COASTER, it only went in a circle.

I nodded harder at Evie.

'I want to go on.' I said.

Evie scowled at Rizla.

'Well done, idiot.'

'She'll love it,' he said, putting an arm around my shoulders and steering me toward the entrance. My hand was jerked away from Evie's, and I panicked, looking back for her. She scowled at me.

'I'm coming on with you, Moo, but if you're a baby I'm taking you home. I don't care what mum and dad say.'

'Okay.' I said nodding and grinning back at her. My knees shook as we joined the end of the queue, Evie was back to laughing with her friends as we waited, but I knew she couldn't take me home.

Something was going on at home.

Something with mum.

Dad said that she hadn't been VERY WELL, so she had to SEE SOMEBODY, and that it would be better if we were both out of the way.

Evie had moaned like crazy. She was going to the fair and didn't want to take me with her. I, however, REALLY wanted to go to the fair. I had never been allowed before. They were BAD places with too many people. Dad explained last year that mum had once got so sick after being in the crowds that she had been in bed for SIX weeks.

SIX, Meredith, he had said. And I knew why he said it

—six weeks was almost a world record. No one could stay in bed for six weeks; it was far too boring. Even ill people got bored. I knew I would be okay because I couldn't SIT STILL for too long, as mum always said.

The fair crowd wouldn't make me ill.

I wondered what was wrong with her now, and would she stay in bed for six weeks again? Not if she hadn't been to the fair, I supposed.

I wondered who was going to the house to see her. Dad said she was going to see A MAN ABOUT A DOG. Of course, I wanted to be there for that, but he still said no. It was a shame because if the dog was going to be ours, I would have liked to have met it too. And what if mum turned it away without me even getting a say. Would there be a puppy when we got home? Was it a surprise? Was it a healing dog? How would it make mum better?

I turned to Evie.

'Do you think the puppy will be home when we get back?'

'What?' she yelled, and crouched down next to me, putting her ear next to my mouth.

'I said, do you think the puppy will be at home when—'

Evie jerked back and looked at me like I had swallowed the goldfish.

'Moo, it's just a metaphor. Of course, there'll be no puppy. Mum is sick, she's seeing a doctor.'

I shook my head.

'Dad said—'

'I know what dad said,' she yelled, cutting me off, 'He's joking. There is no puppy, now drop it, dopey. Don't be an idiot.'

I didn't know what was wrong with mum, but I do know what dad said, and he definitely mentioned a dog. I decided to pray to God a few times throughout the night and maybe I'd be right. Mum hadn't seemed like she needed a doctor to me, she had seemed okay. But dad had said that she had been extra grumpy, and a lot more shouty lately, because of the illness, the DISEASE.

I supposed she had been both of those things, but Evie's SMART MOUTH had gotten her more whacks than I'd had. I had only had two, that had been enough, but I had heard Evie's from my room several times this week.

I said a quick prayer to God that the dog would be there, and that it would make mum better.

'Off we go,' Rizla said, laughing as he pulled me up onto the boards, 'Come on, cupcake.'

'Little one in the middle,' a man with a huge belly, and a cigarette in his mouth, yelled to us.

Rizla stuck his thumb up and headed for an empty CAR.

I didn't think it looked much like a car, but I did catch sight of some wheels as we climbed in, so maybe.

'Follow me, cupcake,' he said.

I climbed in after him and was relieved to see Evie climb in after me. Squashed between the two of them I felt braver. This would be fun. They would look after me.

The man with the belly pushed the bar down and clicked it into place. The others moaned at the bar in their laps, but I wasn't sure what it was supposed to do for me, I could have wriggled out from underneath easily. Something told me it would be better to hold on instead.

Rizla seemed nice but I couldn't understand why he couldn't get my name right. I looked up at him.

'My name is Meredith,' I said, 'not cupcake.'

For some reason he laughed really hard at this. Sammy and Jo did too, although Evie just did her scowly face that said that she thought I was being annoying.

'Nice to meet you Cupcake Meredith,' He shouted, as a loud voice joined the already loud music.

Ladies and gentlemen, hands, and feet in the car at all times please. Hold on tight, Heeerrrreee we go.

I grinned at Rizla. I don't think he got it, but cupcake wasn't so bad. I could go with it for tonight.

The car started to move, rising a little before falling down a small hill, the car rolled to the side, spinning us round and then rocked gently in place. Up the next rise it went again and rolled down the other side spinning us again.

On the next hill the car spun all the way round before rocking.

This is good, I thought, relaxing back into the seat. Then the car went faster, up, and down, spinning down each incline. This was a little scarier. The spins were faster, the car jerky, and I was being pushed into Evie or Rizla depending on which way it spun.

I held onto the bar tightly now, frightened by the jerks, but as the others were laughing, I decided that this must be normal, so it still wasn't too bad.

And then the man with the belly strode over to us. How he kept his balance on the moving floor was beyond me. I wanted to call out, to tell him to be careful, but then he grabbed the back of our CAR and pulled.

I screamed but the breath was whipped from my mouth. Slipping down the seat, my face mashed into Rizla's arm. My hands gripped the bar above, knuckles white. The world spun, faster and faster, and the car seemed to want to spit me out.

'Evie!' I tried to shout but I couldn't speak. I tried to get her attention, but everyone was laughing. All of them.

How were they not bothered about falling out?

Belly man grabbed the car again.

'No!' I tried to yell.

'You want to go faster?' He yelled, looking right at me. I tried to shake my head, but the man pulled anyway. The car lift into the air and fell with a clunk before spinning fast. My face was now completely stuck against Rizla, and Evie was pressing painfully into me. I felt like every bone would break if this lasted much longer, but I knew if I let go, I would be tossed from the car and probably DIE.

I sided with the broken bones. Holding on for dear life as

I began to cry in fear and pain.

When would this end?

Belly man was coming for us again. I screamed a scream he either couldn't hear, or just thought I was screaming for fun like everyone else. He pulled. The car bounced and spun. I cried. My hands shook as I tried to hold on to the bar but sweat was making them slip.

Belly man was back again.

'No,' I screamed, 'I can't hold on. Please!'

He pulled anyway, not hearing, or not bothered. The voice was back over the loudspeaker.

Scream if you want to go faster!

Screams erupted around them, only Meredith screamed with fear. How much faster could they go before she flew out? Couldn't they see that she wasn't strapped in properly?

Belly man pulled. I felt my body losing control. I felt dizzy, sick, tired. My eyes started to close as Evie's body pinned me to the seat. I would die. I knew it. I couldn't care less anymore anyway. I wanted to.

And then the ride slowed. The music seemed to get louder, and the car stopped, rocking gently as it had done to start with.

The man opened the bar, but I couldn't get out. Every bone ached. My stomach cramped and lurched, and my legs were jelly. I couldn't walk.

Rizla laughed and picked me up, carrying me painfully off the ride, where everything spun, and my lunch came up onto the grass. I threw up over and over, and finally flopped on the steps crying.

My body shook. Rizla rubbed my back laughing, but Evie stood with her arms across her chest, a scowl firmly in place.

'I knew this would happen. I just knew it. Bloody hell Meredith, it only went in a circle, God knows what you'd be like on a big ride. How do you get sick on the bloody Waltzers?'

I cried harder as she used God's name in vain. I hoped

she wasn't jeopardising the new dog for us as she did it. I also knew that I would never step foot on a fair ride again. As long as I lived.

I let out a loud, heaving sob, and Evie stomped a foot.

'This is stupid! What a baby you are Meredith, I told them you shouldn't have come.'

I cried harder and Evie turned on her heel and stomped off into the crowd. Sammy and Jo followed laughing.

'Evie, don't leave me!' I called after them.

'Just shut up and stop ruining my night,' Evie called back over her shoulder. 'It's just a ride, it's not like you're *dead*!

CHAPTER TWENTY NINE

It's not like you're dead.

Meredith sat bolt upright in bed, her heart pounding. Disorientated, darkness all around her, she tried to remember where she was.

Hotel. I'm in the hotel room. It's okay. I'm okay.

The room slowly came into focus, the dark shapes of furniture appeared around her as her heart slowed to a dull thud. The room was silent and warm. The bed made warmer by the fact that she was still fully dressed right down to her shoes.

Why am I dressed?

She brought a hand to her head in realisation. The footage. The message. It had been early morning when she got back to the room, and she hadn't intended to sleep before calling Mrs Grey.

Mrs Grey!

She picked up her phone, lighting the screen, the clock said 5.10am and her stomach plummeted.

You've barely been in bed for an hour?

With a sigh Meredith snuggled back down into the soft duvet, pulling the covers up to her chin. Tired, but with worry about her mum and remnants of the dream still nibbling at her subconscious, she turned onto her side and thought about the events of the night before. Of the footage and the strange message that the Ghost Box had revealed.

What did it mean? Was it even a message? How could Meredith know the truth?

It just doesn't make any sense.

Matt had a point though. There was nothing she could do about it anyway. She would just have to call Stephanie and...

…and what?

Tell her she had to excavate the cellar for bones?

And what if she didn't find any? Not only would they have wasted money and made themselves a big mess, but it would have achieved nothing. Stephanie at least was counting on her to help them out, and she was so desperate that Meredith was sure that if she said Elana's bones had to be found she would go ahead and have the cellar dug up.

Meredith ran a hand over her eyes with a grimace.

The only other option is to do nothing.

Is that even an option?

She huffed. She was already feeling guilty that they wouldn't have contact with Stephanie and Orla again, and that they probably believed that Elana had been dealt with as Meredith had said that her spirit had been quiet during the vigil…

…Why had she said that?

Maybe I'll phone and check they're okay anyway when I get five. Then I'll think about whether to tell them or not. If I end the call without saying anything, I'll let it go.

Her thoughts drifted to the strange white orbs on the footage and the way they had danced around the edge of the screen. Twice? Three times? She couldn't remember now. It would be good to see that footage again and really have a look. They didn't seem to…

…A familiar smell floated to her nostrils, faint but just enough to raise the hairs on her arms with goosebumps.

Lilies.

Cold fingers tapped down her spine as the smell grew stronger.

There was a faint tick from the other side of the bed, and Meredith stared into the darkness.

'Who's there?' she whispered, her heart thumping, although, she knew damn well that there was nobody there. No one at all. She was alone.

'If anyone answered, Meredith, you'd run like your heels were on fire!'

She chuckled at her own joke, but her laugh sounded strained and forced. Alien in the early morning silence.

Her laughter trailed off as her unease grew.

*There **is** something here.*

She shook her head.

No.

The Lilies. The smell intensified until it smelled like an over burned Joss stick. Making her twitch and hold her nose at its overpowering acrid smell.

Lilies, but not Lilies. Not flowers. Perfume.

Meredith closed her eyes, the hair on her head seemed to stand on end.

'No, no. Not again. Please. I can't do this Evie,' She whispered. 'Leave me alone, I can't help you yet.'

The smell intensified, no longer a soft flowery smell but the acrid smell of decay. Meredith coughed and gagged, pulling the covers up around her mouth and nose. Her eyes watered. She blinked as darkness closed in around her and finally, she could take it no longer.

She leaned to the opposite side of the bed and flicked the light switch. The lamp came on immediately springing the room to life.

Meredith narrowed her eyes as she squinted around the room.

Nothing seemed out of place.

And yet the air felt out of place. Stirred. Heavy.

She shuddered as she looked toward the bathroom and the little passage that led to the hotel corridor. The end was in darkness, she could just make out the door in the gloom.

Right now, she wanted to run for that door and get out of this room, but to where?

Her heart struck up a steady pounding on her ribs, there was nowhere to go to. She was stuck in this room with whatever would happen next.

She tried to take some calming breaths, but the smell burned at her throat.

Come on Meredith, shit, you spend all night calling spirits forward, egging them on, and now you can't take the one in your room?

There's nothing in the room, she tried to tell herself as she glanced around.

Of course, there's something in the room, you know it and I know it. It's exactly like at home. It's exactly the reason you tried to do a parapsychology degree, and it's exactly the reason you fought for this job.

'To get away from home. From this, and from mum. To learn to communicate. To find out what Eve wants.' She said quietly.

And you're still just going to run when you feel anything?

'You weren't supposed to follow me up here, Evie,' she whispered, her own voice sending goosebumps scattering over her body. 'You were supposed to stay home until I was ready. This isn't funny anymore.'

The room remained charged, but silent.

But she is family, and she won't hurt me, right? She hasn't up to yet, so why would she?

Meredith felt her heart slow a little, although the intensity remained in the air and in the smell.

Meredith sat up and crossed her legs, trying to control the shakes that hit her as the room plummeted in temperature.

Okay. You can do this. Just pretend it's a shoot, Kevin is in the corner urging you on.

She nodded her head slowly.

'Okay, Evie? I'm listening. What do you want?'

Meredith swallowed hard. Why was this so hard without the crew around her?

'Evie?'

She waited, hearing the blood rush past her ears with

each pounding beat of her heart.

'If… if you're there, can you do something? A… anything. Make a noise?'

The temperature dropped further, and she shuddered, her breath clouding. The shakes hit her hard, tremors taking her over from head to toe.

This is good Meredith, calm down. You know how to get a response, just go with it. You know what to do.

Meredith took a breath and blew out a cloud before her, glad to notice that the smell was fading now, and back to Lilies. Perfume Lilies.

'Evie, please can you t…'

No! She stopped herself.

Touch me? You were actually going to say touch me? And if she did, you'd be gone like a shot! Just noises for now. Just noises.

She nod her head lightly in agreement with herself.

'Evie, can you make a noise, just let me know that—'

She broke off as a tap came from the corner. The shudders came on full force and she tried to control her muscles.

'Okay, good. Could you do it again? So—'

The tap again. Twice.

Meredith's stomach plummeted and she wanted to cry.

Evie is here? Oh, oh God, Evie is here.

Not feeling calmer, but more in control now that she was getting a response, Meredith was about to offer a tap once for yes, twice for no communication when a series of raps came from different directions all around the room.

Meredith's head felt like it was on a swivel, and her breathing came hard and ragged as she caught sight of the window for the first time since waking.

A faint light was breaking outside. Dawn was on its way, but Meredith hadn't noticed, because the curtains were closed.

Closed. Shut tight.

Meredith scrambled out of bed, getting as far from the window as she could. She leaned up the bedside cupboard panting heavily as she assessed the curtains.

Shut. The damn curtains are shut. I never shut curtains, why would the curtains be shut? Did you shut them, Meredith? Think! Did you shut the bloody curtains? DID YOU?

Feeling herself getting hysterical she closed her eyes and took some breaths. No, she wouldn't have. Never had since Evie, and never would until she was gone. But there could be any number of explanations. The maid could even have shut them when she cleaned. It's no big deal. It's no big deal. It's no big deal.

But it *was* a big deal.

As Meredith stared at the curtains a shape started to appear behind the curtain on the left. Not too small, adolescent like.

Rooted to the spot, tremors gripping her whole body, Meredith stared. The shape became more prominent, and the smell of Lilies became stronger.

'No,' she whispered. 'No, Evie, please. I can't take it again.'

There was a ripple of flowery laughter and the curtain began to move.

Meredith's heart jumped up into her throat and stuck there, cutting off her air and her scream simultaneously. Her eyes wide, she stared as the curtain came forward, slowly billowing out into the room, the figure behind it moving out of focus as it moved away from her.

Meredith closed her eyes.

Shhh, it's okay. It always does this when the curtains are closed but it's nearly over now. You know what happens, the curtain billows and then she leaves. Go with it. Keep your eyes closed if you must but go with it.

The oppressive air continued, and Meredith finally opened her eyes. Enough time had passed that the curtain had usually taken on its passive form.

Or so she thought, but tonight was worse. So much worse.

Tonight, the curtain began to pull back, just the left side from the middle, just under halfway down. Not only did it pull back, but Meredith could swear she saw a small hand appear to grasp the material.

And that was when she lost it.

With a screech she suddenly found her legs and ran to the door, not thinking of anything but getting away from the thing in her room that was supposedly her sister. Her dead sister.

The door slammed shut behind her and while she was flapping in fear it seemed her brain had half control. Within seconds she was pounding on Matt's door. A second longer and she had fallen sobbing and screeching into his arms.

In the empty bedroom down the corridor, all was still. The curtain back in place pulled neatly against the other, shutting out the daylight that was forming outside, as if it had never been touched.

On the bedside table Meredith's phone rang, cutting through the silence.

It buzzed merrily, rattling against the wood of the table. Its merry tune played and stopped three times before cutting off and falling silent.

The screen showed three missed calls and one voicemail. The name displayed bright and clear in one damning word:

Eve.

CHAPTER THIRTY

Meredith's eyes drifted closed, her mind heavy and numb. There was no room for any more information in there today, what was available was fuzzy and obscure.

Kevin's voice became a drone in the background, a buzzing fly to the blissfulness of slipping away. Nothing to do. Nothing to think about. Just sleep...

There was a sharp dig in her ribs, and she took a breath, jerking awake just as Kevin looked her way.

'Do you think you can handle that, Meredith?'

Meredith blinked, she had no idea what she was to handle, but she nod her head anyway. Was there ever a no where Kevin Spalding was concerned?

Kevin stared at her, forcing her more alert than she had been in the last forty minutes. Adrenaline surged around her body.

'Good.' He said, turning away and moving onto Gwen's role for the day.

Stanmore Lodge was just a few miles down the road, and they couldn't receive visitors today due to a wedding that had exclusivity of the site, which meant that tonight would be free.

But not free of work, of course.

There was to be a further meeting at 3pm, where they would have a chance to go over the use of some of the newer tech, including Spookbuddy, and to get an overall picture of where the show was at so far. Anything that needed a change with script, performance, or interviewing would be implemented.

These next four locations were to be made even better than the previous two.

'Everyone got it?' Kevin said, slapping his pen onto the table with a thud. Meredith's eyes got a little wider.

'Yes, Mr Spalding.' she said, along with everyone else.

The group was quiet this morning. Donald rubbing his head, Gwen doodling something on a pad. Helen looked as tired as Meredith felt. Steve too, although he had a smile that only a new relationship could bring.

Meredith stopped herself.

Did they get together last night? Or did I dream that? I don't know whether that happened.

She raised her eyebrows but couldn't find the answer.

'Good,' Kevin said to the group. He hadn't been too bad this morning. He was serious, grumpy, and strict, but all of that was normal. The fury of the last few days seemed to have blown over, and Meredith was glad. She couldn't have coped with that this morning too.

Not after the curtains.

Which will be open if I have to stand there and keep them open myself tonight.

And then she blew a breath of relief.

You won't be in that room tonight!

Well, maybe I'll hold them open in the next room anyway, just in case.'

'Right. If everyone is good with the itinerary today, let's get on the move. We'll meet out the front in half an hour ready to go. Questions?'

Everyone shook their head. Even Steve was out of jokes this morning it seemed.

'Good. Dismissed.'

Meredith raised an eyebrow and got up to leave. She had to pack yet; she hadn't even been back to the room to change her clothes before the meeting. She wasn't looking forward to going back in there alone, but Matt had his own things to pack, and she had a strategy.

In. Pack. Out.

That simple.

And that quickly if she could.

Luckily, most of her clothes were still in her case. Only toiletries and odd bits and pieces were unpacked. She would change and freshen up at the next hotel, not here.

Gwen and Donald went into their rooms, and Steve and Helen were off down the next corridor. She absently waved them all off as she neared her own room.

She was mentally going through the things she had put out, and where, when Matt spoke from behind her.

'Want me to wait while you pack?'

And that was all it took for her resolve to crumble.

'Would you?' She said, turning to him.

'Of course,' He said with a smile. He looked tired too, although he had managed a few more hours sleep than Meredith, who had only slept for little over an hour.

In Matt's bed.

With Matt.

Clinging onto him for dear life, she had insisted he didn't leave her alone, even to go to the other side of the room. Even in his arms it had taken her a while to drift off.

He must think I'm an absolute lunatic.

'Thank you.' She said, and she had never meant a thank you more in her life. She would take the lunatic title and wear it with pride over going into this room again alone.

He held out a hand for the key card. Her hand shook as she gave it to him and he swiped it against the door, entering first and switching on the lights, although the room was light enough now that daylight filtered through the curtains.

'Everything looks okay in here,' he said with a smile, as she followed him in.

Meredith scanned the room. He was right, everything was as it should have been. She swallowed hard, her gaze turning to the curtains, which looked harmless right now as Matt pulled them aside.

'Want me to help?' he said.

'No, I won't be two minutes, I haven't unpacked much,'

She said, pulling her suitcase into the middle of the bed and unzipping it.

She threw in a couple of books that she still hadn't got around to reading, and gathered the toiletries from the bathroom, putting them in a small wash bag and throwing them on top of her clothes. Last night's pyjamas were on top of the bed, unused. she grabbed them, folding them on top before flipping over the suitcase lid and zipping it shut. Then she stood, hands on hips, scanning the room for anything she may have missed.

'I think that's it,' She said.

'So, can we get rid of the elephant now?' Matt said from the edge of the bed, where he sat watching her.

Her fuzzy mind tried to piece together what he had said. She rubbed a hand over her head.

'Elephant?'

'The one in this room. As in, what the hell went on in here last night?'

Meredith glanced to the curtains. It wasn't that he would think she were mad if she told him what had gone on. He had seen it almost every night for the last week and a half. But there was still something that stopped her.

She wrung her hands over each other absently as she thought. Matt finally got up and put his arms around her, encompassing her in a tight warm hug which sent tears she hadn't known were waiting spilling over her cheeks.

She didn't just cry. She sobbed. He held her, waiting until the tears had diminished a little, before saying anything. Finally, he moved his hands to her shoulders so that he could see her face. Meredith tried to look away, but he brought her gaze back to his with a gentle hand at her chin.

'Okay, Meredith, listen. I don't mind the wake-up calls, the helping you out with your crazy ideas, the watching out for you, the telling you what Kevin wanted you to do when you're half asleep—which was to be nicer to the ghosts tomorrow, by the way—and if you really want to share a bed, go for it. I don't mind any of that, but what I really do mind, and what bugs me, is not knowing what is making you feel so bad. So wired. So uptight. Isn't it worth sharing? Sometimes it's good to talk it out.'

Meredith found herself shaking her head.

'I can't,' she said.

He narrowed his eyes.

'Can't, or won't?'

Meredith hitched a breath. 'Well, I don't know.'

She looked up at Matt, and he looked right back, waiting. She shook her head again.

'I just... I suppose I just wouldn't know where to start. It would take so long, It's so much more than a half hour story. Matt, you're an angel, really. And I do appreciate you being there for me but it's such a mess, it would go on forever and I'd be a blubbering wreck. It would drag us both down, and we only have another few weeks together anyway. You could go on your merry way and leave not being any the wiser. And that would probably be for the best.'

Matt stood silent, his hands now down at his sides. Meredith reached a hand to touch his arm.

'I know you mean well,' She said, 'but this is so much bigger than just a small gripe or issue. This is one whole messed up family and I just think...' She blew out a breath. 'It needs sorting, I know that. I just feel I'm not in control enough to sort it. If you know what I mean. That's why...' She struggled for the words to finish but Matt filled the gap for her.

'That's why you're like a dog with a bone here, that's why you're focused, and that's why you push.'

It wasn't what she had been going to say, but he was right all the same.

'Yeah, probably. It keeps my mind off the rest. I've always been like it, ever since... well, ever since my sister died. That's when it all went to pot really.'

Matt's eyes widened.

'Okay, there's a big thing. When did your sister die?'

'Oh, years ago now, I was six. She was sixteen.'

Meredith flapped a hand at him as though it were nothing, but it still hurt to say it aloud, even after all this time.

Matt watched her.

'I'm so sorry,' he said, 'Sixteen? That's young, what happened to her?' He stopped himself, shaking his head, and holding up a hand. 'No, I'm sorry, this is what you didn't want. You don't have to talk about it.'

Meredith felt her guard lower a fraction.

'It's okay,' Meredith said, feeling anything but. The familiar suppressed grief rolling its way around her stomach. 'It's not the whole issue by half. In fact, I'm not sure what happened to her, I think there was an accident. I went to school as normal, came home and she was gone. I never saw her again. We were making snowflakes. It was Christmas…' She blinked as tears filled her eyes again.

Come on Meredith, what is wrong with you? Pull yourself together.

'You weren't told how or why she died?' he said, his face crunching into disbelief.

She shook her head, brushing the tears away and looked back to Matt.

'No, and I've never asked, not really.' She let the answer linger between them before continuing. 'Anyway, you have to go pack, we've spent too long here already.'

'Come with me.' He said.

She looked up surprised. She had been going to the reception, even if she had to sit on her case for half an hour, it was better than sitting in here.

'Come with me,' he repeated, 'I know you don't want to talk about it, and we'll drop it, that's fine, but that hurt Meredith. Shit, that hurt a lot, I could hear it. Have you ever thought of speaking to someone about this?'

'I saw a bunch of psychiatrists when I was little, it didn't do any good.'

Matt blew out a breath.

'I'm really dropping it now, but just listen to me first. When you were running the other day, and yesterday, it was problems with your mum wasn't it?'

Meredith nodded but said nothing.

'Right, which means not only do you still have your sister to deal with, but your mum too. Your mum is still with us I take it?'

'Yes.' Meredith frowned. What was he getting at?

'Okay, which means there's a whole heap of bad stuff going on in there.' He placed a hand high on her chest, by her throat. His hand was warm, but the pressure felt constricted there—as it always did. She could hardly ever relax, that was why she read. Not that she did much of that at the moment either. 'A whole heap of stuff you need to get out. You have a massive barrier up all the time. You come across strong, feisty, and hard. But I just don't believe that's you. At all.'

Meredith felt her eyes well up again as the truth hit her heart, causing its familiar ache. Within seconds the barrier slammed back up, her protection from more hurt.

'Matt…' She started but couldn't finish. That was okay, he was still going anyway.

'You need to speak to a professional, get this out. Promise me you'll speak to someone when you get home.'

Meredith felt a stab of anger flare.

'I've spoken to a professional, Matt, it was useless. He was useless, and the next one, and the next. So, you can see why I don't speak about this. To anyone. I'm fine, I'm strong, I can deal with it. I *will* deal with it. I just need to figure out how.'

'Then speak to *me*, please.' Matt put a hand on her arm, but she shrugged it off.

'No.' She said, picking up her case and dragging it to the door, leaving Matt behind in the middle of the room. 'I'll be waiting in reception.'

She pulled open the door, took the key card, and left,

letting it slam behind her as she strode down the corridor with a mixture of horror, terror, grief, and rage flooding her system.

This was the problem with people. They always thought they knew best. And knew best for her situation. Well, they didn't, they knew jack-shit.

Matt knew jack-shit.

And he won't be finding out anymore.

From now on it would be strictly professional. No more late-night talks with chocolate, or late nights in his bed. If Eve did decide to visit again, she would deal with it. She could deal with it.

She heard the door open down the corridor and Matt call out.

'Meredith! Meredith, you forgot your phone!'

Meredith faltered mid stride, the remark throwing her thoughts.

Fuck. Of course, I couldn't just walk away like Rhett Butler, there had to be something.

She stopped as he caught up with her and handed it over.

'It was by the bed, obviously slipped off the table.'

'Thanks,' she mumbled, pocketing the phone.

He put his hands in his pockets, shrugging his shoulders up to his ears.

'I'm sorry, I didn't mean to cause any offense back there. I apologise.'

Meredith looked at him.

'It's okay. I just don't know what either of us would get from my stupid confession about a stupid life, that's all. It's not worth the pain, Matt, I'll get over it.'

Matt nodded.

'I won't mention it again.'

He placed a hand on her arm briefly before turning and heading back up the corridor.

Meredith stared after him. Sorry that she had jumped before the gun had gone off and left someone feeling bad because of her actions.

He was only trying to help Meredith.

But what for? What were his motives?

Does he need a motive? Maybe he just cares.

Meredith shook her head, who knew what they were. She turned and tugged the suitcase as Matt called again.

'Oh, I forgot to say. You have some missed calls. I don't know whether they were important. Somebody called Eve. I'll see you at reception in a while.'

Meredith felt the corridor tilt. Missed calls.

Eve?

Surely that couldn't be right. She didn't know anyone else called Eve. She pulled the phone from her pocket and stared at the display.

3 missed calls
    Eve

The corridor seemed to shrink around her, closing her in and closing off her air. Her heart thumped as she swiped open the phone. She frowned at the display. There was no mistake.

Three missed calls from her dead sister.

Not only three missed calls. Oh no, that would be plenty for Meredith's sanity, so of course there was more. Just enough to tip her over the edge.

Three missed calls… and one voicemail.

Meredith threw the phone onto the corridor floor as though it were on fire.

CHAPTER THIRTY ONE

OCTOBER—63 DAYS UNTIL DEATH

My legs were doing a shaky jig. They trembled and ached as I sat perched on the arm of the sofa. The prey was just beneath me, still and unknowing.

Just a few more seconds.

I tilted my bottom in the air, and waggled it slowly from side to side, ignoring the wobble in my knees, as my imaginary tail swished.

The prey, a small piece of forgotten rolled up paper, blew in the cold breeze from the open front door as mum carried the bags of shopping in from the car.

Dad put the bags he had carried down in the kitchen.

'Any more, love?' He shouted.

Mum answered with a grunt, and he came into the living room with a couple of magazines that Evie and I had chosen from the counter.

He swatted them at my bottom with a small *thwack* as he passed, and threw them on the coffee table, before he returned to the hall.

'Get your coat off, Meredith, you look like you're not staying.' He said, throwing a look over his shoulder.

I ignored him. I had to be silent, or my prey would know I was here, would know that I was about to eat it whole and spit out the bones, because that's what cats did.

'Where's my magazine?'

I heard Evie from some dark corner as I made my move. It was now or never. The prey was starting to roll again. I hunched back into my legs and pounced, flying from the arm of the chair down toward the paper, but instead of the paper I flew right into Evie's legs as she came into the living room.

'Ow! For God's sake Moo, what the hell are you trying to do? Break my legs?'

She shoved a foot under my belly, sending me scooting back into the settee with a grunt.

'I wasn't pouncing on you I was getting the paper, you just happened to get in the way.' I moaned, holding my sore belly. I twitched my nose, which smarted a little from bashing into her, the nails of my right hand tingled too.

Evie looked at the long scratches down the front of her leg.

'Ooowww, look at the state of my leg you little idiot!'

Evie brought a hand up ready to strike. Going into cat mode, I hunched back and hissed through my teeth. She swung, getting the air above my head as I ducked. Then I pounced and grabbed with my clawed hand paws, catching her arm with a yeowl.

I had injured her on the arm. Good. It would teach her not to mess with a mountain cat. I sat back on my haunches waiting for her next move.

'You little shit.' She hissed, swinging for me again. This time she hit, I yelled, and stars clouded my vision as my head snapped back.

The cat wouldn't put up with that. I brought my head forward and hissed through my teeth. I was mad now and ready for a fight. But Evie was too. She swung a hand again. This time grabbing hold of my hair and dragging me onto the floor.

I yelled, and then mum yelled.

'What the hell is going on in there?'

She stomped in from the kitchen, wiping her hands on the tea towel. We were on the floor, me under Evie as I scratched and clawed, her on top as she pulled at my hair.

'Stop that, this instant!' Mum yelled. She crossed the room in two strides and whipped the tea towel across Evie's back three times.

Evie screamed and immediately let go of me.

'Mum, it was all Meredith's fault, she jumped on me. Look!'

Evie showed mum the results of our fight. Long scratches down her left leg, and smaller ones on her wrist.

'I don't care whose bloody fault it was. I am trying to put the goddamn shopping away. I've been on my feet for hours, the crowds at the store pissed me off, and now you two are going the same way. Quit the bloody fighting before I knock you both out!'

I cowered back against the bottom of the settee, eyeing mum warily. She looked at me, and I hissed. Mum stepped forward, towel raised, and as quick as the cat had appeared, it disappeared. I was alone again, cowering at the base of the furniture.

'What the hell is wrong with you, Meredith?' she said as she swiped the towel across my cheek. The slap stung and I felt my cheek get warm. 'Why can't you just behave like a normal child? Get upstairs. I said now!'

I assessed my chances of getting past mum into the hall without either a kick from Evie or another whip of the towel from mum.

Slim, to none.

But it seemed that luck was on my side. Mum's attention had already turned to Evie, and boy was she getting it. I ran past on silent cat like feet, because the cat was back, I reached the bottom of the stairs and waited, watching through the doorway. Stealthy. Still.

'You should know better, Eve. A sixteen-year-old tackling a six-year-old to the ground? How would you like it?'

'But she jumped at me on purpose… hurt my legs.' Evie protested. But mum was already on a roll. She slapped Evie across the face. Throwing the towel down, she slapped again, and then again.

'Well? How do you like it?'

Mum rained blows down on her head, back, and neck, as Evie hunched over crying.

'All I wanted to goddamn do was put the shopping away and sit down for five minutes, but what am I doing? Sorting everyone else's fucking mess. Again!'

There was a series of dull thuds as mum punched at Evie's back, and Evie curled into a ball on the floor.

I bit my lip and slid further up the stairs so that I could watch from behind the spindles. My eyes were stuck to the fight, as though they were glued, until dad appeared from outside, and ran down the hall.

'Hey. Hey. What the hell is going on. Nancy! Nancy! Stop it!'

He grabbed mums' arms, stopping them from moving and then he looked to me.

'Upstairs, sputnik.' He said.

I didn't need telling twice. The cat disappeared now that the fear had come back, I scuttled upstairs and shut my door tight, jumping into bed and placing my hands over my ears.

—///—

'What do I have to do?' I asked Evie a few days later.

It was after school, and both mum and dad still had to get home from work. Until 5.30pm it would be just me and Evie, and that was how I liked it for the most part.

We were in the kitchen, Evie standing by a small wooden table, the centre decorated with square ceramic tiles. We always ate there, although it barely fit the four of us round it. I had climbed onto the brown kitchen counter to fetch the first aid kit, where Evie told me I would find something called DEEP HEAT. I didn't know what deep heat was, but it sounded naughty. Like the video's stacked on top of the kitchen cupboards. I had only ever played one. It had been called Cinderella's Secret Garden, but a few seconds in I realised that someone had taped something VERY RUDE over the fairy-tale, and I quickly put it back. I had never looked up there since, but now DEEP HEAT was giving me funny feelings that I didn't like.

'Just find it first, put some on, and I'll find a lip gloss for you. It's simple. Come on, Moo. It's hurts.' Evie said.

Lip gloss. Of my very own. Provided she didn't come into my room and take it back.

I decided I would hide it in my secret spot behind the desk. She hadn't found that one yet. With a grin, I rummaged through the tub and came up with a long red box. I looked at the letters D.E.E.P.

'D-eeeee-p.' I whispered, breaking the word down as we had been taught at school.

H.E.A.T.

'H-ee. Then A-t.'

I frowned. I wasn't sure of the second word, but the first was right.

'Evie, is this one right?' I held the box up to her and she turned, her whole body turning, like her neck needed some WD40. She moved very slowly. Almost like a sloth. Almost, but I had been learning about sloths in school and sloths didn't have a temper like Evie's. They were pretty chilled out.

Evie didn't look as good either. She held her right shoulder almost up to her ear. If she held it normal it hurt her. Mum said she was being DRAMATIC, but Evie still held it there anyway. She also had a yellow bruise just above her left eye, which had been swollen, but was now going down.

Evie said she had fallen and hit the table on Sunday, but Sunday had been the day of the cat, and I knew that she was lying. She always lied after mum had hit her, I didn't know why. Mum was a grown-up. She couldn't get into trouble anyway… who was going to tell her off?

Even as little as I was, I knew the table could not have made bruises all over her body like that. Even if she had thrown herself at it repeatedly. Which would have been

STUPID.

'Yes.' She said. She didn't nod her head, it was more of a jerking up and down from the waist, her head and hands still, but bobbing with the motion. She looked like a funny kind of duck. A slow duck.

She turned away from me to hold the table with her left hand, which was good because giggles were coming up from my belly at her duck move, and I knew she would shout. I jumped down from the side and placed a hand over my mouth to stop the giggles coming out. When I had managed to push them back down, I placed the box on the table in front of Evie.

'So, what do I do?' I asked her, taking the tube of cream from the long box, and taking the cap off.

The smell made my nose wrinkle.

'Just put some on your finger and rub it, see?'

Evie squeezed some of the cream onto her finger and rubbed it into my arm. A small burn started at my wrist.

'Ow,' I said, rubbing at it, 'It burns.'

'You're such a baby, Moo. Not for long, it makes muscles better, just rub it here.'

She pointed a finger to her back, although her hand didn't reach there. Her shoulder was too close to her ear to get round to her back, it looked like it was super glued too high on to her side.

'Just rub it all over, you probably won't see anything because it's inside. Just watch my bruise.'

'Okay.'

I lifted her top slowly, trying not to recoil from the bruises that littered her lower back. The one where she had asked for the cream, crawled just above her BACKSIDE like a monster, in a horrible black, purple, yellow, and green.

I hesitated. It looked like it needed more than cream.

'Come on Moo!'

'Here?' I said pressing lightly into the centre of the bruise with a shudder.

Evie recoiled immediately pulling in a breath through her teeth.

'Yes, there. Just avoid that bruise, it kills for my top to even press on it. It's on the edge by my hip, can you see?'

'Er…'

'It's not that hard Moo, for Christ's sake, just rub in the cream, will you?'

I said a small prayer apologising to God for Evie's blasphemy, and put some of the cream onto my finger. I started to rub lightly onto Evie's back. Evie tensed like a rod and I saw her knuckles turn white as she grabbed the tabletop.

'No! Ooh, Meredith, what the hell are you doing? That burns.'

I pulled my finger away.

'I'm only pressing where you said.'

'It hurts Meredith, is that the right cream?'

I quickly held it up in front of her contorted face.

'Ow, something's wrong, that's not good. My back hurts. It hurts.'

'What shall I do, Evie?' My heart was pattering behind my ribs. Evie was really hurt. Something in my head told me it wasn't muscle, and it shouldn't hurt this bad. 'Shall I put more cream on?'

'No! Holy Christ, no.'

'Wash it off. I can wash it off. I'll get a cloth!'

I ran to the sink as Evie moaned.

'No, don't touch it Moo. I mean it. What the hell is up with that?'

Evie tried to reach her hand back but winced with pain.

'Moo, I need to see. Can you get a mirror?'

'There's the long one in the hall.' I said.

'Yes, but I can't turn, get the one from my dressing table, the small one. You can hold it in front of me to reflect the mirror behind.'

I didn't know what the heck she was talking about, but I

scrambled upstairs as fast as I could, banging through her door and grabbing the brown handheld mirror from the table. Running back downstairs I saw Evie in the hallway, her back to the mirror.

'Good,' she said. 'Give me the mirror and you can lift my top for me.'

Taking the mirror in her left hand, she reflected it back toward the big mirror. She shifted and winced.

'Okay,' She said.

Slowly, with moans and gasps I got her top high enough to reveal the bruise that spread across her back. She gasped and her mouth dropped open.

'Holy shit.' She murmured.

I panicked.

'It's bad, Evie, isn't it? It's really bad! It's bad! We need a doctor!'

Evie huffed a small laugh, but her face was pale and drawn.

'Nah, it's just a bruise, Moo, stop being so dramatic.'

She didn't look sure though, her eyes looked big and frightened.

I'd had bruises, but this was much more than a bruise I thought. Maybe she had broken bones inside. My lip started to quiver.

What if Evie *died*.

A tear slipped down my cheek as she moved away from the mirror slowly. She huffed a laugh as she saw my face.

'It's just a bruise Moo, I'll live. It's okay, idiot.'

I nod my head feeling better as she hobbled into the living room.

It was just a bruise. If Evie said she would be fine, then she would be fine.

CHAPTER THIRTY TWO

The journey to Stanmore was quiet and uneventful, Meredith slept most of the way, slipping into dreamland almost immediately, and being woken gently by Matt when they arrived at the hotel just twenty minutes later.

They had half an hour to make themselves at home. The brief would be brought forward, taking place just before lunch, and then time was their own until tomorrow morning when they would get an early start, having lost this afternoon already.

Meredith dragged her suitcase out of the boot of the car and made her way up to her room. As hotel rooms go this one was nice. Bigger than the smaller and more modern Hotel's they had stayed in, this was a large room, with a four-poster double bed, two comfortable chairs, a coffee table, sideboard with complimentary tea and coffee, and a large television, which the other rooms hadn't had. The whole room was decorated in burgundy tartan which, far from being overpowering, gave Meredith a homely feeling. This was more than a hotel. This was a place that was loved. A home first and foremost, a bed and breakfast as an offshoot.

She pulled the suitcase into the middle of the large room and flopped onto the bed, trying the mattress.

Cosy. I hope Evie hasn't followed me here, I could really do with a night off to sleep.

She closed her eyes, feeling herself drifting as the warmth of the bed closed itself around her.

Not now, the meeting is in less than half an hour. I'll make sure to get an early one tonight.

She swung her legs off the bed. Watch TV, or call mum?

She knew what she needed to do, what she should do after the call again last night—well, this morning—but the thought of speaking to mum just made her angry.

Before they had set off Meredith had spoken to Mrs Grey, who had called back within five minutes to say that Nancy was fine and well, in her dressing gown watching this morning on television. No, she hadn't been drinking, and yes, she was calm and cooperative, even offering Mrs Grey a brew.

So, what the heck was all the fuss at 4am? A blessed cat, after all?

Anger had punctuated her tiredness and she had thrown her phone, now complete with crack down one side, into her case and zipped it away.

Now the case sat in the middle of the floor. Passive, but holding a huge annoying beacon that had to be dealt with at some point.

Meredith grunted in frustration. May as well do it now.

She fetched the phone out of the suitcase, wishing she could erase the words that blared from her screen each time she lit it up, just as she had erased the missed calls. She couldn't bring herself to listen to the message, it gave her chills just looking at it.

She hesitated, finger over the contacts button, and then dialled the number before she could think further. Mum answered on the second ring.

'Meredith! Hi sweetie, how are you? It's so good to hear from you, you don't call enough these days you know. I miss you down here all alone, how long has it been since I spoke to you?'

Meredith closed her eyes.

Could be worse, at least she sounds lucid.

'Yesterday, mum.'

Mum let out a series of titters on the other end of the line.

'Yesterday! Really Meredith, I think I would remember

speaking to you just yesterday. How hard are you working up there? It sounds like you could do with a rest, sweetie.'

You don't know the half of it.

'It was definitely yesterday.' She said aloud, 'In fact no, not even yesterday, it was 4am this morning.'

Meredith couldn't muster enthusiasm to chivvy her mother on, her voice was deadpan and unamused, she just couldn't help it. She knew it was wrong, and she should appreciate her mum being in a good state and not murdered by some man who was leaving her lilies for the second time in two days. She knew it was wrong, but she had no strength to try to change it.

'4am? Meredith, listen to yourself, why the hell would I call you at 4am? How ridiculous. I was tucked up in bed, fast asleep, I assure you.'

'No, mum. You called. Granted it was a quick call, but you did. You said the man was there again, and then you cut me off and wouldn't answer my calls. I have been going out of my mind.'

Meredith felt the anger crawling up from her gut. Slowly but steadily. It would overflow if the call went on too long. If anger had scales and slithered, this one was a beast, it would slide out with no noise and no warning.

Keep a check on yourself, Meredith. She's okay, and that's the main thing. At least you can carry on today without the worry.

'What?' mum said. She sounded aghast, and if Meredith had been there, she knew the look that would be pasted on her mother's face right now. Wide eyes, frown indented in her brow, mouth pulled back.

'Uh-huh. Exactly that.' Meredith replied.

'A man? What man?'

'The man who leaves you lilies on the dressing table I suppose. You didn't elaborate which one, is there more than one?'

There was a sigh from the other end of the line.

'Meredith, I haven't had a man since your father died, who the hell do you think is coming round? And who would leave me flowers? Have you seen me lately? I'm hardly Miss Knockers of Knockville now, am I?'

Miss knockers of Knockville?

Meredith felt her mouth twitch as her mother continued.

'I'm not a catch anymore. I don't have legs right up to my arse, and my tits are hanging round by my knees. Old age, Meredith. I'm old. No one wants me.'

Be that as it may, you still have legs up to your arse mother, we all do.

Now Meredith was grinning, and although the mood was a pleasant relief after the morning she'd had, she needed to get to the bottom of this man and why her mother insisted on scaring herself and Meredith to death every few days.

Especially if it wasn't her ass he was after.

'So why the calls about the man? Yesterday you said—'

'Oh, for fuck's sake Meredith, there's no man! And do you know what?'

Mum waited, and Meredith supposed she was waiting for a reply.

'Huh?'

'Well… I said do you know what?'

'No?' Meredith said. She frowned, squinting her eyes.

What am I supposed to know, now?

'No! No, that's right. You never know!'

Meredith shut her eyes and ran a hand over her hair pulling it back from her face. She flopped onto her back, staring at the material ceiling of the four-poster bed. Mum was starting to wind up, and whatever she was about to fly off the handle about, Meredith knew from experience that she wouldn't get a word in edgeways.

'I don't—' She started, but mum cut her off and Meredith shut her mouth with a snap.

Here goes.

'You always think the worst of me, don't you? Always.

Do you know what you are Meredith? Do you?'

Meredith raised her eyebrows.

'Spiteful,' mum spat from the other end of the phone.

Meredith nod her head and made a noiseless 'ah' with her mouth.

'You are downright spiteful! So what if I've had a man here anyway? So what? Do you know how long it's been? I've been on my own since your dad left and decided to top himself.'

Meredith winced.

'There has been no one. Do you hear me? So what if I have had a man round? Would you deny me a little pleasure at my time of life after all I've been through?'

Now Meredith frowned as her eyes followed the line of the tartan in the folds of the material.

'Would you deny me that?'

The line went silent.

Am I supposed to answer?

She cleared her throat and propped up onto one elbow.

'Er, no? Mum, are you saying that you've been having a man round there? That the man who left you lilies is someone you're seeing?'

'I asked if you would deny me that? I did not ask for accusations!'

'And I said no, I wouldn't deny you that, no mum.'

Meredith pushed herself up to sit on the edge of the bed. If this man was someone mum was seeing Meredith would hit the roof after being told he was an intruder two nights on the trot.

'Oh, I know you would. You've never wanted to see me happy. You want the house, don't you? That's all you're after, isn't it!'

Meredith's mouth dropped open.

The house? What does that have to do with anything?

'Mum, I—'

'Oh, don't you dare deny it. That's the only reason

you've never left home. Scabbing off me, your poor old mum, who's fed and clothed you and put a roof over your head all of your ungrateful little life. After all I've been through!'

Meredith felt the anger start to bubble over. Scabbing off a drunk who couldn't look after herself, while I paid the mortgage and fed and clothed her?

Keep your cool Meredith, just keep your head. End the call and try again later.

'You're an ungrateful little SHIT, Meredith. You always were. I have got a man! And I've left him everything in my will. You get nothing, do you hear me? Don't even bother coming home!'

'So, you do have a man. You're admitting it?'

'He's getting everything. Every last penny. You get NOTHING!'

Meredith closed her eyes.

All the worry has been for nothing?

'So, there is a man, mum? Tell me, because I really don't want to be bothered with intruder crap again. If there is a man, there's a man. But do not tell me you are about to be murdered by him as he leaves you flowers.'

'I said nothing of the sort. If I want to see someone and shag him naked on Mrs Grey's ceramic plant pot in the front yard, I FUCKING will!'

Meredith closed her eyes again with a grimace.

Nice.

'Okay,' Meredith said, trying to keep calm, 'so there's a man. And next time you call and tell me you have an intruder I can relax because you're busy shagging on Mrs Greys pot, not being murdered. Thank you, that's all I needed to know. Mum, I'm busy, I have to—'

'Of course there's no FUCKING MAN, Meredith! Do not patronise me. Shagging on the pot, how utterly ridiculous. Why would a man want me? Have you seen the state of me? It's been so long it's a wonder I've not grown a hymen back over down *there*. There is no need for your smart mouth.'

Meredith flopped back onto the bed with a huff, the relief trickling away.

No, it was never going to be that easy. It never is. And now here we are, back at square one.

'Mum, I need to go,' she said, the tiredness flooding back into her every pore.

'Oh, don't you dare, Meredith. Don't you bloody dare. How could you be so rude to me after not speaking for so long. I don't even know where you are, or what you're doing. I've been worried sick, and this is the response I get when I call you?'

'I called you, mum.'

'Oh, if you say so, Miss I'm so FUCKING prim and proper. You called me, did you? Well take your time calling back won't you, you ungrateful little SHIT.'

With that the phone line went dead.

Meredith stared at the phone before lowering it down to her lap. Tears stung behind her eyes, but she wasn't about to let them fall over her mum again.

Why does everything have to be so hard? Why?

Meredith thought of Mrs Grey's talk just the other day, and her advice that Meredith wasn't responsible for her mum's behaviour, and that she could leave at any time.

Well, that's never felt like such an appealing option.

A lone tear spilled down her cheek, and she knew it would never be possible. She wouldn't be able to do it, because for all Nancy Knight was a complete mess, she had much reason to be, as did Meredith. And besides that, she was her mum, and her only family.

I'll just have to deal with it then. I've got through bad patches before, and I can do it again. We can do it again.

With a little more resolve, and with the firm notion that her mother was fine, at least for now, Meredith looked at the time on her phone, and realised that she was nearly fifteen minutes late for the meeting.

'Oh, shit!' She yelled with dismay.

Aware of being amid Kevin's wrath again, she jumped off the bed and ran for the door.

Why, oh why, could she not seem to keep herself out of trouble. Everything she did just turned into a big mess.

Every bloody time.

CHAPTER THIRTY THREE

Pumping her arms hard, feet slapping on the tarmac, Meredith pushed harder. Her heart pound, her chest hurt, and a stitch was starting up in her side.

Still, she pushed.

The children on the small village park were taking no notice of the woman who had sprinted several laps of the playground like she was being chased by a hungry sabre-toothed tiger. The parents, however, were probably a little more wary of the woman who was circling their children like a shark.

Well, I don't care what they think, they don't have a dead sister, a dead father, a mother who I'm sure should be classed as clinically insane, never mind a recovering alcoholic, a boss who's head barely fits in a room, and a colleague who was supposed to be nice, but turned out to be just like everyone else. Oh, and a voicemail from their dead sister to boot!

Why, oh why could I not just have a normal friend to talk to, without the judgement and the accusation that I may need psychotherapy.

Her feet pound, her lungs burned, and sweat dripped from her forehead and dribbled down her cheeks as she pushed harder, angrier, trying to push out all the energy that threatened to eat her up.

Why does that normal friend who turns out to be a twat have to be one of the nicest people I have met for a long time, and one I get on with so much better than most? Why does he have to be so damn hot? Why does this happen to me? Every. Damn. Time.

Pound... pound... pound... pump... pump... pump...

There goes all the fun Meredith. There goes the light-hearted 'leaving the mother and shitty life at home' stuff. I may as well pack up and go home now.

Except that she had to get to the bottom of the whole Evie mess. This was exactly why she had pushed for the job in the first place.

Honour thy sister, Meredith.

Yeah, I'm starting to think to hell with that too.

She grit her teeth and pumped harder. The pain in her side now running across her middle and up to her chest.

Careful you don't have a heart attack, eh, honey?

Maybe that would be for the best. If she dropped dead mum would have to sort herself out, and she wouldn't be coming back to haunt her, she would leave that to Evie and enjoy the peace.

Hey, if you had a heart attack and died at least you could communicate with Evie properly, without the crap of flashing balls, Ghost boxes, and voicemails.

A grin spread across Meredith's open mouth. That was better, she could feel her emotions calming as her body exerted itself to a capacity Meredith was sure that she had never pushed it to before.

She pushed more, the pain coursing through her legs and arms now too.

On the playground, a few of the children and most of the adults had stopped to watch her run. One of them had a phone up following her round like they'd never seen anyone running before.

She scowled at it before looking forward and pushing on.

She would have told them all to mind their own business, or something stronger—especially to the ignoramus with the phone—she was only running after all. But she didn't have the breath. Mouth now pulled back in a solid grimace as she ran, her legs feeling like they didn't belong to her body, Meredith heard a voice.

'Meredith! Hey, Meredith, wait!'

She swung a glance left, over a patch of green toward the small park gate, and saw Matt walking across the grass, a hand up to her.

Great. Fucking great.

She turned back to the path and pushed more, completing two more circuits before her body threatened to give out entirely. She slowed to a walk, gasping breath, and holding her side which felt like someone had cut her in two.

Coming round the bottom of the park, where the children and adults were now back to usual park business, the phone put away after obviously deciding that she wasn't the bionic woman, after all, she saw Matt again.

He sat on a bench at the side of the path, waiting for her to come full circle as he puffed on a cigarette.

He'll no more give those up again than my mother will stop lying about the alcohol, she thought. And then she wondered why it even mattered.

'Meredith,' he said as she came within earshot.

She considered ignoring him, but when she thought about it, what had he done wrong anyway? He'd asked her to see a psychiatrist. So had many other people. And probably many more to come.

Still heaving in air that her lungs had thought they'd never get again, she looked at him. She said nothing, but then, she couldn't have even if she'd wanted to. She could barely breathe, let alone talk.

'Meredith,' He said again, standing and stubbing out the cigarette with his shoe.

She nod her head at him but kept walking. The momentum was good, and it was evening out her breath and heart. If she stopped, she had a feeling she may just drop down dead.

He met her as she passed him, and strode next to her, keeping pace.

'Meredith?' He said again, and Meredith rolled her eyes.

'Just talk,' she said between gasps of breath. 'I... I

can't.'

He nod at her as they walked, slowing a little now, but still at a healthy pace.

'Okay.' He said. And then he fell silent.

Meredith listened to the birds, the children, the cars from the road, as Matt gathered his thoughts, or whatever it was he was doing.

'Meredith,' He said again finally.

She thought if he didn't follow up this time, she might just bop him on the nose.

'Can I apologise? I want to apologise. I was out of order, I have no idea what is or has gone on in your life, I can only imagine that it was pretty bad, and probably more than you're letting on with your sister and your mum too. I shouldn't have presumed, and I shouldn't have taken liberties to assume what you needed. So, I really shouldn't have said anything at all. I said I wouldn't meddle, and I wouldn't push, and then I go and tell you what you need anyway. It was stupid, and wrong.'

Meredith felt her anger drain away as he rambled on next to her.

When was the last time anyone had apologised to her? Never mind apologising for sticking their nose in, but at all?

I can't remember one.

She blinked as Matt carried on.

'…the thing is, Meredith, I like you. A lot. And we have to work together. I like the laughs. I like the foursome we have with Steve and Helen. I never wanted to upset you; I just care that's all. I can't imagine what you've been through, and I promise I won't bring it up again. I'm so sorry Meredith, I don't like this atmosphere between us, I want to go back to being friends. Please?'

Meredith took a sideways look at Matt.

He kept pace with her easily, striding along, his hazel eyes focused, not on her, but ahead. His jacket was zipped up around his chin, hands stuffed in his pockets as he walked.

I think I like you a lot too.

She felt a flutter of affection, and purely on instinct, linked a hand around his jacket, holding his arm at the elbow.

He turned to her with surprise that she almost laughed at, but she stuck to a smile which he returned as he took his warm free hand out of his pocket to squeeze her cold one.

'I totally didn't expect that,' he said.

Meredith shook her head.

'You're lucky I had a run, or you wouldn't have got it.'

'That magical huh?' He said with a grin Meredith found herself mirroring.

She nod her head.

'I told you, you should try it, instead of doing yourself damage with those cigarettes. They'll kill you, you know.'

Matt started to laugh.

'Oh, Meredith, if you could have seen yourself running around there. I would have put money on you keeling over from your healthy jog way before I did from the fags.'

Meredith cocked an eyebrow at him.

'I may have pushed a little harder than usual.'

'I hope so, because for a minute there I was trying to recall the CPR protocol, just in case.'

She grinned and he looked at her.

'Do you really need to go so hard?' he said.

'Nah, not usually. Today… well today has just been one of those days I suppose.'

'I'm sorry. Really, I am.'

Meredith looked back to him with a smile.

'Don't worry, you don't have to take all the flack for it. You were probably the least frustrating argument of my day.'

'Kevin went pretty hard, didn't he? You didn't deserve that.'

'I did. I shouldn't have been late. I know I've pushed my luck with him already.'

'Yeah, well, even so. He shouldn't have balled you out in front of everyone else.'

Meredith shuddered, now she was no longer running the sweat on her body was turning her damp clothes cool.

'It doesn't matter. I hardly heard him, to be fair he wasn't the worst of the day either.'

Matt looked at her, pursed his lips, and then looked away.

'Your mum?' he said hesitantly.

'The one and only. And yeah, she pretty much beat seven bells out of you, Kevin, *and* me. All at the same time.'

Matt nodded but asked no more.

Meredith thought when they had time that she may tell him after all. Not here in the park though. The man with the phone may have them on mic.

Matt sighed, and Meredith tucked her arm in so that she was closer to him, linked elbow to elbow, her cold body lending some of his warmth. He squeezed his arm, pulling her in close.

'It's okay,' she said.

'It's not.'

Meredith nodded. 'It's done now.' She said.

They walked almost a lap of the park before Matt broke the silence.

'Want to look at the footage again later?' He said.

'What?' she asked losing the thread of the conversation.

'You said something about strings and whatnot, and we have free time if you want to look.'

'Of course I do! But I don't want to push you, I understand if last night was a one off. I know you're wary of Kevin, that's understandable.'

Matt shook his head.

'Kevin lost a bit of respect this morning the way he handled you. To be honest, it's been going down since the start of the shoot with the way he treats all of us. But more-so you for some reason. He's not doing himself any favours. If you want to see the footage, we have all the time in the world now if you want to.'

'It's early, Matt. What if we're caught?'

He shrugged. 'It doesn't matter.'

Meredith stopped, pulling Matt to a stop with her. He turned to face her.

'Why the change of heart? I told you it doesn't matter. I wouldn't mind seeing some of the other footage for sure, but not if you're in any way uneasy.'

Matt shook his head.

'I'm good. We can go now if you like. I'm not doing much else. You?'

'Nah, just killing myself with a run. It can wait.'

He tucked a stray lock of hair gently back behind her ear with a smile.

'Good. Then let's get back.'

Meredith nodded with a grin, and then she threw her arms around him.

'Thank you, Matt. Not only for the footage, that doesn't matter, but for being a good friend, and the apology, and the laughs, and for making life easier on shoot with Kevin. You are a superstar!'

She planted a kiss on his smooth cheek, and he laughed, circling his arms around her in a tight hug.

'I'll take that over being in the doghouse.' He said, giving her a squeeze, before letting go.

She linked an arm in his as they made their way back to the hotel and the fun that would be the footage of ghost communication.

CHAPTER THIRTY FOUR

Meredith squinted at the screen, her nose almost on the glass with frustration.

'Zoom in,' she said.

The picture pixelated on the hotel television screen.

'That's as far as it goes.' Matt said with a frown of frustration, 'it would do no good to go any further anyway, we'd just end up with larger pixels on screen. I think we were better on the smaller camera screen.'

'But we couldn't make it out on there either.' Meredith sighed and sat back on the chair, hands behind her head. 'It's so bloody frustrating.'

'Hmm,' Matt said, rubbing a hand across his chin.

'What the hell is that black strip?'

'Well, aren't orbs of all shapes and sizes anyway? I mean, what would you see if you zoomed in on any orb?'

'Not a black strip, probably. They're mainly light I think, why would a black strip run through them, at that angle? Every time, on each frame?'

Matt raised his eyebrows with a shake of his head.

'I can reduce the frame speed instead of pausing. It may give us a different perspective of the movement if we slow it right down. We may get more of an idea of its... what... behaviour?'

Meredith grinned. 'You'll make a paranormal expert yet. Yeah, that's a good idea, lets run it through again.'

'Big screen? Little screen?' Matt said, looking to her.

'Cardboard box?' she answered, recalling the old rhyme from childhood. Matt rolled his eyes and she chuckled.

'I think that was fish, not screens, or orbs.'

'Yep. Let's keep it on the TV first as it's all hooked up.

If we don't get a notion of it on here, we'll try the small screen.'

'Right. Then what? Then it's just an orb?'

Meredith chewed her lip.

'Maybe. It just doesn't look like any orb I've seen before. It's not totally spherical, which is not unheard of, especially depending on light, but I've never known an orb to comprise of two such distinct colours. I mean, it's almost black and white. It just isn't sitting right with me.'

Matt gave a sigh as he messed with the frame rate for playback. Meredith wondered if he'd rather be doing something else with his free time, in a pretty village, with sunny, if not cold, weather.

'I'm sorry.' She said, as she watched him tap the camera screen. He glanced up at her, surprise lifting his features.

'Sorry?' he said.

'I know I'm a pest. Mum always said I was like a dog with a bone when I came to a decision.'

Matt laughed. 'I could have told you that after the last week. What are you sorry for?'

'Making you do this for me on a nice day, when we actually have free time.'

Matt was looking back at the screen.

'Nothing I'd rather be doing.' He mumbled, tongue flicking between his lips in concentration.

Meredith highly doubted that. She watched him in silence as he paused playback just before the first orb came into view.

'Got it.' He said, 'ready?'

'Shoot.' She said, and he tapped the screen.

The TV came to life and Meredith appeared on screen. *Will I ever get used to that?*

Meredith moved her mouth, but no sound came out, Matt had muted the sound when they had first put it on the TV, and now the sound would just be distorted anyway.

Truth be told she didn't want to hear her making an ass

of herself any more than she had to.

The picture jerked through slowly, almost frame by frame, and the flash of white appeared in the bottom corner. It came into shot from the left in four frames, left by the same angle in four frames, and then moved out of shot as the footage slowly ran on.

'So precise.' Meredith said with a frown.

Matt left the camera on the side and came to squat by her chair in front of the TV. He rest an elbow on his knee, placing a fisted hand to his mouth.

The next orb came into shot. Same black and white colour, same shape and same four frames in and four frames out. There was something very wrong with this orb. Meredith leaned forward in the chair with a frown, unease picking its way around her chest.

'What is it?' Matt said.

Meredith shook her head.

'I don't know,' she said. 'Something isn't right. It isn't behaving very orb like. Maybe I just got it wrong, what else could it be?'

Matt shrugged and shook his head.

'Shall I take it back again?'

'No,' Meredith said, her hand shooting out to catch his arm as the orb appeared on screen again. The same motion, right to left but this time more frames in and more out. This time Meredith's breath caught. The shape was familiar.

She gasped.

'Is it me, or did that orb look distinctly like a—'

'Shoe.' Matt finished with her. 'Yeah. It did.'

Meredith blinked.

'Okay, well there goes the orb theory. I suppose there was a simple explanation after all. A goddamn shoe.'

Meredith looked at Matt, and then they were both laughing.

'Oh man, I'm sorry Matt. What a waste of time. I mean, who the hell has white shoes anyway, especially on a ghost hunt?'

'Kevin.' Matt replied, with a nod of his head, 'Kevin was in white shoes. I remember thinking it was a strange colour for him to go for. So yeah. Kevin goes ghost hunting in white shoes.'

They laughed harder. The release was refreshing for Meredith. How long had it been since she had completely let go and laughed this hard?

She couldn't remember, and that had her laughing harder.

'Fancy a drink to celebrate the solved mystery?' Matt said as his laughter subsided, and he rose to fill the kettle.

'Yeah, why not. Tea would be good.'

Meredith rubbed her tired eyes. It would be nice to get a full night's sleep tonight—if Evie let her anyway.

She watched as Matt made tea for both of them.

Maybe there was no foul play after all, maybe we were just lucky with the locations and the level of activity. Which is good news for project communicate with Eve, right?

Maybe she just needed to bury this bone and move on. Finish the filming, get used to spirit conversation, get on with finding out what Evie wanted, and setting her to rest, which was the real reason she was here after all.

'…were you thinking about doing with the message?' Matt was saying, and Meredith looked at him.

'Huh?' she said.

'The message, from Elana, apparently, have you given that any more thought?'

'Not really, I think I'll just phone Stephanie, tell her the message and leave it at that. It's not like Elana is going to be featuring from now on, is it?'

'Let's hope not,' Matt said.

'I'll give her a ring when we're done here.'

'We are done,' Matt said with a laugh, 'are you sure you want to stir it up with them again?'

'I can't imagine Elana has gone anyway. They'll still

have trouble as long as Asha is prone to encouraging it.'

Matt nodded his head toward the bed, and for a moment Meredith wondered what he was getting at. She was about to contest when he turned back to her.

'My phone is on the bed if you don't have the number. It was put into mine before we came up here.'

Meredith raised her eyebrows as she moved to the bed to get it.

'Before we came to Scotland?'

Matt nodded as he stirred the tea. 'Kevin wanted to make sure I had all the numbers, just in case anything happened to his phone.'

Meredith passed the phone to Matt to unlock.

'What, like the presenter cracking him over the head with it in a fit of rage?'

Matt grimaced as he passed her the phone back.

'I wouldn't like to say that was out of the question.' he said.

'It's not.' She replied, pressing the dial icon on the screen.

He put the tea on the side next to the TV and watched her as she waited.

'Let's hope they answer.' he said.

Meredith crossed her fingers and held them up to him as Stephanie answered the phone on the third ring.

'Hey Stephanie, It's Meredith, from the—' was all she managed to say before Stephanie cut her off.

'Oh, thank God.' She said, 'Thank God you called, Meredith we're in such trouble here. This nightmare just gets worse and worse. Is there any way you can come back?

CHAPTER THIRTY FIVE

NOVEMBER—38 DAYS UNTIL DEATH

'Power's out.' Evie said slipping out of her room. 'Stay here Moo.'

We were home alone. Mum and dad had a DO to go to tonight at the local Working Men's Club, which was great. Evie was in charge which meant I could stay up with her as long as I wanted. And I wanted.

I had been having nightmares about Evie's bruises and the bad man for weeks now. I was tired and scared. I wished the bad man had never come here, but here he stayed, and now apparently Evie had BIG PLANS for Egor.

The bad man's lair.

While mum and dad were out, we had to do SURGERY she said. When I asked what that meant, she said she was going to cut Egor open. She had a plan to figure out how to tell what the bad man was up to, how to listen to him.

My belly screwed up tight at the thought of opening the bad man's lair, and although I knew that Evie would be mad, tears came to my eyes anyway, running down my cheeks before I had chance to block them.

'I'm scared Evie. Don't open Egor.' I said, my voice wobbly.

'Oh, Moo, don't be such a baby.' She huffed. 'This is ADULT work. If you can't hack it, get out and go to bed. I'm not scared.'

I was going to tell her that she looked scared. The black circles were still under her eyes, and the bruise on her back, although fading, still made her wince when she moved too fast, or jerked at an odd angle.

She winced now as she hobbled to the wardrobe and pulled Egor from the top shelf, but just as she got the scissors and cotton from the dresser, the lights went out. Evie said she had to flip the TRIP SWITCH down in the cellar.

I didn't know what that was, but if it made the lights come back on, I was all for it.

Since the day of the cat, things had been quiet. Mum had been quieter than usual. Even letting me have extra chocolate after dinner—which was UNHEARD OF. Dad said that she had some tablets to make her feel better. I would have preferred the puppy, especially now that I was alone waiting for Evie to come back. In Evie's room, in the dark... with Egor, who was somewhere in the darkness.

I hugged my knees to my chest as I sat on the furry rug by the bed, holding them tight as I exercised my eyes to make them see better. Ever since that day Evie had played the trick in the cellar, I had noticed my eyes got funny in the dark. I thought maybe grandad had been so angry I had broken his cane, that he had left a piece of himself inside me. It was my PENNANCE.

'Sorry, grandad,' I whispered into the dark, and my eyes began to work a little better. I began to see things in the room. Shapes and objects...

...Egor, only a hand stretch away, lying on his back.

My stomach somersaulted and I swallowed too hard. I crushed my legs in closer to my chest, feeling my heart knocking against my knees.

'Evieee!' I yelled.

'Just a sec.' She called back from downstairs. 'It's not the trip switch, we need candles.'

I looked back to Egor. He didn't move, he looked like a normal teddy bear, but I knew better.

I grit my teeth and frown hard at him, my hands clenched in my lap.

'Don't you dare move or I'll give you a BUNCH OF

FIVES.' I whispered.

I hoped I sounded brave because I didn't know what a BUNCH OF FIVES were. It was something mum said to Evie quite a lot these days but usually with a rude word too. At first, I thought Evie was getting those notes with the number five on. I told mum I wanted a bunch too. She had shaken her fist at me and shouted that she'd gladly give me some if I carried on being INSOLENT. I don't know what INSOLENT is, but I do know it's a good job I didn't carry on, because when I spoke to Evie about her FIVES, she told me to be glad I didn't get any, they weren't money, they were a BAD THING.

I stared at Egor, watching for any movement. Would his eyes glow green again now I was alone?

I didn't know and I wasn't going to find out. I closed my eyes fast; he wouldn't get me again.

'Here we go,' Evie's voice came back into the room, flooding my body with relief. 'Oh my God Meredith, what are you up to?'

I opened one eye. Evie had two candles in her hands that cast the room into shadow.

'Ooookay.' Evie said, putting the candles down on the floor next to them, 'when you've quit being weird Moo, we'll carry on. Are you ready to stop being a baby?'

I nod my head, my mouth felt too tight to answer her.

'Right,' she said, leaning forward with a wince. 'Listen, there's no need to be scared of the dark, it's just the same as the light, except without the lights on. Nothing has changed.'

She was trying to make me feel better, but I knew different. Everything changed in the dark. Things lurked in the shadows, and night creatures came out. The bad man came in the dark, Evie herself said so. It wasn't the same as the light. Not at all.

'Okay?' She said.

I nod my head at her trying to be brave.

'Good. Let's get back to it,' she said, sitting slowly down

next to Egor with an oof sound, and picking up both bear and the scissors.

A whiff of her lily perfume reached my nose and my eyes stretched wide.

'What are you going to do?'

'Surgery. Then you won't have to worry about the man again. We'll know what he's up to.'

'Are you going to cut him up?'

Evie laughed softly. 'No silly. If I cut him up the bad man will have no lair, he will go back into you.'

'Why?' I said, close to crying baby tears again. I swallowed them down hard and rubbed my fists into my eyes.

'Because if the bad man's lair is destroyed then he automatically goes back to the last place he was. That was you. And you won't be destroyed until you are dead, he'll be in you your whole life, Moo.'

My breath caught in my throat. I eyed Egor, and the bear eyed me back.

'That's why we have to take care of Egor. Forever. He must never be destroyed. *Never.* Understand?'

I nod my head hard and know that I will never get rid of Egor. I don't want the bad man back. And now my heart is POUNDING.

'Evie?' I said, the wobble back in my voice.

'What is it?' she said slipping the scissors into Egor's back and beginning to cut through his fur. White stuffing fell from his cut onto the floor like cotton wool snow.

'If the bad man is in there, Evie, won't he come out?' I said, my voice too squeaky.

Evie shook her head as she thrust her tongue between her lips and cut up to his neck.

'The scissors are silver. The bad man hates silver.' She said, 'A bit like a vampire. Here, hold him a sec.'

She thrust the bear at me and reached back under her bed. Egor bounced off my knee and I scuttled quickly backward, eyeing his little brown body on the floor, scissors in his back, white blood spilled on the rug.

Here.' She said, bringing out her Walkman cassette player. Her favourite. One she could record on as well as play. I watched, my mouth dropping open as she pulled out the headphones and threw them back under the bed. She checked the tape was inside, checked the batteries, and rewound the tape to the start. Then she pulled Egor back to her and moved his stuffing to place the Walkman inside. Finally, she stuffed most of the white stuffing back inside his body and took the cotton and thread to sew him back together. I sat quiet, mortified that she had ripped open the bad man's lair and placed an object inside that he may not like.

Would he be mad?

'Evie,' I whispered.

'Yes.' She said, with a small sigh.

'Is he still in there?'

'Of course, he is. Now he has a voice too. We can record what he's up too. Get me up.'

She held out an arm and I got up to tug it, pulling her to her feet with a grunt.

'Evie?'

She huffed a sigh and rolled her eyes in the low light.

'What is it Moo?'

'Why do we want to know what he's up to?'

Evie huffed a sigh.

'Do you want to know if he's in there or not? Do you want to know if he's ever back in you? You couldn't even tell the first time, Moo. Now we can check.'

My knees started to knock in the candlelight as Evie gave me the scissors and picked up a candle.

'I don't want to check, Evie. I'm scared.'

'I'll do it, baby.' She said rolling her eyes.

'Can't we just throw him out? The BIN MEN can take him, can't they? Far, far, far away. And then the man won't be here anymore.'

'It doesn't work like that. If we throw him out and Egor is destroyed, he will go back to the last place he was. We had this discussion just, Moo.'

'If he's far enough away though…'

'There is no place he won't come back from. He's tied to you, like a string, but we can't see to cut it. So, you see how important this is?'

I swallowed hard and nod my head. She stared at me, candlelight flickering in her eyes.

'Do you want him back inside you?'

I shook my head hard.

'That's why we have to keep him close. If he's in Egor, and Egor is safe, then so are you. We are double safe now though, Egor can listen and speak. We just have to look after him. Forever.'

She moved to the wardrobe and placed Egor back inside on the top shelf.

'We should probably move him back to the cellar, he'll be safe there, but not in the dark.'

I nod my head and chew on my lip not trusting my voice to speak. Evie laughed.

'Don't look so scared, you're safe. I promise. I wouldn't let anything happen to you, would I?'

I shook my head, as Evie laughed again.

'Let's go downstairs.' She said heading out of her room.

I followed closely, trying not to look at all the shadows that jumped around the landing as we walked.

We had done surgery, and I knew with my big sister watching over me, that everything would be all right.

I was too scared for it not to be.

CHAPTER THIRTY SIX

Meredith hung up the phone and stared at it. Her heart was hammering, and she had no idea if she had just done the right thing.

'You did the right thing,' Matt said.

'Did I? I'm not so sure.'

'There was no other option was there? How can we go back to Lynton now? Kevin would never agree to it, it would throw the schedule, and he's being an arse as it is. You were right, we can't go back, we'll get the name of someone who can help and call her back. It's the only thing we can do.'

Meredith chewed her lip and looked at Matt. She felt torn, and a little wired.

Matt put his tea down on the side and came to sit next to her on the bed. He took the phone off her, placing it on the side before turning to her.

'Meredith, really. There was nothing more you could do. Nothing more we *can* do.'

'I know, but Matt, she was really upset. Like really freaked out. Elana has been going mad. I feel like I provoked her, I made her worse. This is all my fault, and now I just get to walk away? It doesn't seem fair.'

'So, what do you want to do?'

Meredith ran a hand over her face. She shook her head and shrugged.

'I don't know. There's nothing. Except try to find a reputable professional to send their way. There's nothing more, I know that.'

Matt took one of her hands in his, and she turned to look at him.

'This is not your fault,' He said. 'You don't need to take

responsibility. Google a service and phone her back, then forget it. It's done.'

Meredith wondered how many times she would be told in her life that she wasn't responsible, and how many times she would feel it anyway. Matt was right though, and she had promised to call Stephanie back within ten minutes.

'I'd better get looking then,' she said.

Matt nodded.

'I'll tidy up the camera, don't forget your tea.'

He gave her hand a squeeze before letting it go, then he left the bed to start removing wires from the television.

Meredith googled paranormal experts. Funny how many of them there were when you were looking. She wondered just how many were fake—like they were really. An uncomfortable feeling settled in her stomach as she scrolled.

Even if we are fake, it was me that Elana sent the message to, me she wants, me Stephanie wants too. Us. Our team.

No time to worry about that, just get a name down and get back to Stephanie.

She clenched her jaw, there was no way around it, they weren't going back to Lynton. Case closed. Get over it. She concentrated on looking at a few reviews and finally came across a firm that seemed reputable as Matt cut the silence.

'Meredith!' her name came out as a hushed gasp.

She looked up from her phone in surprise. Matt was looking at her with his mouth half open.

'I've just had a thought,' he said. 'Didn't you say the orbs on the footage came at particular times?'

Meredith blinked.

'What are you talking about?'

'The orbs, which aren't orbs at all, came at certain times. Something happened around the time they appeared, didn't it? You said earlier, only I wasn't paying much attention. What was it?'

She thought back to the footage that they had watched

earlier.

'Yes, there was. The servants bell, I think. Why?'

'I don't know. I just...' He trailed off with a frown. 'Let's watch it through again, now that we know, more or less, what the orb actually is. Something is niggling, that's all.'

Meredith looked back to her phone with a nod.

'Okay, let me just write this down.'

The footage started up on the hotel TV screen, from the point just before where the real action had started, and the first orb had appeared. This time Matt turned the sound on.

Jeez, you can't wait?

Meredith took a screenshot of the details as Matt watched the screen intently, waiting for the orb shoe with focused concentration. Meredith felt a little of the amusement that she supposed others felt around her when she got her teeth into something they didn't yet understand.

The orb shoe appeared on screen and the servants bell clanged in the distance.

Matt frowned and spun to her, index finger pointing to the TV. Meredith bit back a grin as she nod at him, wondering if he required an answer, but he spun straight back to the screen.

The orb shoe appeared a second time, and again the servants bell went off, clanging in the distance. At the same moment, a bell went off in Meredith's head as she suddenly got what Matt had figured out. She stood, fixated to the screen, the phone falling to the carpeted floor from her lap. She ignored it as the scene played out ahead of them.

And then it came again.

The orb shoe, followed almost immediately by the clang of the servant's bell.

Meredith's mouth dropped open as Matt paused the footage, and turned to her, his face held the same shocked expression as hers.

'I think you may be right.' he said.

Meredith's heart took up a steady patter.

This was big. Really big.

She nod her head.

'Strings,' she said.

'Strings.' He repeated.

Meredith blinked, trying to understand the enormity of what they had discovered. After accepting that no one was faking, they were back to almost hard evidence that someone was. And that someone was the director—if the shoe was indeed Kevin's.

Well, there's no one else's it can be is there? We were all in the circle, Matt was behind the camera, Steve had been over the other side of the cellar. Only Kevin had been by the door between the two rooms.

A sour taste climbed up into her mouth. So much rested on the fact that she was learning to interact with real spirits, having real experiences. It was the whole reason she was here in the first place. If nothing was real, then Kevin had officially ruined everything, and she was wasting her time. All of this would be for nothing, she still had no idea how to communicate with Eve, and now mum was drinking again too.

It's a disaster, Meredith, like everything you do…

'I don't get it.' She said to Matt, trying to keep her voice neutral. She didn't want to let him know how invested in this she was, or the real reasons it mattered so much.

Matt shook his head, staring at the paused screen, and then he rolled his eyes.

'Well, I mean I do get it, he needs to make a convincing paranormal show, so in that respect yes, I get that he would possibly try to fake activity. But we already had good communication going, why the extra input?'

'Unless he somehow faked everything?'

Matt huffed a snort.

'I'm not sure Kevin is good enough to fake a levitating ball, or the frequency of a Ghost box, or a Ouija board that spills secrets. That would take some serious skill.'

Meredith nodded, wondering just how much Kevin knew about her background anyway. He could have been the one to propose the questions, if someone else moved the planchette on the board, right? Kevin would only need an assistant, and Kevin was pretty persuasive when his wrath came into the equation.

The ball, and the Ghost box were different, but the Ouija? Yes, someone could easily set up that one with the right information.

Her heart banged with disappointment and injustice.

'Meredith? This looks bad, but I just don't think he could fake it all. It's not possible.'

'Not without help.' She said, leaving the statement hanging.

Breathe Meredith.

Mum is drinking…

None of this is real…

I feel sick…

'A levitating ball?'

'Well,' she said, bringing her focus back onto the moment before she passed out. 'Maybe we'll get to the ball and the Ghost box, but the Ouija, and the other things, for sure. It's totally possible.'

Matt scratched his head and ran a hand back through his hair. He blew out his cheeks, and then held his hands up in a shrug.

'I don't know who, or how you would ever—'

'Donald.' Meredith cut him off mid-sentence as Donald's activity and uninspired possessions came to her mind.

'Donald?' Matt balked at her. 'Donald? Really?'

Had that come across harsh? Meredith flapped a hand at him.

'Hearsay obviously, but his possessions are a little OTT if I'm honest. I don't know how we'd check though.'

Matt gazed at her in thought.

'Surely, the footage is the only way, and yet, I can't see

what it would show up. If he's a good actor, he's a good actor.'

Meredith thought back to Moweth Manor, and Cara's father, whom Donald had shouted about and then fainted in a magnificently dramatic performance.

'Hmm,' She said, trying to ignore the pounding of her heart. 'You remember when I first asked you to see footage? I was wary about Donald's performance at Moweth, we could go back to that night and view it?'

She looked at Matt, and suddenly remembered that he had been unhappy about viewing any of it at all.

'If you're happy to,' she added.

Matt stood with his hands linked at the back of his head, elbows out, eyebrows raised. He waited a beat before answering, taking his time.

Finally, he nodded slowly.

'Yeah, let's go back over it then. I'm as intrigued by this as you are.'

He powered up the laptop and set about finding the footage from that night. Meredith followed to watch him as he clicked the folder containing the relevant scenes.

'Right then, where did you want to see from?'

'I'd like to see from the start of the glass on the table until the end where the father came through.' Meredith said over his shoulder.

'Okay, well, I've got the edited version, or you can see the whole thing laid bare as it happened. I guess that version will be better for catching anything untoward.'

'Yes, perfect.'

He tapped the laptop screen and the file loaded into the editing software.

'Okay, well, here goes.'

Matt clicked the mouse, finding the frame times he needed and then pressed play. The scene ran out exactly as Meredith remembered. The four of them, Meredith, Helen, Gwen, and Donald linking hands around the table and their serious faces as they put their fingers onto the glass. She watched the action when they were apparently communicating with Cara Crawford. Watched the glass slide and tip around the table. Everyone was solemn, no one seemed to be moving the glass, or trying to move the glass as far as she could tell. The moments where the glass stopped, everyone seemed pensive, waiting, even Gwen stalled before answering the 'no's' as if waiting for movement. There didn't seem to be anything untoward or anything that could have been rigged for those particular shots. She watched until the table tipped, and the glass flew, smashing behind them. She saw Donald shout and fall to the floor, saw Gwen leaning over him, and then the low roar as the commotion continued. She watched herself shout that they needed to stop filming. Watched her hair whipped in a sudden breeze and then watched as she shouted at the spirit and the room fell silent. She saw her hair fall flat again, undisturbed, hearing the roar cut off instantly as Helen's screams continued.

'Shit.' Meredith said, thumbs under her chin, tips of her fingers touching the end of her nose like she was in prayer. 'That was a hard scene, both being there and watching it back. I felt so out of control!'

'You didn't look it though.' Matt said, keeping his eyes on the screen.

Her heart was thumping hard. She remembered how scared she had been, how out of control she had felt, but Matt was right. She didn't look too bad on camera. She had felt a lot worse than she had come across.

Matt played the scene again, and Meredith swallowed as she took in the events as they had unfolded again before her. There was hope though.

How can this be anything but real?

Matt stopped the playback as the footage blacked out. They sat in silence, Matt either letting Meredith mull over the events she had witnessed or mulling over them himself. And then it hit her, and she almost groaned in frustration.

She swung to Matt.

'Did you hear that?'

'What?' Matt said.

'The roar. Rewind a little. Just after Donald falls to the floor.'

Matt found the frames he needed and then pressed play.

Donald dropped to the floor, Gwen leaned over him and then it came again. A low roar, muffled, and stunted.

Matt paused the footage and took it back again, and then again.

'Do you hear that?' Meredith asked.

Matt nodded slowly.

'I hear it, and I get you, but it has to be coincidence. Steve is as clueless as we are, you can see him in the footage.' Matt played it through again. There was a glimpse of Steve looking shocked as the table tipped and Donald fell. Whoever, or whatever, was making the noise, it couldn't be Steve. In full shot with his mouth hanging open before the camera panned away.

Meredith frowned.

'So what then? Because that sounds very much like—'

'Like Steve's snore, yes,' Matt said, 'only muffled. Which sounds ridiculous, said out loud.'

Meredith nodded.

'Exactly, and yeah it does. The other thing is, if Steve is there with his mouth wide open then it can't be Steve, but it does sound human. Can this be a coincidence?'

'Can it be anything else? I think you're looking into it too much.'

She frowned again, the noise sounded more human than ghost like, but there was nowhere else it could be coming from surely. Everyone was fully in shot.

Everyone except…

'Donald?'

Matt raised his eyebrows.

'I still don't get this Donald stuff, Meredith. Donald is the team psychic. He was brought in through his own company whose reputation has been built up over many years. Why the hell would he be faking a noise? Surely he's the one person who wouldn't.'

'Lots of psychics fake things. It adds to the glamour of their career. They look better for it.'

'Well, yes, but there was already activity, and he had already handed talking to Cara over to you. He passed the reins; he could have glammed up his ability by taking control then.'

Meredith ran a hand over her mouth, thinking as Matt continued.

'Also, there is the table, the glass, the wind that whips up from nowhere and disappears again. The roar was only a section of the whole. If we were already experiencing that, then why the roar? Why bother?'

'Like, why bother with the servant's bell?'

'Yeah, I suppose so. I guess it's kind of the same.'

Meredith looked back to the screen where the end action was playing out.

'You tripped, or something.' She said.

Matt looked perplexed. 'Tripped?'

'Yes, as the table tipped and you ran to get the action on the camera, you tripped.'

'I didn't.'

'Look again.'

He backed up the footage with a good-natured sigh and they watched it through again.

As the table tipped, the camera swung sideways, and the shot wobbled before carrying on in a steady fashion.

'What was that?'

Matt frowned, and then nodded.

'Yeah, I remember now, I felt something tug my foot as I moved, I looked down but there was nothing there, so I carried on, that was it.'

'Nothing there. Or something there.'

'Could have been the ghost?'

She pursed her lips.

'Could have.'

'Could have been strings.'

Meredith looked at him, his lips were pursed too.

'Could have been that too. You really can't remember?'

'I wasn't looking for foul play. All I can tell you is that I didn't trip or feel anything around my feet again as far as I can remember. If strings were around, they were broken, or the action was real, and the ghost tugged my foot.'

Meredith closed her eyes and thought. Amid her despair, there was an opportunity here.

The more she thought about it, the more it shone clear and bright.

We can find out the truth and eliminate the two people rigging sets easily, can't we? The door is open we just have to enter.

'You know there's a way to find out for sure, don't you?' she said.

Matt nodded.

'I know what you're going to say, yeah. We go back to Lynton and check the bell over. Maybe we deal with Elana too, and at least leave those guys with the name of a professional as we go.'

Meredith grimaced.

'Exactly.' She said.

'Does it really mean that much to you?'

She nodded holding his gaze, imploring him to understand just how much it meant to her.

If there was no real contact at Lynton now? Then Elana was Asha's doing, Kevin and Donald were rigging sets, and she was going home to deal with her drunk mother before things got any worse.

Evie would just have to wait.

CHAPTER THIRTY SEVEN

Steve flicked his eyes between Meredith and Matt, a look on his face that said he may have had them both locked up in an asylum, if he could only get out of this room.

'Well?' Matt said.

Steve continued to stare, and Helen kicked his ankle from next to him on Steve's bed.

'We'll do it.' She said, looking to Steve. 'Won't we dufus?'

'Yeah, yeah.' He said, 'Let me just get my head around this.'

He frowned, drawing his eyebrows together, and pointed to Meredith.

'You, Bangers, I'd accept this from. Expect it even. You love to follow trouble.'

Meredith felt her mouth fall open. She started to retaliate but Steve held a hand up to her.

'I'm not saying it's a bad thing. Hey, fun is my middle name too. But you...'

His finger now switched to Matt.

'Man, I've known you a lot of years. And never once have you liked trouble. Where the hell did you get this crazy ass idea from, Meredith, and what have you done with Matt?'

'It was my idea, initially,' Matt said. 'Meredith had already called Lynton and they'd asked us to come back, but when we found the bell going off after Kevin's foot appeared... well, it makes sense to see if there was any way he could have done it, and the only way to do that is to go back to Lynton.'

'Kills two birds with one stone.' Meredith added.

Steve laughed.

'Number one, what the hell does it matter if Kevin rigs the set? Who cares? And number two, we don't owe the guys at Lynton anything. We don't have to go back.' He looked from Meredith to Matt again. 'So, what's the story guys?'

Meredith felt her heart begin to thump. Not only did she not want to tell everyone her business, but they didn't really have time right now for the crap and questions that it would throw up.

Matt placed a hand at her back.

'Yes, there's a story.' He looked to Meredith, who thought she may just knock his block off if he told them anything about Evie and her trouble with mum. 'I don't know what the story is,' he continued, 'But I know it's important to Meredith. And that's why I agreed to suss this out with her. If we get to know the story? Great. If not, we've helped anyway. Isn't that what friends do?'

Meredith could have kissed him. The warmth of his hand on her back sent warmth through her soul. All her life she had spent running, keeping people at a distance, finding reasons she couldn't go out, couldn't have friends' home, couldn't get close.

Only now, with Matt's kind words, did she realise just how much she needed someone else to share this with. It had been getting hard to deal with alone, and even with Mrs Grey's help it wasn't the same. Mrs Grey wasn't someone she could break down on and pour her heart out to. Although she was certain the old lady wouldn't mind a jot.

Just Matt though. Not the others. Not yet.

One step at a time, Meredith.

She pulled her attention back into the room as Steve went on at Matt.

'…Okay, I get that. I do, but you guys know what happens if we get caught, right?' He looked to each one of them and made cutting motions across his neck. 'None of us will make it out of the show alive, and probably not with our reputations in-tact. Are you all willing to risk that?'

Meredith nodded, she wasn't a presenter anyway, and although she had enjoyed the whole hunting down spirits to a degree, she hadn't enjoyed the strictness of the filming process. She would rather take Matt, and a handheld camera and see what happened for however long it took. She also realised that that wasn't a professional approach—it would never make a television show or any money.

Helen nodded too, her face shining with excitement. She was looking forward to breaking the rules. A side of her that had been slowly coming through as the show had gone on.

Matt gave a nod too, and Steve raised his eyebrows.

'Matt. Man, are you sure? This could really fuck up your career.'

Matt frowned a little and looked to Meredith. She held his gaze and could see him struggling with the implications of what he was being asked to do.

On one hand she wanted him to be there more than anything, it couldn't work without him. On the other she didn't want him to risk everything just for her.

'You don't have to,' she said, 'we can stop this right now. All we've done is look at footage so far, and half of that was with Kevin's blessing originally. I—'

'I'll do it.' He said, cutting her off with a smile. 'I know what could happen and I can deal with it. I want to do it, I'm in. One hundred percent.'

Matt looked to Steve.

'What about you? You stand to lose a career too.'

Steve started to laugh.

'A career holding a pole. Look, man, as much as I love my job, I could change career like that.' He snapped his fingers. 'I could be a comedian and be in front of the camera. That would be pretty cool, actually.'

He looked off into nothingness, his vision before him, until Helen swatted him around the back of the head.

'Give over, you're no comedian. Your jokes aren't even funny.' She grinned as he put a hand to his heart looking wounded and Meredith found herself grinning too.

'Oh, wow, that hurts.' He said.

'It's also true,' Meredith said, she curled a hand around her chin as she thought. 'I could see you in a cult zombie series though.'

'Ah, now *that* would be cool. I could blow away fake zombies all day.'

'I think she meant as one of the undead,' Matt said with a laugh.

Helen laughed too. 'He wouldn't even need much make up.' She added.

Now Meredith was laughing, all of them but Steve.

'Hey, hey,' he said, holding his hands up, 'I work all night on a paranormal shoot, the lack of sleep will do that. You should see me when I do sleep. I'm a regular Chris Pratt.'

'A regular Forrest Gump.' Helen said, and Steve pulled her into a headlock, forcing her down onto the bed with a laugh.

Matt was the first to break the mood and get back to business, which was a shame because Meredith was enjoying the laughs immensely. Although it had been just days, it seemed like eons ago that she had last laughed properly. She calmed with a little regret as Steve and Helen got up, both brushing down their hair, which was wild from scrubbing the bedclothes.

Meredith tittered again. They made a good couple.

She wondered if she would ever make a good couple with someone, and turned back to Matt, her heart jumped, and she pulled her gaze away.

Bloody hell Meredith, where is this coming from? Focus.

Matt went over a strategy he had formed, almost instantly it seemed, of what they would do next, and when and how they would sneak away. Focus and authority only seemed to make him more attractive, and Meredith's concentration waned as she chewed on her lip, taking him in.

I've really enjoyed his company today. He's different. Mature, capable.

She vaguely wondered what it would be like to kiss him, and then she shook the thoughts away.

Woah, Meredith, calm down. Matt's cute, laid back, caring, and considerate, but this is just a job, and in a few weeks he will be gone. No point getting all fired up about someone who will be leaving soon, best to squash any feelings down.

She was used to that anyway, adept at it. And then he met her eyes, forcing her attention to him fully.

'Sound okay?' He asked.

Meredith hadn't got a clue, but she nod her head anyway. Luckily, he went into summary mode, all the years working with Kevin rubbing off on him.

'Okay,' he said, looking at his watch. 'It's four-thirty now, we'll aim to leave around eight tonight. After dinner we go to our rooms, if we don't go to the bar, I can't see Donald, Kevin and Gwen staying up to have an evening drink together. They'll hopefully head back to their rooms too, so we should be safe from anyone seeing us leave. Meredith, you call Lynton back and tell them we'll be with them by half past eight. Steve, you and I can load all the stuff into the van when it gets darker. Nothing excessive though, it'll just be handheld camera and Mic really.'

Meredith nodded, as he continued.

'Helen, Meredith, I don't know whether you want to get together and go through a plan or not?'

He held his hands out, looking from one to the other. Helen looked straight to Meredith.

'No,' Meredith said. 'I don't see the need, we're quite good at winging it together.'

Helen grinned and nodded.

'I'll grab my pen and pad, anything else to bring from our

point of view?'

Meredith shook her head.

'No, we should be good.'

'Great,' Matt said. 'I think that's about it. Everyone got it?'

There were two yeses from Meredith and Helen, and a loud whoop from Steve which made them all jump.

'Woah,' Helen said looking at him, 'what's that about?'

Steve looked at her with his mouth open.

'What's that about?' he said indignant, 'We're going on a secret road trip, and if we get caught our asses are toast. Fucking *love it,* baby.'

His voice rose to another whoop as he broke into a big grin and pulled everyone into a group hug.

Meredith felt a trickle of excitement amongst the affection she felt for these three people who were going out on a huge limb for her.

Friends, they really are my friends.

CHAPTER THIRTY EIGHT

There was a bang from upstairs as the man retrieved the heavy woolen cloak from the shelf and wound it around him in the darkness, feeding his arms gracefully through the armholes and clasping it at the front, taking the time and care to smooth the join delicately with no rush, feeling the fall of the wool for confirmation that it hung right. There were no mirrors down here, he didn't need one, God's hand would steady his, the rest he could make out in the half light from the upper floor of the house.

Pulling the hood up over his head he took the rosary from the shelf and held it in his hand, closing his eyes as his fingers closed on the cool wood.

'Father. Thy work will be done, on earth as it is in heaven. I am your willing slave, obedient servant, grateful son. What is your wish?'

The man stood in stillness in the dark, emptying his thoughts and listening to the quiet in his mind. Sometimes it took a while to hear God's word, but it would come, it always did. He closed his eyes and fingered the rosary, passing through all 101 beads before hearing the reply.

He was shocked. He hadn't been allowed to touch the woman yet. He hadn't expected it to come to this so soon, but God's wish was just, and he would uphold it in accordance with his duty to his life's work and his master.

'As you wish.' He whispered, a trickle of excitement running through him. Electricity through his veins.

There was another bang from upstairs. A yell. And he knew he would have to sedate her further before he began. It was a shame. She should be made to understand the devastation and depth of her sin, that would be *his* wish. But

God's was to have no one else interfere with the work, and so she would be calmed.

'Thank you, Father.'

The man crossed himself, kissed the beads, and added them to one of the cloaks deep pockets. Then he turned to the shelf which held his cloth roll. The old white linen just visible in the low light. He pulled it to the empty part of the shelf where his cloak had been folded.

There was another yell from upstairs, the devil's talk, but there was no need to rush where God's work was concerned, there was only need for diligence, faith, and careful consideration of the work to be done. The woman was contained. Ignoring her attempts for attention the man reached for the gloves and slid them over his hands feeling the cool leather caress his skin. There would be no contact between himself and the woman, accidentally or otherwise. It was forbidden. Unholy.

Carefully, he untied the small knot at the side of the roll and rolled it open from left to right. Inside were many implements for his work. Some used, some not. It was God's wish what was planned, and tonight there was only one instrument to be used on the woman. He pulled the small leather handle from its clasp and untied the long end of string letting the sliver of rope fall out long and flat, it's tufted end falling to the floor at his feet. He ran his hand down the length of rope, feeling it's gentle firmness until he arrived at the tuft, soft and smooth at the end.

The man smiled. Such a strange thing, perception. This soft, gentle, yielding implement with its silky end would harbour no pleasure for the woman tonight. For as soft and yielding as it was, it had a bite, and he knew from experience that it's bite was ferocious and greedy.

He placed the handle into his right hand, drew it high and with a quick flick of his wrist sent the rope out to bite into the darkness with a satisfying snap.

A snap that would snake across the woman's skin, it's

bite leaving wounds that would bleed only sin.

Feeling in his pocket for the small media player he put the earbuds in his ears and pressed play. Classical music filled his ears, relaxing his very being, bringing him closer to God, his Father, and drowning out the woman's evil words.

He crossed himself again and folded the long end of the whip into his fingers.

'I am ready.' He said and made his way to the stairs.

CHAPTER THIRTY NINE

The atmosphere at Lynton Castle was tense, and Meredith was glad they had decided to go back—glad they'd found reason to. It was almost as though they walked through a barrier as they entered, a barrier of unease and darkness.

If it didn't feel haunted before, it certainly feels haunted now, all right.

Goose bumps broke out on her flesh as she followed Stephanie into the living room. Orla stood by the fireplace, wringing her hands before the flames. She turned as they entered the room, and Meredith's mouth dropped open at the pallor and lines on her face.

'Hi Orla.' She said, the hair at the back of her neck standing on end, as the woman nod her head and turned back to the fire without a word.

'I'm so glad you came back.' Stephanie said, 'Half a team is better than none, and to be honest I feel better without Mr Spalding. He makes me tense just being in the same room, and I'm so tense now I may just uncoil and go whizzing off into space at any second.'

She laughed politely. Meredith smiled, presuming the others had done the same behind her as no one had joined in.

'You're welcome,' she said, biting back a comment about them being the better half of the team. A sudden thought crossed her mind. What if Kevin had set this up and put cameras here?

You'll be in trouble if he finds out anyway, Meredith, may as well get your backside back to London. Do not pass go, do not collect £200. Anyway, you called Stephanie remember, she didn't call you.

Stephanie turned to face the group, not offering them a

seat. Her eyes flit around the room, and her head jerked toward sounds it seemed only she could hear.

Meredith felt her stomach turn over.

'Are you okay, Stephanie?'

Stephanie nod her head, just once.

'Yes,' she said, looking over to the door, 'Yes, better now.'

Meredith took a step forward, placing a gentle hand on her arm, bringing her gaze back to Meredith's own. Meredith saw the fear in her eyes, almost smelled it coming from her pores.

'What the hell happened?' she whispered.

'I don't know… I mean… I don't know where to start.'

Tears filled her eyes, and in that instant Orla broke into loud sobs by the fireplace, her shoulders heaving. Stephanie visibly restrained her own emotions and moved to Orla, taking her into her arms, hands rubbing her back.

'All right, 'she soothed, 'It will be all right, darling. Meredith will sort this whole mess out, I promise.'

Meredith balked. She turned to Matt, who was right behind her. He pursed his lips with a small shrug. What can we do about it? The look said, and Meredith knew he was right. All they could do was their best, but right now everything seemed up in the air. There was no control. That was the part Kevin was good at, and with Matt quiet, and Helen and Steve looking positively horrified behind him, Meredith supposed they could have done with a plan after all.

Well, take control, Meredith. Let's see what we can do for these people.

She turned to the others.

'Okay, would someone go and make us all some tea?' she said quietly. 'I'll calm them down. We need more information.'

Steve nodded. No jokes for now. 'I'll go.'

'I'll help,' Helen said, grabbing his arm and turning him to go.

Meredith was about to contest, Helen had the pad to write down anything important that they said, but Matt shook his head.

'We can handle it,' He whispered with a wink, placing the camera bag down at the side of the chair, and moving over to the women. He gently coaxed them to the settee and sat them down together, reciting to them how they liked their tea, and with how many sugar's, as though he had known them years.

'I'll make sure Helen and Steve know what they're making and be right back.' He said, walking toward Meredith, who hadn't budged an inch.

'I promise,' He whispered as he passed, giving her arm a squeeze, and nodding his head toward them. 'You've got this.'

Meredith composed herself, smiled, and hoped they wouldn't hear the banging of her heart. Sitting opposite them, in the other chair, seemed too formal, the chair too far away for intimacy. So, she perched on the coffee table, taking a hand from each of them, and holding it in hers.

She met Stephanie's eyes.

'What happened?' she said.

Stephanie swallowed hard.

'It's been awful, Meredith' she whispered. 'I… we've had to send Asha away. We didn't know what else to do. It was just… Oh God, when you said you couldn't come back… Oh, I just didn't know where to turn. You don't know how grateful I am that you're all here. Truly.'

She gripped Meredith's hand so hard that her knuckles pressed painfully together.

'I'm so sorry about that.' Meredith said. 'We had to get Mr Spalding's approval. This part may or may not be on the show. We want to take this more seriously tonight, and without him here, it's difficult to say what he will do with any footage. We have the camera and microphone, as before, but everything else we've left. It will just be us trying to get to the bottom of this Elana business. Okay?'

'Yes, yes. That's fine. Just help us, please.'

'I'll do my absolute best, that I can promise you. And if for any reason we can't help, we'll leave you with the names of some reputable people who will be able to.'

Stephanie's eyes widened and Meredith knew she had said the wrong thing.

'You have to help, you have to be able to do *something*, dear God.'

Orla let go of her hand with a wail, placing both of her hands over her face.

'All Meredith meant is that sometimes spirits are hard to shift. For the most part they go without too much fuss, but if Elana doesn't want to play ball, there are professionals more experienced in exorcism who can, and will, help.'

Meredith blinked.

She hadn't even heard Matt come back into the room, but here he was deftly getting her out of a hole that she was busy digging herself deeper into. Tiredness and worry about Evie and her mum were eating the best part of her brain tonight. She smiled as he perched on the coffee table beside her.

'Exactly.' She said, with a reassuring squeeze of Stephanie's hand. 'So, tell us, what has happened since yesterday?'

Once Stephanie began to talk, she couldn't stop, pouring out the whole episode with emotion that tugged at Meredith's heart. She knew what fear of the unknown felt like. She had been living with it all her life between her mother and Eve. She had a spirit of her own to contend with that had frightened the wits out of her too, although Evie had done nothing in line with what Elana had been up to since they had left early this morning.

She had started with small things just after the children had arrived back after breakfast. Bangs and footsteps in the cellar that couldn't be explained, and then they had found

Asha down by the boiler area again. This time in some sort of trance. After leading her out, they had padlocked the cellar, and she had returned to her normal state, but an hour or so later she had done the same again. The cellar fully open. Door swung wide.

Meredith bit her lip.

Easy to play the part, she can reach the keys to the cellar. Do they know that?

Steve and Helen bustled in with the tea, interrupting her thoughts as they handed out cups of steaming liquid, before sitting themselves on the settee by the window. Stephanie murmured a thank you and continued on.

'We double padlocked the door after the second time, but within the hour she was there again, this time she was *digging.*' Stephanie licked at her lips and ran her free hand through her hair. 'She said that she was finding Elana's bones. That the truth had to come out, and that Elana needed to rest.'

A chill snaked around Meredith, and she blew out a small breath. She must have given away something on her face because Stephanie hesitated.

'What is it?' she said.

Meredith shook her head.

'It could be nothing. But it may be worth looking in to. Did Asha find anything?'

'Just dirt,' Orla said, her hands winding over themselves, voice whimsical and distant, as she looked past them to the window.

Meredith nodded.

'I may as well tell you now. I was going to tell you over the phone but with us coming here anyway, it seemed silly.'

Stephanie's gaze bored into Meredith, and Orla's head swung back, her face ashen.

Meredith pulled in a shaky breath.

'Have you heard of a Ghost box?' she said.

Both women shook their heads. Meredith wasn't

surprised.

'It's…' she stopped. What the hell was it when you had to describe the thing?

Steve cleared his throat, bringing their attention to him.

'It's basically a small computer that uses radio frequency sweeps to generate white noise, which, in turn, can generate the energy needed for a spirit to communicate. It's called Electronic Voice Phenomena, or EVP.'

Orla looked blank, but recognition swam behind Stephanie's gaze as she looked at Steve.

'So, they can speak to you?' She said.

'In a manner, yes. We had one set up for the investigation last night, and we found some interesting frequency changes, and a voice.'

Stephanie's mouth dropped open, Orla seemed to shrink back into the chair, half closing her eyes, as though she didn't want to hear.

'A *voice*?' Stephanie whispered.

'Yes,' Steve confirmed. 'Sometimes it's difficult to make out, but we sat until sunrise this morning, comparing the footage with the box recording, trying to figure what Elana was trying to say. Sometimes they answer what you're asking, you see?'

Now Orla's eyes closed completely, her face paled further. Stephanie nodded, pushing him on.

'What did you find?' She said, 'What did she say?'

Meredith swallowed hard as Steve hesitated, catching her eye, and she took the baton back.

'We looked at the footage over and again, and we're almost certain of what was said. But please be aware that this was only what we came up with. There could be a million other things that she really said or meant that we didn't catch on to.'

'Meredith, please.' Stephanie said, fingering the cross at her neck.

Meredith held her gaze as her heart thundered.

Was she ready to hear this? Was Meredith ready to say it? It was too late now, either way. She licked her dry lips.

'We think the message was 'You, Meredith, know the truth. Dead bones cellar.' Now obviously it could be two—'

Stephanie cut her off.

'Dead bones cellar?'

Meredith nodded with another large swallow. Her head beginning to ache with the tension in the room.

'But that's what Asha was trying to do? She was trance like. Do you think that Elana took her over to find her bones? Is that what she wants?' Stephanie was speaking faster, her words tumbling over each other. 'If that's what she wants then we'll do it. We'll tear up the whole goddamn cellar, won't we Orla? We'll find the bones if she wants to rest. We'll find them Elana if you please just leave us and Asha alone.'

She was shouting now, and from the direction of the kitchen a door slammed with a heavy thud. In the silence that followed, there was a small, ominous, creak, and Meredith turned to the living room door, which was open, but moving slowly.

She blinked and stared at the wood, wondering if her eyes were deceiving her, when there was a neat 'whoooosh' and the door slammed shut with a loud bang.

Meredith jumped up from the table with a yell, noticing that Stephanie and Steve had done the same.

'Are the children here?' Meredith said, although she had seen no one by the door.

Stephanie shook her head.

'No. We've left them with someone in the village until this mess is sorted. It's not safe for them here. This has been going on most of the afternoon.'

Meredith turned to Stephanie, hairs now standing up on her arms as ice seemed to move down her spine.

'So, the castle is—'

'Empty, yes,' Stephanie confirmed. 'Aside from us,

anyway.'

'You have a poltergeist.' Meredith murmured, remembering the cat ball levitation from last night.

There was a moan from behind, and Meredith swung around to see Helen pointing to the fireplace, where one of the photographs hung in the air. Meredith just had time to see Asha's smiling face before the frame flung toward her and Matt, missing them both by millimetres to smash against the wall with an unearthly screech that Meredith swore couldn't have been made by any living thing on earth.

CHAPTER FORTY

The moaning came and went like the waxing and waning of the moon, the door still rocking into its hinges as bangs, crashes, and screeches were heard from all over the castle. Orla sat sobbing with her hands over her ears, as a very pale Stephanie went quickly over the rest of the activity, including the near drowning of Asha in the bathroom just after lunch, after which the children had been sent away while they decided what to do. By the time she had finished the account, Meredith felt sick. She didn't want to leave the room, let alone open the door to the destruction outside, and complete a vigil in the cellar.

'That's everything?' Meredith said, hoping there was more, as Helen scribbled on the pad on the settee.

'Everything so far,' Stephanie said with a nod of her head.

'Okay, well let's get this over with then,' Steve said, rising and moving to the door without his usual joviality, but seemingly none of the all-encompassing fear that Meredith felt. As he pulled the door open all noise instantly stopped. The silence was eerie, deafening, leaving Meredith feeling as though she had been out in a tornado and was now sitting in the eye of the storm.

'Maybe we should walk the castle together first,' Matt said, 'just to see how much has been upset, and what we can put right?'

Everyone agreed, staying together as they toured the rooms, only to find everything in place. The only salvageable piece of evidence to what had just happened was the broken photograph of Asha, which was left on the floor where it had fell, no one wanting to touch it.

Far from calming Meredith, the whole situation left her feeling frightened and on edge. After what had gone on already, she didn't like to think what was to come down below, but it was time to find out regardless.

After the castle walk through, they gathered the equipment and started for the cellar. It was agreed Stephanie and Orla would go with them. They didn't want to be alone upstairs, and Meredith felt better with more people around down here.

All was quiet as Matt and Steve set up the equipment, even Steve was devoid of his usual jokes. Meredith had a feeling that they were all thinking pretty much the same thing. Even if Kevin was rigging paranormal activity, he was in no way rigging this. This was about as real as they could hope to get. And Meredith wasn't sure at this point that any of them were hoping for real at all. Why had she been so determined to find out what Evie was doing anyway? A flutter of the curtains was nothing compared to this.

Buckle up, honey, it's about to get rough. I think you're about to find out just how scary the paranormal can get. And Elana is after you. You're in the firing line. Suck it up you lucky lady.

Meredith sniffed, and rubbed her eyes, on edge as Matt got the camera ready and set it on his shoulder.

'Ready to go.' Steve said as he set up the mic.

Meredith swallowed as her body began to tremble. She wasn't ready to go at all. What she wanted was to go home. She wondered why it had seemed so important to come back, just to see wires on a servant's bell that they still hadn't checked.

You wanted real activity, maybe in future be careful what you wish for.

Matt was about to start counting them down when Steve suddenly yelled, making everyone jump.

'Oh, wowowow, woah.' He held up a finger. 'Wait a minute.'

He disappeared from the room as Helen let out a mirthless chuckle, hand to her chest.

'Holy cow, thanks Steve, I nearly shit a brick.'

Meredith let out a nervous chuckle herself, and Matt grinned.

'Glad you didn't, I hadn't got the camera running.'

The nervous laughter became giggles, even from Stephanie, and Meredith felt a little of the tension run off her. It was okay. She was with friends, and whatever happened they would be okay. Bad stuff could happen, but no one had ever died from a ghost hunt—as far as she knew anyway.

She shook her legs out, stamping the cold from her feet, and jazzing herself up.

Come on, Meredith, you've got this. You know what you're doing, stay professional. What's the worst that could happen?

On second thought don't answer that.

'Come on, Steve,' she said, 'what's he doing?'

Matt shrugged.

'Who knows?' Helen said, as Steve came back into the room with the one thing that Meredith could have done without.

Spookbuddy.

Fabulous. You want to make the night any worse Steve?

Steve smiled from ear to ear as he held Spookbuddy at his chest.

'Couldn't leave the little fella out now, could we?' He said.

Helen glanced at Meredith, who gave her a small smile and a shrug.

'I guess he can't do any harm,' she said.

'What the hell is that?' Stephanie said as Steve switched him on and explained what the bear did.

'A ghost hunting teddy?' Orla said, her voice shaky.

'Yep,' Steve said, a hint of proudness in his voice that

was reminiscent of a father talking about his small child, 'I thought Buddy may help, what with Elana being young?'

He looked directly at Meredith. She gave him a nod.

'We'll see, I suppose,' she said. 'Is he ready to go?'

She flinched as Spookbuddy read out the stats of the room in his childlike American accent.

'Jeez, Spookbuddy,' she said, heart thumping. 'We are not going to be friends if you're going to keep shouting out at nothing.'

'Hey,' Steve said with a laugh, 'He's statting the room, leave him be. Ignore her Buds, she's stressing about Elana.'

Whether Spookbuddy was to be a bind or not, he had certainly broken the tension again, and Meredith was feeling more in control by the time they were ready to go. More like herself, and ready to deal with Spookbuddy too.

'Okay.' She said. 'We all ready?'

Five yeses came from various parts of the room as Steve got the mic and Matt began to record.

'Let's get this show on the road,' Meredith said, 'I think we'll just do some calling out and see what we get. Elana already seems to be fairly active tonight so I shouldn't think it will take much. If that doesn't work, we'll try—'

She cut off, her breath catching as the feather light touch of a small hand ran across her cheek and back into her hair.

'You okay?' Matt said.

Meredith nod her head.

'Yeah, I just got stroked across the face, anyone else feel anything?'

No one had, but Steve's jokes were back, and Meredith had never been so glad to hear them.

'You lucked out. The way you spoke to Elana yesterday I'm surprised she didn't give you a damn good slap.'

There was a ripple of laughter, that Meredith couldn't help joining in with.

He's right, it could have been a whole lot worse.

She took a breath and continued.

'Yeah, sorry about that Elana. So, as I was saying, I think we'll go for—'

She cut off as her hair was given a sharp tug.

'Ooh, you bugger. Steve that was your bloody fault.'

Steve looked at her with amusement.

'What the hell did I do?'

'I saw that.' Helen said with a spreading grin.

'I felt it,' Meredith said, 'She tugged my hair. If it is Elana anyway… ouch!' she said as her hair tugged down sharply again.

'One tug for yes, two for no,' Helen said with a giggle. Steve and Matt broke into laughter as Meredith looked at her horrified.

'Thanks. She isn't gentle. One tug on my hair for yes, two on Helen's for no, got it Elana?'

The room rippled into laughter as the tension ebbed, even Stephanie smiled, and then Helen held her head, her eyes wide.

'Two tugs!' she said, as Meredith grinned.

'That's a no, I guess she only wants to tug my hair then.'

She laughed as she felt a tug and her head dipped back.

'I got that on camera,' Matt said with a laugh.

'That one hurt,' She said, feeling a lot more relaxed that she had when they had entered the cellar. This may turn out to be okay after all.

Let's just Ask Elana about the message, get to the bottom of what she wants, check for strings, and get the hell out of here.

'Okay. So, it seems we won't have to call out for anything. I guess the hair tug will suffice if that's how you want to play it, Elana. As Helen says, one tug for yes, two for no. Have a go at Helen's for no if you like, spare my scalp, will you?'

Matt gave her a thumbs up and grinned at her, she deduced that was either because she was looking in control for the camera or because she was doing well under the circumstances.

She would take it either way.

Helen gave a yelp, and then a laugh.

'Two tugs, nope, she's definitely not going to spare you tonight.'

'Fabulous.' Meredith rolled her eyes with a smile.

Looks like we have a mischievous young lady in with us tonight. I still prefer that to the one we had the night before last on the Ouija board.

'Okay Elana. We were with you last night, asking you questions, do you remember.'

She closed her eyes as her hair was tugged back.

'That's a yes then,' she said to the camera. And then she saw Steve, the mic over his shoulder toward them as his back shook up and down rhythmically.

Matt cocked an eyebrow at her.

'Someone has the giggles.' He said.

'Steve?'

Steve turned, wiping tears from his eyes as he apologised.

'Sorry. Sorry. This hair tugging is hilarious.'

'For you,' Helen snorted. 'It really hurts.'

Steve howled with laughter, before mimicking her and Meredith almost perfectly.

'One tug for yes, two for… ow, fuck!' he finished, holding the back of his head.

They all laughed, even Stephanie and Orla who had been standing watching quietly, joined in this time.

'All right, all right. I get it, I'm not mocking,' he said. 'We have a little joker in with us tonight, don't we?'

When the laughter had died away Meredith tried again.

'Okay Elana, we don't want to hurt you, we just want to ask you some questions about last night, and something you told us, would that be okay?'

A tug on her hair told her yes, and she repeated it with a grin, glancing at Stephanie, who smiled back looking a whole lot better than she had just half an hour ago.

'Okay Elana, you spoke to us last night. You gave us a message. I'll say it loud; can you confirm for us that this is what you said?'

A tug, lighter now, barely felt but there all the same. She stated a yes for the camera. This was going far too well, she wondered whether the little girl was sated now that the attention was on her, or whether she really would let loose at some point.

Oh well, for now all is good. Go with the flow.

'Thank you. The message. You said...' She stopped swallowing hard, 'You said 'you, Meredith, know the truth. Find bones cellar.' Is that right, Elana?'

There was nothing, and Meredith looked to Helen, expecting a 'no' reaction, after all the words didn't make a lot of sense when said together. Helen didn't move. She frowned at Meredith and shook her head.

Meredith tried again.

'Elana? Can you—'

Meredith cut off as the door adjoining the two rooms slammed shut with a metallic clang, despite being made of wood. It sent echoing reverberations around the foundations of the old building, which seemed to Meredith, to literally shake.

She bit on her tongue to stop her screech as Matt yelled and Helen and Orla screamed. Everyone dropped to the floor, and Meredith sat in a crouch, hands over her ears, her heart drumming against her legs as she waited to see what was next. Silence fell around the room.

Followed by Spookbuddy.

'Brrr, it's cold in here.' He said cheerfully.

CHAPTER FORTY ONE

NOVEMBER—24 DAYS UNTIL DEATH

I giggled behind the floor length curtain in the living room, putting a hand over my mouth to stop the noise coming out. It didn't work, the noise coming through my fingers anyway.

'Where are you Moo?' Evie called out from the hallway.

She was getting close now and I had a plan to trick her today. There were only two windows in the living room, it was obvious I was behind one, but not the same one as usual. It was important that I stay quiet, but my giggles wouldn't stay down. I huffed them out in a series of blows through my nose.

'Moo, how can you have disappeared? It's impossible, I've looked everywhere.'

I knew she had come into the living room, her voice said so. I closed my eyes and thought about Grandad and how he was in HEAVEN. That stopped the giggles, but now the tears were close instead.

I sniffled, making more noise than the giggles did, and rubbed at my nose. Maybe grandad wasn't a good thought after all.

The settee made a pffftt sound as someone sat down. I wondered if it was Evie, and then she spoke.

'Well, I guess I have the afternoon to myself as Moo has vanished and I don't have to look after her anymore. How exciting, what shall I do?'

The telly flicked on and a woman began to cry.

'Oh Jack, how could you?'

Jack began to answer, along with a sad wail of music, but I ignored him, I was tensed. My muscles ready.

This was all part of the game. Evie knew exactly where I was, and in a second, she would pull the curtain across with a loud HA!

It used to scare me, but not anymore. Now it just made me laugh. Now it was Evie's game to try to come as quietly as possible, to see if she could make *me* jump.

I stared at the curtain, the stain on the cream lining from where dad had spilled his coffee one morning when opening the window.

Mum hadn't been pleased about that at all.

My back hit the low windowsill and I had a marvellous idea.

I would climb on, sit stealthy like a cat and pounce on Evie as she pulled the curtain back.

That would make her jump, all right. I would have to jump to the side to miss her though. I wouldn't want her to fight me as she had that day a few weeks ago.

Evie's bad bruises were healing now, although there was a new one on her shoulder I noticed while she was getting dressed yesterday. A yellow and blue one. Mum used to say they were the WORST ONES.

I asked Evie about it, but she told me it was nothing.

She still wasn't RIGHT though. Not really Evie. I wondered if she was sick, like mum. Maybe she needed PILLS to make her better too, but she said no.

But then mum always said no too. Even though dad had said first about the dog and then the pills to make her better. Mum had swiped him around the head for filling my head with THINGS BIGGER THAN ME, but dad said that I NEEDED TO KNOW. I don't know why, I'm not a doctor, I can't make her well.

I wondered if Evie would ever get fully better. It had been weeks now, she still had potato sacks under her eyes, and her lips were still devoid of lipstick. The lack of makeup made her skin pale, and I didn't like the zombie look that she was giving off. Her short skirts had stopped too, which was a shame because they were pretty. Now her legs were always covered in jeans or leggings to hide the marks.

Hearing the woman on the telly, and the sad music that played, I remembered my plan, shook away my thoughts, and focused on trying to climb onto the windowsill before Evie got to me. She was taking her time today, but then she seemed to be slower lately. She always seemed to move funny to me, too. Jerky and slow.

Maybe she's becoming a real live zombie, after all?

My eyes widened and my mouth pulled back.

I didn't think I wanted a zombie for a sister.

I turned to hop up on the wooden windowsill and came face to face with Egor, propped against the glass with a bear grin, legs stretched out toward me.

My breath caught in my throat and I stumbled back, pushing against the floor length curtain behind, which shifted under my force.

My scream didn't materialise, but a heavy moan came from my throat instead.

From the other side of the curtain came a thin scream that I knew was Evie.

The bad man! Had he got out of Egor? Had he got Evie?

Panicked, I turned, getting a face full of curtain. I pushed at the heavy velour with my hands, trying to get it out of my way. To get to Evie, to see what was wrong.

The scream lasted. Shrill and loud. And then I found the edge of the curtain and pulled it aside with my hand, freeing myself from its folds, and from Egor. I let it swing back, covering his furry face as I looked to Evie. The scream stopped but Evie's mouth still hung open. Both hands clutched her chest as she stared at me.

'What!' I said, horror mounting in my chest, causing my heart to beat so fast that I thought it may jump up and out of my mouth. And then Evie's face crumpled, and she blew out a breathy sound. I wondered if it was a laugh or a sigh.

'Oh,' she said, 'Oh Meredith! You scared the SHIT out

of me!'

My eyebrows jumped into my hairline at both the NAUGHTY WORD and the fact that I could possibly have scared her.

'But I'm always behind there,' I said.

The breathy sound turned out to be laughter as Evie fell to her knees and put her hands over her face, her shoulders shaking and jumping like the bones in the operation game when you set the buzzer off.

Evie's laughter was something I hadn't heard for weeks and I started to laugh too. Glad I had caused it, even if I didn't know why.

'God, Moo. You're always at the other window. When you moaned and started to push the curtain, I thought you were… well, I don't know… a ghost or something.'

I laughed harder.

'That's silly Evie, Mum says there are no such thing as ghosts.'

'Well, you looked like one. You gave me a right good scare, I'll tell you.'

Evie pulled me down to her and scrubbed the top of my head with her knuckles.

'Nearly gave me a heart attack,' she said.

I didn't understand really, she knew I was behind one or the other. I would have known if it had been the other way round, but then Evie had been taking her time, and her mind seemed more muddled lately. Or maybe she was letting me win this time. That was more like Evie than she had been in ages.

I put my arms around her neck for a cuddle, giggling at her.

And then she hissed through her teeth.

'Bruises, Moo, be careful,' She said.

And I remembered she wasn't back to Evie at all. Not by a long way. I pulled my arms down, and then remembered Egor.

'You scared me too, dummy.' I said with a grin, trying to push down my fear and force my thoughts away from Evie's bruises. Trying not to be a BABY in front of her. I would have swatted her chest, but I wasn't sure where I could touch these days, let alone hit, so I didn't.

Evie frowned.

'Scared you how? I didn't do anything, idiot.'

'You did. You put Egor behind the curtain. *You* nearly gave *me* a HEART ATTACK.'

'You're too young for a heart attack.' She said. 'And I didn't put Egor anywhere.'

She leaned back, placing her hands beside her, and stretching her chest towards me with a groan.

'God my old bones,' she said, in a voice just like mums. 'Egor is in the wardrobe, Moo, where he always is.'

I shook my head and jumped off her lap to pull back the curtain.

Egor sat passive, in the same position, legs stretched toward them.

I gave a huge sigh of RELIEF. At least he wasn't moving like the time I was sick. And then I looked back to Evie.

'See?' I said.

Evie got to her feet, pushing her lips between her teeth, as she grabbed Egor from his perch.

'You shouldn't be messing with him, Moo. The bad man is not to be messed with.'

She looked the bear over.

'Is the bad man still in there?' I asked.

'I'll check the recorder later,' Evie said. 'Probably. Don't touch him again, it's not safe.'

I frowned.

'I didn't take him, Evie, I promise.'

'Then who put him there?' she said.

'I don't know, I thought you did.'

Evie gave me a long look, and then glanced to the bear.

'We need to put him in the cellar, contain him properly. I'll figure it out.' She picked him up by a paw. 'I'm going to put him back upstairs. Stay here and we'll get some noodles for lunch and watch some telly until mum and dad get back. Sound good?'

I nod my head, Egor forgotten now that he was safe with Evie. Noodles were my favourite, and I knew as I'd been scared, that Evie would let me watch what I wanted and cuddle next to me.

There was no better way to spend an afternoon.

CHAPTER FORTY TWO

Silence reverberated around the cellar, and Meredith slowly brought her hands down away from her ears. They rang, leaving a high-pitched whine in her head. The others were looking around slowly too, although no one had risen from their spot on the floor yet. She caught Helen's eye, and Helen looked fearfully back into hers. They held the same question.

Was it safe? Had Elana finished, or was there more?

There was a strange air around Meredith that she couldn't quite put her finger on. The air seemed to swirl, encompassing her, although there was no breeze felt on her skin, no stirring of her clothes, and no hair on her head moved. It was a gentle non-breeze, if that was even a thing.

Like the *impression* of air.

Meredith felt the pressure of it, which made her feel a little lightheaded and out of focus. When nothing else happened, one by one, everyone got to their feet. Meredith felt she had been crouched for years, but it had probably only been seconds, her knees groaned and creaked, and pins and needles ran through her left foot. She shook it out gently with a grimace.

'Everyone okay?' She said.

There were a couple of yeses, and more nods, but the relaxed atmosphere had gone. The nerves of the group were well and truly back.

Let's just keep everyone calm and see what we can find out.

She let out a long breath. Seeing it cloud before her sent her heart rate notching up a gear.

Fabulous.

And then she checked herself. This was what she needed, wasn't it? What she was here for. If Elana was here, then there was no better time to get started, and she may as well delve right to the crux of the matter, hadn't she? It was better than Elana not showing up at all.

Possibly.

'El—'

Meredith opened her mouth to speak to Elana, but Spookbuddy also took the opportunity to state a fact that everyone knew.

'Brrr, it's cold in here,' he said again.

'No shit, sherlock,' She mumbled.

'Ignore her, Buds,' Steve said, rubbing his hands up and down his bare arms. Why he hadn't brought a jumper was beyond her. He not only lacked a jumper but his usual jokey vigour.

Meredith looked to the bear, sitting in the corner it's green light vibrant on its chest. Looking so much like Egor, but with one green eye, not two.

Down at his feet three small red lights began to flash. Three to one, and back again.

'The lights are flashing, is that…'

'EMF.' Steve said, 'She's still here. What are you up to Elana? You want to play with the bear?'

Meredith suddenly felt a surge of inspiration.

'Yes, Elana, Spookbuddy would love to play. See if you can touch him.'

There was no response from the bear, but the EMF lights flickered to four.

'I know you're here Elana. You can play with the bear if you like. He's here for you.'

Silence fell over the room again.

'Maybe it's not her?' Helen whispered. Her voice sounding a hundred decibels in the quiet.

'It's her,' Stephanie said, her thick Scottish accent cutting the air, making Meredith flinch. 'There's nothing else in this castle I assure you.'

Meredith raised her eyebrows at Helen, and then Spookbuddy broke the silence, giggling like a small child.

'That tickles!'

'Tickles?' Meredith looked to Steve.

'A response to being touched,' Steve said. 'Touch Spookbuddy again Elana, he loves to be tickled.'

The bear laughed again, responding perfectly.

Right, we have her back and responsive, maybe her attention aimed at the bear is a good thing.

Matt swung the camera back her way, and Meredith thought they had better get on with this, or they'd be here all night.

'Elana, will you talk to us now? Can we maybe go to tapping? One tap for yes, two for no?'

No response. Meredith waited a beat before asking more.

'Okay, how—'

Spookbuddy cut her off again, this time with questions of his own...

'Hi, I'm Spookbuddy, What's your name?'

Meredith swung her head to him, raising her eyebrows.

'Are you finished?' She muttered, but here in the cellar it reverberated around the walls, causing giggles amongst the others in the room.

'I think he's done,' Matt said with a grin.

Spookbuddy stayed passive, blinking EMF lights from his feet.

Meredith eyed the bear—*Egor... No, Spookbuddy*—and felt her heartbeat raise.

Why a damn teddy bear? Of all the things?

She gave herself a mental shake and brought herself back to task.

'Elana, If you're still here, one tap for yes, two for no, Okay?'

Everyone was still and a hush fell over the cellar.

'There.' Helen said. 'Did you hear it?'

Meredith shook her head with a frown.

'Upstairs, a small thud.'

'Okay, if that was you Elana can you tap again? Just so we're sure.'

There was a loud clang, like a boot kicking against the metal Aga upstairs. It sounded like a gunshot in the silence.

Meredith blinked.

No need for sarcasm, Elana.

'Thank you, Elana, that was perfect.' She said with a forced smile for the camera, 'Can we get back to the question from before? I understand if you're a little angry but we're only trying to find out what's keeping you here. If we need to find your bones then we can help, but not if you start to throw and bang things around. Do you understand Elana?'

There was a small tap from upstairs again. Meredith looked to Helen, who nodded a yes.

'I heard a tap,' Stephanie said, from the other side of Meredith. It took Meredith all of her steel not to jump as she swung her head to Stephanie with a nod.

Stephanie had moved toward them, away from the door where she had been standing with Orla, who was now fingering a rosary necklace, eyes closed, lips moving in silent incantation. Stephanie gave a small shrug and Meredith smiled reassuringly.

'Elana, thank you. Can you tell us, did you die here?'

There was a stirring of air to match the already chill air in the room. This time Meredith's hair lifted, and she pulled her coat closed, zipping it with a shudder.

'Elana?' She said.

There was a thud from the kitchen.

'Yes.' Helen said. Meredith felt a pang of sympathy for the little girl.

'All right, sweetie, I'm sorry about that.'

'Someone get Meredith her pills,' Steve said from one corner of his mouth.

'Shhh,' Helen said, waving an arm at him. Meredith could have kissed her, the joke was funny, but right now she didn't want to break the atmosphere.

'Was your death an accident?'

A knock from upstairs.

'Yes?' Stephanie whispered.

Meredith frowned.

'Okay, that's good Elana, you're doing well, but now I'm confused…'

There was another knock which sounded further away in the castle, or maybe she was just tapping lighter now. Meredith carried on.

'Asha said that your bones are under the boiler. Is that right?'

A thud. Louder now, back above their heads.

Helen shifted. 'Why are the bones under the boiler if it was an accident? Why wasn't she buried properly?'

Meredith shrugged. This wasn't making any sense at all. Meredith supposedly knew the truth of something she had no idea about, and Elana's bones were under the boiler—but it was an accident. Where the hell was this going?

'I don't know, how can we ask? We need the Ghost box back.'

Stephanie let out a small ooohhhh on her breath.

'Maybe her death was concealed, poor mite.'

There was a thud from over their heads again, and a swirl of cold wind wound around Meredith's legs.

'Anyone else get the cold wind?' She said.

'Me,' Helen said, and Matt, Steve and Stephanie nodded.

Good, all in unison. Either all having a paranormal experience, or all experiencing that phenomenon called a draft.

Tonight, Meredith couldn't hear the wind though, it was pretty calm outside and there hadn't been a draft when they first came down.

'Just to confirm Elana, your death was covered up?'

There was a beat of silence where she thought there would be no reply and then a single knock. Further away, but there all the same.

'Why was it covered up if it was an accident?' Meredith mumbled, wondering where to go with a line of questioning that would give only a yes or no answer.

'Protection maybe?'

Meredith met Matt's eyes.

'How?' She said.

'Like, protection of the person who committed the crime. I mean was it someone she knew? Someone who…'

The door to the room flung open, bouncing off the wall, with a screech that emitted so loud and long that they all had their hands over their ears.

'I guess we got it,' Steve said, as the door hit it's housing and clicked quietly shut again.

Meredith had a faint memory of trying to shut the door while they were here last, and not being able to budge it.

'Okay, Elana, we've got you. Just answer yes or no. Did someone kill you? By accident?'

A scrape, over in the corner. Meredith took that as a yes.

'Did you know them?'

There was a small tug on Meredith's hair, and she felt a sadness wash over her. This was just a little girl by all accounts. She wished she could give her a hug. For a fleeting second, she wished she could put a face to a name, but only came up with Asha's sneering features.

'Yes,' Meredith said aloud.

'I didn't hear anything,' Matt said, adjusting the camera on his shoulder. There were murmurs of agreement from around the room.

'The hair tugs are back,' Meredith said.

'Fantastic,' Helen responded.

'Communicate how you want to, Elana,' she said, smiling at Helen, who poked out her tongue.

'Was this person who had the… the accident a friend

Elana?' Helen's hand flew to her head. 'Ouch. That's a no.'

'Not a friend,'

Meredith fell silent and frowned in thought.

'So, this person was known to her, but not a friend.'

There were footsteps upstairs in the kitchen, loud and clear. Not the steps of the paranormal, but the steps of a person. Meredith swung to Stephanie, her mouth dropping open.

'Is there someone else here?' She said.

Stephanie shook her head, and then turned to the corner where Orla was now missing.

'Orla!' she shouted, her voice reverberating around the room.

'Fuck!' Steve whispered under his breath and Meredith grinned as he clutched at his heart.

'I can't do this any longer,' Orla called from the kitchen area.

'Do what?' Stephanie said.

'I can't be down there. Carry on without me, I'll be in the living room.'

'No, Orla,' Stephanie said, lunging for the bottom of the stairs, just visible from the doorway. 'The pictures keep being thrown. I don't like the thought of you up there alone.'

'Elana is down there with you, I'll be fine,' Her voice faded as her footsteps disappeared across to the carpeted hallway.

Stephanie gave a huge sigh and placed a hand over her face, Meredith felt a tug of pity. Orla had never shown as much care for Stephanie's feelings as Stephanie had shown for hers. People were different, and Meredith was sure that Stephanie knew and loved her exactly as she was, but right now, this seemed callous. Orla knew how worried Stephanie was about her, and yet she went with no compromise.

'Come on Stephanie, She's right about one thing. Elana is with us. She'll be fine.' She said.

Stephanie looked unsure. She glanced to Meredith and

back up the stairs again. Steve, Matt, and Helen watched her, impatient to get on with the investigation.

Meredith looked at her watch.

9.45pm

Already?

They had to wrap this up, or leave soon, or they risked not being up in the morning to get to Stanmore.

'Stephanie?' She urged.

Stephanie nodded and returned to the group, coming in closer, between Helen and Meredith.

'Okay?' Helen said.

Stephanie nodded.

Meredith took one of Stephanie's hands, glad to see that Helen had followed suit and taken the other. It was an energy building comfort exercise Meredith thought.

'I like hugs!' Spookbuddy declared from the corner.

'Motion trigger, he's been touched,' Steve said.

'Okay, let's get back to Elana,' Meredith said, conscious of the time.

'Right, so we know that she knew this person, but they weren't a friend.' Helen said.

'A friend of your parents, Elana?' Meredith tried. There was no response, and Meredith looked to Helen for a hair tug, but Helen shook her head.

'Was this person close to you, Elana?' Stephanie said.

There was a tug on Meredith's hair.

'Yes,' she said, turning to Stephanie.

Stephanie gave her a sad smile.

'Usually the case,' she said with a shrug. 'I wonder if…'

'I like good stories, please tell me one.' Spookbuddy piped up.

Meredith closed her eyes.

'Steve, I'm starting to think Spookbuddy is a liability. Really.'

Steve looked over at the bear with a pout.

'Don't say that, he's just doing his job. He's coming good. Trust me.'

Meredith shook her head, more inclined to get the investigation over rather than argue about a bear. She turned back to Stephanie.

'Go on,' She said.

'Do you want to play?' Spookbuddy said.

'Steve!' Meredith said.

Steve held his free hand up to the ceiling.

'Elana must be around him. He's being a good ghosthunter.'

'Why is he interrupting us? It's the most annoying thing I've ever had the misfortune of working with… and I include Kevin in that remit.'

Steve shrugged as Helen tittered. Matt turned the camera to Steve with a grin.

'More annoying than Steve?' He said.

'They're level pegging at the moment. Do something with the bear. Really.'

Matt chuckled as Steve turned Spookbuddy off, and then switched him back on again. Meredith waited until his annoying, but necessary start-up sequence had finished before she turned to Stephanie again.

'Let's try again, what were you saying?'

'Brrr it's cold in here.' Spookbuddy announced. Meredith gave Steve a black look.

Steve grimaced and shrugged but made no move to switch him off. Meredith let it go for now, not only annoyed at Spookbuddy, but Steve's nonchalance, and Matt's amusement at her reactions.

'I wonder if the person was family. Close but not a friend… it would make sense would it not?' Stephanie said.

A breeze gust around the group, and Helen pulled her coat closer to her.

'Okay,' Meredith said, 'Elana? Was it a—'

The breeze seemed to whip around Meredith, making her

dizzy as there was a small tug on her hair. She wanted to say yes but the air had become so oppressive and heavy, that she felt pushed down. Laden with weight that shouldn't be on her shoulders.

Her knees hit the floor first as the room spun and then a small girl appeared in her vision. A girl who reminded Meredith of herself as a youngster.

The girl looked solemn. Her large brown eyes filled with such sadness that Meredith let out her own sob. The girl's blonde hair hung in strings as she placed both hands over her mouth and proceeded to emit the loudest, most piercing scream Meredith had ever heard.

Meredith felt her head hit the concrete floor, felt the bounce, heard the yells of the others but couldn't see them. And then the world turned off.

CHAPTER FORTY THREE

Meredith walked through the castle, yet not the castle. She knew where she was, and yet it was different. Unsettling, and very, very cold.

The girl walked in front, through the hallway, and to the stairs which wound up to the first floor.

She turned to Meredith at the bottom, giving her a look that made her heart pound. Stringy hair stuck to the side of her face with something wet, possibly tears by the streaks of dirt that ran down her cheeks and neck, dirtying the collar of her cream tartan dress.

The colour was off. The girl was pale enough as it was, and this made her look almost grey.

Why would her mother put her in something that made her look so... dead?

The dress shifted and Meredith was drawn back to its thick material, Cream with red check, hanging just below her knee.

No—black, just above the knee.

Black?

Meredith blinked.

Cream tartan. Definitely tartan.

Meredith felt her head spin and a throbbing pain over her eyes as the girl looked at her. There was something behind those eyes, something that shifted and changed in the expression. One sad and melancholy, the other terrified and pleading.

Meredith brought a hand to her head and rubbed, closing her eyes.

When she opened them, the girl was more than halfway up the stairs. She felt a pull in her abdomen and started up behind the girl, holding the handrail for support. Her head swam and the low light seemed to flicker. Meredith looked down to see the rail flex and change under her hand, from one rail to another. A familiar rail, and yet one she couldn't place.

She wanted to ask the girl who she was, but when she opened her mouth to speak, no sound formed the words, so she dropped quiet.

At the first floor, the girl continued down the corridor. The plush deep red carpet, at once soft under her feet and then threadbare. Red and plush, and then a dirty mustard. Her feet were both quiet and clomping on floorboard below her shoes. She heard them, and yet it was silent.

The corridor spun and she put a hand to the wall.

'Wait,' She called to the girl soundlessly, as the tartan dress disappeared round a corner.

The landing flickered and changed around her, and Meredith thought she may be sick. Scouting her surroundings and seeing nothing in the way, she closed her eyes, trailing a hand on the wall as she moved forward.

What the hell are you doing Meredith, get out of here. Who the hell is this girl?

The words seemed to float out of her mind as she trailed forward, eyes closed, pulled by some indiscriminate need to find out what was going on, and what the girl needed to say.

Her foot tapped something ahead and Meredith opened her eyes.

Wall. Where the corridor turned, where the girl had turned, where Meredith now turned, hoping to see some sign of where the child had gone, and hoping that the walls would stay still.

What she didn't expect to see was the girl herself.

Right in front of her.

Black hair hanging in her eyes, black t-shirt, and skirt. Her eyes, rimmed with kohl, looked urgent and terrified.

'Oh!' Meredith said without sound, her heart jolted and

began a marathon as she stepped back, bumping the wall behind her. She jolted forward again with an oomph that was silent in the corridor and looked back to the girl.

Blonde, cream tartan.

She put out a filthy hand to Meredith and then curled her fingers back, nails rimmed with dirt as she beckoned.

Come this way. Come see.

Meredith wasn't sure she wanted to see at all, her heart was jumping now, and her breathing was ragged—except without sound.

The girl turned and Meredith felt the pull again. She started down the hallway after the child, careful not to get too close, blinking her eyes at the stuttering hallway.

It was like being inside an old black and white movie, the picture stalling, and cutting, and jumping, except that this movie was in full colour. Meredith wouldn't have been surprised to hear the old projector clicking away in the background, but there was only silence.

Real, deep, deafening, silence. A silence that consumed everything, and made you question your own sanity. Everything had a *noise*, didn't it? This was like she had no ears, but even then, wouldn't she hear her internal swallows rushing past them?

She swallowed.

Feeling but no sound.

Help me Doctor, I'm insane.

Meredith tittered silently as they climbed more and more stairs.

Is this the actual stairway to heaven?

The girl trailed ahead four or five steps above, these steps stuttered and stalled as the others, but these went from carpet to concrete and back again, carpet going up, concrete going down, the picture flickering and stumbling over itself. Meredith stopped and looked hard at them. Swaying slightly as she held the rail.

Carpet. Going up. Same plush deep red. No flickers. No

concrete.

She frowned and realised it didn't matter.

She felt like she had been drugged. One of those drugs that kept you lucid and awake, while not caring if your leg was being cut off.

She cocked her head to the side, and then looked up to move on.

Black hair, over a pale face, right in front of her. Black eyes pleading and red rimmed under black kohl.

Meredith stumbled back with a silent yell and looked up to see the pale tartan dress disappearing around a landing at the top of the stairs.

'What in the hell?'

Her mouth moved, but the words didn't appear, just circled in her head with no way out, and then the drug pushed them away.

It doesn't matter. It doesn't matter. Follow the girl like a good little Meredith. Are you good Meredith? Are you? Are you really?

She paused a beat to consider, one foot hanging above the next step, figured that she didn't know, and continued on.

Up you go, up you go, Round the corner, round and round the corner, round, and round like a spinning top. Wwwwwweeeeeeeeee!

Meredith stopped to shake the tumbling thoughts from her head.

Doctor? Doctor? Where for art thou doctor?

Frustrated and dizzy, the floors now shifting and changing size in a stuttering pulsating rhythm, Meredith took a breath and slammed her right foot down on her left. Hard.

She shouted silently, but the focus was back. The thoughts gone.

At the end of the corridor ahead, the girl in tartan stood. She faced Meredith, her back to the door to the tower.

Ah. Of course.

Keeping a hand to the wall, Meredith moved toward her.

The girl reached out a hand to open the wooden door.

'No, it's locked sweetheart,' Meredith said, mouth moving with no sound.

The girl opened the door easily and quietly.

Of course she would.

A thick Scottish accent flood into Meredith's ears, the sudden volume forcing her backward. She placed her hands over her ears.

'Rose? If you're up there again so help me God, I'll give you a belting. The tower is not a place for children!'

There was singing behind the woman's rage. Low and soft. A child's voice, singing a child's rhyme, but not in a language Meredith recognised.

The girl started up the stairs and Meredith was unable to do anything but follow.

At the top she saw a blonde girl, knees on the seat, arms hooked over the back to look out of the window over the mountains as she sang her song. The same blonde girl that she had followed through the funhouse, aged around nine. The name came to her in a flash.

Elana.

The girl on the bench spun round and Meredith looked into the girl's big brown eyes, much the same as her own. Meredith was fully focused and alert now. The walls in here weren't shifting. The tower was as it was when she had been up here with Stephanie earlier in the week.

As she looked at Elana a tear slipped down the young girl's cheek. Meredith moved to smooth it away, but Elana wasn't in her world. She was stuck in her own time. She stopped singing and turned to listen to the shouting woman, who was now coming up the stairs from below.

Eyes widening, the girl scrabbled off the bench, trying to find somewhere to hide in a small round room with no furniture but the wall seat. Then it was too late, the woman was here.

'I knew it! I knew you'd be up here. How many times do

you have to be told? Get the hell out of this room!'

The woman ranted, Meredith stared, because the woman that had entered through the doorway was small and stooped, long hair hanging over her face. As much as she looked elderly and infirm her voice said otherwise as she bellowed.

'Do as I say!'

Elana was shaking her head in mock defiance, the terror behind her eyes obvious, and for the first time Meredith heard her little voice. Not the voice of the Ghost Box, but Elana's voice.

'Never!' she shouted, following with a string of her own language.

'You'll speak our language here. I know you understand me, and you know to stay the hell out of this tower. Now get!'

Elana shook her head.

'No! I hate you!' She screamed.

And the rest was like slow motion.

The stooped woman shot out a hand, grabbing the small child by the arm and swinging her toward the doorway. Meredith was sure the intention was to forcefully show her back to the stairs, but the stairs were just too close, the woman too strong. Elana fell back, her head falling over the stairwell, the momentum driving her down. With no hands to break her fall she bounced to the bottom as the woman at the top fell to her knees.

'Rose!' She screamed, but it was too late. They all knew it was too late. Meredith peeked down the stairs, saw the blood spreading from the child's head, and looked away, closing her eyes.

When she opened them, the scene was gone. The tower empty.

No, not quite.

Empty of everything but ghost Elana who was staring down the stairs, tears silently coursing down her cheeks.

'Ma-ma.' She whispered in broken English.

And Meredith broke out in goosebumps.

Her mother.

An accident.

Meredith looked back to the small concrete stairs. If Elana had fallen down any other set of stairs in the castle she would probably have survived, but this set were so small. Narrow and crooked.

She shook her head. It was sad, and it was tragic, there was no doubt about that, but that wasn't where the story ended.

'I don't understand.' She said, surprised to hear the words as she said them.

She turned to Elana, and Elana looked back, eyes red rimmed and filled with tears that still spilled over, wetting her face, running into the collar of her dress.

She extended a dirty hand to Meredith. Meredith looked at it. The intent was clear, but she was unsure. Elana pleaded with her eyes, her bottom lip wobbling.

'Please.' She whispered.

The hair stood up at the back of Meredith's neck at the small girl's innocent, almost sweet voice.

How was this the same Elana with the attitude. The same Elana that had threatened and poked at her at every opportunity.

Another large tear fell over onto her cheek and Meredith could take it no more. She extended her hand to meet the child's. Warm fingers meeting cold.

Elana nodded to the stairs and again the intent was clear. Meredith was to go first. Her heart thud against her ribs as she moved to the stairwell, determined to protect the little girl, whatever was to happen next. But at the top of the stairs Elana tugged back, pulling Meredith to a stop as her foot hovered over the first step.

'What's the matter?' she said, looking back over her shoulder.

Behind her Elana flickered, black top and black skirt,

huge black eyes, made worse by the streaking kohl that had been dragged around them.

Meredith gasped and tried to pull her hand from the girl's, but the grip was tight and firm.

The girl took a step forward, her terrified eyes boring into Meredith's, and then she opened her mouth.

'Know the truth.' She said.

Meredith blinked. Was this still the same Elana, a darker side of Elana, or another spirit entirely? Heart hammering now, her clammy hand shaking in Elana's, she didn't move. The girl moved closer, cocking her head on to one side, her face inches from Meredith's.

'THE TRUUUTTTHHH!' The girl screeched.

Meredith took a step back, teetering on the top step of the stairs.

And then the girl screamed, her mouth stretched wide to expose her broken teeth and chapped lips, her terrified, crazed expression, sent Meredith stepping backwards into air.

There was a moment when she realised what she had done, and then she was falling.

CHAPTER FORTY FOUR

DECEMBER—15 DAYS UNTIL DEATH

'Evie!' I yelled as my foot slipped and I felt myself FALLING.

I hit air, which whistled past my ears as my hands whirled, trying to grab hold of something, anything, and then my backside hit the floor with a painful thud.

I saw Evie's outline in the light of the doorway but there was no other light down here in the cellar. The light had GONE Dad said. I wasn't sure how a light could GO anywhere. It wasn't like it had legs, and the bulb was still there, sitting in the white light bulb holder which hung from the ceiling.

I had tried to tell dad the light was still hanging a few days ago, but the NEWS was on, and he had simply waved a hand that meant I was to be quiet.

'What the heck are you doing Meredith?' Evie called down.

There were two Evie's I noticed. One at the top of the stairs, covered in darkness, and one that draped down the stairs, elongated and stretched by the light from behind.

'Ow.' I said, tears forming in my eyes. 'I fell.'

Two triangles of light appeared either side of Evie, outlined in a black line that stretched from her shoulders to her hips.

'Well, are you okay? Or are you being a baby?'

'I'm okay,' I mumbled at the floor, not wanting her to see my wobbly bottom lip and the tear that splodged onto the floor. I wiped it away quickly as I got to my feet.

My BACKSIDE and leg hurt but I ignored them as I

climbed up to Evie. She rubbed my head as I got to the top.

'Dad should fix the light,' she said.

When we had come down to the cellar earlier Evie had flicked the switch up and down, but the bulb hadn't lit so we had come down in the darkness, putting the hall light on and holding the door open with a box of kitchen stuff that mum cleared out months ago. The name on the box said CHARITY.

I didn't know who CHARITY was, but I wasn't sure they wanted our old stuff as they hadn't picked them up yet. The box had a layer of dust on the top that we had blown off after Evie had written her name in it. Then we had pushed it out of the kitchen and against the open door to the cellar.

'That'll do.' Evie had said.

And we had gone down using the light from the hall which she said would have to be enough.

'Right, Moo.' She said now, brushing dirt from my back. 'If you're okay, shall we get him?'

I looked up at her and nodded my head once IMPORTANTLY. Dad said that all IMPORTANT nods had IMPORTANT BUSINESS, and I felt that this task should certainly be classed as IMPORTANT BUSINESS.

'What the hell is this mess?' Mum said as she came out of the living room. Her hair was wild, like she hadn't brushed it for years, and she was still in her pyjamas, even though it was after school now. I noticed the big stain that had splodged on her top like a decoration and wondered what it was.

'What mess?' Evie said.

I stared at mum and wrinkled my nose. She smelled like vinegar, although why she would be drinking vinegar was beyond me. Unless it was part of her illness.

'This,' she said, waving a hand toward the door and the box that we were standing by, 'and probably all of the mess you've left down there.'

'No, we haven't, we were just, er, playing...' Evie shot

me a look and I said the words before I knew they were coming out of my mouth.

'Hide and seek.' I said.

Evie's eyes went wide.

'Exactly,' she said, 'Hide and seek.'

Mum waved a hand to cut her off.

'Ah, what the hell, you never listen to me anyway. Get it tidied up when you're finished or there will be HELL TO PAY.'

Mum shuffled off into the kitchen and came back with a small beaker of water, leaving a trail of the vinegar smell behind her.

I made a mental note to remind Evie to clean up the box afterward because I really worried about PAYING HELL. If I was paying HELL, and that was a place, then surely I would be paying whoever was the boss. And that was the DEVIL. Not only did I not intend to meet the Devil EVER, but if I happened to in this instance what was I supposed to PAY him WITH? I had no money, and I wasn't sure what the DEVIL would do with money anyway. Would he keep me down there, in HELL, if I had nothing to PAY with?

I chewed the side of my mouth with my teeth and frowned, thinking hard.

'Moo? Are you even listening?'

I blinked and looked to Evie who was staring down into my face, hand on her hips.

'You didn't hear a word I said, did you?'

I shook my head, and then I could hold it in no longer.

'Evie, what would we PAY HELL WITH? I don't get it.'

Evie rolled her eyes and swept her long dark hair over to one side where it hung limply over a shoulder.

'Meredith, why do you worry about the stupidest things?'

'Mum said that there would be HELL TO PAY—'

Evie stared at me, and then gave a small titter.

'Ah,' she said, 'Moo, don't worry about it, really. I heard dad saying that mum had already made a deal with the devil last night. It's fine, lets…'

My mouth dropped open, and my heart seemed to stop.

'Mum has made a DEAL with the DEVIL?'

Evie raised her eyebrows and glanced to the living room.

'Shhh, and no! It's just an expression, silly Moo. No one has ever even seen the devil.'

'Cassie Jones' mum has,' I said, horror filling my stomach and lining it with lead. I remembered the conversation I had overheard between Cassie and Holly at school. 'Holly said that Cassie's mum had DANCED with the DEVIL before. I don't know where, maybe—'

Evie burst out laughing and I shut my mouth, hurt that she would find something so serious so funny. The DEVIL was a NASTY BUSINESS. Even I knew that.

'Moo, you're such a card, really!'

She laughed loudly until mum shouted from the living room.

'Play somewhere else or shut up will you, I can't hear the damn TV over you girls.'

Evie slapped a hand over her mouth and cocked her head to the side, motioning to the stairs. We climbed them together up into Evie's room before letting our giggles come out.

'What's got into moody Margaret?' Evie said.

Moody Margaret made me laugh harder. It suited mum and I wondered why her name would be Nancy, and not Margaret which suited her better.

'Shh,' Evie said.

I stopped my giggles as I looked at her.

'Okay, Moo, this is the important bit. Are we ready to do it?'

I nod my head getting back to the IMPORTANT BUSINESS.

'Let's get him,' I said. 'Egor is toast.'

CHAPTER FORTY FIVE

Air whooshed passed Meredith's ears as she fell—for far too long to be possible—down, down, down the small spiral staircase. She had a moment to wonder how she hadn't hit the walls at all, when the blackness and falling sensation disappeared, and Meredith was standing, upright and motionless in Lynton Castle's living room.

She looked around with a frown, the girl in the tower and the sensation of falling still with her even as her feet stood on solid ground.

Except that it wasn't solid.

The stuttering film was back. The living room at Lynton constantly shifting and interchanging with somewhere else. The thick, plush, dark patterned carpet at Lynton shifting with an equally patterned but thinner carpet. This one tufted and unforgiving. The sort that salesmen called hard-waring, tough, hard, but not comfortable.

Meredith looked to the fire to see that it was doing the same. The roaring open coal fire of Lynton stuttering and flickering, changing places with another smaller fireplace. Brick, electric. The sort with the small cream element bars that heated to an angry read when the fire was lit, laying horizontal, contrasting with the small vertical steel bars of the outer casing and protection.

It was a weird contrast, and one that was so out of joint it made Meredith's head spin.

What is going on, and why does nothing stay still?

She looked left and saw the girl in the cream dress beside her. Tartan. Blonde hair.

Elana.

Elana was staring at the heavy oak door. No, white.

Heavy oak. White…

Meredith closed her eyes and shook her head.

No more.

Sobbing. There was sobbing from somewhere in the castle. A touch on her hand brought Meredith's eyes back to Elana, who looked to Meredith and then to the door, which swung open, and shut with a bang as the shuffling woman entered, a handkerchief over her face and phone to her ear. She limped to the fireplace, almost standing on her own thin floor length dress as she stared down into it with a sob.

'No, John. No. I can't. I won't. How can I?'

She paused a moment before her voice took a pleading tone.

'Is there no other way? There must be. There must be something!'

She moved the handkerchief from her face and placed the back of her hand to her head with a sniff.

As Meredith watched, the woman flickered with the room, the roaring fire replaced with the small electric fireplace, the woman lost the dress and gained faded baggy jeans and an oversized cream jumper. Her back was to Meredith, as was the woman in the dress, but she seemed to be wringing her hands. Meredith strained forward to see, but the image was there for mere seconds before changing back to the room at Lynton.

The woman placed a hand on the mantlepiece, her fingers pushing pictures, her dress almost in the fire itself.

'Oh, dear Lord. I can't… Oh, John… I can't do this.'

She collapsed into a heap before the fire, sobs wrenching at her body. The woman in the jeans and jumper sobbed also, but standing, and then back to her knees as the dress returned, like some strange flick book.

'I know. I know it. Yes, I can say she ran away.' There was a pause, and then 'I understand.'

The sobs were subsiding to snuffling as the woman nod her head. Lank hair bobbing around her hunched shoulders.

'Yes. Yes, there's the cellar. I know a place. I can guarantee her not being found. The cellar is to be newly concreted next week.'

The room flickered and the woman and a new man changed places.

It was dark, the floor hard under Meredith's feet, only a small shaft of light falling on a concrete stairway, the fireplace gone.

Meredith frowned and clenched her jaw with a silent grunt.

I can't keep up, what the hell is going on?

As the scene flickered, it looked like the man was on his knees, he was shroud in darkness, but appeared to have his head in his hands. The woman in the jeans and jumper put her own hands on his shoulders.

Meredith scrubbed her eyes with the heel of her hand and shook her head.

What was wrong with this picture? And something about that damn fireplace was lending itself a creeping familiarity through Meredith's confusion.

She turned to Elana.

'I want to go,' She said, 'I know what happened to you here, I get it, I'm so sorry, I am, but I'm done.'

They were back to silence. No sound, just words that went to nowhere. Whether Elana heard or not she shook her head slowly and pointed back to the fire.

The woman moaned, an awful moan of deep despair, and simultaneously the man moaned at the woman's feet, the picture shifting and jerking. Meredith felt sick, there was nowhere steady, nothing solid to keep hold of. Her vision and stomach were rolling, and she didn't know how much more she could take.

'I said I'll do it. I can do it.' The woman said angrily, all tears stopped now. 'It won't come to that. I have the story. It was a bloody accident for God's sake!'

Her voice was rising to a rage, and simultaneously the

woman in jeans took her place. Her voice was also a rage.

'It was a bloody accident, just leave it! Leave her alone!'

Meredith's vision flickered, her head spun, and everything dissolved and went black. She felt herself falling to nowhere, as a piercing screech joined her.

'YOU KNOW THE TRUTH!' It screamed as another, stronger, voice joined it.

'FIND MY BONES!'

Meredith clamped her hands over her ears, blocking out the sound with a scream of her own.

CHAPTER FORTY SIX

'Meredith? Meredith! Wake up.'

Meredith became aware of something hard and cold underneath her. A cold so dense it penetrated her bones. She had to get up.

Her eyes fluttered open and blurry outlines appeared around her.

'Meredith!' It was Matt's voice, but he wasn't quite in focus yet, 'Water, get her some water.'

One of the blurry outlines moved and Meredith tried to get up.

Hands pushed her back down.

'Don't move, you hit your head.'

'I'm okay,' she said, struggling to a sitting position as her vision finally decided it belonged to her. Matt crouched straight ahead, hands now on her shoulders, Helen was to his left, Steve to his right. Stephanie was missing, and Meredith deduced that she was the one who had gone for water.

Thank heaven, because her throat was drier than a desert, and seemed to be full of as much sand. She turned to the side spitting not sand, but dirt.

'How are you feeling?' Matt said with a squeeze on her shoulder.

Meredith gave herself a mental scan. Yes, there was a patch that ached on the back of her head. She put a hand up to it and felt a small lump under her hair. Nothing major and no blood. Her knees also felt a little sore, other than that she felt good. Just confused.

'I'm okay,' she said again, feeling a little more with it. Lynton. She was at Lynton Castle, in the cellar.

On the floor?

344

'What happened?'

Steve stood and shook out his legs.

'Thought you were doing a 'Donald' on us, Bangers,' Steve added, 'One minute you were talking to Elana, the next you seemed to go funny. I thought 'aye, aye, here comes the takeover' and then you dropped. Out cold. Gone. No possession, no Meredith.'

Helen shook her head and rolled her eyes.

'We don't know,' she said, crouching back onto her heels with a sigh of relief now that Meredith seemed to be okay. 'Steve is right, you were communicating with Elana and then seemed to just... go down.'

'A fairly slow fall to be honest, which was lucky, could have been so much worse,' Matt said. He gave a visible sigh of relief and grinned at her. 'Imagine having to explain that one to Kevin in the morning!'

Meredith smiled but something was sitting on the edge of consciousness. Pushing and nudging. Something she should remember.

She zoned out, thinking as the others talked, to her and over her.

Elana, I was talking to Elana...

She crinkled her forehead in thought. It was right there if she could just reach out and grab it.

And then images came, thick and fast.

A flash of a tower. The girl. The hallways, the stairways, the living room.

Lynton.

'Elana!' She said getting to her feet so fast that Matt had to scoot back or be knocked over. A rush of adrenaline coursed through her as Stephanie came back with the water. She halted uncertain, in the doorway, and Meredith called her through with a flick of her hand.

If there was one thing more important than Elana right now, it was water.

Stephanie came forward and Meredith took the water,

downing the whole glass in one.

'Wow, I needed that,' She said pushing the glass back to Stephanie, 'Thank you.'

Stephanie looked at her in amusement, and then they were all laughing. Meredith wasn't sure what at, so she smiled at them. The kind of smile you would give the lunatics in an asylum when they thought they had said something hilarious, and you had no idea what was going on, but didn't want to be murdered over the fact.

She waited for the laughter to die away.

'What's so funny?' She said.

Helen giggled and wrapped her arms around herself.

'The way you said Elana, like it was the most important thing on earth... until a glass of water showed up.'

Elana. Of course.

Meredith smiled and then heaved a sigh.

'Well, I guess it is important. As is water.' She looked to Stephanie. 'Elana, yes. You'll need your cellar digging to lay her to rest. She's down here for sure.'

Stephanie's mouth dropped open.

'What?' Her face offered a mixture of relief, horror, and confusion. 'I don't...'

'I saw it... I think. I'm fairly sure.'

Steve heaved a laugh from the corner where he was checking over Spookbuddy.

'She was doing a Donald after all.'

'Not a possession,' she said. 'More like a dream, but a very real dream. I saw Elana pushed down the stairs in the tower. Her mother did it, she was shouting at her, saying she shouldn't be up there, but it was an accident, she didn't mean to push her down. There was a phone call after with a man. She discussed burying the body in the cellar as it was to be newly concreted. She said it would never be found here.'

'Guess she was wrong.' Helen said.

Meredith nod her head.

'Newly concreted?' Stephanie said.

Meredith turned to her. She shuddered. She thought she had never been so cold. Her hands were like ice.

'I don't know who she was talking to obviously, but she seemed to be reassuring him that Elana would never be found, and that she would make up some story that she ran away. She must have been around nine or so, poor thing. Incredibly young.'

Meredith put a cold hand over Stephanie's, warmth radiated into hers, but Stephanie didn't seem to notice.

'She just wants out. She hates it down here, I suppose. That's all she wants.'

So, we need to dig the cellar, find the bones, and bury them.' Stephanie said lightly. 'Where do we start?'

'The boiler?' Matt said. 'Asha always had trouble with the boiler, didn't she?' He turned to Meredith who nod her head, looking back to Stephanie.

'I'd say it's a good bet.'

Stephanie was nodding.

'Right,' she said. 'I'll sort something first thing tomorrow. Let's get you all a warm drink before you go, you're freezing Meredith.'

The group shuffled from the cellar, Meredith bringing up the rear, she stopped to look at the old boiler boards as she passed. There was a gentle breeze that wound its way around the cellar. Warming. Almost a caress on Meredith's cheeks.

'You're welcome Elana,' Meredith whispered, a sense of calm washing over her.

* * * * *

Orla had gone to bed and the teacups were in the sink before Matt nudged Meredith with his shoe. She turned to him. It was after 11pm and she was exhausted but relaxed. She was sure that Elana would cause no more trouble now that the cellar was to be dug. Stephanie and Meredith had swapped numbers so that the family could keep her updated, and she really hoped that this would be the end of it.

Meredith clamped a hand to her mouth, concealing a yawn and feeling like she could sleep dreamlessly for a thousand years. Matt cocked an eyebrow.

'Did you want to look at the servant's bell before we go? I'm sure Stephanie could do with some rest, and we certainly could too.'

The servant's bell hadn't entered Meredith's thoughts since they entered the cellar, but now it jolted her awake.

'Oh, yes!'

Now that Elana had been dealt with (fingers and toes tightly crossed, because this family deserved some respite) Meredith felt her interest at Kevin's rigging coming to the fore again. Now they'd had real, conclusive, activity tonight it wasn't important for Meredith going forward, but it would be interesting to know either way. Was Kevin duping them all?

'The bell?' Stephanie said. 'What's happened with the bell?'

Meredith looked to Matt. He gave a small nod to go ahead. If there was any damage to be done by finding this information, it had been done by now. It was unlikely Kevin would speak to Stephanie or Orla again anyway.

'The footage we shot here, and the Ghost box activity, all appeared to be legit, except the servants bell. It appears that Mr Spalding may be rigging activity, but we just wondered if we could check. Has anyone been near the bell since we were here?'

Stephanie shook her head, perplexed.

'We don't use the bell. It was disconnected a fair while ago. No one has been near it for years.' Stephanie said, glancing at it sitting innocently on the wall. Pitted brass, unpolished, dusty with age. 'There were others back in the day, but most had been removed before we came here. We like it, it adds character and history, the chime ball is inside, but it doesn't work.'

'May I?' Matt asked, motioning to the bell.

'Of course,' Stephanie said, 'It makes no difference to us now that we know what we must do, just handle it carefully, it's very old. Stand on a chair if you need to.'

Matt nodded and Meredith, who was nearest the bell, got up to offer him her seat to stand on. She leaned against the wall so that she could see the bell as he looked. He hadn't touched it before he looked down at her, lips pursed.

'How long would you say it's been since this was touched.' He asked Stephanie.

'Oh God, we don't even clean it unless the dust is an inch thick, we forget it's there. It's got to have been a good few months now.'

'Enough to have a layer of dust then at least?'

'At the very least,' Stephanie said.

He looked back to Meredith.

'No dust?' She said.

He shook his head.

'Nothing. It's shiny on top.'

'Not possible,' Stephanie said.

Meredith frowned as Matt leaned over to look underneath at the small chime ball that still hung inside.

'Ah,' He said.

Meredith's heart kicked up a flutter of excitement.

Foul play, Kevin Spalding? Really?

She grinned as Matt traced his hand down something invisible, his thumb and forefinger pinched.

'What is it?' Meredith said, hardly able to keep the excitement out of her voice.

Matt flicked his hand, and the bell gave a resounding bong making everyone jump.

Helen stuck her fingers in her ears.

'You could have bloody warned us, Matilda.' Steve said wiggling a finger in the ear nearest the bell.

'Wires,' Matt said.

'What?' Stephanie got up off her own chair and moved

to Matt's side, putting her fingers up to his. 'Fishing wire, I should think,' she said, 'How in the hell did that get there?'

'Mr Spalding.' Meredith and Steve said together.

'But why?' Stephanie said, crossing her arms over her chest. 'And when?'

'Probably when we were setting up and doing interviews I should think,' Matt said, stepping down from the stool, 'It wouldn't take him long, it's only tied loosely around the chime.'

'The why is harder when we had activity anyway,' Meredith finished.

'So why would you think it's him?' Stephanie asked.

'We saw him. Each time the bell rang on the footage his shoe appeared.'

'He wasn't supposed to be in shot at all,' Helen said, 'And he was standing outside of our view obviously because he surely would have to have lifted his foot quite high.'

Matt shook his head. 'He was only just outside of the shot. I had wondered whether to ask him to move. If I hadn't been concentrating on you guys, I probably would have seen him do it, but it wouldn't take much of a flick to set this off.'

Meredith was intrigued. Did the wire go all the way into the cellar? And how did Kevin ever find it again and rig it to his shoe without them noticing?

'I want to find the end.' She said, looking to the cellar door.

'Go for it,' Stephanie said with a yawn. 'You've solved one mystery tonight, it's the least we can do.'

Meredith thanked her and then she had the wire in her hand. It was fairly tight, not much play in it and she couldn't understand why until she reached the floor, where it was loosely taped to the old skirting with clear tape.

'Ooh, he's crafty,' She said.

From the floor she followed the wire to the cellar door, where it was taped again and finally down the cellar steps. She was in the boiler room, tracing the wire to its large loop on the end before, she realised that the others had followed her.

She held it aloft.

'Looped.' She said. 'He must have slipped it over his foot. What an idiot.'

'Why bother?' Helen said.

Meredith shook her head and handed the loop to Stephanie. 'I guess you'll need this to take it down, I'm sorry our director is such an ass. He probably would have removed it after the shoot if we hadn't been gathered in the kitchen with the Ghost box footage.'

Stephanie smiled as she took the wire.

'Not such an ass, he let you come back and help us tonight, that is very much appreciated. Much more than you'll ever know.'

Meredith glanced to Matt and Steve, who were huddled together, arms folded against the chill.

'He doesn't know we're here,' Matt said to Stephanie, 'If he calls to ask—'

'I haven't seen you,' Stephanie said with a smile, nodding her head toward the teddy bear that still sat in the far corner. 'Listen, I'll let you collect your things while I wash the cups, I guess you need to get back, and I need some sleep. I have a feeling tonight will be a quiet one thanks to you.'

A chill worked its way around Meredith's legs, and she felt a sense of Deja vu. She looked to the bear.

Spookbuddy could stay in this cellar forever for all she cared, and all the help he had been. She watched as Stephanie grinned at them and turned, heading back up the cellar steps leaving the four of them alone in the cellar.

Meredith shuddered, unsettled, but couldn't put her finger on why. Elana had been dealt with, hadn't she?

'Meredith?' Helen said.

Meredith shook herself of the menacing air that seemed to permeate the room.

'Let's go,' she said quietly, still looking for shadows that weren't there.

'You okay, Bangers?' Steve said.

'Yeah, just… I don't know, it's weird down here, it feels…'

'Haunted.' Helen finished, and Meredith turned to her.

'Yes, and this place has never felt haunted.'

Helen shook her head with a frown. 'No, but it was. And it feels haunted now it isn't anymore?'

'There's something not right here.' Meredith whispered.

Something I've missed. Something I can't put my finger on.

What have I missed?

Meredith felt icy hands creep up her spine as the group fell into silence. The air felt charged, heavy, and the chill was getting colder.

The silence hung.

Swelled.

Oppressive.

'Brrr It's cold in here.'

Meredith nearly expired at Spookbuddy's childlike voice emitting from the corner. Her heart thud so hard, and so fast, that she thought it could have battered its way out of her chest and ran the four-minute mile on its own.

With no legs.

She also had a feeling that she wouldn't have been far behind it.

'Fuck!' Steve said, a hand over his own heart, as the anger surged from Meredith's gut. Were they not all scared enough, without being scared by a damn teddy? Had she not been scared enough by a damn teddy all her life?

Before she could check herself, she stomped over to the bear and gave it a swift kick up its backside. Spookbuddy flew into the air and she saw Steve, mouth open in aghast horror as he placed himself under Spookbuddy's line of trajectory. He caught the bear deftly and safely.

Unfortunately.

'Woah, woah, Christ! That's some expensive kit, Bangers.' He said his eyebrows almost disappearing into his receding hairline. She glowered at him.

'One more hunt with that bear and it will come down to me or him. It's that simple.'

Steve's face fell, doing a very good impression of someone who just had his dog kicked.

'What's up with you? Look at him.'

Steve grasped Spookbuddy around the chest and held him up in front of his face. He waved Spookbuddy's furry arms.

'I'm so cute.' He said in a squeaky voice.

'Fuck you, Spookbuddy.' Meredith said, pointing to the bear. 'If you speak out of turn again, you will meet your end.'

Steve still in play mode, bear before his face, didn't miss a beat.

'That's okay, sweetie, I'll see you on the other side.'

Helen and Matt sniggered. Meredith fumed.

'That's what bothers me.' She said moving past Steve, who was laughing as Spookbuddy chose that moment to start himself up.

'Hi, I'm Spookbuddy, and I'm ready to investigate.' His childlike voice said cheerfully.

'You're a bit late, buddy, show's over.' Steve said, whipping the bear around to face him, and then he leaned forward and whispered into Spookbuddy's ear, 'and you're lucky you haven't been fired. Pipe down, huh?'

He clicked the button in his backpack, turning him off, as Matt, Helen, and Steve laughed at his timing.

Still on edge, Meredith found she couldn't even draw a smile as she stalked out of the cellar, leaving them to follow up behind.

CHAPTER FORTY SEVEN

Sweat dripped down the man's face as he slipped into the cellar. The exertion of the light whipping not as breath taking as the excitement of the sliver of rope across her skin. Welts were all he had left her this time, although in two places he had got carried away and split the skin. Red oozing from the wounds as she had thrashed and screamed.

When God commanded he stop, he had given her more tablets from the kitchen, with more of the devils juice that he had brought from the corner shop, until she lay unconscious on the bed. Then he had carefully removed the binds from her hands and feet and left her to come round alone. She would remember nothing of the event when she awoke, and that was the way it had to be.

In the cellar he removed the robe and folded it, placing it on the shelving at the back of the boxes. He rolled the whip and placed it back into the strap on the roll, then he moved his hand down to locate the lash.

He had drawn blood. Not a lot, but that hadn't been God's plan. Now he would pay for his sins. Pay for his over excitement.

Thicker and shorter than the ungainly whip he unwound the leather strap and placed it on the shelf ahead of him. Then he found the large white cloth and placed it onto the floor, just able to see it in the darkness around him.

He sank to his knees on the cloth, mumbled a prayer, and picked up the lash.

His naked body ran with goosebumps in the cold of the room, but he barely noticed as he gave the lash a flick.

'Divine and heavenly father, I give my body and soul to you, cleanse me of my sins so that I may do your work with purity. Make all that is unholy, holy. Make all that is impure, pure. I am at your service father and I cleanse myself in your name.'

He flicked his arm up and the strap landed across his back with a sharp snap. He ground his teeth together with a growl, and pulled the strap up again, and again.

By the sixth snap of the lash, he felt nothing but comfort and joy as his sins were released.

Tomorrow he would be ready. God had bigger plans. Tonight, he would sleep in the cellar.

CHAPTER FORTY EIGHT

Meredith pumped her arms, focused on the path, her breaths even and controlled as she ran. Steady, today. Not frantic. But still as satisfying for thinking things through. She made a mental note not to kill herself again. It made no odds to the outcome of the run.

She had completed six laps of the park before she noticed Matt on a bench, elbows on his knees, watching her as he blew smoke. She waved and he held a hand up in return. Deja vu, she thought.

I'll do one more lap before I join him.

She ran the last lap harder, finishing on a high, before plopping down beside him.

'You're up early,' she gasped between breaths.

'Hmm, didn't sleep too well.'

Meredith sat back to re-tie her ponytail, studying him. The dark circles under his eyes telling of the evening before. She wondered how much Kevin would notice.

'How come?' She asked lightly.

'Just one of those nights. Bad dreams. How'd you sleep?' He took another cigarette from the pack. Meredith was about to chastise him, but he seemed a little down this morning.

'Good, for once, 'she said. 'I was out cold… until 5am anyway.' She nodded at the packet, 'You want to be careful; you'll give yourself a habit.'

Matt nodded but smoked anyway.

'Why the 5am wake up?'

Oh, nothing much, just the smell of Lilies and my phone ringing as my dead sister tried to call… again.

'Early riser.' She said. 'I don't often sleep past six am.'

'Unless you're doing a paranormal shoot…'

'Exactly. I think it was going to bed at an almost normal time after a pretty chilled day. Even with what went on at Lynton. So, you had nightmares?'

'Kevin found out what we'd done.'

'Ah. Not good.'

Matt smiled. 'It seems less of a scary issue in the day, believe me. What would really happen could be no worse, for sure.'

'Grim.' Meredith said.

'Yeah.'

Matt took a long inhale of smoke, looking back to the park. Meredith watched him. His eyes weren't as bright as usual, and he didn't seem so quick to smile.

Maybe he's more worried than he let on about Kevin finding out… does he blame me for all this?

Her heart flipped, she didn't want to be in Matt's bad books, nor the cause of any of his suffering. She put a hand on his arm, and he turned to her.

'You sure you're okay? Are you having second thoughts about what we did last night?'

Matt blew out smoke. 'Absolutely fine, don't worry about it.'

Meredith watched him absently turn his attention to another early park runner.

'So, what's really wrong?' She said.

'What do you mean?' He said, turning back to her, but she caught the look of knowing. There was something. She held his gaze wondering if he would give it up. He opened his mouth to speak, thought better of it, and then closed it.

Meredith waited quietly, giving him time to think as he took a last drag of the cigarette and crushed it underfoot.

'My Grandad.' He said finally. 'I got a call to say he died in hospital last night. Mum is distraught.'

'Oh no, Matt I'm so sorry.' Meredith's hand found its way over her mouth as she stared at him. Matt shrugged.

'We've known it's been coming for a while. It's been a long hard battle; one I guess he finally lost.'

It could have been anything, but Matt's choice of words gave the game away. Everyone who had 'fought a battle' in illness was fighting the same thing, weren't they?

'Cancer?' She said, swallowing hard.

'No.'

Maybe not, Meredith thought as Matt pulled in a breath.

'The alcohol got him. Demon drink. He was an alcoholic for many years, this was only a matter of time.'

Meredith felt the world stop spinning, and time slow down.

'Alcoholism?'

Matt nodded and ran a hand through his hair. Meredith grabbed his free hand. This was something she could certainly sympathise with, and maybe she shouldn't be so quick to judge that Matt couldn't understand or handle her problems either.

'I'm so sorry,' She said.

Matt smiled squeezing her fingers. 'I'm not, he was a lying, cheating, cantankerous old bastard. I've been waiting for that last breath for the best part of five years so that mum can have a life. All of our lives he has consumed the drink and then consumed our family, it's all I've known since I was a child. He's been seriously ill for a few months now, completely taking over mum's life, and I've hoped and prayed every day since that that day would be his last. It's mum I'm worried about, he's still her father, after all, but I feel only relief that he's gone.'

He took another breath, and then reached for the cigarettes. Meredith took them from his fingers, he looked from the pack and back to her, but didn't take them back.

'Chain smoking will send you the same way, and you know who you'll meet up there now, don't you?'

She smiled and he gave a small laugh, more of a huff.

'I want to delay that reunion for as long as possible.'

He rest his elbows on his knees looking at the floor as he scuffed the gravel with his shoe.

'Have you asked Kevin if you can go home for a while?'

Matt looked up, and then sat back on the bench.

'Nah, it would disrupt the whole show, we're on schedule and I'll be home in a few weeks. Mum will be fine. I have four brothers and a sister who will be rallying round after her now. She knows that's the nature of the job and she expects nothing less. When I spoke to her the others hadn't got there and she just didn't sound good, that's all that's worrying me right now. When I know she's not alone, I'll be fine.'

Meredith frowned.

'I'm sure Kevin will give you a day or two. What about the funeral?'

Matt smiled. 'I don't need it Meredith, and I wouldn't go anyway. I'm not grieving after him, he doesn't deserve it. When the others get to mum, and I know she's being looked after, I'll be good. That's all I need.'

Meredith stared at him, trying to assess whether he was being truthful about his lack of grief. This was his grandad after all.

'It's callous, I know.' He said with a small smile. 'But I'm not sorry. Mum knows where I stand on this, she's accepted it, we've spoken about it lots, and the others will all go except Lila, my sister. She's the same as me, won't go near it.'

Meredith swallowed and dipped her head. Callous or not, she had often wished the same of her own mother. Especially when she relapsed, and they had to start over. And if she hadn't now been an only child, she may have fobbed off the funeral too.

No, you wouldn't. This is your mum, it's completely different. You're like Matt's mum. She is still your mother.

Matt kicked at a stone with the toe of his trainer.

'I know you must think—'

'No,' Meredith said. 'Don't you go there, and don't feel

guilty either. I get it. I really do...'

Matt frowned, his narrowed eyes questioning, as her phone's shrill song cut her story short. Matt watched as she checked the display. Her shoulders dropped.

Mum. Great. Speak of the devil and it shall appear.

Best to get her over with now than to anticipate the call back. She blew out a breath.

'Are you okay if I take this?' she said to Matt, 'I won't be long, I promise.'

'Go ahead,' he said, linking both hands around the back of his neck with a sigh, then he smiled. It didn't reach his eyes. Meredith placed a hand on his raised arm as she rose, pocketing the cigarettes as she walked across the path to the park railings opposite. She checked the time as she swiped to answer. 6.15am, plenty of time before they met for the brief at 8am.

'Hey, mum. You're up early, how—'

'Meredith, this has to stop. I can't do this anymore.'

Mum sounded weary, downbeat.

'Er, okay? What's up?' Meredith said, for lack of anything else that seemed appropriate without getting down and dirty with her mother in a public space.

'What's up? I'm fed up, I'm ill, I'm out of pills, and I'm being harassed. I'm done with this SHITTY life, Meredith. Done. And you've abandoned me!'

A chill travelled down Meredith's spine, but she hoped mum wouldn't do anything stupid. They had been through this before, and they could get through it again.

'Don't be silly mum,' she said, 'I haven't abandoned you, it's only a few more weeks and I'll be home. It'll be okay, listen, there's a repeat prescription with Mrs Grey, give her an hour or so and she'll go with you to the doctor to get—'

'I don't need the *pills*, Meredith. That was merely a statement. You asked what's up, that's only one of the things *up* but it's not the worst one.'

No, the worst one is that you need a drink. That's the

problem isn't it, mum?

Meredith closed her eyes. She wondered if she could skip going home for a few years. And then she thought of Matt's poor mum, she would have been the same. Mum's voice rambled on in her ear until one word caught her attention.

'...Harassment, Meredith! The worst one is the harassment. I am sick of the messing about in my house. The flowers, the noises, things out of place, the games, the man, the music, and now I'm marked!'

Meredith blinked.

'Marked? I don't—'

'Yes marked! My body is covered in marks. Cuts! Where the hell did they come from, huh? Where?' She lowered her voice to a whisper which shook with emotion. 'Stop with the innocence, it's you, isn't it? Are you doing this, Meredith? You want to get rid of me, don't you?'

Meredith blinked.

'What?'

There was silence on the other end of the line and then the ting of glass and two large gulps. Meredith felt her heart sink, she put a hand up to her forehead.

'What are you drinking, mum?'

'Water. What else?' The reply was instant but accusing.

'Are you sure?'

There was a desperate grunt on the line and glass smashed in the background. 800 miles away in a park in Scotland, Meredith flinched.

'Am I sure? Am I bloody SURE? Did you hear what I said? This is NOT about ME, Meredith. This is about YOU.'

Mum's voice was instantly at fever pitch and Meredith leaned her elbows on the top of the railings, running her hand over her face. Meredith listened to the sounds of her kitchen. A cupboard door, another glass, the chug of liquid, and the screw of a metal cap. Water didn't come with a screw top. Drink, for sure, mum must have poured it with the phone in her hand. It was both goading and depressing to hear from all the way up here, knowing that she could do nothing about it.

Heart sinking, she wondered how much this time as mum took three large gulps of whatever it was. The glass tinged back down.

'Well?' mum said, her voice calmer.

Meredith sighed.

'I'm not doing anything, mum.'

'The FUCK you are. You're playing games with me, and I am a sick woman!'

'Mum, I'm not playing games—'

'You are playing FUCKING GAMES, Meredith. Are you trying to give me a heart attack? Get rid of me? Well, I won't go down so easily. I don't care how many lilies you place in the damn room, or how many men you hire to harass and mark me in the night. And I don't care if you try to throw me off the scent with the classical playlist. I WILL NOT GO DOWN!'

Meredith shook her head, a little confused, but now her heart pumped with worry too.

Who the hell is this man, and what does he want?

'It's not me, mum, I promise. Is this man still around? Have you seen him? Do you want me to call the police? Or get Mrs Grey to help you? Please, mum, I'm worried.'

'Oh, she's worried,' mum said in a singsong fashion, the slight slur now evident. 'Listen everybody. First, she pulls the games on me, then she's FUCKING WORRIED about it. Fucking off to Scotland when I'm ill wasn't such an issue, but now she's *worried*. Maybe I'll give you something to worry about. I might just top myself while you're up there. You can't play your little games if I'm not here. Where are my pills…'

Meredith heaved a breath.

'Mum, please—'

'Bye, Meredith.'

The line went dead.

'Mum? Mum!' There was no reply.

Meredith stared at the phone. She could call her back but what would be the point right now? She was obviously drinking—and drinking hard again if she had fallen and not known.

I'll call her later, hopefully she'll have sobered up.

She stared across the play equipment, her heart thumping as she chewed on a nail. Harassed and marked? Who the hell was in the house? Or was it that she had been drunk and fallen and now she couldn't remember. Did she need the police to go out, or not? Would Mrs Grey be able to help if mum was spiralling out of control again so fast?

She felt a hand at her back and turned to look at Matt.

'Everything okay?' He said his eyebrows pulling together into a frown. Meredith gave a small nod, but Matt shook his head at her.

'You're not, I can tell. What's going on, Meredith?'

'No, Matt, I'm not doing this to you right now. You have enough to deal with.' She sniffed and swallowed the lump in her throat before it turned to tears. She handed him his cigarettes and turned back to the play area, but he forced her to face him, turning her by the shoulders.

'What is it?' He said ignoring her, 'Your mum? Is she ill? what's up with her? Meredith, please tell me. I want to understand.'

Oh, I think you'll understand all right.

She blew out the breath she had been holding, looked at his concerned face, and gave in.

'Alcohol.' She said.

Matt's face stretched both ways comically. His jaw dropped open, and his eyebrows shot up.

'Alcohol?' He repeated.

'She's an alcoholic. She was recovering, I guess now she's not. Again.'

There was a pause before his eyes widened as the penny dropped, and then he pulled her in roughly for a tight hug.

'Oh, shit, Meredith,' Were his only words.

Meredith thought that she couldn't have put it more eloquently herself.

CHAPTER FORTY NINE

It was cold now, the wind seeping through her coat as they sat on the bench, the early morning sun doing nothing to warm the Autumn air. Meredith stuffed her hands deep into her pockets.

'…Not only that, but you have absolutely no idea what happened to your sister?' Matt was saying next to her.

She shook her head.

'None. I mean, I remember bits. Like mum saying that she was taken to hospital from home, but then I remember dad saying that it was an accident. I always thought she had been hit by a car or something. Out in the street? It happened when I was at school. Although it was still fairly early when they called me home.' Meredith shook her head and blew out her cheeks. 'Everything seems so mixed up in my head.'

'How old did you say you were?'

'Six.'

Matt stared at her. 'And your mum started to drink back then?'

Meredith began to nod, but a memory was trying to nudge to the surface. A dog. There was a dog and the pills, the day of the fair.

'No. Well, yes, the drink I suppose she hit hard after Eve, but she must have had problems before then looking back. A few months before the accident mum was prescribed Valium and antidepressants which she still takes in varying doses. She runs out frequently though, and because she's Agoraphobic, she relies on me or the neighbour to help her to get them. She has other pills too, but she doesn't take them much because of the side effects. I don't know what they were for, she never allows me inside the doctor's office with her, I presume the Valium are for anxiety to help with the Agoraphobia, as well as Eve's death.'

Matt chewed the side of his mouth.

'Agoraphobia too, huh?'

'And anxiety, and the obvious mood swings, she can really trash the house, especially when she's looking for booze. She's ill, though Matt. It's an illness.'

'You sound like my mum,' he mumbled looking down at his hands.

'It is though. The thing is… now…' Meredith ran her hands over her face and hitched in a breath.

'It's okay, take your time.' Matt said, taking out another cigarette, Meredith couldn't help but see his hands shake as he lit up.

'You know, maybe we should just get back. We don't have that much time, I don't know how to get this out, and I don't want to be in trouble again. We can do this another time.'

Matt checked his watch.

'We've plenty of time, don't worry. So, what's happened now?'

Meredith tried to get the jumble of thoughts trying to clamber out of her mouth into some sort of order.

'Well, I guess she's always had a nasty side. She can get quite personal, and accuses me of all sorts of rubbish, but this is weird, even for her. I'm not sure what the truth is, and it worries me that she's down there alone. I almost wish I'd never taken this job.'

Matt waited, shrugging his jacket up around his ears against the chill.

'She thinks there's someone in the house, at first only leaving her gifts but today—just—she said she'd been *marked*, like cut. But she can't remember it happening.'

Matt nodded nonplussed.

'Blackouts were always a thing with Grandad. And the accusations and violent moods too. Sounds like the drink to me.'

'Did he ever hallucinate?'

He thought for a beat before shaking his head. 'No, not that I'm aware of, but if he drank enough, he would imagine something had happened that didn't, or, like you say, he'd end up with a bruise or injury that he couldn't remember. He was always adamant about those things, even though *we* usually knew what had happened.'

Meredith felt her shoulders relax a little.

'Mum said there was a man in the house the other day. She was whispering. She said he'd left lilies on her dressing table, and… God, Matt, I've been so worried.' She cut off, her voice faltering with emotion that sprung from nowhere.

Matt placed an arm around her shoulders and Meredith found herself leaning in to him for comfort and warmth.

'Listen, this all sounds remarkably familiar to me.'

'So, you wouldn't call the police?'

'The police? What for?'

'The intruder… if there is one.'

'There's the clincher, right there, is there one at all?'

Meredith sighed pulling back from the warmth to see his expression.

'He could be all in her head, and part of me thinks that's exactly what's going on. But then a tiny part of me thinks what if he's real? If he's real, mum is vulnerable, and I'm not protecting her.'

Matt chewed on his lip and then he nodded slowly.

'Right. I get you, and I do think the intruder is in her head too, but for your piece of mind is there any way you can check for sure?'

Meredith shrugged.

'I asked Mrs Grey the neighbour to check before, but she said mum was denying all knowledge of a man. Since then, I've not really spoken to mum in a coherent state.'

Matt raised his eyebrows. He didn't need to say any more. Meredith nodded.

'I'm being silly. There's no man, is there?'

'I wouldn't say silly, you need to cover all avenues, she's still your mum. You wouldn't be normal otherwise. Is this what's been eating you?'

Another runner was taking the park at a fair few knots and Meredith suddenly had the urge to join him.

'Pretty much,' She said. There was still the stuff with Eve, but maybe that could wait for now. She felt a huge weight lifted just being able to discuss her mum with someone other than Mrs Grey.

Her phone pinged, and she looked at it, seeing a text message from a number she didn't recognise.

Quiet night. Excavators are in today. Thank you so much for all your help. Thank the others for us too. We'll keep you updated with progress, message us on this new number any time.

Orla.

Meredith smiled and Matt squeezed her back in close.

'See, something is going right. It seems the ladies are finally getting some peace now. I think you may have exorcised your first spirit. She was a feisty one too, you almost met your match!'

Meredith laughed and Matt kissed her forehead.

'That's better,' he said, taking her cold hand in his.

There was a beat of silence as she leaned her head on him and the butterflies let loose in her stomach. She thought there was nowhere she would rather be, and then a voice shouted across the park.

'There you are! Christ, is this how far you'll go to keep a bloody secret. I'm sure Kevin wouldn't have seen you a little closer to the hotel you know. This is extreme!'

They pulled apart and turned to see Steve panting across the grass.

'Meetings early. I've been sent to find you. Didn't

expect it would take a search party though.' He put a hand to the back of the bench gasping breath as Matt stood and pulled Meredith up. She stamped her feet trying to shake the cold from her bones.

'Dude, the hotel is about 200 yards away. You need some exercise,' Matt said, patting Steve's stomach.

'Yeah, yeah,' He said. 'Come on, before Kev gets on the war path. I'll be speaking to you both later, don't think you're getting away with this deceit.'

He started off ahead as Matt rolled his eyes at Meredith. She grinned.

'Feeling better?' he said when Steve was out of earshot. She nodded and linked her arm with his.

'Thanks for listening.'

'Anytime.'

'Come on, lovebirds. Kev will be blowing steam from his ears and performing that trick with Gwen's glasses before we get back if we don't hurry.'

'Chill out, we're coming,' Matt said, whether he deliberately ignored the lovebirds comment Meredith couldn't be sure, but she quite liked it. It had been a while since she had been called anyone's lovebird.

She was feeling more relaxed than she had in a while until Matt broke the spell.

'Oh, I don't know whether you noticed, but you have three missed calls from that Eve now, you going to call her back?'

Of course, got me a line straight to heaven.

'They're voicemails,' she said, 'I just haven't got around to listening to them yet.'

'I don't mean to pry, I just thought they could be important.'

Meredith shook her head. 'They're not, I don't know anyone called Eve.'

Not living anyway.

'You do. You mentioned an Eve earlier I'm sure you did.

What were we talking about now?'

Meredith felt her heart drop. He had too good of a memory.

'My sister.'

'Yeah…' he said. Then he stopped and looked at her. She let the information click together in his mind as Steve vanished into the distance.

'But Eve is dead.' He said simply.

'I know, that's why I don't want to listen.'

CHAPTER FIFTY

DECEMBER—9 DAYS UNTIL DEATH

'Listen to me, Meredith,' Eve's voice came through the small speaker of the walkie talkie, 'Stay at the top of the stairs. I'm at the wardrobe now. I'll pounce on him and we'll take him down together. He's a slippery sucker remember so there could be some foul play.'

'Roger, over and out.' I said with an IMPORTANT NOD to nobody. I was all alone at the top of the stairs. I could hear mum in the living room, or rather I could hear songs of praise. She always said religion was a great stinking PILE OF SHIT, so why it was on I had no idea. I hummed along to 'The Lord is My Shepherd' as I waited.

'Moo,' the speaker crackled, 'I have him. I'm on my way out. Oh, and stop with the over and out, we're not in MI5.'

'Okay, reading you loud and clear. Over and Out. I mean... oh, er... over and out. Over and out.'

I shook my head taking my finger off the button so that Evie could reply.

'Great.' Evie said, the disdain in her voice clear. I scrunched up my nose. Stop with the over and out. No more over and out.

Got it.

'Over and out.' I said into the speaker and scrunched my eyes closed as Evie came into view on the landing, expecting a telling off that didn't come.

I opened them again and swallowed hard. Egor was under one arm, his legs and arms poking from either side.

'I said stop with the over and out, idiot.' Evie said, rolling her eyes as she moved past me. I turned to follow her, looking over the bannister to check for mum in the living room. Her slippered feet located and in a crossed position, I gave another nod.

'Safe to proceed.' I said to Evie, but she had gone. I caught the tail end of her shirt disappearing down into the cellar and took the rest of the stairs at a run. I didn't want to go in there by myself with the light GONE.

Evie was at the shelving when I got to the cellar, pulling a box from the top shelf. Her fingertip scraped at the bottom, edging it nearer until it tipped into her hand, pulling the old clown along with it.

'Here should be good,' she said.

I stayed back, I hated the clown, his rosy cracked cheeks and big smile didn't fool me. This was where the man had been for a long time until he got into me. The clown tricked me when I was alone down here and frightened. I watched as it slipped further forward, tilting, and wavering on the edge.

'Moo, quick get the—'

The clown fell, twirling over as Evie grabbed the box and fell to her knees. The box slipped, crashing to the floor, its contents, a couple of old newspapers, and what looked like metal plates and an old light, spilled out, as Evie grabbed for the clown, missing by a HAIRS BREADTH as mum always said.

I watched motionless as the clown hit the dirty floor, his rosy cheeks shattered into pieces and flew up into the air. His smile cracked into three, and small chunks of scalp containing sprouts of orange hair flew across the floor. Only his soft body was intact, his fragile hands and feet had also gone.

A grin spread across my mouth. The clown had been destroyed, and he was the main reason I hated the cellar so much. Egor would be in here now, but in a way, the clown was worse.

There was a shuffle from behind me, as Evie threw her

hands in the air.

'For fuck's sake, Moo, now look what you did! I told you to get the damn clown.'

There was a rush past me, and a dark figure loomed over Evie and pushed her aside. She fell onto her side as mum screeched.

'What the hell do you think you're doing?'

Evie scooted back on her butt as Mum picked up bits of the clown as though they may crawl away and be lost at any second. I narrowed my eyes in case any did.

'Your father will be so mad! This clown was his favourite toy when he was a child. Not only that but it was our safety net, you idiot!'

'It was an accident,' Evie said, still on the floor, 'I told Meredith to—'

Mum swung to Evie, bits of clown flying from her hand. I watched as they hit the floor and rolled. 'Meredith was by the stairs. Don't you blame her. I saw you Eve. I saw you; you did this on purpose!'

Evie was on her feet quicker than someone who thought they'd seen a ghost, and mum followed suit, tufts of orange hair sticking out of both clenched fists.

'I didn't... mum I didn't, it was—'

She had no more time to react before mum's fist struck her belly. Evie bent double with a 'urgh' sound that made my heart jump start.

'This was an antique you little shit.' Mum punched, and Evie curled up on the floor. 'A fucking antique, it was worth hundreds of pounds,'

Three more punches landed on Evie's head and side, terror flooded my heart and my lip wobbled as tears spilled over my cheeks. My stomach rolled and I thought I may be sick. I held my hand over my mouth to keep it inside. Mum pummelled away at Evie as though she were a doll as she shouted.

'...Which is why it was sitting safely up on the top shelf.

Out of REACH!'

Mum roared the last word, landing another punch. She looked like a mad animal, hunched over Evie. Evie was crying now, I could hear her, and I could watch no more.

Evie had been helping me with the bad man. She didn't break the clown on purpose. This wasn't her fault, it was mine.

I ran for mum with a yell and threw myself onto her back, punching my little fists against her spine as fast as I could.

'Leave her alone, it was an accident!'

Mum whirled round and up, and I fell, landing against the shelving with a thud, pain shooting up my arm.

'Stay out of it, she needs to be taught a lesson. Maybe you want one too.' She leaned over, glaring at me in the half light. I shook my head. I didn't want one of those lessons.

I prayed that Evie would keep quiet and keep her head down so that this could be over, but when I looked over mums' shoulder, she was edging silently to the stairs. I began to howl causing mum to look over her shoulder.

Without a word mum lunged, pulling her back as Evie screamed. In the light scattered bits of clown fell from mums' hands, orange hair now red. I knew what it was. Blood.

The world muted and tilted wrong, kind of upside down. Evie screamed in silence as mum dragged her back and as she pulled back her fist, I saw it drip to the floor.

Mums' hands. It was mums' hands. Not Evie, not yet.

And the sound came back on, mum and Evie fell to the floor as there was a loud deep bellow. I looked to the stairs and saw an angel.

Dad.

I cried.

* * * * *

'I'm sorry.' I said, my breath hitching.

Dad cupped his arm more firmly around my shoulder, making me wince from the pain where I hit the shelving. The shelving we were now sat against, on the floor, from where I had refused to move, still clutching the walkie talkie.

Evie was in her room, Queen playing loudly from her stereo and Mum was OUT COLD in the living room, from whatever dad had given her.

I rocked. Back and forth like I was on a swing. My hair moved in the breeze and I could almost feel like I was outside. Safe. On a swing. Free.

It was dad who stopped me. Made me get off. I didn't want to, I said that it was nicer out there, but he told me I had to come back to the cellar.

'Listen munchkin, 'he said, 'I know things seem bad right now, but mum is under a lot of pressure. One day the tablets they give her will work. I promise you. This won't be forever.'

'But I broke the clown, I didn't catch it.'

Dad heaved a sigh.

'Well, it is very sad, but it doesn't matter. The clown is in the bin now. It was just a toy.'

'I should have caught it.' I said starting to rock gently again. The swing. I wanted the swing, but dad wouldn't let me. He held me tighter.

'It doesn't matter, Meredith. I promise you—'

'It was my fault. If I'd caught it, mum wouldn't have come in, and Evie would be okay. And mums' hands would be okay. It was my fault.'

Now dad forced me to look at him.

'No. What happened was not your fault. None of it was your fault. Don't ever think that it was.'

I tried to look away, but he held my chin gently.

'Do you hear me?' He said, 'It's not your fault. Say it.'

'It's not my fault.' I mumbled.

'Louder.'

'It's not my fault.'

'Again.'

'It's not my fault. It wasn't my fault.' My bottom lip quivered, and a tear let go.

'Good.' Dad said, wiping it away. Pointless because another came in its place. 'Now believe it, Munchkin, because it really isn't. None of this is. I'm not mad about the clown, and mum will be okay. Everything will be okay. I promise.'

I cried again. This time with relief.

If dad said it would be okay, then it would.

He let me cry, stroking my hair for a while, and then he looked at me.

'Shall we go upstairs in the warm? I can get us some pizza for tea?'

I wiped my tears, feeling better, as he lifted me up.

I held onto him as he walked to the stairs and then it hit me.

'Daddy? Where's the box?'

He stopped.

'What box?'

'The one that fell. Everything spilled out.'

'I cleaned it away. No harm done.'

My heart jumped, as I remembered what Evie and I had been doing down here all along.

'Where's Egor?' I said as dad started to climb the stairs. He stopped again.

'Who?'

'Egor, the bear?'

'Ah,' he said, putting me down and crossing to the box on the top shelf. He opened it up and pulled Egor out by one furry paw. 'This little guy?'

I nodded as dad put the box back onto the shelf.

'No!' I said. 'Egor lives in the box, put him back.'

Dad frowned, 'you want him back in the box?'

I nodded firmly.

Dad shrugged and put him back in the box, pressing the lid down on top. 'Okay?' he said.

I grinned, feeling better.

'Yes, thank you.'

Now whatever happened, Egor and the bad man were where they were supposed to be. Locked in the cellar.

'Come on sputnik.' Dad said ruffling my hair as he passed me.

I followed him upstairs and made my way to my room as dad put a pizza in the oven. I sat on my bed, lifted the walkie talkie to my mouth and held the button.

'Mission complete.' I whispered.

CHAPTER FIFTY ONE

Stanmore Lodge was dreary and smelled bad.

'Bad pipes.' Said the elderly man, in thick Scottish, pointing his stick at the chairs in the small nook by the reception area. 'They'll be needing a good clean out again I've no doubt. Need cleaning every week, bloody place. Sit down, I'll get Elsie.'

The man moved slowly away on his stick as Kevin sat down and the others followed suit. Meredith stood.

Stanmore lodge was a long building, single story, with a central doorway, which meant from here she could scope the hallway from both left and right. The view was as though someone had put a mirror at one end, allowing the other to stretch away like an illusion. Both identical. There was nothing fancy, and nothing homely about this place, and the smell seemed to get worse the longer they were in this area.

Who the hell rents a place like this exclusively? And for a wedding?

Meredith pushed out her lips and caught Steve's eye as she looked over at the chairs. He wrinkled his nose and she nod her head lightly in agreement.

She looked out of the picture window by the desk. The gardens would be pretty in summer if they were planted, but right now they were bare and brown. All dirt, dead leaves, and bark with only the vague outline of what it had been. Probably. Maybe, at some point.

If the inside was this bad, maybe the outside was nothing special after all.

Her thoughts drifted. Bad smells could be paranormal, and this place was smelly, drab, cold, and eerie, even in the day. There could be some more interesting activity tonight.

She glanced at Kevin.

Or we could just fake the lot.

Paranormal Encounter indeed. This show should be called Fake Encounter.

She rolled her eyes wondering what little stunt he had planned to rig here today. It was ironic, really. Thank goodness for Lynton last night or the only thing she would have learned so far is how to fake a possession and rig a television show set. At least she knew that Elana had been a real entity, and she knew that she had dealt with her perfectly. A little more experience now and she would hopefully have the confidence to communicate with Evie.

She thought of the voicemail messages.

Seems Eve is much more adept at that than you are.

Meredith looked at the top of Kevin's head, shiny bald patch catching the light as he scribbled notes in a loose-leaf pad. How could he sit there like that knowing he was doing what he was doing? How could he act so innocent and authoritative knowing that he was faking it, and pulling the wool over their eyes? And why bother when there was real footage to be had anyway?

She looked away before she worked herself up again, she really didn't need Kevin's wrath for the fourth day in a row.

Makes no difference anymore anyway, let it go.

At the end of the corridor a door banged, and Meredith turned to see an older lady walking toward them. Long grey skirt swishing around her ankles, long grey cardigan hanging from her shoulders, a shock of thinning wild grey hair fanning her face. As she got closer, she smiled at the group, and Meredith saw it was a warm face, friendly, and welcoming.

'Hello there,' she said, in as thick an accent as the gentleman had spoken before her. 'So, you're the ghost hunters, eh? You'll find a lot to appease you here, they don't come any more haunted than Stanmore Lodge I assure you.'

She grinned, and Meredith found herself grinning back.

'Perfect,' Kevin clipped as he stood, looming over the lady, and almost shook her hand right off her wrist. 'Activity is exactly what we need for a good show. Kevin Spalding, director and producer of Paranormal Encounter.'

Meredith raised an eyebrow.

And if activity we don't get, we shall just fake it, don't worry.

'Pleased to meet you Mr Spalding,' the lady said without missing a beat at Kevin's intimidating stance, 'I'm Elsie Stewart, Owner of the Lodge.'

'Now if we could get on—'

'Excuse me, Mr Spalding, I shall take you to the rooms in due course, first I have some safety information for all of you.'

Kevin stopped in his tracks, his mouth making a surprised 'O'. Meredith concealed a smile. She was starting to like Elsie already.

'Go ahead, Elsie, safety is of the utmost importance, and we wish to be respectful of you and your property while we're here too.' Meredith said placing a hand on the arm of the lady, who placed her own hand over the top. She pointed out each of the team in succession, slowly and thoroughly, a job Kevin had neglected. 'I'm Meredith, the presenter, this is Steve, sound guy, Matt, Camera man, Helen, assistant, Gwen, the historian and Donald, show psychic.'

She caught Matt's raised eyebrow and knew he was amused, but also worried she was going to wind Kevin up again. She had no such plan today, however. It was just rude that Kevin had only introduced himself... again. Elsie gave her a warm smile as Kevin reddened and shot Meredith a look that she ignored.

'And a pleasure it is to meet all of you. Now, I must warn you it's been a while since we had investigators in here, a good while since we've had many people in here. The wedding was unusual to say the least, bunch of *goths* do you say? Dressed all in black, couldn't see most of their faces for the black make up, bride included. Still, they were paying guests and seemed to enjoy it. I don't know why many people would enjoy it these days, the rooms are—'

'Could we move forward, time is of the essence. We have equipment to set up when we know what we're doing here, we've already lost an afternoon.'

Meredith felt herself redden at Kevin's self-important request, and although Elsie politely agreed, her pursed lips gave away her annoyance at his rudeness.

'Aye, well then, let's move forward, shall we?' She smiled at the rest of the group.

'Please.' Kevin clipped.

'Your director sounds like he has a pole up his arse, maybe someone would like to remove it before he returns later,' Elsie said as she turned to walk back down the corridor. 'This way.'

Meredith shot a smug smile at the back of Kevin's head as she saw Helen and Steve exchange a look.

'Have a little attitude do we, Elsie. Are you always this polite to guests?' Kevin said, and Meredith cringed. Elsie was doing them a favour, why couldn't he just be pleasant?

'Oh, no dear, not all of them.' The lady retorted with a smile, 'The attitude is all yours. Just remember that you are in my house, and as a non-fee-paying guest, I can remove you and your team at a moment's notice. Although your team seem perfectly able to remember their manners now, don't they, so who will spoil the show? An apology for your rudeness wouldn't go amiss if you wish to bestow it.'

Meredith didn't know if it was the reference to the show, but Kevin did indeed apologise, although he made it seem hard work, and his red face could have given a comic relief red nose a run for its money. He made an excuse about being on a tight deadline and not having the chance to be here yesterday.

Elsie merely shrugged.

'Well, life likes to kick us in the rear occasionally, nothing you can do about that.'

If Meredith had a chance, she thought she may well just give Elsie a high five for being so utterly unaffected by Kevin's intimidation. It was refreshing to see. Elsie shuffled off down the corridor leaving them to follow.

Kevin usually brought up the rear of house tours, more for his own gain Meredith thought, now that she knew the truth. This time she hung around, pretending not to notice him ushering her forward, until he gave a small sigh and went ahead. Meredith finally let the smile she'd had trouble concealing out.

Elsie explained that there was activity in pretty much all areas of the four-hundred-year-old hunting Lodge, but two rooms seemed to be the main focus. The dining room, and bedroom six.

She opened a door to the right and a musty smell hit Meredith's nose. The dining room looked like it had been in a time warp. It was large, Elsie informed them that it would cater for sixty or so guests in total, not that many dined in here now. The tables and chairs looked melancholy in the dim morning light, a skim of dust covering each one, the room quiet, their voices echoing in the space.

'This room seems pretty sedate right now, but we've had things thrown at guests in here, chairs pulled from underneath them, plates of food thrown, things hidden. It got so bad that I've another makeshift dining room down the hall. I don't use this room for guests anymore, unless they're paranormal investigators of course. This room is bound to throw up something for your investigation, if it doesn't, I'll eat my hat.'

The room did seem oppressive even in its large space.

No, not oppressive, alive. It feels like it's pulsing with energy.

Meredith shut her eyes, rubbed them, and opened them again, to no effect.

It's like an electric charge in here, a strong force that's lying dormant—until we wake it and plug it in anyway.

A small flutter of fear bat in her chest. Or was it excitement? She couldn't tell. Her eyes scanned the dated tables and chairs.

Should be interesting if nothing else.

Elsie ushered them out and motioned to the right down the same corridor, shutting the door behind them. She made her way past the unusually quiet group.

'Okay?'

There was a general consensus of mumbled yeses and nods before Elsie turned and led them down the corridor.

'Not many people will spend the night in bedroom six,' she said, 'it's a room I generally keep closed up, unless it is asked for.'

She reached the far end of the corridor and turned left into a small wing. There were three doors leading to three rooms, Elsie told them that the other side of the building was identical. Room six stood at the very end of this corridor. Room 13 was its mirror image on the opposite side of the building.

'Ironic that room 13 is the room with the least activity, and yet it's the one that most guests don't want to sleep in. Superstition is a funny thing.'

'I suppose to most people you could say that superstition is more believable than the paranormal.' Gwen said.

'Oh aye, but most people are stupid. The paranormal exists, superstition is bunkum. This place has taught me many things. That is one of them.'

'How long have you lived here, Ms Stewart?' Helen said.

'It's Elsie, please. Thirty-five years and counting. It was my husband's inheritance, unfortunately he stopped sharing the load when he passed over six years ago. It's a lot to manage alone, and the history and activity certainly don't help with hiring staff, but I'll never give it up. I'll die here and join the party on the other side, the spirits have never bothered me, that's for sure.'

Meredith smiled at Helen who was now swinging her head back to Elsie with a frown.

'Oh wow, you own this place alone. So, who—'

Kevin gave an irritable sigh, which Elsie ignored.

'The man who saw you in? The handyman, and butler, and general hired help for any other duties. Egor.'

Meredith did a double take, and her heart skipped.

What are the bloody chances? Really? Is this goddamn bear ever going to leave me alone?

'Egor?' Gwen said, head tilted to see Elsie over the top of her glasses, 'Not a typically Scottish name.'

Elsie smiled, and Kevin shifted his weight with another deliberate huff of breath.

'He was originally from Italy, bless his soul, but that was over fifty years ago now. He's the only staff I've been able to keep for a length of time, he's not at all bothered—'

'All right, let's see the room.' Kevin said cutting her off,' we're coming back to set up in three hours, the historical talks are scheduled to happen then, not now.'

Elsie lift an eyebrow, and Kevin lift one back. For a moment Meredith held her breath in the standoff.

'Please.' Kevin finally said, with a smile so false Donald's teeth must have felt positively real beside it.

'Of course,' Elsie said. 'I hope you don't think that the spooks will perform to schedule Mr Spalding because I'm afraid that you will be sorely mistaken.'

'We've had good success so far, that's exactly what I'm counting on,' he replied.

With a little help from you, of course, Meredith thought.

'We'll see,' Elsie said, motioning to the door ahead of them. 'Room six.'

Meredith turned her attention to the bedroom door, and felt an involuntary shudder run down her back, leaving goosebumps down her arms and legs in its wake.

The door looked forbidding—not in reality, it was just an

oak door with a silver number six on it. A little worn but solid and fit for purpose—but it seemed to dance in front of Meredith's eyes, to distort and blur. She rubbed at her eyes as they reached the room and Elsie put a hand on the door handle.

The corridor stuttered, as Lynton castle had done when Elana had shown her what had happened. Light possession Donald had called it when she had spoken to him about it earlier—not in context of Lynton of course—nothing to worry about, he said, but it still put Meredith on edge. Now Elsie and the door flickered ahead of her. She closed her eyes.

'Many people have quite a strong reaction to this room, some don't feel anything. I've seen it all don't worry. I wouldn't mind hearing about what you pick up in here.'

'Interesting,' Donald said, 'People usually don't wish to know.'

'I've told you, dear, the spirits and I have a deal. They don't bother me, and I don't bother them. Doesn't mean I'm not interested now, does it?'

Meredith opened her eyes, to see the corridor as it should be, and Donald rubbing his hands together with a nod.

'Fair enough.' He said. 'I suppose it adds a more realistic element to the show if we don't know anything in advance.'

Meredith gave a wry smile.

Realistic! Ah, Donald, if only you knew.

She thought of the footage.

Unless you're part of it and you do.

Elsie nod her head at Donald, her wild hair following at a slower beat, making her look like granny from Fraggle Rock.

Meredith felt a pain begin at the front of her head, just by the temples. Voices of Elsie and the team seemed to be filtering into her head in waves.

Not a good time for a headache, Meredith.

She made a note to get some paracetamol before they came back later.

'I'd advise taking a breath now,' Elsie said.

She opened the door and Meredith was hit by the smell of something dead. Very dead, and very rotten. She gagged as the others walked into the room ahead.

Kevin gave a cough and a sniff. Donald didn't seem to notice. The others covered their nose and mouth with their hands.

'Wow, this room is, er… er, really being left to decay,' Steve said, wrinkling his nose up and down under his hand.

'Well, not so much,' Elsie said, 'The room is always cleaned and changed, and we have trouble with the pipes up here, so the bathroom is bleached and cleaned once a week, even when it isn't used. This smell appeared a few months ago, and I just can't get rid of it. I've had everything checked over, and I've tried all sorts of air fresheners. Nothing seems to shift it.'

Meredith saw two plug-ins' just inside the room, and a pot with diffusing sticks on the windowsill, none of which gave off any sort of smell over the rancid air now taking up residence in her nostrils.

At the threshold of the room, she stopped. Elsie was still talking in an alternate world, but that world was now muted. A buzzing started up in her ears as the group moved further inside, but Meredith found that she couldn't put a foot into the room.

It was as though there was an invisible barrier she couldn't physically move past. A glass doorway that she couldn't move through, couldn't hear through. The rest of the group were no longer with her, they were in this other world that she could see but no longer interact with. She put a hand up to feel the solidity of the invisible wall in front of her, this was a phenomenon she had never really heard of. Interesting.

'Meeeerediiiiith.'

The voice whispered sweetly from behind and the hair on her neck prickled. She mentally counted the crew inside the room. All accounted for.

Fabulous. Maybe this isn't so interesting after all.

There was no way to get to the safety of the group, she understood that she was alone out here with *it*.

And *it* knew her name.

A shudder shook her body and a bead of sweat trickled down her forehead and into her eyebrow.

'Mer-e-dith.' The voice said again, singsong, playful, and a pressure seemed to bear down on her, the electric charge of the dining room sending static into the air.

She closed her eyes and waited.

A tickling crawled over her scalp (fingers?) and she bat at it three times frantically, before shaking her hand down beside her.

A giggle. Childlike, but not childlike. An older child.

Goosebumps raised the hair on her arms and her heart pound frantically in her chest as she began to shake uncontrollably.

'What do you want?' she mumbled, still looking inside room 6, at the crew who were now silently laughing at something, hands still over their noses.

'Mer-e-dith.' There was another giggle and Meredith slowly turned her head.

At the end of the corridor was Elana.

Not cute blonde Elana. Dark Elana. Elana who was all in black aside from her pale skin and cracked lips. Elana with kohl smudged so far around her eyes they looked like deep black holes.

Like the goths who got married here.

Meredith's breath caught in her throat.

Elana smiled. A horrible, dark smile. A smile that slipped away like the flick of a switch.

'Go home, Meredith,' She whispered. Sharp, urgent.

Meredith focused on the thumping of her heart, trying to keep it steady and stable.

It's okay, She's just a spirit. You can deal with spirits.

You know what to do, you've done it before.

'You go home Elana.' She said, 'I did what you asked. Your bones are being excavated; you'll be laid to rest. Now leave here and leave me alone.'

Elana cocked her head jerkily to one side and giggled again. The sound hollow and dark. She flickered and stuttered under the low wall lights in the windowless corridor. Or was it the light that flickered. Meredith couldn't tell. She remained focused on Elana, unable to look away. Terrified to turn her back.

There was a stutter, a patch of darkness and then Elana was suddenly closer. Lots closer. Meredith took a sharp step back but hit the glass of the doorway. There was nowhere to go, and now that Elana was closer, she looked older, and scarier, and not very Elana like. Meredith put a hand out.

'Don't come any nearer, Elana.'

Elana smiled, and then the smile seemed to melt from her face, dragging her lips down and her eyebrows up and together in a terrified mask. Her arm came forward to Meredith, fingers clawed, and her dark pooled eyes began to well and get wider. Meredith gasped. She had trouble drawing breath as her heart thumped and the blood washed past her ears. There was a constant buzz, like interference in her head.

'You know the truth.' Elana whispered, her voice urgent and desperate. And then her face collapsed into a menacing glower, teeth bared. 'YOU KNOW THE TRUTH!' she screeched, and then she screamed, her mouth stretched into a wide 'O' as she rushed toward her.

Meredith clamped her hands over her ears, closed her eyes tight, and was about to join her when the sounds of the Lodge came back.

Elsie was talking to the crew in the room, there was shuffling, then Helen's voice, and then Matt, just behind her.

'Meredith? Are you coming in?'

She opened her eyes to an empty hallway and gulped

some breaths of air.

Gone. She's gone. Shit! What the hell does she still want? And why has she followed me here?

'Meredith?'

She turned to see Matt motioning her inside, there was a question in his eyes, concern? She willed him not to bring it up now, and mercifully, he didn't. He smiled, urging her inside again as Kevin grilled Elsie about set up. She vaguely wondered how she would explain not being able to enter the room, but the invisible barrier disappeared as she stepped easily over the threshold, and back into the world of putrid smells.

She gagged.

'Bad, huh?' Matt whispered, his curled forefinger under his nose. She nod at him, but the smell wasn't bothering her too much. Elana had topped the charts for that prize.

She turned her attention to the conversation, watching but not hearing. Thinking only of Elana.

How the hell did she follow me here? And why? Has she attached to me? Does that mean she is going to stay with me and terrorize me for good?

For the first time since Meredith had taken this job, she wished she'd never bothered. Everything was going to shit. Kevin was making up his own investigation activity, mum was a fully-fledged drunk again, there may or may not be a man terrorizing her in the house, Evie was around as much as she had ever been and Meredith was still none the wiser as to why, and now it seemed an angry spirit had attached itself to her and was determined to terrorize her too.

As Meredith listened to Elsie's strong tones, the last thing she wanted to do was film another investigation. She didn't even want to go home.

All she wanted to do was get out of this stench, curl up into a ball, and cry until it all went away.

CHAPTER FIFTY TWO

'Meredith? We're ready.'

She turned to see Helen in the doorway, fluorescent book in her hand reflecting the carriage light in the darkness as she peered around the corner of the building.

Meredith held up a hand as the ringing continued in her ear, and then the answer phone cut in again.

'Hey, it's Meredith. Again. Please could you give me a call when you get this message. Thanks.'

She cut the connection and placed the phone in her pocket with a tremor of unease.

First mum, now Mrs Grey? Why is no one answering?

'Meredith?'

She looked up and smiled at Helen, hoping she wouldn't see just how shaky she was.

'Coming.' she said.

They made their way out of the damp dark fog of the evening and into the warm, but smelly, air of the Lodge.

'I didn't mean to interrupt,' Helen said. 'Kevin sent me to find you so that we can interview Elsie and then get filming by 10pm.'

Meredith nodded as she checked her watch. 9.05pm.

'Plenty of time.' She said, as Helen marched down to the dining room.

It was unusual to do an interview so late but having lost the day before Kevin was on a schedule warpath to keep the shows filming exactly on time. They entered the room to find Matt facing Kevin.

'It's fine. It'll be good. Her mum is sick, she's just checking on her, that's all. She'll be in—'

Kevin flung an arm up in the air.

'I don't have time for sick – ah, Meredith, welcome to the investigation.'

Meredith stood in the doorway. Hackles up and senses on full alert. Matt gave her a relieved smile which she didn't return.

What has he told Kevin?

Kevin spoke first.

'Matt, go check where Steve is. I think Donald was having a walk through. Tell him fifteen minutes. And for God's sake will someone find Gwen. Why is it so hard to keep this team together and on time? Helen, Elsie was in the other wing, go find her and tell her we're finally ready.'

Matt and Helen left the room. Helen almost at a run, Matt with more reluctance.

Which left Meredith and Kevin alone.

Meredith's heart bumped. She wouldn't be able to hold it together if he started on her now. She stared at Kevin as he held her gaze, his mouth a hard line. Finally, he huffed a breath and placed his folder down on a table with a loud thwack. Dust rose into the air and spun in the lamp light.

'What to do, Meredith. What to do?'

She wasn't sure what kind of answer he would want, so she watched him instead. Waiting.

He pursed his lips and raised his eyebrows, his hands clasped together at his chest.

'How *is* your mother?' He said.

Meredith was taken aback by the question. She opened her mouth to say 'fine' as she nearly always did and then realised that it would be counterproductive after what Matt had said.

'I don't know. I haven't been able to get hold of her.'

He nodded, solemnly.

'It's a worry, then. May I ask what is wrong with her?'

Meredith clenched her jaw, she didn't want to tell him, but there didn't seem to be any other option right now.

'She's an alcoholic. She's not been well for a couple of

days.'

'An alcoholic?' For a moment Meredith thought she saw a hint of humanity in his eyes, but then she realised she was mistaken. 'So, this isn't an illness at all then. It's self-inflicted. I thought she was at death's door the way Matt was banging on.'

'She could be. I don't know what—'

'Was she at death's door a few days ago?' he cut in.

Meredith flinched. 'No.'

'Well why would she be now? Does she have someone who cares for her?'

'Yes, me.'

'Well, that's useful, isn't it? Because you took a job that would involve you being away for at least two months. Did this cross your mind when you left?'

Meredith gaped.

'Yes, of course! She was recovering, and there's a neighbour that helps out. I thought she would be fine. She's obviously relapsed... I...I...' she cut off and swallowed the lump in her throat. She would not cry, right here and right now in front of this asshole. She stared at the floor, the bright red check in the carpet dulled by the sunlight and the dust.

'Well, it's pretty simple from where I'm standing.'

Meredith frowned and looked to Kevin.

'Get on the phone to the neighbour—'

Hackles rising, Meredith snapped, cutting him off.

'I have! She isn't answering her phone either. If I could get her checked and know she was doing okay, then I wouldn't be in this predicament, would I?'

Kevin's cheeks reddened.

'You have been in this predicament all the way along, Meredith.' He boomed.

'What? I—'

Kevin held up a hand, his jowls wobbled on the collar of his shirt.

'You have had an attitude since we started this shoot.

It's always you with the smart mouth and the bad time keeping. You do not run this show, Meredith, I do. You will do as I say and keep on my schedule whilst you work for me.' He glanced at his watch. 'The infuriating thing for me is that when you're present you actually do a damned good job, but unless you can sort out this problem with your mother and be fully present to do it, then you shouldn't be here. It's that simple. Are you in, Meredith, or are you out?'

Meredith's mouth dropped open.

Was he firing her?

'I'm in.' She mumbled.

'Then for God's sake call rehab, get your mother admitted so that she can get the care she needs, and then you can focus on your goddamn job instead of making my job harder.' He pointed a finger at her, wagging it in her face. 'This is your last warning, Meredith. Your last.'

Picking up the folder he stomped from the room, leaving Meredith alone, her heart pounding behind her ribs. If dealing with her mother were that easy, she would have done it by now. They didn't have the money for a fancy rehab clinic, and Alcoholics Anonymous meetings hadn't worked three times. She was both furious and appalled at Kevin's attitude and complete ignorance of such a debilitating disease.

I could leave. Just walk out. Forget the job.

Except I don't want to.

Kevin was an ass, but he was right. She had only been half here while she was worried for her mother. He was the boss, this was his show, he had a right to demand a hundred percent from his team, however he demanded that. And even with his trickery this was the most exciting thing she had done in way too long.

Years.

She was out in the world, meeting new people, making new friends, investigating something she loved. Even when Elana was scaring her half to death, she still felt alive. She felt like Meredith, not just her mother's carer, and she felt nearer to being able to deal with Evie.

Even up here she was letting her mother rule her life. From 800 miles away she was still managing to drag down her days and almost get her fired from her job. A job she was enjoying, with good people, whose company she was enjoying.

A stab of anger ran through her.

'It's just eight weeks.' She whispered to the room, 'eight weeks, and still, she gets the upper hand?'

She shook her head.

No, she thought. They had been through all of this before, and no doubt they would go through it all again in the future. But these eight weeks, or the six that were left, were hers alone. She would be present here, as Kevin said, and deal with the fallout when she got back.

I'm not chasing you anymore mum. I'm only going to give you a thought when I'm not working, and if you can't be bothered to answer your phone, then we don't speak. Tough.

Even with her steely resolve a flutter of worry ran through her.

Well, I'll do the best I can, and that's all I can do.

With a mental note to try Mrs Grey tomorrow morning, she turned off all thoughts of her mother and went to find Helen and Elsie for the interview.

CHAPTER FIFTY THREE

The room was warm and would have been comfortable if the smell of decay hadn't been rife. Meredith gagged as Matt and Helen placed the cat balls around the room. Three of them. One in the centre where everyone could see it, one by the bathroom door, and one by the bedroom door.

Tonight was Room six, tomorrow would be the dining room, and Meredith thought that she would take poltergeist activity any time over this awful smell.

She heard a muffled gulp beside her and looked round to see Gwen, white napkin over her mouth and nose, tears streaming down her face.

'I'm not at all sure how long I can be in here.' She whispered.

'As long as it takes.' Kevin said from his place by the door to the room.

Meredith moved a few inches left so that she could keep an eye on the director. Unfortunately, this also meant that she had full view of a certain bear who sat blinking between the door and the bathroom.

She huffed.

Why, oh, why did Steve have to find the stupid bear?

'Are we all ready?' Kevin said from the doorway.

Meredith nodded, joining the murmurs from the others, but saw that he was looking directly at her. A flush ran up her neck and cheeks. He was going to be all over her like a rash from now on, she could feel it.

So just focus, Meredith. Let's do this.

Kevin counted down and signalled for Matt to start rolling.

Meredith opened her mouth to speak but Spookbuddy got

there first, making his debut on a real shoot, unlike the one that shouldn't have happened the night before.

'That tickles.' His chipper childlike voice said.

He had been touched already? Meredith took a breath, it looked like they weren't going to have to call any spirits forward in this room, they would come without coaxing.

'Okay, it would appear a spirit is with us already. Thank you for that. If there is a spirit wishing to communicate, could you do that again, please?'

'Like we need a sign,' Steve mumbled. 'The bloody smell is sign enough. It's been a while since this spirit took a bath.'

Meredith grinned at him as she continued.

'Could you touch the bear again? Make the—'

The cat ball by the doorway immediately went off, strobing its disco lights around the room.

Too soon. Surely too soon.

'Thank you.' She said feeling for all the world like she was being played as she waited for it to stop strobing. 'Could you do that again for us?'

The words were barely out of her mouth when the ball went off again. As she turned to it Kevin shifted very slightly to the left. Meredith narrowed her eyes. In previous shoots she would have taken him to be moving out of shot, but now she wasn't so sure. And if it was him, why was he being so forward? At least in the other places he waited for actual activity first.

Well, you thought it was real activity, but was it?

'That's amazing thank you!' She said, trying to be enthusiastic, probably over the top, as Helen wasn't really reacting either. Did she have the same thought? After all, she knew what Kevin had been up to as well.

'Are you the man who died here, in this room?' Gwen asked from under her napkin, 'Tap once for yes, twice for no.'

There was no response, but Meredith had an idea, if this *was* Kevin there was a way that she could play this out to test for certain.

'Give us a sign if you are Alfred, the man who died in this room,' Gwen was still pressing. 'Alfred are you there? Can you hear us?'

Meredith looked to Gwen, catching Helen's eye in the process. Helen had her own hand over her nose and mouth, but the laughter was in her eyes.

Don't laugh Meredith, just sort politely.

Meredith bit back a smile, wiggling her own nose to try to get rid of the smell, and only succeeding to make it worse.

'Gwen, we haven't given the spirit an outlet to communicate. We don't even know that it is Alfred yet.'

'I said, tap once for yes, and twice for no.'

'Okay, and he—it—didn't tap. Give them chance.'

Gwen shrugged.

'Sorry, I just want to get out of this godforsaken smell. I wasn't thinking.'

'It does smell, but sometimes that can be exactly what we're looking for. Smells and temperature can both be evidence of spirit activity,' she said, more for the camera than for Gwen.

'There's smell and there's goddamn smell. This reeks,' Steve said, Matt trained the camera on him. 'I mean, this is an unholy stink, man.'

Meredith had to agree, she shrugged.

'You want to hold my hand?' Spookbuddy said cheerfully from the corner. All eyes turned to the bear.

'Something definitely wants to play with the Budster,' Steve said, 'I'm not sure it would be a devious murderer like Albert, though. I would imagine it would be more a child?'

'My thoughts too,' Helen agreed, turning back to Meredith, eyebrows raised.

Meredith felt her stomach plummet.

Could be Elana, guys. She followed us seven miles down the road to continue her quest of harassing me, how about that?

'Well, let's keep going and find out,' Meredith said, pushing the thought down.

And that's one more thing that I have over Kevin, at least. He isn't aware of Elana, and there were no other children brought up in the history of the Lodge. So, will he play the child card, or just keep setting the ball and the bear off?

She glanced at Kevin who gave her a rolling motion with his hand. Get on with the show, it said, we don't have all night.

Gwen coughed and gagged, and Meredith waited until she had composed herself before moving on.

'Okay, Spirit if you're still here, could you tap once for yes, twice for no?'

There was no response.

'Are you Albert? The man who died in this room?' Gwen questioned.

Meredith was about to correct her again when she thought better of it.

Okay Kevin, I'll give you a chance.

'Albert, if it is you, could you maybe make one of the balls light up, or touch the bear again?'

Meredith watched the ball by the doorway, eyes boring into the small sphere, but it didn't light, and Spookbuddy didn't make a sound.

She pulled in a breath that she regretted and looked to Helen, her eyes watering as much as Gwen's had as she tried not to gag.

Matt panned the room, turning further away from Kevin and the bedroom door to face most of the small crew by the bathroom door.

The ball went off, strobing colours around the room.

'Guess it is Albert after all,' Donald said. Meredith turned to him as the ball strobed again.

'Thank you, Albert,' She said, 'could you do something else to show us it's really you? Make the ball in the centre here light up, or the one by the bathroom door.'

Meredith turned her face to the bathroom door, but flicked her eyes left, toward Kevin. She hoped he wouldn't notice in the half light. He didn't, and she was rewarded by his arm flicking, almost unseen, just behind his leg. A second later something small dropped by Spookbuddy.

'Do you want to play?' Spookbuddy said, on cue.

Meredith felt her heart bump.

Was that foul play Meredith? I think it really was. Kevin is giving us the run around. Shit.

She swallowed hard. Her heart bumped with both excitement and fury. She had to stay on track. Focus.

'Thank you, Albert. Could you try to move one of the other balls in the room. Set the light off somewhere else for us?'

The ball by the door went off as everyone's attention was focused on the other two. Clever.

Meredith nodded.

'I think this is too easy a game for you, Albert. Let's have a proper conversation. Knock on the walls for us. One knock for yes, two knocks for no. Can you do that?'

There was a faint knock and Meredith asked Gwen to take the lead with the questions for the first time. She knew more about Albert's history, and Meredith was more interested in Kevin and his games. She bit her lip, trying to conceal her anger every time there was a knock (from the bedroom doorway, of course) or Spookbuddy or the one ball went off. So far, the other two balls hadn't been touched.

Anger was rising from her gut, she tried to swallow it down, but the spirit of the hunt was lost tonight. Literally. There was a living spirit doing the talking for them. She found herself getting more irritated the more Gwen questioned.

There had been a lot of activity from the show's point of view, but here in the supposedly haunted Lodge, none of it so far had been real to Meredith's knowledge.

This is supposed to be a very haunted room. What the

hell is he playing at?

She tried a change of tack.

'Okay, thank you for talking to us Albert, that's a lot of information you've given us. We're very appreciative, but I'd like to ask you to step back now. Are there any other spirits that would like to come through to talk to us?'

There was nothing for a beat, Kevin was behaving himself as Matt panned back around the group, and then the ball by the bathroom went off.

Meredith's heart skipped.

At last. A real presence. Hopefully not the real Albert.

'Come forward,' she said, 'we don't wish you any harm. Do you want to communicate, do you have a message for us?'

The strobe went off by the doorway again and Meredith had to bite back a sarcastic comment.

Fuck off Kevin, let me speak to the spirit.

All eyes were drawn to the doorway and Kevin caught Meredith's eye his hand whirling in a circular motion.

Wind it up? Was he kidding? No chance.

Even as she knew she would be getting into trouble again she continued on, determined to talk to the real spirit finally here with them.

'Do you have a message for one of us?' She said, avoiding Kevin's eye.

The ball in the centre of the circle flickered and rolled toward Meredith. Her heart pumped harder.

Okay, there was wanting a connection with the room to piss Kevin off, and there was Elana, and Meredith wanted no more of Elana tonight.

'A message for Meredith?' Helen said, taking her hand from her nose and mouth and turning to Meredith with a puzzled look.

The ball strobed again, rolling nearer. It took Meredith all of her will not to take a step back, to put some distance between herself and the ball.

There was a huff from the far side of the room and Meredith looked into Kevin's steely gaze. His wind it up was now more feverish, and his face showed restrained anger. His movements tense. Meredith was all for winding up if this was Elana, but Helen took the reins, leaving her no choice.

'Can you set the ball off for yes if we ask you a few questions? Maybe just keep quiet for no?' Helen said, unaware of Kevin's mounting anger as she took the lead. Meredith looked to Donald as the ball strobed.

You're quiet tonight. Why is that?

'What message do you have for Meredith?' Gwen asked, and then closed her eyes and shook her head. 'Stupid question, sorry!'

Spookbuddy was more forthright, however.

'Do you want to be my friend?' He asked.

Meredith felt a chill creep down her spine. Surely Kevin wouldn't be playing now, and if this was Elana, it was downright creepy.

'You want to be Meredith's friend?' Helen said, raising her eyebrows at Meredith.

Spookbuddy seemed to falter, to start to say something and then fizzle out.

'Is he supposed to do that?' Donald said, 'He sounds a little sick.'

Steve took a step toward the small bear.

'I. am——' Spookbuddy said, not so cheery now. Meredith's heart was at full gallop and she barely disguised a shiver as Steve stopped midstride.

'I am?' he said, turning to the rest of the group.

Only Kevin seemed unaffected. He huffed, coughed, and finally said.

'Cut, everyone. We're done here.'

Meredith blinked.

Done? But it was just getting... she had been about to think interesting, but terrifying was probably more the ticket.

'But Mr Spalding, we…'

'No arguments Meredith, we have enough activity. This place hums and I can be here no longer. Gather the equipment, we'll spend longer in the non-smelly dining room to make up footage tomorrow.' He bent to pick up the file that he had propped against the wall. 'Matt, you can switch off. I'll meet you all in the morning 11am sharp.'

Kevin turned on his heel as Spookbuddy continued.

'Mere-dith.' He stuttered.

The hairs on her neck stood on end as she stared at the bear.

'Go. Home.'

'What was that?' Steve said, shooting a look at Meredith 'That's not in the repertoire, Bud.'

Meredith stood in fight or flight mode, rooted to the spot, unsure whether to listen to Spookbuddy, who was scaring the hell out of her right now, or follow Kevin out of the room.

Why isn't he interested in Spookbuddy, Meredith?

She glanced to the now empty doorway, seeing Kevin's retreating back as her fury grew. Hot and white.

Has he rigged this too? To scare me? To get me to leave? Asshole!

Meredith, go hooooo…' Spookbuddy said, his voice trailed off as his voice mechanism gave out and smoke began to pour from his backpack.

'Goodness, he's going to set alight!' Gwen said from behind her hankie.

'Woah, woah!' Steve shouted, picking up the bear whose lights were now flickering, not to show activity, but to show failure of his mechanism. 'Don't die on me little buddy.'

Meredith looked to the bear and suddenly, she was certain that this was all Kevin's doing. He had rigged the bear. He had seen her reaction at Lynton and now he was playing his own game with her.

Did he know that she knew?

Well, he's about to find out.

Heaving large angry breaths, she stepped around Helen and strode out of the room in three short strides,

She was vaguely aware of the relief of being out of the smell, but rage pushed her on anyway.

Elana stood at the end of the corridor and Meredith stormed down toward her without missing a beat.

The girl stretched out a hand, her face a mass of menacing black. But Meredith was already too far gone.

Maybe Kevin had rigged her too.

'Fuck off, Elana.' She said as she marched past the girl and headed for the door.

CHAPTER FIFTY FOUR

DECEMBER—1 DAY UNTIL DEATH

'Fuck *off*, Meredith,' Evie said.

'No.' I scowled at her. I was watching Transformers on the TV. It was one of my favourite cartoons, not because of Bumblebee like my friends, I watched for Optimus Prime. He always seemed to have the answers and he was bigger, stronger, and wiser than the others.

'She's all right, aren't you, cupcake?' Rizla said, leaning a shoulder up the doorway to the living room. His short hair greased into spikes that ran down the middle of his head, cigarette behind his ear, denim jacket sporting badges that showed lots of skulls and weird writing. The one on the top pocket had a spelling mistake. Even I knew Korn was spelled with a 'curly c'... and the R was backward too.

Dad would say that the person who made that badge was a JOBS WORTH. I didn't know what that was, but I thought Rizla was a JOBS WORTH for wearing it anyway, unless he couldn't spell.

I looked back to the screen, where the Decepticons were coming for a fight.

'She's not. We have to talk' Evie hissed to him, 'She'll tell mum and dad.'

My ears pricked up. What would I tell mum and dad?

'They'll be back soon,' Evie continued.

'I'll be gone by then, babe, and if I ever see your mum, I'll rip her fucking arms and legs off.'

My stomach clenched on the floor and I turned my head to look at him. Evie nudged him in the ribs.

'Only joking, cupcake.' He said with a croaky laugh.

I squinted my eyes at him. People on the telly did this when they wanted to see people better, and right now, I wanted to see Rizla. Not who he was standing there with his fake smile, yellow rats' teeth, and spotty skin, pretending to be nice. I wanted to see through to the other Rizla. I wanted to ask him what he was doing with my sister and I wanted to tell him that if he touched my mum, I would get dad to rip *his* arms and legs off.

'What'cha watching?' He said, coming into the room and trying to squat beside me. The Christmas tree filled the space by the window now, and with the coffee table pushed to the side there wasn't much room where I was on the floor. I watched as he shuffled the plastic tree branches and finally sat still, one red glittery bauble hanging down the middle of his head.

'Transformers.' I said watching the baubles swing where he had pushed at the tree. The red glittery one bounced off his hair, but his hair didn't move at all, it was stuck still and hard in the air. I wondered if it was a wig.

'Is that *your* hair?'

'It's gelled. You like it?' He grinned showing his yellow teeth, his blue eyes had lightening red veins trailing back to his head. I shook my head, eyes going back to the screen which suddenly clicked and went dark.

'Hey!' I yelled getting to my feet.

Evie had the remote in her hand and now she held it out of reach.

'I said fuck off, we have important business.'

'Why can't I hear?' I said folding my arms tight across my chest.

'It's not for babies, now scat. Up to your room.'

'Make me.' I said knowing full well that she couldn't. Even just moving from one side of the room to the other seemed to be a chore for my zombie sister. At least today she looked half alive, but I knew it was just MAKE-UP. She had a dark red lipstick to cover the cracks in her lips and the black pencil was smudged around her tired eyes again. Mum said yesterday that if her EYE BAGS got any bigger her eyes would fall into them. I thought mums weren't too far behind.

Evie didn't seem bothered though. She had grunted and walked away—limped away, really—something she was doing a lot now. It was like there was no fight left in her. Not only that but no FUN, no SMILES, no JOKES. I wanted to ask Evie where my sister had gone. It worried me that the bad man had come out of Egor and gone into her, but when I asked her, she said that the bad man was still safe in Egor in the cellar.

When I pushed her further—*But how did she KNOW?* —she had yelled and banned me from her room.

Just like she was banning me from the living room right now.

The cushion connected with my head, the zip catching my ear.

'Ow!'

'Get out.' Evie said through clenched teeth. Then she scrunched her nose with a hiss and her hand flew to her side. Rizla climbed out from under the tree.

'All right, babe, calm down. Off to your room, cupcake.' He said with a flick of his head.

I went. Not because he told me to but because I didn't want to hurt Evie anymore. She hurt enough on her own.

What they didn't know was that I only went as far as the landing. I banged my door shut and crept back to lie just above the top step of the stairs, where I could just see Evie and the edge of Rizla's jacket through the spindles of the bannister.

'Have you got all your stuff?' Rizla said, his voice hushed.

'Everything is in the bag. I don't want anything else it just reminds me of here. Of *her*.' Evie's mouth curled up like she had eaten a worm.

I squinted my eyes at Evie. Did she mean me? My heart started to patter, and my stomach gave a funny swirl.

'Okay. Tomorrow then. Come round the back of the old Scout Hut at midday, I'll let you in. Mozza should have the car in the hour then you're home free, babe.'

HOME FREE? I frowned struggling to understand what was being planned. Home was always FREE, wasn't it? That's why it was HOME.

'I need to get far really quick. He can do that, right? I don't need to be found.'

'He'll take you as far and fast as you want to go, babe. He may want more payment though.'

'I can pay.' She said. 'Thank you.'

She leaned forward to kiss him like they did in the movies. Evie had told me once that it was called a FRENCH KISS. She hadn't told me that she had ever done one—or why it was FRENCH. I wrinkled my nose as Rizla's claw like hand snaked around her back and slid down to her BACKSIDE. I thought of mum last year sitting me down on the settee to tell me that a girl my age had been touched in the private place under her pants by a NAUGHTY MAN three streets away. Mum said that no one was to touch DOWN THERE, and if they did, I was to scream as loud as I could and kick him hard in the BOLLOCKS. I had nodded importantly and promised I would... but then I had to admit I didn't know what BOLLOCKS were. Mum had rolled her eyes with a laugh and said, 'just make sure you aim right between his legs, Meredith'.

Now, I waited for Evie to scream and kick, but she didn't, she seemed to like it.

'Right, I'm off babe, I'll see you tomorrow.' Rizla said as he stopped the kiss with a wet slurp that made me want to gag. 'How good does it feel? You'll never have to see her again.' He slapped her private place and she limped behind him to the hall with a laugh.

'Good.' She said.

It was then that my slow brain began to click things together. My breath caught in my throat and my heart galloped like a thousand horses.

My friend Chelsea's sister had run away a few months ago. They found her a week later only a few miles away because she RAN OUT OF MONEY. If she hadn't, she may never have been found they said. Chelsea said that was fine—she didn't want a sister anyway, but I loved Evie. And who would protect me against the bad man if Evie was gone?

I didn't want Evie to run away. Was she going to run away?

The door clicked shut, and I was on my feet.

'NO!' I yelled, running down the stairs.

Evie rounded the edge of the hallway with a wince and put a hand to her chest.

'For God's sake, Meredith, you scared me to death.'

'You can't go!' I said, with a silent apology to God for her blasphemy which seemed to come out every other word these days, just like mum.

Evie's face got all red. It was the most colour I had seen in it for weeks.

'I told you not to listen.' She spat. 'It's my business what I do, not yours.'

'But Evie, I don't want to be here alone.'

'You're not, idiot, you have mum and dad.'

'I want yoouuu.'

'Tough. Look Moo, I won't be gone long, silly—'

'He said you'll never see me again!' I wailed, 'What did I do Evie? What did I do? I won't do it again, I promise I won't, I promise.'

Evie's face softened a little, she looked tired and weary. She sat on the settee carefully running a hand over her face.

'Not you, silly.'

'Who?'

'No one. I'm not going anywhere.'

'You're not?'

'No, I've decided against it.'

'But you just said—'

'Forget it, Moo!' she snapped, getting angry again. I shut my mouth with a snap and my bottom lip wobbled. I tried to stop it, but it had a MIND OF ITS OWN.

'I'm scared Evie.' I whispered.

Evie pat the settee next to her, I scrabbled up, and she put an arm tentatively around my shoulders. I snuggled in for a cuddle, mindful of her bruises and catching them anyway.

'Ow, Meredith, that hurts. Everything fucking hurts, I'm so sick of this. I'm so tired.'

I didn't understand the edge to her voice, but her speaking of being tired was making me tired too. I yawned.

'I'm tired too.'

Evie gave me a sad smile and pulled me closer with a shake of her head. We sat quiet for a bit, she held me longer than she normally did, but it was nice. Like the old Evie was back. Happy and cuddly.

'I'm glad you're not going Evie, I don't like Rizla much, and who will help protect me against the bad man?'

Evie gave a long sigh, and then she pulled away, putting her hands on my shoulders. She squeezed a little too hard but as she wasn't going away, I wasn't too bothered.

'Oh, Moo stop being so dramatic. There is nothing more to do now. The bad man is in Egor, who is in the cellar. He is stuck. Leave him alone and you'll be fine. He can't get you, right?'

I nod my head, looking up at her watery eyes. One was bloodshot, I hadn't noticed that earlier.

'Evie—' I began.

'The bad man can't come out of Egor. Don't touch him, don't get rid of him, don't destroy him. Those are the only rules, and you will be safe forever. I promise you. Can you remember that?'

'Don't touch, don't get rid, and don't destroy.'

'You've got it, you'll be fine, Moo. I promise.'

'Promise?' I said snuggling back into her black jumper.

'Promise. I love you Meredith Moo, don't ever forget it, whatever happens.'

'I love you too, but nothing will happen. You're not running away now, right?'

'God, Moo, you're like a dog with a bloody bone, let it go, will you?'

'But you're not going, right?'

'Right.'

CHAPTER FIFTY FIVE

Meredith stormed after Kevin, catching the door to his car just as he was pulling it shut. She yanked it from his grip, and he sat back in the car seat dramatically, shooting his hands up into the air as though she had pulled out a gun.

'Meredith,' He hissed through clenched teeth, 'Whatever it is does it need to be quite so dramatic?'

'You know what the hell it is! Really? I believed it all, what the hell are you playing at?'

She banged a fist on the car roof, and he leaned forward on the steering wheel looking up at her. He opened his mouth, shut it, and huffed a sigh.

'You were supposed to believe it, how the hell do I get real reactions if everyone knows what's going on?'

'How about getting a real reaction from a real paranormal event. Isn't that what we're supposed to be doing here?'

Kevin looked at her as though she had just told him she had four nipples.

'No, Meredith,' He said with controlled calm, 'it's not what we're doing here. What we are doing is making a paranormal television series and the logistics are remarkably simple. Get a crew, find a spooky place and shoot some spooky footage of ghosts—'

Meredith heaved a harsh laugh cutting him off, hand still on the door.

'Ghosts! There are no ghosts—'

'Precisely!' He cut her off with a shout, banging his hands on the steering wheel, and she felt herself bristle.

'If you'd let me finish,' she said. 'I was going to say that there are no ghosts in your bloody series. Which, incidentally, is called Paranormal Encounter. Paranormal Encounter my ass. All I've encountered so far is a bunch of amateur tricks.'

Kevin ran his hands over his face pushing his palms into his eyes.

'What else did you expect to encounter?'

'The paranormal?' She said, unable to hold back the sarcasm.

Kevin laughed, shaking his head. In the cars light Meredith caught the flecks of grey through his hair and the shiny skin of his scalp through the thin patch at his crown.

'I can't see what's so funny.'

His head came back up to rest on the back of the seat, eyes closed briefly.

'What is so funny? I'll tell you what's so funny. There are no such things as ghosts, Meredith, the little 'paranormal encounters' have to be faked because there is no paranormal. These things have been faked for centuries; don't you think if there had been anything out there it would have been recorded by now? People have been investigating the paranormal for hundreds of years, and what do we have to show? The odd faked photo or tampered video? Nothing solid. No real proof. Because there's nothing to show. Fake. Gimmicks. Trickery. It has held people entranced since the dawn of time, only the people who know how to pull the strings are in control.'

'Bullshit. There is some very convincing evidence out there, and technology is more advanced now, we have more chance of capturing the real thing than they ever had all those years ago. Why do you not even want to try?'

'I'm on a timescale. If I had all the time in the world to humour you, I'd still not pursue it. We have two days in each location and activity needs to be recorded in each location for the series to be a success. Just as a small tip, that activity needs to reach some kind of crescendo at the end of the series. A little more of the frighteners. Unless of course, we do find the real thing, eh?'

'But we've been getting activity, and every time we do you yell bloody cut. What the hell is that all about?'

'I yell cut because it is my show. Whoever is faking the bits I know nothing about is not under my control.' He gave her a look that said he knew exactly who was controlling the other activity. 'I have control Meredith, at all times. You'd do well to remember that.'

'I'm not the one faking anything.' She spat.

'Congratulations.' Kevin depressed the clutch and slammed the car into first gear. 'Then you won't mind when I yell cut in future.'

Meredith grit her teeth as the car started forward

'I'll tell them it's all fake.' She shouted, swinging a hand to the building.

The car stopped almost before it began to move. Kevin flicked it out of gear and swung around, getting out of the car so fast that Meredith had to take a step back or be steam rolled by his forty-inch waist. She looked up at him, his eyes glinted with anger. She swallowed hard.

'You will do no such thing. This is the nature of a shoot. Nobody needs to know anything. I need real reactions—'

'Then find real experiences.'

His hand shot out and grabbed her arm painfully as he brought his face down to hers. His breath reeked of stale coffee and cigars.

'Meredith, I'm warning you. If you ruin this show I will ruin you. That's not a threat, that's a guarantee. Now, it's late. I'm tired. I don't have to explain any damn thing to you. You're here to do a job, and that job is to present my show in any way I see fit. I'm in charge and you will do as I say, or you will be hightailing it back to London on the next bus with your P45 in your hand. Do you have a problem with anything I just said? Because there will be no further warnings. You will be out.'

Meredith closed her eyes and shook her head. Her heart

was pounding with anger and injustice. She didn't like that she had been conned and she didn't like that the audience would be either, especially when she knew that real activity had come forward. She did, however, want this job.

You know he fakes it. It doesn't matter. You know you can deal with Evie now, enjoy the break, chill out, have fun.

'Everything okay out here?'

Kevin let go of her arm, stepping back as she rubbed at it.

'Fine, Matt, everything packed up?'

Matt looked from Meredith to Kevin.

'Not yet, I heard shouting, I—'

'You're mistaken, there was no shouting. Meredith and I were just having a difference of opinion, that's all.'

Matt looked at Meredith and she raised a smile and a nod that she hoped was reassuring enough for Kevin, then she looked away busying herself with re-tying her blonde ponytail to hide her anger.

Kevin heaved an irritated sigh.

'This goes no further, Meredith. Not now, not ever. I need this show to be a success, it needs to pull in the numbers, it needs to cover costs, or my ass is on the line. Get the kit packed up, get to bed, and pretend this never happened. You too, Matt. Oh, and while we're at it explain to her how a bloody show works would you?'

He jerked a thumb at Meredith, who shook with anger as he calmly got back into the car and started the engine. He leaned his head back out of the window as the car idled.

'We go over tomorrow night's schedule at 11am sharp in the lounge. Don't be late.'

Matt simply nod his head but Meredith, already wound up, was chomping at the bit.

'Maybe that schedule could involve planning some real activity.' Meredith snapped.

Kevin banged the steering wheel so hard it rocked the

car.

'Why is it so important to you to find the truth?' He shouted, red cheeks wobbling with the force of his words.

'Why is it so important to you to conceal it?' Meredith shot back, her own cheeks probably just as red.

A sharp tug on her arm almost toppled her backward and she cast a scathing look back at Matt. Kevin sat stony faced in the car.

'Is there anything more you wish to dig your grave with tonight Meredith?'

She opened her mouth to reply.

'Meredith,' Matt warned behind her.

Swallowing her words, she closed her eyes and shook her head, saying nothing.

Matt loosened his grip and pulled gently at her arm and she allowed herself to be lead away from the car a few steps as Kevin thrust into first gear with a crunch.

'Wise decision. See you in the morning, and don't be late.' He said looking pointedly at Meredith as he stepped on the accelerator.

Meredith bit back a thought, pursed her lips hard and then found it flying out from between them anyway.

'I hope you can see every string in your precious footage!'

The brake lights lit up as the car screeched to a stop, and Meredith held her breath, heart thumping, as the car sat purring.

Then the lights went off and the car disappeared slowly down the gravel and turned out onto the road. Meredith stared at the empty driveway, breathing hard.

'That was never going to be the best way to end that conversation.' Matt murmured behind her, his hand still on her arm.

Meredith spun to face him.

'I don't care. He was moving the cat ball and setting off the bear. I bloody saw him!'

'I know, I clocked him doing it too.'

She stared at him.

'But you said nothing?'

Matt looked at her steadily.

'What was I supposed to say, Meredith?'

'Well, I don't know, how about 'hey I know you're an ass, and you're rigging the set, but could you tell the guys instead of making them all look like idiots? I mean, how pathetic was all that crap in the room back then? Everyone getting all excited about a ball Mr Big Shot Asshole was moving all along, speaking to a dead man who probably doesn't exist, and if he does, he was so busy laughing at our ridiculous attempts to fake contact that he couldn't be arsed to come through to a bunch of amateurs anyway.'

She flung her arms out in frustration, heart banging with anger. Matt caught her hands gently in his own.

'Meredith, calm down. I don't know why you're so mad. We knew this already, didn't we? Why does this matter so much? This is television. I know it's not what you wanted, but he isn't trying to make everyone look stupid, he's trying to make a television show. That's all.'

'And we're supposed to be ghost hunting. Whether the ghost appears or not is surely the whole point of the series. It's about proof and finding real evidence, not trickery and faking events.'

'Well, not finding the ghost would be a bit pointless on a show called Paranormal Encounter—'

'Now you're sticking up for him? Matt, the premise of my job was to host a series which investigates the existence of the paranormal. *Investigates the existence of the paranormal.* Forgive me for thinking that we may have a stab at doing just that. I mean what the hell is the point, if no one is bothering to find out the truth then we could have done this in a studio in half the time. Fake sets with fake ghosts. Because that's about as real as it gets on this show anyway.'

Matt looked down at their hands, quietly intertwining his

fingers with hers. Meredith wanted to be mad at him, to pull them away, but while her mind raged, her stomach was busy exploding fireworks, and her body shook with the effort of not putting her arms around him and pulling him close. She liked the feel of his soft warm hands holding hers, holding her upright, a sense of steadiness when she felt like she may lose control.

'Meredith, beautiful, you need to calm down.' He said stroking his thumbs over hers. 'Kevin will have his reasons, and whatever they are we aren't in a position to question him. This is his show, he can do it in whatever way he wants to.'

'Or I can have my P45 and get on the bus back to London, right?'

Matt shrugged.

'That's just the way it is. There were girls hustling for your job. You could be replaced within hours. As much as you want to fight this, just think about whether it's worth it, because, unfortunately, you're not indispensable. And I'm not saying that to be mean, none of us are. He could replace any one of us with very little trouble or disruption, whichever way you look at it he's in control, he holds all of the cards. Sometimes it's better to keep your mouth shut, do your job, and move on.'

'Well, I have a hard time shutting my mouth. I didn't come here to faff around on fake sets. The reason I fought so hard for this job was to have a real shot at finding the truth. I'm not like the others, Matt, I don't need five minutes of fame, this isn't my dream job, it just happened to pass under my nose. I saw an opportunity and grabbed it.'

Matt nod his head.

'Right. Now turn it around. Kevin also has a job and sees an opportunity to give people the drama and scares that they love to watch. That's what makes a hit show after all. If we're all sitting around in the dark with nothing happening, then where's the show? He needs a good show. If it needs a helping hand then so be it. That's why he's director and producer. He's been in the industry a long time and he knows what works. What people want to see.'

Meredith huffed through her nose with a harsh *Hah*.

'What people want to see? Fake ghosts? Is that what people want? If that's the case, he should have told Donald just to wear a bloody sheet over his head and say boo to the camera. There's the ghost, eh? Bish, bash, bosh. Job done.'

Matt tried to disguise his grin, biting at his lip but Meredith caught it anyway. She took her hands from his.

'So, Mr Big Shot Asshole gets away with it and I get to keep my mouth shut. That's the long and short of it. I get it. Let's get the bloody equipment and get out of here.'

Matt put a hand on her arm, turning her back to him.

'For what it's worth, I'm sorry Meredith, I am. The world of television disillusions you very quickly. It's not glamourous, and most of the time it's either fake footage or the people you work with that are fake. It's hard, it's long hours, people are tetchy. It's about what works, not what's real.'

Meredith gave a nod. It was nothing she hadn't learned. A steep learning curve at that.

'I'm not trying to piss you off.' he said.

'You're not, I'm pissed off at myself for expecting more. Let's get the equipment.'

Matt was quiet as they walked back to the small medieval door and Meredith kicked herself that she had managed to make him feel bad again, on top of the news he had last night.

How much of your shit do you think he'll take, Meredith? He'll be glad to see the back of you in six weeks at this rate.

To make the matter worse, he walked with her to the door, he didn't go off ahead, he didn't lag behind, he didn't tell her she was an idiot for expecting more, he didn't try to take back anything he had said to make her feel better. He acknowledged that she was angry, even if he didn't agree that she should be, and stuck steadfastly by her side anyway, allowing her to have the moment.

It made her feel respected, and it made her feel like an ass.

She wanted to tell him she appreciated the way he handled her, appreciated his honesty. She wanted to tell him that she didn't blame him for any of this, and that he was the least fake person on a set she knew. She wanted to tell him how he made her feel.

But there was no time, and with lack of anything else to vent her frustration at, she shot a foot at the wall of the Lodge with a loud grunt, wincing at the pain that shot through her toes at the lack of protection from her converse trainers. Matt turned, hand on the door, eyebrows raised.

'I'm not sure kicking a seventeenth century lodge is going to help much, but if it makes you feel better…'

'It doesn't.'

'Right.' He said as she passed him, trying not to limp.

CHAPTER FIFTY SIX

Meredith was putting on her trainers when the phone rang the next morning. It was 6.02am, there was only one person ringing this early.

Mum!

She snatched up her phone, hesitating when Stephanie's name appeared on screen.

Stephanie?

'Hi Stephanie, Everything okay?' She said.

'Meredith? Hello. Sorry it's so early. Yes, things are going well with the excavation now that they've finally started, but good? Well, I don't know about that.'

Meredith's heart sank. She knew the feeling in the cellar at Lynton hadn't been right when they left. The place had felt more haunted than it did when they first arrived, and the presence of Elana at Stanmore yesterday only cemented the fact.

Not again, please, we can't go back for more, we move on to Aberdeen tomorrow. It's too far. Besides, I just don't think I can take anymore, I have too much of my own shit to deal with.

'What's up?' She said, putting a hand to her head and closing her eyes to push out the thoughts.

'Lots. I don't know whether you can even help me here, I'm not sure how much you remember. Elana is still active, Asha has been in the cellar again, and Orla is acting strange. Since the first night you guys came, she has been... well, off. I suppose the trouble with Elana has unsettled her, but honestly, she stopped the dig yesterday. She said that you hadn't given enough evidence to dig the foundations, and she said that you had only stirred Elana up, and that you were probably just a bunch of crooks. I'm at my wits end, I don't know what to do—'

'Well, that's strange. I had a message from Orla yesterday,' Meredith said with a frown—ignoring the crooks comment. Amateur yes, crook she could take offense to. 'She said that Elana had been quiet, and the dig was going well. She thanked us.'

Stephanie was quiet for a moment.

'What? Are you sure it was from her?'

'Hundred percent. She said you had a new number and to message on that one from now on?'

'Now why the hell would she do that? No, actually don't answer. I have a feeling I know why, it's the reason I called.'

'What do you mean?'

'Something niggled after you came round in the cellar and told me the story Elana had shown you. I didn't want to admit it, so I pushed it away. Now…' she gave a long sigh, 'Now, I just don't know.'

Meredith waited, she had no idea what Stephanie was talking about, and wasn't up for guessing right now. She yawned and rubbed the sleep from her eyes.

'Can you remember any of the details of the… the… what would you call it? Possession? Dream?'

Meredith frowned. 'Either I suppose, and yes of course, that's not something I'll forget in a hurry, believe me.'

'Right, well, could you clarify the details for me.'

'Which ones?'

'I'd rather not lead you. I want to be as sure about this as I can be, my heart is breaking right now.'

Meredith thought back to the tower, and then the living room, all the details of Elana's story (Rose?) were as clear as they'd had been two nights ago. Even the flicker of the floor from red to paisley mustard, the woman in the oversized jumper, the electric fireplace…

Meredith gasped in a breath, slapping a hand to her head, as her mouth dropped open.

Meredith, you knew this! How did you not link the goddamn carpet? The stair rail. Mum, dad. The fucking fireplace. Home, Meredith, it was home you idiot! You should have known! Fuck!

'Meredith? Are you still there?'

She swallowed hard.

'Yes. I'm just going through it in my mind to make sure I have it right. It was in the tower, Elana's mother pushed her down the steps—'

'Yes, I know that bit, sorry,' Stephanie cut in, 'I mean how did you know it was her mother? And you said she was speaking to someone after?'

Meredith raised her eyebrows.

I thought you didn't want to lead?

'Yes, so, Elana said that the woman was her mother—well, mama she called her. Afterward Elana showed me the castle living room where her mother was speaking about covering up the accident.'

Oh, dear Lord. I can't… Oh, John… I can't do this.

'John,' She said as the conversation came back to her. 'It was a man called John, definitely. First, she said that she couldn't handle it, he seemed to be pushing from the other side. Eventually she said that she would do it. She would say Elana ran away and the body could be buried in the cellar. She said that she would never be found as the cellar was being re-cemented. That was it.'

'You didn't get a year, you know, some sort of idea of time?'

Meredith thought of the cream tartan dress that could have belonged to any era in the last century. Dark Elana was practically modern she supposed remembering her from the lodge last night.

Dark Elana, or Eve?

Meredith's heart bumped against her ribs.

'Er, not really.' She said, 'She had a knee length dress, so I suppose twentieth/twenty-first century sometime? I wouldn't like to put an era on it, I'm rubbish with that sort of thing.'

'Right. Were there no other details you can give me. I just want to be sure I have this right.'

What did mum say? What did she say to dad by the fireplace?

Meredith shook her head.

'Er, well. I suppose the woman had on a long skirt, mousy hair, thick accent. Elana was blonde, brown eyes. Actually, come to think of it, she wasn't Scottish, she didn't even speak English bar a couple of words. It was a language I didn't know. Russian maybe? I don't know.'

Stephanie seemed to choke and yell at the same time.

'Are you okay?' Meredith said.

'I don't know. You said the mother had a thick accent?'

'Scottish.'

'Are you sure?'

Meredith hesitated with a frown. Come to think of it she didn't really remember the voice.

'I think so.'

'But you're not sure?'

'Well… I suppose I couldn't put money on it but I'm fairly certain.'

'Okay,' Stephanie sounded a little relieved. 'It's just that to an untrained ear the Scottish accent can sound a lot like—'

'Rose!' Meredith said cutting Stephanie off. 'I knew there was something else weird. Elana was showing me her story and called the woman mama, but the mother called her Rose, not Elana.'

Stephanie was silent. Meredith could hear the tick of the small clock on the wall. Twenty seconds, thirty.

'Stephanie?'

There was a sniff.

'Yes, I'm still here. Thank you. That's all I need. Thank you for your honesty.'

Meredith turned her phone to stare at it before putting it

back to her ear.

'Honesty? All I can tell you is what happened. Does it mean anything? What's the matter?'

'It means a lot. A hell of a lot. It means I know who the child was, and I know her mother. I know her very well indeed.'

Meredith's mouth dropped open.

'You know? Was it an ancestor?'

'No. My family would do no such thing. It was Orla.'

Meredith blinked, went to speak, and found she didn't know what to say.

'What?' she whispered. 'I mean… what?'

'I had my suspicions when you said about the floor being done. We had it screed over a little over three years ago now. Just before Asha was adopted.'

Meredith's breath caught in her throat.

'I work part time helping refugees. Three years ago, there was a boatload turned up from Greece, one little girl had lost both of her parents and a grandparent on the way. She had sat with the bodies for some time. They thought she was around nine, she had no family, nowhere to stay until the government could decide what to do with her. Orla and I offered to foster her until a decision was made, and a more permanent home was found. The charity know us, we've done this thing short term before and so we took her in. She didn't know any English at all. We didn't know her name, her birthday, any details, and so…' Stephanie gulped a sob, 'so we opted to call her Rose.'

Meredith closed her eyes, her hand finding its way over her mouth.

Oh shit. Orla? No.

She frowned and thought about the woman in the tower, her hair, her frame, her accent. Stephanie was right – Irish was so similar to Scottish unless you had a trained ear. Had Meredith been confused?

Oh shit!

Stephanie gave a sniff and then she continued.

'I had been out with the boys until late that day, when I came home Orla said that Rose had ran away. We had the police and the charity involved but she couldn't be found. She wasn't legal in this country, no records and no legal citizenship. It was presumed that she had tried to make her way home and that she or her body would turn up somewhere. We were heartbroken for her. Heartbroken, Meredith, when Orla knew that the poor girl's body was in our cellar the whole time. She knew because she put her there!'

Stephanie let out a moan, Meredith didn't know what to say. Shocked didn't come close.

'That's why she didn't rest.' She whispered, 'We didn't give the whole story.'

'That's why Orla wanted to stop the excavation, and why she messaged you to stop you speaking to me. That's why she wanted to lock both doors on the tower from then on. Oh God, Meredith, Oh dear, dear God. What do I do?'

'I don't know, I'm so sorry, I just don't know.' Meredith answered truthfully. Even with what she was going through herself she wouldn't trade places with Stephanie right now.

'Asha has never taken to Orla you know. Oh, I know she acts it, but she plays her. All the time.'

'I know, I saw it.'

'Does she know? Did Elana show her too? Has Orla threatened her?'

'I don't know,' Meredith said again, feeling a little useless after a revelation she could do nothing about.

'I have to go. Now I know the truth I have to sort this… mess. Thank you, Meredith.' Stephanie said suddenly.

Know the truth.

'Stephanie, if this is the truth, I can't tell you how sorry I am. I didn't mean or want to bring news like this to you. I'm so sorry.'

'I'm not, I wish you'd come sooner. I had no idea. What

if she had… had killed one of the others? Oh, I can't think about it, really.'

'No, Stephanie. It was an accident,' Meredith said confidently. It was, she had seen it. If Orla had done this then her crime had been deciding not to call an ambulance and burying the body for reasons only she knew. 'I can tell you that for certain. It wasn't cold blood. Yes, there was an argument, but she didn't mean to push her. It was an accident.'

'Thank you, Meredith, but you don't have to protect her. I'll be in touch. Take care.'

'You too, please call if you need anything. Anything at all.'

'Thank you again, for everything. Bye now.'

The connection was gone, and Meredith sat with the phone in her hand as her own mother's words came back to her.

It was a bloody accident, just leave it! Leave her alone!

Meredith broke into a cold sweat, as the dream/possession passed through her mind like a movie. Two Elana's, two places, two situations, two stories. Running parallel.

Elana's story, Eve's story.

Eve.

The black. The kohl, the chapped lips, the pale skin.

Dark Elana was Eve. Eve was trying to connect too.

Why wouldn't she?

It was Eve she had seen at the lodge yesterday. Eve screaming at her to know the truth.

Two separate messages.

You, Meredith, know the truth.

Find bones cellar.

One was on its way to being dealt with. But what of Eve's message? Of Mum's voice as she sat in the darkness, dad by her side.

It was a bloody accident, just leave it! Leave her alone!

You, Meredith, know the truth.

Meredith clenched her jaw, pulled on her jumper, and headed for the park as incriminations filled her head.

Fuck. Oh, fuck, Meredith. Why did you think you weren't told what happened? Why did you think you were shipped to all those therapists? Why is it you Eve won't leave alone? What the fuck did you do?

CHAPTER FIFTY SEVEN

Meredith's arms pumped and her feet slapped the ground.

Accident.

Harder, faster, driving out the words.

Leave it.

Breath coming in hard gasps.

Leave her.

The man appeared from nowhere and Meredith ran headlong into him. She spun around, a staggering hop on one leg and he stumbled back a few steps and turned to look at her.

'I'm sorry.' She said, holding a hand up to him 'So sorry, it was an…'

Accident.

'No bother but look where you're going in future.' The man said, 'you could have knocked me off my feet.'

'I will. I'm sorry.'

She turned away from him and set off at a brisk walk, all breath and inclination to run gone. Today was the first time the problems had outlasted the run. Today they clouded her thoughts even as she knew her muscles were spent, her calves tensed, chest aching.

Today she could curl up into a ball and cry. Except that she couldn't, because now there was new information that she had to sort, and she had no idea where to begin, but she had to know either way.

It's why Evie came back, it's why she'll never leave you alone, Meredith, she'll never rest because her little sister was probably the one that killed her—and what can you possibly say to make that better? How can she ever rest?

'Are you okay, hen?' A voice puffed at her side.

Meredith looked up to see another runner, a woman, slim and blonde, hair in a ponytail, not unlike herself, jogging on the spot next to her. A comrade of the early hours park brigade.

She had stopped walking, she realised, and was now standing in the middle of the path staring off into the tree line toward the road.

'Yes, thank you. Just catching my breath.'

The runner nodded, knees coming almost to her waist in a silent still run.

'I'll be away then, enjoy your run.'

'You too,' Meredith shouted after her as she moved off, hand in a backward wave as she picked up speed.

I must look like the lunatic of the park this morning.

She tried to smile at her own joke, but it wouldn't come. Her heart pound even though she had stopped running a while ago now, pounding for different reasons than exertion. She was shaking too. She looked at her watch. 6.45am. Near get-up time for the world, but nowhere near time for Kevin's meeting at 11am.

She shuddered and looked back toward the hotel. It was cold but she didn't want to go back, not to where she was couped up alone with only herself and her thoughts. This morning she thought she may just go insane—if she wasn't already.

She began to walk, easing her cold and tired muscles into movement as her mind ran.

My fault, it was my fault. All this time they've been protecting me. I pushed Evie. I pushed her and she didn't come home, no wonder mum is in such a state, no wonder she blames me. How did I not connect it before?

Am I normal? Can I do such a thing and still be normal? Even if I didn't know?

And yet, deep down she thought she must have known, it was always there, just on the periphery of consciousness.

She had always felt to blame for Evie's death, even if she hadn't known why. On the bad days, when mum really got a hold, she had even thought it would be easier if someone had just blamed her, told her off and held her accountable. But it hadn't worked out that way, everything had been concealed. They had protected her.

It had been an accident, they said. And she had believed it, her six-year-old mind not equating the two incidents. Not putting the pushing, and the death together.

'Six,' She whispered, her voice shaking. 'God, I was only six, and so, so, scared. They said it was an accident, they gave me a get out of jail free card. An accident!'

An accident through which mum had been forced to drink and mental issues.

'Leave it alone! Eve is dead, Meredith, dead!' Mum screamed throwing her whiskey glass at the wall where it shattered into a thousand pieces as Meredith hid behind the settee.

Issues not only from the loss of a daughter, but by living with the daughter that had taken her life.

I pushed her down the stairs. I killed her.

Meredith stumbled for a bench and sat down hard as more memories surfaced and she struggled for breath.

'Why do I have to constantly be reminded of the daughter I lost by the one that is living!'

Not only that but Meredith had killed her father too. Not outright, of course, but he had taken his own life because he couldn't bear to live with her any longer while trying to grieve and trying to look after his wife.

'Unless you can bring Eve back, you'll get the fuck out of my sight. I can't stand to look at you, Meredith.' Mum

screamed throwing the broom up the stairs after Meredith.

Meredith. Me.

'Why do you keep bringing this up? You need therapy Meredith, you're not right! You're not right in the fucking head!' Mum spat the last word, her drink sloshing over the glass onto the floor. 'People who are sick need fucking help.'

Me.

'It's okay Sputnik, it wasn't your fault.' Dad said. His arms warm and safe, quelling the fear.

So why did you go to a barn and tie the rope around your neck, dad? Why did you leave me and mum alone? What father abandons his six-year-old daughter at such a time?

One that knew the truth. One that could never look her in the eye again.

It was your fault, Meredith. It's always been your fault.

Warm tears fell onto Meredith's cold hands, clasped tightly in her lap, and she gasped in a sob.

Was it any wonder Eve couldn't rest? Was it any wonder she was trying to scare her? Was Eve trying to get her to admit it? Or did she just want revenge?

'I'm so sorry, Evie,' She whispered, tears coming faster, 'It was an accident, I'm so, so sorry. I loved you so much.'

The phone buzzed in her pocket.

Mum! Finally!

Meredith sniffed and pulled the phone out, taking a few deep breaths as she looked at the display…

And then her heart stopped.

Eve.

Her heart threatening to pound out of her chest Meredith's thumb hovered over the green answer icon. She swallowed hard.

If she wants to have this out, do it, Meredith. You owe it to her. Answer the call.

Meredith grit her teeth and pressed the answer icon.

'Hello?'

CHAPTER FIFTY EIGHT

The mirror on the dressing table reflected the early morning sunlight, casting the man's shadow back into the room and over where the woman lay. The man cocked his head as he moved forward, and the shadow released her body from its grip.

The woman didn't move. She was sleeping heavily, he had made sure of it, as he did every time he visited her room. An empty bottle of pink gin lay lightly in her fingers as her hand trailed off the bed and down toward the floor. Gin that had been laced with something that would keep her sedate, yet lucid, while he prepared to do his work. Pills prescribed for her own demons, but these would never touch her particular demon. The devil was too strong.

The man looked over to her, fingering his rosary beads as he recanted a small prayer, head bowed in respect. He would like to have dropped to his knees to show his appreciation but in this room of unclean filth he stopped himself. He would simply have to pray and flagellate with more vigour later in recompense. For now, the prayer would do.

His mutters faded away and he crossed himself three times.

He looked to the woman, drawing the cloak around his face. For now, her snores penetrated the room, long and loud. She wouldn't be snoring for long, but the man took no pleasure in the fact. That was all it was. Fact.

He turned to the dresser, replaced the old lilies with a new bunch, and lit a single lily scented candle. Leaning forward to cup the flame between his hands, he inhaled deeply. The scent merged him with God, and usually gave a little light to his work, although the sunlight was an unusual bonus today. In fact, the Sunlight was an unnecessary worry, and now he would have to be extra careful that the woman did not see his face, but after a cold night in the cellar, God's word had been strong this morning.

Today would see the completion of his mission.

There would be two sessions for the release of the woman's sins. One this morning and another later today. After that, his work here would be complete. He would be free to leave, free to retreat back to the shadows, until his next assignment was spoken.

He inhaled again, the sweetness filling his nose and lungs as he tilted his head toward the flaking painted ceiling. He pulled his hands slowly together in prayer and closed his eyes.

'With your divine guidance and instruction, I complete your work with diligence, joy and love. You are the master, and I your willing slave. So is my duty in life. Thank you, father.'

And now to finish his work. This morning she would bleed, tonight she would release her sins for good, and he would leave.

He approached the woman on the bed and gently pulled down the bedclothes that had been keeping her vile stench and uncleanliness covered. When the whole of her was laid bare, her naked, scrawny, useless body set out before him, he pulled on his black leather gloves and unrolled the small cloth pack he had placed by her head.

Wrinkling his nose at the stink of her, he reached for the leather binds, and then leaned to take her arms, binding them one at a time to the top of the bed by each wrist.

The woman moaned and grunted, but the man continued, she wouldn't wake yet.

Next, he tied each leg to the bed post at the end of the bed, spreading her legs wide, touching her as little as possible.

Finally, he lift her head, securing the cloth gag inside her mouth with a tight knot that pulled her cheeks back in a macabre grin.

He stood back and surveyed his work.

Good. And now it begins.

He moved his cloak aside and pressed play on the small media player in his pocket, placing the earbuds into his ears. Classical music, calm and flowing, filled his soul. He smiled.

He retrieved the small brown handle from the cloth roll and untied the rope on the end to let it fall out long and flat. The small tuft of fur scraped the floor. He ran his free hand from handle to the end of the rope, caressing it, becoming one with it.

He flicked his wrist and the rope curled, snaking down to the small tuft with a soft *thwack*.

'And so, help me God, help me rid this woman of the unclean sins of the flesh, so that she may live in peace until the cleansing begins again.'

He brought his hand up high and drew it down to his side with a firm flick. The rope snaked across the woman's bare midriff in a long line, with a firm, hard, thwack.

Her eyes flew open, and she howled against the gag, trying to sit upright in her shock. The bed pulled and rattled as her hands caught the ropes and pulled her back down to the mattress.

Her eyes rolled and she moaned, as a long weal of red snaked across her abdomen. She was lucid, but not fully alert, the effects of the pills put into the gin not yet worn off.

He pulled the whip up and let it go again. This time further up, across her breasts and those small, sin inviting nipples.

He curled his lip in disgust.

The woman bucked again and screamed. The man reached into his pocket and raised the volume of the music. It would need to be raised a few more times before this cleansing was through, but that was normal. He hummed to the melody as he brought the whip down across her milky skin, again and again. Her screams getting louder as he hit his stride, her thrashing against the restraints was violent, but the glowing red welts on her skin were satisfying.

To him, anyway.

The woman bucked and screamed, long and loud, baring her teeth at him. Her hair slicked back, body a sweaty sheen that told him of the pain she was enduring.

He turned the music up.

Ah, Beethoven's symphony No5. One of his favourites.

He closed his eyes, letting the music sooth him as he drew his hand up again.

CHAPTER FIFTY NINE

The phone blast static into her ear and Meredith jolted thrusting it away. It sounded a little like the Ghost box on steroids, getting louder and softer in bursts. Between loud bursts she gingerly held the phone closer.

'Hello?' Meredith said.

The static remained, and after another loud screech, Meredith disconnected the call with a sigh.

So much for that plan.

She stared at her phone, watching in half thought as the screen scrolled a message with a buzz.

1 new voicemail.

Meredith frowned. What was the point in static voicemails?

Oh well, at least you know what they are now.

'I'm sorry Eve. If you're trying to say something, I just can't understand you through the noise.'

She stood, shaking out her frozen feet and legs, feeling numb as she looked at her watch again. 7.04am. Time crawled when you were having such fun. Each minute seeming like a thousand.

Why don't you listen, get rid of those voicemails, and take it from there?

She agreed with herself that it was a good idea, but not out here. It was simply too cold. She didn't fancy the hotel room alone either, but she couldn't do this in public, what if Eve did manage to communicate?

Back we go then. Let's get this over with.

* * * * *

Back in the cosy hotel room, Meredith made herself a tea and sat down with her phone, a headache starting to brew as she called her mailbox.

You have five new messages. Hold to listen, then press one to save, two to listen again, or three to delete.

Meredith held, heart drumming and hands shaking as the first message clicked in. There was the hiss of static, not much different to that which she had heard on the park bench, her thumb was just about to press the three when she heard it.

The thin sounds of a voice.

Thinking her heart may jump right out of her throat, Meredith waited out the message and then pressed two to listen again. The static came again but this time she turned up the volume full, put the phone on speaker and placed it back to her ear.

The voice came again, and Meredith narrowed her eyes. It was female, but it certainly wasn't Eve. Then again, the playback was so dull and scratchy on the recording that Meredith thought she would probably never place the tone, so she listened for the words instead. There were only two of them before the message cut off.

Fucking bear.

Meredith reeled.

What?

Who the hell was that? Who *was* that, and what did it mean?

There was static on the phone and she realised that the second message was playing.

Listen to the rest, let's see if they make more sense.

Heart banging, she pressed two to start the message again. More static, and then:

Pushed... little shit.

Meredith felt winded. That one hit home. The voice was mum.

She shuddered.

Mum? No, not the mum of now, the mum of then. Like the scene at Lynton, it was old, the words scarred into history. Meredith's stomach clenched and rolled over as the third message began, static and then voice, same scratchiness as the previous two. This one was longer, but parts were familiar.

It was a bloody accident! Leave it! Leave her... Leave her alone, she didn't mean it.

Lynton. That sounded like the scene at the castle, Meredith thought trying to keep emotion out of her thoughts. If mum was protecting her here, then why had she seemed to be determined to make her life hell ever since?

Meredith put a hand to her face. Her head swam, pain thumping above her temples.

The fourth message held a male voice. She knew who the man was immediately. Another voice that she thought she would never hear again after the incident in Cornwall. It wasn't quite as faded and scratchy as the other voices, easier to make out. Dad.

Not your fault, Sputnik.

Meredith's eyes clouded with tears and her heart seemed to physically drag down through her chest.

I wish that were so, dad, I really do.

She swallowed hard as the last message clicked in, recorded at 7.03am this morning. It sounded far away but was much clearer than any of the previous recordings. This was definitely Eve, her lullaby voice sending the tears spilling over Meredith's cheeks as it took her back nearly twenty-five years. Shame the words weren't quite so nostalgic.

You know the truth, Meredith.

I do, Meredith thought as tears dropped onto the phone screen.

'What do you need me to do, Eve?' she whispered. 'What can I do?'

There was a chill, a soft breeze that sent prickles down Meredith's arms and legs. A breeze that felt charged.

Meredith held her breath, determined not to run anymore. It was too late for that.

The phone suddenly burst static, loud, and then quieter as a scratchy voice came through the speaker.

Fucking bear

Meredith nearly passed out on the bed until she realised the mailbox was playing the messages round again. She picked up the phone, wiping the sheen of sweat from her forehead.

Bloody hell, Meredith, you'll give yourself a heart attack. Just turn off the voicemail system.

Wiping her tears, she ended the call to the mailbox and placed the phone next to her on the bed.

It rang immediately. The shrill tune making Meredith yell out. She looked at the display expecting Eve, but this time it announced Mrs Grey.

Meredith huffed out a relieved breath.

Thank God. At least I'll find out about mum now.

She answered with a hello that was as cheery as she could muster, but she needn't have bothered. Mrs Grey was panicked, speaking quickly into the phone with a low voice.

'Meredith! I think we have a situation here. There were some strange… noises… earlier, so I've been round to see your mum this morning, but she's not answering the door again. I peeked in the living room window and... so help me God,' Mrs Grey paused, and Meredith heard her heart thumping in the silence.

'What?' She whispered.

Oh, Meredith, I think there's a man in there. I saw a man pass the doorway.'

CHAPTER SIXTY

DECEMBER – DAY OF DEATH

'You said you wouldn't! You promised Evie,' I screamed pummeling my fists against my sisters' stomach. I didn't care whether I hurt her. I *wanted* to hurt her.

Evie grabbed both of my hands in just one of hers and placed a hard hand over my mouth.

'Shush. You'll wake mum and dad.' She said hissing into my face.

'I want to.' I tried to say but my voice was little more than a mumble under her fingers. I bit at them, catching the skin on her palms.

'Ow, you little shit. Moo, don't be an ass, I'm not going away for long, I'll be back soon, just shush, okay?'

'You said you would never see me again if you went! Then you promised you wouldn't go away at all.'

Evie raised her eyebrows and sat on her bed with a huff.

'Will you keep your voice down. That was then, this is now. I'm not going to be long, moo, I'll be back soon.'

'Then why do you have the same bag? You said you would see Rizla today, and now you have the bag, Evie!' I wailed.

Evie tried to calm me, making shushing noises like mum used to do when I was little, but I knew better. My tummy was swirling, and her words didn't sound right in her mouth. She was LYING. Mum said LIARS went to hell, and I wasn't so sure I cared about Evie going to hell right now, as long as she was with me until she was old enough to go there —which was very old.

'This is the only bag I have, you idiot. Of course, I'm

taking it.'

'You're meeting him, and you won't come home.' I shouted, 'you're RUNNING AWAY, Evie, just like Chelsea's big sister.

Evie placed a hard hand over my mouth.

'If you muck this up for me, Meredith I swear to God I'll —'

'You'll what?' Mum stood in Evie's doorway, hands on hips, cigarette in her mouth. Her hair was mussed. Once, when my hair had looked like hers, she asked if I had been DRAGGED THROUGH A HEDGE in the night. 'What's going on? It's five-fucking-thirty in the morning!'

'Nothing,' Evie muttered looking down at her hands. She did this with mum a lot now, like mum was stuck in her hands, not in the doorway.

'Am I on glue, or do you have make-up on?' Mum squinted closer to Evie, and I squinted my eyes at her feet. No glue. But before I could tell her, mum was already speaking to Evie again. 'Make-up, no uniform, a coat, and a bag? What's this?'

'Nothing, it's non-school-uniform day. We can wear what we want.'

'No, it's not.' I said. That was two LIES, double Hell for my LYING sister.

A sharp elbow dug into my ribs.

'How would you know, idiot?' Evie spat, her nose scrunched at me. 'Do you go to my school?'

'You're not even going to school.'

'Of course, I am.' Evie laughed, rolling her eyes at mum, who scowled in the doorway. 'Where else would I be going?'

'To the Scout Hut to meet Rizla, then you're running far away. You said so.'

Evie's face went red before she exploded.

'Why would I do that you stupid idiot? Where—'

Mum cut her off mid-sentence with a laugh. She laughed so hard she couldn't get her breath. Evie and I watched. I was always wary when mum acted STRANGE. Usually something equally strange and not very nice happened afterward. What was she laughing at?

'Running away?' She finally gasped, 'Where the fuck are you going Eve? The cineplex? The roller drome?'

She sneered as Eve looked away toward her wardrobe.

'I'm not running away.' She mumbled, scowling at me. She didn't say it, but I knew what she wanted to say with those eyes.

Thanks a bunch, idiot.

I didn't care. I was glad mum knew, maybe now she would sort Eve out and she would stay at home. I stuck my chin up and folded my arms as dad did to mum to tell her the CONVERSATION WAS OVER.

'Open the bag.' Mum said.

Evie's mouth dropped open, and she reddened. 'No, it's just school stuff. For *school*.' She said looking pointedly at me. I looked up at the ceiling, arms still folded.

'Open the bag.'

'No.'

And that was when ALL HELL BROKE LOOSE. Mum rushed into the room; her teeth bared like mine on the day of the cat. She grabbed Evie by her coat, her fist under her chin as she pulled her to her feet and placed her nose almost on her own. I scuttled to the pillows on the bed, crouching out of the way, my heart thumping wildly.

'If you're going to school, why do you have your coat on at five thirty in the morning?'

I saw Evie try to swallow, saw her face go pale, and I almost wanted to take back what I had said to mum. Maybe dad would have been better. He would have sorted things calmly.

'I was just trying it on.'

Mum pushed Evie back on to the bed with a fist. Evie's head bounced off the wall behind with a sickening crack. I screwed myself up tighter into the pillows, arms around my knees, seeing her eyes roll almost to the WHITES as mum screamed.

'Open the fucking bag, NOW!'

Evie blinked and put a hand to her head with a grimace.

'NOW!'

I flinched as mum snatched the strap from Evie's hands, pulled the zip open and stuck her hands inside.

'What the hell is going on?' Dad said from the doorway, rubbing his mussed hair, like he was in a loop motion of exactly what mum had done just minutes before. Mum was now throwing clothes and shoes from the bag onto the floor, the underwear she threw at Evie like she hadn't heard dad at all. I sneaked a glance at his face, but he had a confused, tired look, like he was still asleep.

'Knickers? How many pairs do we need for school today? One, two, three, four, five, six,' she counted them out as she threw. One landed on Evie's head. I would have laughed if I hadn't been so terrified. Mum leaned back in towards Evie, bag still in her hand, 'What sort of fucking education is this? WHORE academy?'

My breath caught. Mum was always calling the people she didn't like DIRTY WHORES. Did that mean Evie was firmly in her don't like pile? But how could she not like her own daughter?

'Woah, woah. Nancy, calm down. Have you had your tablets this morning?'

Dad was rubbing his eyes so he didn't see the look mum gave him, like she would gladly cut him into pieces and feed him to Mrs Grey's cat. She swung around, the near empty bag banging off Evie's knees.

'No dear,' she said with one of her fake smiles, her teeth were clenched together like they were glued, 'It's not yet six and I was supposed to be sleeping. The girls woke me up with their incessant squabbling, and a good job, because one of our little babies was about to become a stowaway.'

'Huh?'

I rolled my eyes at my knees, my arms hurting from holding so tight. Sometimes dad could be so SLOW, and now mum was winding up like a clockwork doll. Once the key was fully wound, she would go off like a bomb, and that was the time I didn't want to be here. I swallowed.

'Dear little Eve was running away.' Mum pulled more stuff out of the bag and finally came across an envelope. She threw the bag aside and opened it up. Inside were more notes than I had ever seen in my life. My eyes widened as Mum pulled them out and stared, and dad finally began to catch up.

'Running away? Eve is this true? Sweetheart I've said —'

Mum cut him off with a roar. 'Fuck me Eve, where did you get all this?' Evie's eyes grew as wide as mine as she shook her head. 'If this is mine and your dad's... If you've been stealing... I'll cut each of your thieving little fingers off with a bread knife. One by one. Where did you get this money?'

'It's mine,' Eve muttered, her bottom lip shook, and she looked like she may cry. Her hand was still holding her head like it may break at the back.

'Nancy, let's just—'

'Yours? Yours! Where on earth would *you* get a wad of cash like this?' Mum's lip curled in a sneer and Evie looked back at the bedspread.

'I saved it.' She said.

'Saved it from where?'

'It's mine... I saved... I sold some stuff.'

'What did you sell? Your fucking BODY? You dirty, dirty little SLUT—'

'That's enough, Nancy!' Dad shouted over her, his feet thudding into the room. Mum swung to him, thunder on her face, and I slipped out of the door to huddle on the landing. From here I could watch to see if everyone was safe but run to my room if things got too bad, like they had last week when Evie had come back late.

'What? Do you have any other fancy pants ideas about where the hell she got it from?' mum raged.

'Why don't we calm down and let her tell us…'

'She FUCKING SAID. She said she SOLD STUFF. What fucking stuff? Can you tell what the hell she sold?' Mum raged around the room throwing items off the shelves and pulling the wardrobe doors open so hard one ripped off a hinge and hung like a broken limb.

Dad motioned Evie behind him, and she stumbled out of the room, standing just in front of me at the top of the stairs. As she listened to the whirlwind that was our mother destroy her room, a single tear ran down her cheek, and she looked so sad, that I gulped down my own tears.

I'm sorry. I said silently to her, hoping she could read my lips as dad tried to calm mum in her room.

She gave me a sad smile and a small shrug and then dipped her gaze down to her fingers.

In the room, war raged. There was shouting and banging, and then mum was flying toward the bedroom door with the curtain pole, complete with one curtain that was hanging on for dear life. She looked for all the world like she was hoisting the OLYMPIC FLAG, just like they had done on telly last summer. Mum looked past dad, raising it high, and all of a sudden, I knew what she was going to do.

This was all my fault, now I had to help Evie, who was looking down at her nails not knowing what was going on just a few steps behind her.

'Noooo!' I screamed, pouncing off my cat legs and lunging at Evie, knocking her off balance as the curtain pole crashed onto the bannister just behind my head. I turned to look, and then turned back to Evie, but she was gone.

Falling.

I screamed but no sound came out as she rolled over and over, bouncing and crashing against the wall and the bannister, which shook as though someone had let off a bomb

outside. Then she reached the bottom with a small 'oof'…
and she was still. So still that she looked like one of my dolls,
her open mouth a small 'o'.

In that moment it seemed as though everyone was still.

Mum stared from the landing, hands still on the curtain
pole which hung over the bannister, curtain draped like a flag
with no wind. Dad's mouth was open in the bedroom
doorway, his face looked like he had seen a ghost, and was
just as pale. I turned back to Evie, my mouth saying things
that I couldn't hear. The world was silent, and Evie was still.
I felt my legs crumble as dad's hand scooped me around the
waist, taking me down the stairs with him.

'It's not your fault Sputnik,' he was saying. 'Not your
fault. Evie is fine, it was an accident, she's fine, It's not your
fault.'

CHAPTER SIXTY ONE

Meredith's hands shook as she closed the suitcase and zipped it shut. She looked around the room, a quick glance to see if anything was left, and then she put the case on the bed and left the hotel room, walking down the corridor to room 101.

Kevin's room.

She tried to calm her nerves as she rapped on the door, but thoughts of the man flood into her mind at every opportunity. When pushed, Mrs Grey hadn't been quite so certain it had been a man, there had been nothing but the sighting which she agreed was only a flash, the other noises she heard through the wall of the semi-detached were probably just normal Nancy. To top it off, just before she got to Kevin's door mum had finally contacted with several ranting messages that could only be her.

Meredith didn't know what to believe, where to put herself, or what was real anymore. All she knew was that she had to get home as quickly as possible. Her mind tried to work through information she didn't have yet, and it drove her crazy.

Was there a man? Was mum okay? Was this just a ploy to get her home? How would she get home? Was there a train from here? What train was it? What time? How fast could she leave? How many hours would it take to get back? What if the train was leaving NOW and she was HERE? What if there was NO train? Could she get to Inverness to fly home?

The door opened and Kevin stood before her. Stern but not unkempt. This was a man who had been up a while, as she had herself.

Good job he's not a runner, I may have met him at the

park.

'Meredith? What the hell is it now?'

'I need to speak to you.' She said.

* * * * *

Fifteen minutes later she was back in her room. Jobless and thoroughly dressed down. She had told Kevin the situation, told him she was going home—yes, right now—and that she was very sorry, she had to resign, on the spot. No, she wouldn't be back, he would need to call one of her understudy groupies.

Well, she hadn't put it quite like that, but he was angry enough to tear a strip off her anyway. Angry at her stupidity for coming up here with a mother so ill, angry that she had pushed for the job and was now leaving, angry that he had taken a chance on her, angry that she had been such a pain in his ass, angry that she was one of the most competent but aggravating presenters he had worked with, angry that she was not coming back and had ruined a good team, angry that she would have the audacity to leave halfway through, angry that she would jeopardize the ratings of the show.

She had simply listened and then told him that the next presenter would give him better reactions—they wouldn't know of his strings.

Kevin had gone red and fired her on the spot. Her incessant need to poke at him infuriated him, he said, he could take no more.

She had thanked him and left.

Now she was trying to find transport home, but her hands shook so much she couldn't unlock her phone, and her mind was flicking through scenarios so quickly that she couldn't think straight.

She wanted to throw the phone and cry. Instead, she calmed herself enough to leave the room and a few seconds later she was knocking on Matt's door, hoping he was awake. If he was still asleep, she didn't know how she would hold it together. Thankfully, he opened the door quickly, fully dressed, the room smelling like toothpaste and coffee.

'Meredith? What's up?' He started. Then he saw the look on her face and pulled her inside shutting the door. He gathered her into his arms and held her tight.

'What on earth is the matter?' He mumbled into her hair, his voice vibrating through her as she held him back, equally as tight, tremors flooding through her.

'I have to go home.' She said into his jumper. Warmth, stability, cigarettes, and aftershave. 'Right now.'

He pulled back so that he could look at her.

'What? Why?'

'Mum.'

And thank heaven he needed no other explanation. He understood, it was enough, even if it wasn't all of it. He nodded.

'Okay, have you decided how you're getting back?' He said working through his thoughts out loud. 'Inverness has an airport, there's a train station down the road but I imagine you'd have to go to Inverness, maybe Glasgow, to get a train back to London. Coach? Not sure where there's a station though.'

He pulled out his phone and sat on the bed, Meredith sat beside him, shakes and her heart finally slowing as she pulled her thoughts together under his calm authority.

'Whichever is quicker, seriously.' She said.

He nod his head, scrolling down search results, and clicking different sites. She watched him, willing him to have a solution that got her home today, even though he wasn't in control of planes and trains and buses.

'Any preference? Does flying bother you?'

'No, slow bothers me.'

'Okay,' He scrolled some more. 'So, it looks like Inverness is your best bet either way, how far is that from here?'

She waited quietly as he looked it up.

'An hour, realistically. Okay, well the next train leaves at 10am which gives us an hour and a half. Do-able.' He mumbled. 'The next flight is at 2.30pm, but—'

'I'll book the train. I have to get the hell out of here.'

Matt looked at her, eyebrows raised.

'Well, the flight would be better if you want to get home at a decent time today, cheaper too.'

'I'm not bothered about cost. I can't wait here for hours. I need to get out. I have to get moving, sitting around will eat me up. It's eight-thirty, Matt!'

He nodded and took one of her shaking hands, squeezing her fingers as he worked the phone with his other hand. 'All right, I get that, but the train will take around ten hours or so, you'll be in London by, say, eight this evening. The flight is an hour and a half—you should be back in Heathrow by four. It would be Heathrow you'd want, right?'

Meredith nodded as his explanation wound its way into her thoughts. He was right, even by sitting around here driving herself mad until the flight she would be home almost four hours sooner. He tapped at his phone, attention back on the screen.

'I'll take the flight then,' she said. 'I suppose it gives me more time to—'

Sit around and chew over the fact that I killed Eve, and that mum wasn't joking about the man.

'—sort out my ticket and transport.'

'It's all booked.' He said, putting the phone down at the side of him on the bed. 'I'll drive you to the airport, don't worry about that.'

She blinked.

'What?'

'It's done,' he said with a sad smile.

'Thank you, how much do I—'

'Nothing. Really. You're going through enough, it's the least I can do.'

'But this isn't your fault, you don't have to…'

'I want to.'

Meredith snapped her mouth shut with a small nod. Tears filling her eyes at his kindness.

'Thank you.'

He ran a hand through his hair with a sigh and then put an arm around her shoulders pulling her into a hug.

'What the hell happened?' he whispered.

'I finally got hold of mum's neighbour. Mum hasn't let her inside for the last couple of days. She looked through the window and thinks she saw someone inside. A man possibly.'

Matt pulled back to look at her with a frown. 'The man we talked about? Have you called the police?'

Meredith bit her lip. 'That's the tough bit. Mrs Grey couldn't be a hundred percent certain. She thought she heard something earlier but since then it's been normal mum stuff, even down to the television programs she was watching last night and this morning. And look at this.' She unlocked her phone and showed Matt the messages she had received since Mrs Grey had called. 'These are all unprompted since Mrs Grey's call. I haven't been in contact with mum since the day before yesterday, she won't take my calls. This morning, these came through.'

Matt looked through the messages that had passed between them this morning. Mum apologising for her behaviour and asking for Meredith to come home so that she could start again. She didn't want to drink, she said. She wanted to get dry, she wanted them to have a life. She needed Meredith's help.

He raised his eyebrows.

'Well, these certainly don't sound like someone in trouble.' He said.

Meredith shrugged and leaned to scroll down to the next few.

'Well, I'd be inclined to say those weren't mum, incidentally, but these next ones escalate into normal mum talk.'

She felt her cheeks redden and her heart begin to thud as he read over the cutting remarks about how she was neglectful, and deceitful, abandoning her for all this time. How selfish she was for going away to hunt ghosts when she had a mum to look after, and how she wanted her dead, and that she should never come home. All of that and more, despite Meredith saying that she would be home today.

It was all stuff that Meredith was used to hearing and turning off from. A useless conversation, but by keeping mum on the phone, she knew that she was okay. Eventually the messages made no sense and Meredith assumed she had hit another bottle.

Matt said nothing as he read, and Meredith swallowed hard as she leaned to scroll to the last few messages.

'This bit at the end, I think maybe she found something else to drink. But the bits above are her all over. Her words, her expressions, she says this stuff all the time. There's no way this can be anyone but mum, which would suggest that she's okay.'

But Matt wasn't reading into the fact that mum was okay, he was too busy reading the words and their meaning, something Meredith was adept at skimming over.

'Shit, I… I underestimated how bad this was,' Matt mumbled as he scrolled. 'She can't speak to you like this, Meredith, it's not right.'

'It wasn't this bad when I left. It has been in the past, but not when I took the job. She had her moments, but she was doing well. This has spiralled again.'

He shook his head with a frown, still reading.

'Look at this,' he said pointing to the messages between them where mum had apologised for all the man talk and said no one was harassing her after all. She had brought the lilies herself.

Meredith felt tears well up, and she began to shake again.

'I know, this is why I'm constantly worried, I don't know what the truth is. If Mrs Grey even saw a man, is he legitimately there? Is this just another game? I don't know what to do.'

'Exactly what you're doing,' he said, his words punctuated as he passed the phone back to her. 'There's no other way is there? She ran you into a corner and left you no choice. Not returning your calls, leaving you to worry after she's told you about this man, and now she says there's no man—but there possibly is.' He huffed and ran a hand over his face before turning to look at her. 'This is manipulation, Meredith, you know that don't you? It's manipulation and it's wrong.'

'I know, but—'

'I know you'll say she's your mum, and it's the drink and quite probably some of it is, but she can't speak to you like that. Look at your answers compared to what she comes back with. It's like she's having a different conversation. I hope you don't listen to any of that shit, Meredith, because that's not fair.'

'I try not to,' she said, looking down at her shaking hands. She had listened to her mum all her life in one way or another, Mrs Grey had often told her that mum wasn't her responsibility, but no one had ever thought to tell her that it wasn't right, or that she didn't deserve it. It was alien, and it wasn't the reason she had shown him the messages. She had thought that he would just agree that mum sounded okay. She didn't know how to respond.

Matt shifted on the bed and took her hands in his.

'I'm sorry, I'm not angry at you,' he said. 'I'm just sorry you have to go through this, and I'm sorry I said this man was probably in her mind.'

'He could still be.'

'He could, but I shouldn't have swayed you either. I didn't know how bad things were.'

'I thought the same, Matt. There's no other way this

would have played out. Even if I had said nothing, I'd still be at this point right now.'

'Well, I'm pissed you're at this point,' he said with a sigh. 'for you and for me.'

'What do you mean?' she said.

'I mean I really hope your mum is okay, but right now I'm absolutely gutted that you're leaving.'

He pushed back the stray hair that had fallen out of her bobble and ran a hand gently down to squeeze her shoulder.

'I'm gutted too.' She said, trembling from his touch as much as the situation. She tried to smile but wasn't sure it ever reached her lips. 'You'll be fine, there will be another presenter in a matter of hours.'

He stared at her, his fingers caressing her shoulder.

'She won't be you.' He said.

The tension made her want to throw herself into his arms and stay there until this was all over. She felt tears form behind her eyes and tried to deflect the emotion.

'I guarantee she'll be less argumentative. The show will run a lot smoother, and she probably won't keep you up half the night with footage she shouldn't be watching.'

He smiled and then ran a hand over his face with a sigh.

'That's true, it's certainly going to be quieter around here.'

'You'll probably get to smoke in peace too.' she said with a small laugh.

Meredith felt the butterflies explode in her stomach as he moved his hand to her face and brought his forehead to rest on hers. 'I'm going to miss you.' He whispered.

She nodded and closed her eyes as his hand moved gently from her face and wound back into the hair at the nape of her neck. Her heart thumped with nerves and desire. She thought she had never wanted a kiss more, but simultaneously didn't want it either. She had a feeling that she wouldn't see him again after she left, and that she would only be hurting herself by immersing herself in another memory of what she would be missing as she got back to her own miserable life.

Then he moved closer, and she knew she wouldn't be able to resist either way.

God if you're up there, I need a Matt in my life. Preferably this one. I don't care how you do it, but please let this man be part of my future.

His lips met hers gently and she could resist the pull no longer. She wound her hands around his waist, drawing herself closer, surprising herself with the intensity and desire that swirled inside her, as he pulled her in, deepening the kiss. It had been a long time since she had wanted a man, and she had never wanted one this much. She shook with emotion, fighting the desire to go back for more, as the kiss ended too soon, and she was left clinging to him. He wrapped his arms around her, holding her just as tight.

'I wish we'd done that earlier,' he said into her hair. 'and I wish to God you didn't have to go,'

'I wish to God you could come with me.' She whispered.

'I'm half a step away, believe me. If it wasn't for Kevin, and the fact that it's his last shoot and I'd leave him in the shit, I'd jack it in and come with you.'

Meredith's heart flipped over.

Stuff Kevin, come back with me, please. I need you, she thought as she heard her mouth betray her.

'You couldn't, I've got a ton of crap to sort through and you have a show to finish.'

'After the show though?' he said, 'Can I come and see you then?'

'Of course, if you still want to. The next presenter may blow your socks off yet.'

'I'm not allowed to romance presenters, and I don't like trouble,' he said, a grin playing on his lips as he pulled back, cool air circulated where his warmth had been. He kissed her cheek. 'You want a coffee?' He said standing.

'Yeah, that would be nice.' She said, watching him as he

flicked the kettle on. 'For the record, I don't believe you.'

'That I need a coffee?' he said with a grin as he added coffee and milk to two cups.

'That you don't like trouble. You got talked into looking over the footage and going back to Lynton with a fair amount of ease.' She stood and moved over to him. He swung an arm around her as the kettle clicked off. 'I think there's a rebel in there somewhere.' She said, circling her arms around his waist.

'I think you're underestimating just how persuasive you can be, beautiful.' He said with a laugh as he poured the water and stirred the drinks. 'We did have some fun though, eh?'

Meredith nodded, warmth washing over her at the pet name. Even with her mum, and Eve, and the stress of Elana, she had laughed more in the last week than she had in years. He put the spoon down and curled his other arm around her, planting a kiss on her head.

'I hope your mum is okay, Meredith, I do, but it's a real shame you have to go. It won't be half the show without you here.'

She lay her head against his shoulder.

'You mean without the drama, and fighting, and someone for Steve to wind up about the bear…'

Matt chuckled. 'Steve hasn't had so much fun for ages, and Helen has become so much braver with your encouragement. Remember that first shoot when she was so scared that she wouldn't join in any of the activities? Look how she was at Lynton when we went back the other night.'

'She's grown a lot.'

Matt pulled back to look at her.

'She looks up to you, you can see it in her face, in her actions, she follows your lead without question.'

'Even when I'm busy leading you all into getting fired.'

'Yeah, all of us.' He said with a grin. 'Like I said you underestimate how persuasive you are.'

He lift her chin to kiss her softly, deeply, taking his time. She gave herself to him completely, letting go, letting him lead, savouring the feel of him. So familiar and yet so unfamiliar. Relishing every moment, committing it to memory, every nerve tingling at the gentleness of his touch. Then he broke away and encompassed her in his arms with a moan.

'Meredith, this is torture,' he murmured.

Meredith nodded and held him tight. Emotion swirled in her stomach and she couldn't tell if it was warmth or despair, whether she would laugh or cry. In just a few short hours Matt would be gone, and she would be home. Whatever was going on with her, and Evie's death, and mum and this man, she would get her answers by this evening.

Some answers she wanted, some terrified her, but this didn't seem to work in halves—it was all or nothing, and nothing wasn't an option.

CHAPTER SIXTY TWO

'A matter of days ago we were driving up the Cairngorms and I was thinking we may have trouble with you, after the way you had gone off at Kevin the morning after Moweth, remember?'

Meredith smiled at Matt, she watched him as he drove, drinking him in, she didn't want to forget anything about him. Not the colour of his eyes, the shape of his nose, the press of his lips, the feel of his arms. All of it she wanted to ingrain onto her memory forever.

No matter what he said, there was still six weeks of the shoot left, a good amount of time after you had known someone a matter of weeks and were practically living in their pockets, to forget the rest of the world existed. Meredith had certainly tried to forget.

'And now you know it was true.' She said. Her stomach an anxious swirl. Now that they were leaving for the plane it was suddenly real that she had to go home and face mum, and maybe an intruder, and the truth about Eve's death.

'Now I know I completely underestimated you.' He said.

She smiled, looking at Matt's hands on the steering wheel, his arms as he turned the car. She suddenly wanted to be going anywhere but home. Wished she was going somewhere with Matt, away from the world and from the pressure of home indefinitely.

'Don't go to the airport, Matt, take me somewhere far away instead.'

Matt reached a hand across to grab hers.

'If I could, I absolutely would, but you wouldn't thank me for it if something happened to your mum.' He said. 'Kevin also wants me back by three.'

'I'll blame Kevin then.'

'Hey, he let me drive you without much persuading, and he took you aside and said some nice stuff. I do think he liked you more than he let on. You kept him on his toes.'

'Humph.' Meredith said, but a warm feeling crept over her as she thought of Kevin's words and the team's goodbyes.

Matt was right, Kevin hadn't taken much persuading, even telling him that it was a good idea as long as he wasn't late back. Meredith had gone to the meeting with Matt, regardless of her leaving. She wanted to tell the others herself that she had to go, and Kevin had gracefully stepped aside to let her, much calmer after the argument this morning. Possibly something to do with his finding another presenter already. After their exclamations and regrets that she had to leave, Kevin had dismissed the meeting, and pulled her to one side.

She had expected another dressing down and was fully prepared to take it, but he had surprised her. He said that it was regretful that she had to go, she had been right for the show and she would be hard to replace. A natural presenter with a real invested interest was almost unheard of in his field, and as much as she had irritated him, he found her doggedness, and her ability to stand her ground admirable. He also admitted that some of their best footage had been gained after he had yelled cut and thanked her for that. If he had been staying in the business and her mother's condition had been cleared up, he would happily have worked with her again – although threatening her with dismissal every day was wearing thin.

The idea that he would have sought her out to work with her again had been both terrifying and humbling. She wasn't sure what to say, so she had stuck to thank you, and Kevin had wished her well for the future.

She walked out of the room to find Matt waiting outside

the door with Helen and Steve. She told them what Kevin had said as they walked back to her room, where they had an hour of an amazing room service lunch, with reminiscing and laughter and plans for the future, before she and Matt had to leave. It was like the last supper, Steve had said, and then he had hugged her hard.

'I haven't had so much fun for ages, Bangers, we're a good foursome. After this, we should drop the professional shit and make a show together, what do you think, Matilda?'

'I think that sounds bad for my mortgage repayments… but a lot of fun.'

'I'd love that!' Helen said. The most she had to look forward to after this was going back to business school to please her parents.

'What the heck are we going to make a show about?' Meredith said laughing as she hugged Helen just as hard as Steve.

'Ghosts!' Steve and Matt said simultaneously, and then looked at each other with a laugh.

'Yes!' Helen said, 'There's nothing else we could do that would be as awesome, Meredith, really.'

'You guys can say that because you weren't the ones getting possessed by a little ghost girl the other night.'

'Hey, we could ask Donald—' Steve started.

'No!' Meredith and Matt said together. 'Just the four of us,' Matt finished.

'Agreed.' Meredith said, pulling them into a group hug. 'I'm going to miss you guys.' She said.

'It's not going to be the same without you,' Helen said, 'You've taught me such a lot, not least that the paranormal isn't as scary as I thought. And who's going to throw sarcastic remarks about my screaming?'

Meredith laughed. 'I'll probably hear you from London.'

'We need to get each other's numbers,' Helen said, ever the organiser.

Meredith added Matt, Steve, and Helen's numbers into

her phone and then Matt broke up the party.

'We really need to go,' He said rubbing a hand at Meredith's back.

There were plenty of tears as she checked out, Helen and Steve walking down to see them off. Meredith had waved until they were dots in the distance behind, hoping that she would see them again one day, when all the crap was over and done with.

'You okay?' Matt asked, her hand warm in his, only taking it away to change gear before it was back.

'Yeah,' she said. 'Getting nervous.'

'Make sure you call the police when you get there, please don't go inside alone. Who knows who this man is and what he wants, he could be dangerous. I know you may not want to hear this, but you also don't know whether you'll be walking into a crime scene of some sort.'

Meredith nod her head at him. Logical, authoritative, calm, supportive, honest—and not afraid to be.

'I know,' she said, 'that has crossed my mind.'

'I wish I were going with you.'

'Me too.' She said, thinking she had never wished anything more in her life.

'I wish this man hadn't turned up.'

'Me too.'

'And I wish I hadn't told you it was probably imagination.'

'Ah, don't worry about it, it wasn't anything I wasn't telling myself. Do you believe in fate, Matt?'

'Fate? Um, I don't know. Never really thought about it. How do you mean?' he moved his eyes back to the road.

'Like everything happens for a reason, and everything happens when it's meant to, regardless of how we try to intervene.'

'I guess. Like Final Destination?'

Meredith thought of the film she had watched many

years ago.

'Yeah. When it's your time, it's your time.'

'Okay.' He said waiting.

'So, I'm thinking, whatever happens with mum, it was just meant to be. I couldn't do anything more, or anything any more quickly. It was the situation and the events leading up to it. Like the fact that she had stopped drinking and had been dry for months when I took this job. I really think she started drinking again to spite me. To get me home, where she wanted me. I didn't want to go, so I tried to ignore her, and yet here I am. Going home early.'

'That's the curse of living with a drunk.'

'It's also partly fate. Whatever happens from here is just the way it's meant to be. I'm going to try not to worry about it.'

'Well, you certainly couldn't have done any more than you have, no. If she was dry when you took the job, it's only taken a matter of days for her to relapse. You couldn't have known this was the way she would go when you left.'

'No.' She said, looking out of the window at the fields, seemingly endless until finally a small sign announced the airport.

Matt turned into the side road, around an island, and into the car park, pulling the SUV into a space a short walk from the entrance.

'You'll be charged.' Meredith said. 'You should have just thrown me out.'

'I didn't want to throw you out.' He said. 'I want to be able to say goodbye properly without being moved on.'

'I don't want to go.' She said, the shakes beginning to take over her body. 'I don't want to say goodbye at all.'

'I don't either.' He said kissing each of her shaking hands. 'I wish I had time to come in with you.'

'I'm okay, plenty of books to read and people to watch.'

He nod his head and she ran out of words, terrified that she was only a couple of hours from home now, and utterly dejected that they were at the end of their journey together. Matt looked as downcast as she felt.

'Come here.' He said, pulling her into a hug over the centre console. 'I'm really going to miss you.'

'Me too,' she said holding onto him, then she huffed a laugh and he pulled back with a smile.

'What?'

'Just thinking you won't miss the late nights looking at footage, or the early calls, or late nights with chocolate. I guess you may get a half decent amount of sleep each night now.'

He nodded, 'hmm, you forgot one. The one where you banged my door down like a lunatic and jumped into my bed. I also won't miss the fights with Kevin, and the wondering whether I should listen to him, or keep recording, as you ignore his yells of 'cut.''

She laughed. 'Sorry about that.'

'How long have we been here again?' He said, rubbing his chin.

'Feels like months, doesn't it?'

'It does.' He huffed a breath and looked down to his hands, locked in hers. 'Let me know you got home safe, and keep in touch, won't you? I want to know you're okay, and what's going on with your mum. When I get back, we'll get together somewhere to catch up properly.'

Meredith nodded. 'I will. And yes, that sounds nice.'

Matt looked at his watch.

'It's nearly quarter to two, best get you inside.'

He leaned across to open the door for her and then got out himself, pulling her case from the backseat of the SUV and wheeling it round to her.

She looked up at him and he placed a hand on her cheek bringing his forehead to hers.

'You're going to be okay.' He said.

In all honesty she had no idea if she would be okay, and although she had been alone most of her life—a drunk mother didn't count—she had never felt more alone than at this moment. There were no words for how she felt, so she followed her gut and leaned in to kiss him instead. The same swirl of desire and despair circling her abdomen as she circled her arms around his back. He felt the same, she knew it, could feel it in the gentle, but full kiss. A final kiss. A kiss full of both longing and sorrow. A kiss that made her wish they could go back to yesterday so that she could tell him how she felt earlier. A kiss that ended far too soon as they broke apart and he pulled her close.

'Thank you for listening to my craziness, and being patient with me, especially where Kevin was concerned.' She said, head on his coat.

'It wasn't a problem, any of it. I've enjoyed these last couple of weeks more than I've enjoyed shooting any other show. I quite like the paranormal… or maybe it was just the presenter.'

'Good job Kevin isn't here to hear you say that.'

Matt chuckled and pulled away to look at his watch again. A stickler for timekeeping, she thought. Then again, he had worked with Kevin for seven years, and he would have to deal with Kevin's wrath if he was late back.

'I'd better get inside,' she said, 'I'll miss the flight.'

'Yeah. The show must go on.' He said with a sigh, no trace of humour on his face.

'I'm not indispensable, I know.'

'To some,' He said, running his hands down her arms to her hands, and clasping them softly. 'Not to me. I've never met anyone like you before, Meredith.'

'I've not met anyone like you either.' She said a lump in her throat that threatened to open a whole dam of tears.

He kissed her softly and pulled her into a tight hug and the dam opened anyway as she sobbed into his coat.

CHAPTER SIXTY THREE

The bright Scotland autumn of the last few days turned to wet murk as the plane took off and headed back to London. Matt had booked her a window seat, just behind the wing, which was serving her well now. She could look out of the window, ignoring her neighbour and everyone else. Letting the chatter morph into a constant drone, like white noise, with the occasional ding of a hostess call button.

Tears streamed down her face, much like rain had streamed down the window of the plane as they rose into the cloud. Above the cloud there was nothing but a cold autumn sun, fluff below, as though the plane was riding on cotton wool. Meredith wished her tears would subside as quickly, but they didn't want to stop.

There was such a range of emotion inside her that she couldn't settle.

Despair at having to leave her friends and a job she was thoroughly enjoying, even if its purpose had been made obsolete, and the purpose of Eve's haunting was now revealed. Despair at leaving Matt with his pretty eyes, beautiful smile, and calm, easy-going, but honest nature. Despair that she may have done something so bad that it had been concealed from her for all these years. Even a ridiculous despair that she was leaving Stephanie with her own mess and would now be too far away to see her again anytime soon.

There was a deep anger too. Anger at the situation that had taken her away from all of these things. Mum. It simply came down to one person. A woman fully in control and not drinking when she left, who was now an incomprehensible mess. A woman who may now be in trouble, which Meredith may have been more inclined to believe was real, had mum not been in such a state. Now it seemed that the man was most probably real after all.

Which moved the dial to terror. Terror of who this man was, what he wanted. Terror that he was in their house. Terror that he had already hurt mum, maybe even killed her.

Meredith swallowed back her tears with a loud gulp, drawing a glance from her neighbour, whose reflection she could now see in the drying window of the plane.

She pulled out her phone and kept her head down as she read the messages from Mrs Grey, who she had kept informed of her flight details as she had waited to board the plane. Mrs Grey said that there had been no sign of the man since, although mum still wasn't letting her inside. In fact, she had seen nothing from mum in the last two days. She suggested calling the police on the way back, in the hopes they would enter with them to see what was going on. Thinking of what Matt had said about entering a crime scene, Meredith had agreed.

Then she looked at the message Matt had sent as she had checked in.

Deep breaths, keep calm, let me know when you're home or I'll worry about you. Miss you too much already. xx

She ran her thumb over the message, as though she could reach out and touch him that way, but more tears rose to her eyes and she switched the phone off instead, looking back out to the clouds below.

The drop into Heathrow was turbulent, the clouds low and heavy with rain that poured from the darkening sky. Meredith checked the time, three fifty as the wheels touched the ground with a thud, they had made good time, now she just had to get back to Uxbridge and the three-bed semi that she had called home all of her life.

In the back of the taxi, Meredith hovered over Mrs Grey's number, but she didn't press call. Mum was vulnerable, and with drink in her it would frighten her to death to have a barrage of police forcing their way inside, whether Meredith was there or not. She had rung mum a couple of times from the airport in Inverness and several since getting into the taxi, but if she was there, she just wasn't answering. Not unheard of, Meredith thought, trying to calm her edgy nerves.

She sighed and fired off a text to Matt to keep her mind occupied for the twenty-minute drive instead.

Nearly home now, just the last few minutes to the house to go. Thank you so much for today and for all your help I don't know what I'd have done without you. Missing you lots, hope everything is going well up there. xx

She put the phone down. It was just after half past four, they were possibly at the lodge now, maybe setting up and speaking to Elsie again, he wouldn't be able to reply for a while. Proving her wrong and living up to his reliability, the phone pinged a reply almost immediately. Nerves swirled as she opened it.

It was nothing, beautiful, wouldn't have had it any other way. It's going okay. New presenter is nice, very professional, very straitlaced, won't put a foot wrong and won't argue with Kevin. More interested in how she looks than the show, def after 5 mins of fame. It'll be a very ordinary shoot from now on. I'm trying not to think about how much I'm missing you, but messaging is almost torture. It hurts!! You should be here with us. Let me know how it goes even if you have to message at midnight. I'll be up recording some show anyway. xx

He added a winking and a heart emoji to the end. she read

through it again feeling her heart flutter at his words, before replying.

I wish I was up there too, I'd rather be hunting ghosts with you guys, even with Kevin. I'm glad you're getting on okay though. Missing you loads and scared to death. Two streets to go! Dreading what I'll find. Have fun tonight. Xx

She had been brief, and given him a get out clause, letting him off the hook if he was busy, but he didn't take it.

Please be careful, I'm getting more nervous the closer you get! Remember what I said earlier and remember I'm only a phone call away. If you need me—ring. I don't care what time. Message with how you get on either way or you'll be depriving me of sleep... again! Xx

She smiled as she answered.

I will, I promise. Kevin may care what time I call! I wish you were here. Xx

Me too, beautiful. You're right, not between ten and two, any other time is fine. Xx

He followed with more laughing faces. Meredith grinned and started to reply when the driver startled her out of her bubble.

'Here we are, love.'

He pulled up next to the kerb, and she handed him two notes.

'Keep the change.' She said, getting out and pulling the case onto the lit street behind her. She swallowed hard as she stared at the house. The same as it always was, and yet changed all the same. Her heart began to pound as she fished the keys from her coat pocket.

Home, sweet, home.

Shit.

Why is this stuff always worse in the dark?

CHAPTER SIXTY FOUR

The stale stench hit his nostrils as the man swung the door open. He placed a cloth over his nose and mouth. It was dark, no moonlight tonight to cast him some grace. Outside the day was coming to an end, and the cloud covered the sky like a funeral shroud. Tonight, it would be justified.

Excitement rippled through him, and the man forced it down. He would wait for his master's word with patience, his eyes adjusting to the darkness with a speed that could only be God's work. This stench, however, was the Devil's work. This was Satan's lair, and if he'd had any trouble wondering if God had been right in his direction with the woman, he knew it from the smell in this room.

Vile, Unclean, rancid, dead.

He would need to purge after his work tonight. He had been too slow to get the cloth over his face. Some of the putrid air had been drawn into his lungs. He gagged. Forced himself to stop, to breathe, to compose himself. The purging would be for later, right now, he had to finish what God had started.

He crossed the dark room with a purposeful, but steady stride. He never rushed, especially when he had a job to complete. He had learned the hard way that to hurry creates fear, and fear is destructive. In the years since he had found God, he had learned to eliminate all fear. He was in control of this vessel on earth, and God was in control above. As a team there was never a need to hurry, and never a need to fear. Faith was all that was needed, and faith would complete every job successfully. All he had to do was listen.

There was a noise from the bed. A muffled shout he supposed, although under the tight gag it was hard to tell.

She was awake then.

He was no medic, but he thought that much more of the drug would put her out for good.

Earlier, one of the only times he had ever worked in the day, the neighbour had come round, banging on the door, and peeking through the windows. This afternoon he taken the music from his ears and plugged it into her speakers, playing classical music loudly, hoping to defer the lady later. This evening he had tied the woman's gag tighter to further muffle the sound.

The plan for tonight was simply to complete his work with the unclean one and leave, but with the devil waking, he was no longer sure how long the neighbour would keep her nose out if the noise level rose, especially as he needed the music in his ears to work. If the man had been inclined to curse, this may have been a moment when he would have.

Instead, he waited for a sign, then he made his decision.

The devil had to be dealt with. She had to be contained. The neighbour would be dealt with afterward if necessary.

He muttered a prayer before getting to work.

'Thank you, Lord, for allowing me to see the path. The challenges I face today I overcome in your name, to become a stronger, purer man of God.'

He moved to the woman on the bed, reciting the lord's prayer over her, before placing the ear buds into his ears.

Ah, Vivaldi. Thank you for this sign, Lord.

Invigorated by the music he picked up his cloth pouch and began to unroll it, placing it carefully on the dressing table by the flowers.

The woman swung to him with a low growl, teeth bared against the gag. Her eyes rolled back as she thrashed against the restraints on the bed. He wasn't worried, they would hold her firm.

The woman screeched and thrashed again, her eyes wild as the man watched her, hands in prayer at his chest, waiting for the way forward to come to him.

He hummed to the music as it became clear.

Then he looked at the woman, lifted a gloved hand, and brought a fist down into her face. Hard.

She was immediately still, a slither of blood trickled from her nose. He would have to watch he didn't get it on him.

'There now, that's much better,' he said, his voice smooth and low as he retrieved what he needed from the cloth roll. 'And now, for the work.'

CHAPTER SIXTY FIVE

The front door of the adjacent semi-detached opened, and Mrs Grey bustled out into the illumination of her front door security light.

'Meredith!' She said charging over to give her a hug that Meredith welcomed. 'Why didn't you call? I could have called the police. Hang on, I'll go and get the phone—'

'No need, Mrs Grey. I changed my mind. If she's got drink in her she'll be frightened with all of the people, especially as she's not expecting me home.'

'Did you try to call?' She said.

'All the way back.'

The rain had slowed to a fine drizzle – the kind that soaked you to the bone. Mrs Grey wiped the mist from her glasses.

'I've been round five times. I haven't seen the man again, but neither have I seen Nancy. I've tried calling and I've knocked the door each time I've been round.'

Meredith's stomach flipped over.

'That can't be a good sign.'

'It's not all bad dear, I did hear music coming from inside earlier, so she must be okay physically. It wasn't her normal choice though by any means—it was classical.'

Mrs Grey folded her hands over her bosom with a shiver in the damp air. Meredith nod her head, her fear easing as Mrs Grey touched her arm.

'I'll go and get my coat dear, and I'll come in with you.'

Mrs Grey went back inside, and Meredith looked back to her familiar front door, chewing on her lip with a frown.

Classical music. Mum said something about a classical playlist, didn't she?

A shudder ran through her. What the hell was she about to uncover in her own home?

At worst, the man had murdered mum, and was now living in the house as if it was his own—playing classical music. At best, mum really did have a new man, and they had been sitting together, maybe drinking together—playing classical music.

But mum hates classical almost as much as hymns.

Meredith ran a hand over her wet hair as Mrs Grey came back outside, pulling a coat around her shoulders.

'Ready?' she said.

Meredith nodded.

'You sure you don't want the police?'

'Only if they're needed. I want to check it out first.'

'As you wish,' Mrs Grey said as they walked down the weed strewn tarmac driveway.

Meredith unlocked the front door and swung it open into the cool hallway. The house was dark and silent. No television, no radio, no noise. It was as though the occupant was away, maybe at work, maybe on holiday, definitely not home.

Meredith nod her head to Mrs Grey, who suddenly looked older as they entered the house and turned on the hall light.

There was no mess, no sign of a struggle, everything here was as it should be.

'Mum?' she called, and Mrs Grey hissed.

'What if the man is still here? Stay quiet and we have the advantage.'

Meredith nodded. It made sense, although he may have seen the hall light by now.

'Where did you see the man?' She whispered, looking back over her shoulder.

'Going past the living room door.' Mrs Grey whispered back.

'Did he see you?'

'No. I don't think so. His face was covered, he was wearing some kind of cloak. It was most odd.'

'The whole thing has been most odd,' Meredith whispered back, 'I can't understand what this man wants with her.'

Mrs Grey shrugged, and Meredith moved to the kitchen at the back of the house, surveying the mess with growing dismay. The worktops were cluttered, used plates and dishes filled the sink, and a bottle of whiskey was smashed on the floor. Two empty bottles of wine sat on the small table, and a bottle of vodka was displayed among the cleaning products behind the open cupboard door above the sink.

Mums pill box sat amongst the mess on the side. The pills that had been organised and set out into days for a whole three months just before Meredith left, were now more than half gone, the days mixed, the pills possibly too.

Mrs Grey pushed in beside her with a gasp. She put a hand to her mouth and closed her eyes.

'It wasn't this bad a few days ago I promise you, Meredith. I had no idea… she wouldn't let me inside.' A small sob left her lips and Meredith grasped her hand and squeezed.

'It's okay. It all comes down to the fact that she wasn't ready to be left. Obviously, I left far too soon after she got dry. I should have given her more time.'

'No, you mustn't blame yourself, you had a job to do, Meredith. These were Nancy's choices and she's a grown woman.'

'And I'm her only family,' Meredith murmured, scanning the mess.

Nothing that can't be cleaned fairly quickly, I suppose.

'Let's go to the living room,' she whispered, turning back to Mrs Grey, who stepped aside to let Meredith pass.

The small living room with its double windows and long drapes was just as she left it three weeks ago. If she didn't know any better, she would say that her mum hadn't been in this room since the day she left. Only the empty bottle of tequila on the settee, and an almost empty bottle of rum on the coffee table gave away that she had been inside the room at all.

'This is weird,' Meredith said in a low voice.

'It's like she's disappeared.' Mrs Grey said behind her.

'I don't like it.' Meredith said, flutters of terror circling her stomach as her heart pulsed behind her ears.

Upstairs were the only rooms left to search, aside from the cellar. Four. Mums, Meredith's old room, Evie's room, and the bathroom. As she looked toward the stairs, she hoped to God that her mother's body wasn't up there.

Hope to God the man isn't up there… sorry God, I can't help it at the moment.

'Meredith?' Mrs Grey whispered. 'Do we check upstairs?'

Meredith nodded slowly. 'I suppose we'd better. Just in case.'

She heaved a breath and turned to face Mrs Grey, who placed a hand over her heart and closed her eyes.

Is it a bad sign that she's as nervous as I am that we'll find something?

Meredith passed Mrs Grey and paused at the bottom step to look up the staircase.

The staircase you pushed Eve down, you're probably standing right where she lay.

Bile rose into her mouth, and she ran a shaking hand across her face.

Mum, Meredith, just concentrate on mum.

Mrs Grey placed a hand on her arm, almost making her jump out of her skin.

'Meredith, this is lunacy. I should call the police.' She whispered.

'It may be a good idea.' She whispered back, relenting. 'Just in case.'

She turned back to the stairs which suddenly looked a mile high.

THWACK.

Meredith jumped, stepping back into Mrs Grey, who gave a small yell.

'What the hell was—'

THWACK.

Heart pounding, Meredith looked to her neighbour, who was now ashen, her mouth in a small 'o'.

'Call the police. Stay down here,' Meredith mouthed to her, and suddenly all out of curiosity, Mrs Grey nodded, pulled her mobile phone from her coat pocket, and stayed at the bottom step without a fight.

THWACK.

Meredith didn't want to climb the stairs, she wanted to wait for the police. The voice in her head screamed it, her heart demanded it, and yet her feet climbed.

One step. Two steps. Three steps.

THWACK.

Meredith had heard the sound before, not an exact replica she thought, but it had been a long time ago. The snap of the tea towel as mum had whipped it across her or Eve's backsides. Mum found it was one of the quickest ways to get attention from either of them. No one liked the sharp snap of the towel, especially when it caught the face, or the back of the legs. Eve had once howled and had a mark across her face for two whole days after one such whipping.

But mum lives alone. There's no one to whip now.

You're so dramatic. It's probably just mum making the bed up, you do realise that.

Eves was the first bedroom at the top of the landing, next to the stairs and Meredith was rewarded—or sickened—by the fact that the noise seemed to be coming from her room. The door was closed, other than the loud thwack that came in pulsing rhythm now, there was no sound. Meredith pressed her back to the wall next to the door and heaved some breaths. Mrs Grey caught her eye as she spoke in hushed tones—to the police Meredith presumed. She signalled where the noise was coming from, and the lady gave a nod.

Heart in her mouth, Meredith reached a hand to the door and pressed gently. It gave under her touch. Not closed all the way, she wouldn't have to throw it open in ambush, that was good.

Maybe you should just wait for the police.

But now she was here she just had to peek, because if it was just her mum snapping the duvet, or even a towel, she would be highly mortified when the police beat down the bedroom door, and mum would be terrified.

THWACK.

Doesn't sound like the duvet.

Open the damn door if that's what you're doing, Meredith. How is it you can speak to the dead with no issues now, but you can't handle the living?

She felt a tickle by her ear and brought a hand up to wipe sweat off her face. Her heart was beating too fast, and her breath was ragged. At this point she thought she was more likely to pass out right here on the floor than to find out if it was just her mother in the room.

You left a voicemail saying you were coming home. Several. She's doing the bed for you, I'm telling you.

Maybe, but what if it's the man?

There's no man.

THWACK

Mrs Grey saw a man. Through the window.

It could have been mum in a gown. Maybe she has a new one with a hood.

Could be the man.

The BAD MAN.

THWACK

Meredith shook her head, trying to force the tumbling thoughts from her mind.

The BAD MAN is in Egor

There was never a BAD MAN. Eve made him up.
Is Egor still in the cellar?
THWACK
Was the BAD MAN this man all along?

With a silent roar of frustration that stretched her neck tendons as she clenched her hands. Meredith screamed at her own chatter.

SHUT THE HELL UP!

The voices seemed to flinch in shock, silent for a beat. The arguing silenced. Meredith used the moment of clarity to step away from the wall, turn to the door and push it inward before she could think another thought. She had never been so scared in her life—and her life had been a series of scares, let's face it.

The door swung wide, quickly and quietly, coming to a halt with a soft swish on the rug that used to be by the bed, before Meredith had moved the bed to the other wall, where she could see the doorway and the curtains simultaneously.

Now she almost screamed with shock. She clamped her hands over her mouth tight, eyes bulging as she stared into the room.

Before her stood a figure, at such an angle that most of its back was presented to her. She couldn't tell whether it was male or female, but it was dressed in a dark robe, a hood over its head. On Eve's old dressing table were fresh lilies, and a flickering candle which looked precariously close to falling off. As she watched the figure raised a hand and pulled back a long whip, the end almost brushing Meredith in the doorway. After a moment of pause the arm snapped back down and the whip followed crossing the bed with a loud THWACK.

Meredith flinched.

Where's mum? Who the hell is this? WHERE IS MUM?

She felt like a rabbit frozen in headlights. There was no other sound in the silence between the thwacks. Not from this figure or from anyone else. It was surreal, almost more surreal than anything she had experienced on her ghost hunts.

Where is the noise? Where is mum?

THWACK.

She may be on the bed. The figure is hiding the view.

BUT THERE'S NO NOISE!

And as Meredith stood in the doorway, she knew. She knew that this wasn't right. She knew that her mum was dead. That this person—man—had killed her. She was either on that bed at an angle Meredith couldn't see, or she had fallen to the floor at the side of the bed. The whip would snake right over and around the other side of the bed, long enough to hit either way. There was no other explanation for this strange scene with...

...NO NOISE!

Time slowed as Meredith's head spun and her vision swam.

No, there would be no more murder in this house. No more of her family would have their life cut short at the hands of another.

Meredith roared. A rage building inside her so huge that she thought she could have pulled the entire house down if she had to.

Out of the corner of her eye she saw Mrs Grey ascend the stairs in slow motion, her mouth moving at the phone by her ear, her expression full of both fear and horror. And then Meredith lost sight of her as she entered the room. In three long strides she had the figure, placing both hands on small shoulders. With a grunt she pulled the figure back and pushed it aside to reveal the rest of the empty bed.

Her bed.

Ripped to shreds from the rope of the whip that had hit it many, many times with a force that would probably have ripped *her* to shreds if she had been sleeping in it. There were russet stains too. Streaked, dry, and dark.

Blood? Is that blood?

Heart exploding in her chest, she jumped on the bed, ready to see her mother's body behind it, but there was only carpet. She dropped to her knees, looking under the bed, as the chanting began. Low, and menacing.

She hesitated, hearing the force of her breath pulling air in and out of her lungs, and then she peered slowly up over the bed.

In the doorway the figure was hunched over in a crouch, only its hands visible. In the grip of its fingers was a rosary, mumbled words pouring from a mouth hidden by its hood. Out on the landing behind, Mrs Grey was pressed against the banister staring at the figure, hand to her heart. She caught Meredith's eye, and tried to motion something, possibly that it was the same man she had seen. Meredith wasn't interested.

'Who the hell are you, and where is my mother?' She yelled, jumping back over the bed in a single motion, and grabbing the babbling figure by a fistful of robe at its neck.

'I said what have you done with my mother?' she screamed in the figures concealed face.

The stench of alcohol was overpowering as she pulled back the hood roughly with her free hand.

Shocked, she let go of the figure and staggered back into the room, slipping on the dropped whip behind her.

'Meredith?' The figure said.

Meredith stared, her mouth dropping open, a headache forming over her eyes.

'Mum?' She said. The air seemed to leave her body like someone had punched her to the stomach.

The figure that was Nancy Knight dragged the earbuds from her ears and threw them off her as though they were vermin. She looked at her own robe in confusion, held the rosary up high in her hands, and then she began to cry as classical music poured from the small earpieces into the quiet of the room.

'Help me, Meredith. Please, I think I need help. Forgive

me father, for I have sinned.'

In the doorway of her dead sister's door, Meredith's non-religious mother slumped to the floor, held the rosary close to her mouth, and began to chant.

CHAPTER SIXTY SIX

Meredith listened to the ticking of the clock and wondered if she were insane.

The odds were good.

She had a father who had opted out of life, even though he had looked sane enough, she had possibly killed her own sister, and now she had a deranged mother who had been detained for the last week. Dissociative Identity Disorder, amongst other underlying conditions, was the conclusion until the official diagnosis.

The official word was that she would be kept in the facility until diagnosed and treated – unofficially, the doctor was almost certain that Nancy would never leave care. There would have to be a miracle with the medication, not unheard of, but not likely, given the drugs she had already been prescribed over the last thirty years. She was too far gone. Babbling to herself incoherently, hands grasping the beads that they hadn't been able to take from her. Her mind was simply not there anymore, she was too unstable. Too far gone.

Meredith sipped her tea in the quiet living room. She stared at the blank screen of the television and wondered what she had done in a former life to get such a shit deal in this one.

Shit deals come when you do shit things. Eve was your fault, Meredith, you shouldn't have pushed her. Accident or not. What do you do about that?

She knew that no one would ever know what she had done unless she told somebody. The last living person to know was insane. Heck, if Meredith went about shouting the truth now, with her family, and history of therapy, she would probably find herself locked up with her own mother. Who would believe the word of a six-year-old child, twenty-five years later? Especially one who wasn't even there when her sister died. A sister whose death was confirmed accidental at the time.

It was pointless. Futile.

The point now was could *she* live with what she'd done?

She swirled her tea in her cup.

Or what, Meredith? What's the other option? To do like dad and opt out?

Doesn't sound like a bad plan. I can meet Eve on the other side and explain how sorry I am. Maybe over there we get to be sisters again.

Ridiculous. Death solves nothing.

'So how on earth do I process this information and move on?' she said aloud. 'It's impossible.'

There was a tick in the hallway. Just small, light, but enough to get her attention.

Meredith sighed. She was tired, she'd had enough of this to last a lifetime, but here it was again, how much more did Eve want? How much more would she have to take?

As much as she wants you to. It's your fault.

'Eve, please,' she whispered into the quiet. 'I'm home. I know the truth, I get it, I pushed you. Please rest Evie and let me rest too. I'm sorry, I don't know how many more times I can say it. I'm so, so sorry.'

She placed her cup on the small coffee table and rubbed her hands over her tired eyes.

Tick.

A giggle. Soft, feathery, far away.

Meredith fought the urge to cry.

'Mer-e-dith.' The voice was low, whispery, singsong.

Meredith felt her heart turn over, as goosebumps littered her body.

Eve. But stepped up. She had never spoken before. Not here.

Speaking to the dead had opened channels, Scotland had opened channels. And Eve was not afraid to use them.

How was I to know that it would make things worse?

Terror running through her, Meredith got up and went to the hallway.

'Eve, please, I can't do this any—'

She cut off abruptly at the figure stood in the hallway. Her heart giving a jolt and appearing to land in her throat, blocking her air as she gasped.

Eve, or should that be dark Elana, stood in front of her. Short black skirt and top, grey face, unkempt black hair, and black ringed eyes. She stared at Meredith and Meredith stared back, fighting every urge to run and hide under the cushions on the sofa.

You can do this Meredith. Pretend you're on a shoot. Matt's here. He has the camera on you, Steve has the Mic, Helen is by your side. Kevin will be mad if you don't give him action.

Meredith took a shaky breath and let it slowly out, switching her brain into presenter mode. Pretending that this was someone else's house, someone else's ghost. Her friends behind her. She swallowed.

'Okay, Evie…' Her voice shook and she cleared her throat as Eve's presence stuttered like an old movie reel. 'Okay, I'm listening. What can I do? How can I help you?'

Eve cocked her head to one side and then she moved her arm slowly. Already shaking, Meredith thought she may expire with fear if Eve came any closer, but her sister only pointed…

…to the cellar door.

Meredith's knees began to knock, and her legs felt weak as she stood at the living room door. She grabbed the door frame to hold herself upright.

'I can't go down there Evie. I really can't.' She said, shaking her head.

Evie laughed, her figure stuttering as though the sound

caused interference. The scent of lilies reached Meredith's nose and then her dead sister walked *(glided)* to the cellar door. The door swung slowly inward exposing the concrete steps running down. A rush of cool air entered the hall causing Meredith to shudder. She swallowed hard, a cool sweat breaking out over her body.

Why is it always the damn cellar? Why?

Meredith stood firm and shook her head. She wouldn't follow Eve as she walked to the top step, she couldn't, even as Eve looked back at Meredith, her expression so sorrowful Meredith thought she may cry. Then Eve turned and disappeared down into the darkness. Gone. As though she had never been there at all...

...the open cellar door confirmed that she had.

The hair on Meredith's arms stood on end. She took a tentative step toward the dark opening, holding onto the doorframe as she peered, trying to catch a glimpse of her sister, seeing nothing but blackness.

She felt her hand leave the smooth wood, felt her feet move toward the darkness, even as her head protested. Each step she took she wanted to close her eyes and put her fingers in her ears until it was all over. In the possession at Lynton, she had closed her eyes though, and Elana had been stood right in front of her when she opened them. If Eve did that now, Meredith didn't think she would ever stop screaming, and so she forced her eyes open, forced herself to see.

At the top step, she stared into the darkness, feeling exposed as the cold air rushed around her.

'Eve?' she whispered, her own voice raising the hair at the back of her neck. She reached out and pressed the light switch, fully expecting it not to work, but the single bulb illuminated the space below just as it always had.

Meredith's ragged breath began to steady as she looked down into the old cellar. Ahead of her were the racks complete with the old boxes that had always been there. At the bottom of the steps, pushed to the side was the box which Meredith had thought was for someone named 'Charity' all those years ago.

Back when we were putting Egor into the cellar.

The day Evie really got hurt, when mum truly lost it, and the blood from her hands merged with the clown's orange hair.

Meredith shook away the images and peered around to the right where the cellar ran under the rest of the house. It wasn't a large space, but the bulb's light didn't make it right to the end. In the far wall were the steps leading up to a small trapdoor from the garden. The door dad had installed, like the local pub's, after he had trouble getting bulky items down here that wouldn't fit through the door from the hall.

The same trap door that Eve had slipped through the day I had broken her collarbone and grandad's cane.

Cold sweat trickled between her shoulder blades, and Meredith blinked hard, trying to detach herself from the childhood images.

I wanted a spray of her perfume so badly I agreed to sit in the dark down here.

'Are you too scared, Meredith Moo?' Eve's voice said somewhere in the past.

The smell of lilies returned to the top step, and Meredith swayed, her eyes unable to focus, head spinning as memories flooded back. She closed her eyes and took some deep breaths. When she opened them, she was back in the past, sitting on the bottom step with dad's arms around her.

Everything will be okay, munchkin, I promise.

Meredith blinked back tears at the top of the steps.

'Nothing was okay dad, nothing.' She whispered. 'You promised, and even you weren't okay.'

She looked away from the cellar, away from the memories, taking a step back. Her gaze finding the staircase instead, the same yellow carpet, same fleur-de-lys pattern. Everything still the same as that day.

She saw herself at the top of the stairs, crouched against the bannister, hands over her ears as dad pushed Eve out of the room and mum raged. Tearing the room apart in much the same way she had while Meredith had been away this time.

Was it Eve's death that made the difference Meredith? Or was she already mentally ill?

Then she saw the curtain pole ripped from the wall, her mother, murder in her eyes, charging at Eve, dad jumping out of the line of fire with a shout. She saw herself rise with a scream, lunge at Eve, and push her out of the way. She saw her tumble down the stairs, saw the angle and stillness of every limb as her sister lay at the bottom. One foot draped up the bottom two steps.

The sickly yellow carpet, threadbare and broken as Eve.

Except the stairs in the castle dream were concrete, Meredith.

Meredith blinked, her own voice and another forgotten memory coming to her through the haze of her childhood.

Concrete?

The hallway spun and Meredith sank to her heels, putting her head into her hands. As she took slow breaths, she tried to remember the possession. The plush carpet of the castle, the fleur-de-lys pattern of the living room—same as the stairs to save money—mum and dad speaking about… her?

'It was an accident, leave her alone.'

Fleur-de-lys. It was carpet.

And then she remembered the stone steps of the tower going up. The flickering that drove her mad, and the stairs going down.

Concrete.

The steps of the dream possession had been concrete, the living room was the carpet.

There was a small thud from the cellar and Meredith snapped her eyes open. She was immediately back in the doorway.

The light from the cellar illuminating the space below.

Something had changed.

Sitting in the middle of the floor between the shelving and the stairs, innocent and unassuming, was Egor.

CHAPTER SIXTY SEVEN

'It's just a bear,' Meredith repeated to herself as she descended the steps down into the gloomy light, wringing her hands over each other. 'Just a teddy bear. Pretend it's Spookbuddy.'

Except you hated that bear as much as this one.

Well, not quite as much, she thought as she reached the bottom step, her heart thudding in her chest.

She eyed the bear, he looked grey, like he had got older over time, but as she peered at him, she saw it was only dust, covering the half of him that had been out of the box. Egor sat passive, still looking very much like a well-used old teddy bear that had been forgotten in a kid's toy chest.

So why don't you pick him up? Let's get out of this cellar. If this is what Eve wanted you to see, then let's get him and go.

She swallowed. She couldn't seem to move her feet another step.

What if the BAD MAN was...?

Was what, Meredith? She argued with herself. What if he was real? And was enticed from a small girl wearing a cape and a hair clip with a mirror and a blackjack sweet?

She hesitated, tongue flicking to wet her dry lips.

You know there's one way to check for sure. Just switch off the lights.

Meredith thought she had truly gone out of her own mind until she remembered the eyes. The BAD MAN's green eyes.

She rolled her own eyes at her stubborn childishness.

'There is no man Meredith,' she whispered to herself, 'get the bear and go, you're freaking me out.'

I should check first.

She wondered what could possibly be worse than being in a cold, dark, cellar where she had just seen the spirit of her dead sister.

Egor's eyes could glow?

She huffed a breath and climbed the steps.

'Could you be any more annoying?' She said to herself as she reached the door and pulled it close. Not shut.

Just in case.

Swallowing hard she turned out the light and let the darkness settle around her. She stared toward the bottom of the steps for twenty slow seconds that felt like years. Counting them out as she would have when she was younger.

One-elephant. Two-elephant. Three-elephant.

At twenty with no green glow from the bottom of the stairs she turned the light back on, scouted the room, dashed down the stairs, grabbed the bear by the paw in a plume and whirl of dust and ran back out of the cellar. Switching off the light and slamming the door with a bang.

Her heart thundered so wildly she thought she would faint. She leaned back against the door, Egor hanging heavy in her hand. She pulled him up and grabbed him around the waist, forcing herself to look at him.

'Okay Egor, I don't know why Eve wants you...'

She trailed off as she felt the mechanism inside his body. The surgery.

'Egor can listen now, Meredith' Eve's voice relayed in a distant time.

Egor can listen?

Meredith's mouth dropped open. She moved to the now spotless kitchen, and grabbed the kitchen scissors, taking them and the bear to the living room.

The atmosphere felt off, heavy and expectant. A tickle at the back of her neck making her shudder as she pressed the scissors to Eve's rudimentary stitching.

'Okay Eve, I think I finally get you.' She murmured, slicing through the loose stitching, and reaching a hand into Egor's back. All thoughts of the BAD MAN were gone now. Egor simply a teddy bear with ears.

Meredith slid out the Walkman, which seemed ancient in today's modern world. Twenty-five years ago, Eve had told Meredith this was the height of technology, a gadget of extraordinary powers.

How the heck does it read the TAPE, Evie? she remembered asking Eve the day she first got it. Eve had lent her an earphone to listen to the music. Eve had shrugged and smiled.

'Magic.' She said simply.

On the Walkman Meredith saw both the play and record buttons were pushed down. The tape inside had come to its end long ago, now static in its recording function. Frozen in time.

Meredith clicked the stop button and the play and record buttons jumped back out of position together, running flush with the rewind and fast forward. She pressed the rewind, but the tape sat still. Meredith rolled her eyes and slapped her head.

'Whoever heard of batteries lasting twenty-five years, idiot.'

She turned the machine over, removed the battery cover and took out the batteries. It was a homage to the dry cellar that there was only a bit of rust inside where the one battery had sat. She took the machine into the kitchen and cleaned the battery space with some tissue before replacing the batteries and throwing the old ones away.

The tension seemed to mount around her as she hovered a finger over the rewind button.

'Moment of truth.'

She pressed the button down firmly. It stuck with a click,

and the tape cassette inside began to spin, the brown tape disappearing from one side of the cassette wheels and filling the other quickly.

'Magic,' Meredith whispered with a smile. 'Well, okay, maybe just a gear mechanism.'

She pressed eject and the top of the machine rose revealing the cassette tape inside. It was a ninety, which meant an hour and thirty minutes of recording time if she remembered rightly. A short amount of time for Eve to be so concerned with her listening to it, a long amount of time to actually sit and listen. But listen she would. She owed that much to Eve.

She found some wired earbuds in the kitchen drawer and took the machine back into the living room, plugging the headphones into the socket. It was the only way to listen to the Walkman, they weren't made to be played aloud she remembered. She popped the earbuds into her ears and pressed play with shaking hands, watching as the wheels began to turn. A voice appeared immediately amidst the crackle of mild interference on the tape. Mum's voice.

fucking bear.

Meredith was so shocked that she turned off the cassette, pulled out the earbuds and found her phone. She opened her voicemails, playing the first one back.

Fucking bear. Same tone, same voice. Same lady.

Mum.

Skin crawling with goosebumps, Meredith realised that the voicemail must have been a copy of this recording. One mum had obviously recorded accidentally, when Egor had fallen at some point in the cellar.

Out of the corner of her eye, Meredith saw the heavy velour curtain shift, as though in a breeze. She shook her head firmly.

'Okay Eve, you have my attention, but no curtain, please.' she said quietly. The curtain fell still, and Meredith's heart calmed. She placed the earbuds back into her ears, blew out a long breath, and pressed play.

There was a further twenty minutes of crackling nothingness before what sounded like footsteps on concrete, the scraping of a box, and rustling on the shelves. No other noise until fifty minutes in.

Voices. Shouting. Far away.

Frowning, Meredith pushed the earbuds into her ears further, the argument must have been in the hallway, it didn't seem near enough to be anywhere by Egor.

She caught snippets of conversation, and then... Eve.

Meredith hit the stop button. Her heart hammered in the silence.

Eve. That was Eve. My Evie. My sister.

Eve. Speaking from the tape as though she were still here but trapped in time. Doomed to have this argument over and over again.

Her whole body shaking, Meredith pulled in some deep breaths, blinking back the tears.

It's okay, calm down. Just breathe.

When the shakes subsided, she pressed play again.

'I told you I'm not!' Eve screeched in the distance.

Still reeling from Eve's first appearance, Meredith ran a hand over her face, numb as her mum and sister continued to argue in a long-ago time.

'Liar... the bag... skipping school... leave?'

'No,' Eve yelled.

'What are you doing here... bag? No, you didn't think I'd... home... shit.'

Meredith swallowed hard. Her blood running cold as mum's voice rose to a shout, and all of the familiar childhood feelings rushed up to meet her. Feelings of being helpless, useless, powerless, terrified. Vulnerable. Like mum could squash any of them underfoot like a bug, and often tried to with Eve.

There was a bang, a yell.

Meredith flinched.

'Little bitch… here!'

There were more bangs, distant echoes. A scream and then a louder bang, followed by a chunkier thud. Meredith had heard this noise a thousand times—the cellar door banging off the wooden stair rail.

'The outside door is locked. You won't get anywhere down there.'

There was a grunt, followed by a bang.

'Leave me alone—this is why I'm leaving, you deranged bitch!'

Meredith gasped, her mouth falling open. She had never heard Eve say anything like it to their mother before, and knowing mum's temper, it wouldn't go down well either.

The voices were clearer now as the fight headed toward Egor's ears in the cellar. scuffling, a scream from Eve, and a series of thuds that could only be someone, or something, bouncing down the steps. There was an unearthly yell and then silence. Just the crackle of the tape.

Gasping heavy breaths that didn't seem to reach her lungs Meredith pressed the stop button and leaned forward to hang her head between her knees. She was shaking from top to toe, and if she didn't calm her breathing and heart rate, she knew she was in line for a panic attack.

Not only was the exchange as brutal as she remembered the fights being, but the feelings it produced in her made her feel six years old again. She wanted to crouch into a ball, push her hands over her ears, and yell for them to stop it.

As she pulled in deep breaths, concentrating on making the exhales as long as the inhales, she thought of the fight, trying to place her memories of the day alongside the recording.

Mrs Grey had given Meredith breakfast and taken her to school that morning. she had been packed off to their neighbour around thirty seconds after Eve had been pushed, when mum had finally lost all of her anger, and ran to her 'baby' lying at the foot of the stairs.

'The baby whose head you almost smashed in with the curtain pole that you ripped from her own wall.' She whispered with a shudder.

The point is, Meredith, mum mentions the bag. This must be the same morning, which means that Eve went to school too—and obviously came back home to grab the bag. Mum must have stayed home from work that day, probably nursing a headache from her foul temper, and Eve ran right into her when she least expected it.

Either way, Meredith knew that she wouldn't have seen her sister after school that day, but if mum had gone to work as usual, maybe she would have seen Eve again in the future.

The recording accidentally showed the pivot point. The fork in the road.

Meredith lift her head, blinking into the living room as a thought occurred to her.

'Eve went to school after me.' She breathed. A weight that felt like a hundred stacked houses suddenly lift from her shoulders and a sob escaped her lips. 'I didn't do it. It wasn't me. It was an accident after all. A fight when I wasn't there. Thank you, God, Thank you, God.'

She ran her hands over her face, wiping away drying sweat and tears. Cool air circulated around her shoulders and Meredith remembered that her sister had shown her the tape. If not for Eve, Meredith would probably never have even looked at Egor again, and certainly not listened to the tape if it was ever found.

'Thank you, Eve, I'm so grateful you showed me this. You don't know how grateful.'

Meredith felt a shift in the air around her and looked tentatively around the room. There was nothing out of place, no sign of Eve, and yet she felt as though she were being watched. She felt the prickle of her scalp, the raise of the hair on her arms, the mounting pressure... and then there was a loud click.

Meredith almost screamed as the crackle of the tape

filled her ears. She held a hand to her chest as she looked to the tape player.

Must have caught the play button, you idiot.

Just as she was about to flick it back off there was a scuffle, footsteps on concrete.

'Oh, get up Eve, stop the fucking dramatics.'

There was a moan, so small and low that Meredith rewound the tape and pressed play again with a frown.

Definitely a moan. Must be Eve, she was still alive? Oh shit, she was still alive.

Meredith felt her stomach spin over.

'The possession at Lynton showed the steps, surely that was cause of death?' She mumbled to herself.

A shift in air caressed her cheeks as the tape played on.

More scuffling, footsteps, a bang.

'Get the fuck up, I don't know what game you're playing, but it's pointless.'

There was more moaning, a large scuffle like something being dragged, and then a yell.

'Ooowww, no, please.'

Meredith felt a chill run down her spine. She closed her eyes with a shudder.

'I don't have time for this shit, get the hell up, and get to school, now.'

There was a moan that sounded like it may be mum. But mum was already winding up and Meredith had a sick feeling right into the bottom of her stomach. If Eve was already hurt, mum would only make it worse.

'Eve!' She screeched, so loud that it made Meredith flinch sitting here twenty-five years later. 'If you don't get up, I'll give you something to fucking lie down for. Get up you little shit.'

There was a moan and then she heard Eve, clear as the view on a sunny summer's day.

'Fuck you, mother.'

Meredith put her hands up to her head.

'No, Eve…' she half whispered.

She knew mum wouldn't need any further excuse, and then it came, each sickening thud bringing bile into Meredith's mouth.

Whoomph.

The noise sounded deep, almost bottomless hollow, as mum's fist connected with Eve somewhere only her sister would know. Egor only had ears, and right now Meredith had never been so glad. There was another low moan and Meredith began to sweat and shake on the settee, her nails digging small crescents into her palms from her clenched hands. She wanted to tell mum to stop, to leave Eve alone, but no matter what she said or did from here the outcome would be the same. Forever.

'GET.' Mum roared.

Whoomph.

'THE.'

Whoomph.

'FUCK.'

Whoomph.

'UP.'

Whoomph

'You vicious little slut. Why do you try to antagonise me? Always, Eve, it's always you! Get the fuck up!'

There was no response from Eve now, not even a moan.

There was a scuffle, and then mum again, lower this time.

'Eve? Eve? This is not the time to play dead, you are not a fucking mouse, get UP.'

'Eve?'

There was a shuffle, and a thud, a slap of a palm against skin.

Meredith's nails dug deeper into her palms, drawing blood. The pounding in her head matching her heart, beat for beat. She could do nothing but listen. Hopeless. Powerless. Useless. Just as she had always been.

'Eve?' Another slap, and then another voice, louder, the squeak of a door.

'Hey! Nancy, hey!'

Dad.

Meredith closed her eyes, breath catching in her throat, as silent tears rolled down her cheeks.

Oh, God, not only Eve but dad. What are you doing, Meredith? How much more of this can you take?

And yet she listened. For Eve. For Eve to be able to rest after such a brutal ordeal. If this is what it took, then she would do it to honour her sister. She would know the truth, as Eve had asked her to. She wiped at the tears which mingled with the blood on her hands and ran into the cuffs of her jumper.

On the tape there were quick footsteps on concrete. Heavier.

Dad must have come home from work too. Had he been tipped off? Had Mrs Grey heard something? If she did, she never said anything to me.

Slap.

Meredith's attention was forced back into the past.

'Hey! Leave her, Nancy, what the hell is going on? Is she okay?'

There was more scuffling.

'Caught her with the fucking bag—she was leaving. We had a little fight, she tried to leave through the garden door from down here, she fell down the steps, little shit.'

'Eve? Eve... Eve! Nancy, we need an ambulance.'

'No, she's fine.'

'She's bleeding.'

'I just told you, she fell down the fucking steps. She'll be fine, she's just knocked out again, I'm trying to bring her round.'

'From her mouth.'

'What?'

More scuffling, then...

'Nancy, she's bleeding from her *mouth*, call an ambulance. I don't think I can find a pulse.'

'What?'

'Now!'

'If there's no pulse, there's no point.'

Meredith's hand hit the Walkman. Everything stopped, including her heart as she gasped for air. Her stomach ached, her heart ached, her head ached. She thought she had never heard such nonchalance. It was as if mum didn't even care.

She was ill. She is ill.

How long is that going to be an excuse for abuse? For murder?

Before she lost her nerve Meredith pressed play again.

There was more scuffling, an angry grunt, and then the sound of dad in the hallway calling the ambulance. Not all of the conversation could be heard, but Meredith got the gist. She got it far too well. Mum just didn't care; or couldn't care.

The steps grew loud again, and dad's voice was back, shrill, higher pitched than Meredith had ever heard him.

'No! Nancy! Eve! Don't turn her, I've called an ambulance. Leave her alone. Leave her.'

Dad wept loudly on the tape, joining Meredith's tears twenty-five years later, in the living room of the same house, recounting something that happened only feet away from her.

'I told you it would come to this, Nancy. You should have changed the goddamn pills. Why didn't you change the goddamn pills for something stronger? Why didn't you tell the doctor how bad things were? Look what you've done.'

His voice cracked and broke, and in turn that broke Meredith. She sobbed as mum's nonchalance continued in the cellar all those years ago.

'Don't blame me, I didn't touch her.'

'I saw you.'

'I didn't touch her, she fell.'

'You get angry, Nancy. I saw you.'

'She fell. It was an accident.'

'She has no pulse, Nancy. She's not getting up. Dear lord, my baby isn't getting up. Where's the goddamn ambulance!'

'They'll take Meredith away.'

In the living room Meredith sniffed and frowned.

What?

'What?' Dad asked in the cellar.

'They'll take Meredith.'

'They won't—'

'They'll take her, she pushed her. She pushed her down the stairs!'

'You're confused, Nancy. That was earlier.'

More scrapes and a bang

'Nancy!'

'Don't blame Meredith, it was an accident.'

'I'm not blaming Meredith… ow, for Christ's sake. Nancy that's enough, calm down.'

'It was a bloody accident! Leave it! Leave her… Leave her alone, she didn't mean it. She didn't mean it. She didn't mean it.'

In the cellar mum began to wail.

'Nancy.' Dad's voice was tentative.

'They'll take her away. They'll take her away. They'll take me away.'

More scrapes, another sob.

'They won't. Let's just get Eve seen to, we'll talk about it later. maybe they can do something.'

'They'll blame me.'

More scuffling.

'Why would they?'

'They will, they'll take me away.'

'Nancy you just said what happened. You caught her leaving. She fell. It was an accident, let's just leave it at that for now, please.'

'We had a fight, she fell, that's right, isn't it?'

'That's right. That's right. Eve, oh God my poor darling baby, God, Nancy, look at her.'

'We had a fight, she fell.'

'Yes, that's right, Nancy, she fell.'

'Oh, God, Graham, she fell. My poor, poor baby! She fell!'

'She fell.' Dad said, his voice breaking into hard sobs. This time mum's sobs finally joined him.

Meredith sat vacant in the living room, tears streaming down her cheeks.

Mum was ill.

Mum killed Eve.

It was an accident.

It was murder.

Dad helped mum.

Mum killed dad.

Dad killed himself.

Dad couldn't take the truth.

Mum was broken.

Mum broke... me.

Eve is dead.

I'm broken.

I know the truth.

Mum.

On the tape the sounds of the ambulance crew as they got to work, and then the sounds stopped, and the Walkman clicked off.

Meredith flinched, put her head in her hands and sobbed.

EPILOGUE

EIGHTEEN MONTHS LATER.

Meredith drummed her fingers on the windowsill as she craned her neck to check up and down the street. Her heart was thumping double time with both excitement and anxiousness. If he didn't hurry, they would be late; if he didn't hurry, she would barely get a hello before they had to get out of here, and Matt had been gone too long. She was desperate to see him, desperate to hear his voice, feel his soft full lips, feel his arms wrap around her tight, feel the warmth of his skin against hers...

Okay, Meredith, cut it out, definitely no time for that before we leave.

There was a small tick in the hallway and Meredith swung her head to the door of the living room. She listened to the quiet of the house, only realising she was holding her breath when she had to let it out to talk.

'Eve?' Meredith said, checking for the subtle changes that had always accompanied her sister's spirit. The room remained warm and comfortable. No feelings of unease, change in the air, or temperature surrounded her.

Wishful thinking.

She felt her shoulders sag, and yet, she had to check.

She left the living room, glancing up the stairs as she passed, and rounding the hallway to the front door.

'Eve?'

That was when she saw the envelope sitting on the floor. The postman had been hours earlier, it had obviously been hanging onto this side of the letterbox all this time and had finally let go.

The house was still and quiet. Meredith felt deflated, sadness pulled at her heart as she stared at the envelope. The sense of loss still hurt, even after all this time since Eve had been seen or heard.

Don't be ridiculous, Meredith, it's good that she's at rest.

There had been no contact with Eve since finding the tape that fateful day. Meredith had even tried to call her forward, to see if she had done the right thing, the best thing, but there had been no response. The only oddity was a dream five days later where Eve simply smiled at her, saying nothing. It had been a strange dream, but Meredith had woken feeling warm and fuzzy, totally connected to Eve, ready to communicate, ready to see her sister. And then... nothing.

Meredith sniffed, shook the thoughts away and picked up the mail. Nothing important. She placed it on the kitchen table and moved back to the living room window, trying to focus on Matt, and instead finding Eve and the tape running through her mind.

After listening to the tape Meredith had spoken to the doctor at the hospital. She didn't know what she wanted to do with the evidence, and she wasn't sure what Eve had wanted her to do either, but since the day she had found and played the tape there had been no sign of her sister. None. Maybe she had just wanted Meredith to know what had really happened, to know the truth. Maybe now mum was in the asylum she had got her comeuppance already, maybe that was enough for Eve.

Maybe, but Meredith needed further reassurance of what she was supposed to do.

The doctor had only cemented her initial thoughts. He listened to the tape but advised that it wasn't concrete proof that the fall hadn't killed Eve. The damage could have been done initially, and she could have died from injuries caused by the fall. He agreed that it could have exacerbated her mum's mental problems if she had, or if she believed she had killed Eve, but there was no proof that what they had listened to was a murder. He explained that mum was still incoherent, had been since Meredith found her, she spent her days chanting religious passages over and over, while clutching the rosary.

Initially, Meredith had found this strange from a non-religious woman. It worried her that her own religious schooling had sent her mad. There was only one living relative who may know anything, so Meredith had tracked her down, although she hadn't had contact with her aunt since her dad's suicide. Auntie Jean blamed mum for the whole mess, and so she had stayed away, but she had known that a strict religious upbringing, and an unplanned pregnancy had cast Nancy Wallace from her family home and thrown her into the path of her brother Graham knight. The rest was history Meredith knew, although finding Eve was only a half-sister, was as devastating as it was surprising. With a little more piecing together she finally understood why mum had turned her back on religion, much like her family had turned their back on her, and why she had beaten up on Eve as the child that had caused problems between herself and her own parents. She was also the child that hadn't been to a religious school as Meredith had. Not that any of this was Eve's fault, and not that all of it wasn't speculation.

The doctor had also added that Eve's death was officially an accident, a closed case, and mum was too ill to be put through a trial either way. It was Meredith's choice. Did she want to do anything with the allegations?

His words said it was a choice, but his point was clear.

From mum's point of view nothing would come of it. She was unable to speak for herself or defend herself. All Meredith would get was upset and upheaval. She would be the only one left to answer any questions. Had she even been there at the time? How could a six-year-old be expected to remember details with any accuracy twenty-five years later, even if she had been there. The ambulance crew had assessed Eve at the scene, it was determined that she had died from the fall. It would be a hard slog to prove anything different, especially as the tape wasn't conclusive evidence, and was there any point in dragging up the past?'

No, Meredith had agreed. It did seem ludicrous, and as Eve seemed to be out of her torment now, there wasn't a point. And so, she had let it go. Mum was suffering enough, the drugs weren't working, she would spend her life committed the doctor said. She was already in a jail of her own making.

What goes around comes around.

The positive was that Eve was finally at rest. Egor had done his duty, and Meredith felt she had mourned the loss of her sister all over again. However terrifying the curtains had been at night, she almost longed for her sister's form to push them forward again. She now slept with the curtains closed, hoping for a wake-up call, but getting none. No voicemails, no smell of lilies, no moving curtains, not even a cold spot.

Meredith chewed her lip and looked to the clock on the wall of the living room. 7.42pm.

Late. We'll be late, it's a fifteen-minute drive from here.

She looked at her bag on the floor next to her, mentally checking the things inside. It was always packed ready these days though; she knew she had everything they would need. She went back to drumming her fingers on the windowsill, and then the car pulled up outside.

Meredith grinned, and her stomach flipped over. No time for hello, but at least they may make it by the skin of their teeth.

Picking up the bag, she grabbed her phone and keys and left the house, locking the door behind her. She jogged down the path as Matt got out of the car and opened the boot for her to throw the bag in. Then they were both back inside, and Matt was performing a manic three-point turn, before she had even fastened the seatbelt.

'Hi, beautiful.' He smiled when they were finally on their way.

'Hi,' she grinned back at him, worry of being late dropping away at the sight of him. 'Trouble on the roads?'

He knocked the heating down in the warm car and shook his head at her.

'You have no idea. Accident on the M20. Two hours of pure hell. I'm so sorry. I wanted to be here at least an hour earlier.'

'Don't worry about it,' she said, placing a hand on his thigh as he drove. 'We'll be fine. I would have messaged Steve and Helen if you'd been ten minutes more, they could have gone in to explain.'

Matt picked up her hand and kissed it, holding it as he drove, much like he had on the way to the airport to face her future all that time ago.

'I wanted to get back to spend some time with you. I'm truly pissed off right now.'

She reached to touch his cheek.

'Don't be. It's all good. How was your mum?'

He finally seemed to relax as he smiled at her.

'Really good, it's amazing what a little freedom does, you know. She's truly been catching up with all she's missed, she even has a new man. She's so happy, Meredith. She's a different woman.' He turned to look at her. 'Very much like you. Both ladies in my life are thriving, nothing makes me happier.'

'Maybe it's because we both have you.' She said squeezing his hand.

It still amazed Meredith how they had all come back together, especially when four months passed with no contact from her side. She had been busy trying to get her head around what had happened with Eve for the first few weeks and had spent the next few in a fog of tears, before trying to pick herself up and move forward with a life that she had to make from scratch. Because without her mum home, she suddenly realised just how much time she had on her hands, and just how much life of her own she didn't have.

That had changed when Matt had turned up on the doorstep, looking nervous and fidgety. Hands stuffed in his jean's pockets.

'Hey, sorry to drop in on you. I just wanted to make sure you were okay. You've not returned any of my messages or calls for weeks. If it were just me, I'd think you weren't interested, but it's all of us, which only makes me more worried. I badgered Kevin for your address. I'm sorry, I know it was overstepping the mark, Meredith, I just had to see you. If you want me to go, I'll go, just tell me you're okay and I'll leave.'

Meredith had no intention of saying any such thing. She had simply stepped into his arms, where an embarrassingly large barrage of tears sprung from nowhere. After lifting a hand to Mrs Grey, who had been tending her garden next door and had turned to watch, she brought him inside, where she had blubbered her way through the whole ordeal. From faking her degree, to Eve's presence, to mum being not only a drunk, but mentally ill, to finding she may have killed Eve.

If Matt wanted to judge her by her family, her mum's run-down house and surroundings, and run a mile, so be it. Meredith decided that it told her more about him than her. As it happened, he had held her tighter, made her a drink and sat listening quietly, holding onto her hand, until she had talked it all through. He hadn't judged, he hadn't mentioned therapy, hadn't mentioned her needing help, he even told her he thought she had done the right thing with the information from the tape.

After that he had called work to tell them he was sick, something she knew he didn't take lightly, and spent the next six days and nights with her. Letting her talk things through, letting her cry, making her food, making her laugh, doing the shopping, doing the cleaning. Doing what he was good at: taking charge, and generally holding her upright. After that it was back to work, but from that week on, they were almost inseparable. Every free moment Matt had he spent with her, and finally Steve and Helen, who were now renting a house only fifteen minutes from Meredith, began to join them for pizza and movie nights too.

A house that had been filled with violence, anger, illness, and death for far too long, finally began to come alive, and feel like a home, as laughter and love rang around the rooms.

During those evenings, a seed that had been planted in Scotland was batted around. Helen was living off student loans, doing a business degree for her parent's benefit, and hating every minute. Steve and Matt had lost the regularity of working together, and with the retirement of Kevin Spalding, both had quit. Steve had gone into web building but missed the buzz and travel of television, and Matt went freelance for a while, but hated the time it took him away from Meredith when he was on location.

The more they spoke, the more serious the idea got, until 'The Ghost Connection' was finally born. A You Tube channel dedicated to finding REAL evidence of the paranormal. After the concept had been thrashed out, they fell into their roles like clockwork. It was seamless. Fate. And it moved fast.

Before the shoot in Scotland Meredith had been terrified of speaking to the dead, now she enjoyed any interaction she got. Now, she was interested in their stories and providing real proof to the 1.7 million You Tube subscribers that they had gained on their channel in just the first year. Between them they made a good team, Meredith good with organisation and being head of house, enjoyed overseeing the whole business, getting the bookings in, and taking care of relations, social media, and emails. Helen dropped out of her business degree to take a bookkeeping and finance course and found a passion for helping to keep track of the incomings and outgoings of the new company. The spreadsheets she had compiled were intricate, with every financial avenue covered, and she could spew figures on command faster than a calculator, which earned her some ribbing from Steve, and a new nickname. Abacus.

The technological side was left to Matt and Steve. Steve had built them a phenomenally spooky interactive website, incorporating all their idea's perfectly, and getting it to run seamlessly to their specification. He was also good at finding pioneering gadgets to spend their money on, and somehow his bad jokes at timely intervals seemed to endear him to their watchers, who were quickly turning them into catch phrases.

Matt's personable connection skills and flair for editing and marketing was the only reason that they had managed to get their footage in front of so many of the right eyes so quickly. He was a clever communicator, managing to hook the group up with more prominent ghost hunting crews for joint shoots, getting valuable eyes on them through other people's platforms. He was also good at keeping the group in line and assessing their ideas with logic that stopped them getting carried away. Without him, Meredith thought, they would have run the company into the ground more than once.

After only eight months of setting up the phenomenon that was The Ghost Connection, Meredith had offered the house as headquarters. It was getting harder to meet up between day jobs, especially when a run left everyone tired and argumentative. The house was too large for a single person, especially when it was looking less and less likely that mum would ever be released, in Meredith's mind it was a no-brainer. A solution that could just as easily be undone if mum ever did make it home.

Having the house was a godsend. When they were tired or pulling late nights, which was often, the bedrooms were utilised. Time outs were easily scheduled when things got heated around the coffee table, and the pressure of not having to travel at the end of a session enabled them to work over a two or three-day period without the commute. It was useful for Steve's ideas at two in the morning when he got everyone up to explain a new gadget. It also felt nice to get some activity back into the house.

Not long after, the show gathered so much momentum that they left their day jobs to keep the company expanding. Steve added to his income with freelance website design, Matt also went freelance, this time with a small course in online marketing, which almost took care of itself through his many marketing 'funnels'. Helen finally gained some independence from her parents—who were none too pleased with the path she was taking—and took on some bookkeeping for others. With no mortgage, no car, and little spending on necessities Meredith managed to keep at the company full time on the small wage they each took from the show.

One by one they had dropped their part time side hustles to join her, and as of three months ago they were all full-time professional ghost hunters. On the road most of the time, in strange and unusual places, sometimes with strange and unusual people, recording new footage a few times per week.

It was gruelling, but breaks were scheduled every eight weeks to enable them to kick back for a week, chill out, eat crap, knock around ideas and update anything that wasn't working. It was a working break more often than not, but time at home was precious when you were away so much. All of them agreed that they were working their dream job with their best friends, and they made a pact that if that ever changed, they would look where they could make change in the company first. Their friendship was worth more. It was hard work, and often testing, but it was fun. Meredith thought she had never laughed as much as she did now.

Tonight, they were trying something new, combining recording with a Facebook live that would be uploaded, as it stood, to their channel and other social media platforms afterward.

Meredith was adamant that she wanted everything to be as authentic as it could be for the viewer, and for them. She was steadfast that they didn't fake anything. In fact, that was one of their company values and promises, and Meredith learned that Kevin was wrong… people did care about real as much as the drama, especially if Steve stuck a few bad jokes into the quiet.

Even so, they always had a disclaimer in the description. Each video was carefully edited to produce varied footage of the building or place they were at (the spookier the better), interviews with the owners, or just a short history of the building and a video tour locating all of the haunted areas. If there was little activity, they would state the activity with a time stamp in the descriptions, but they made sure each show was no more than an hour. They had made the mistake of uploading a longer video with not much activity, early on, which got slaughtered by viewers calling it a waste of time. It was the only time Meredith questioned her ethics and whether Kevin was right after all.

If they were blessed with a lot of activity, they would upload in parts over a few weeks, the tension had people queuing up for views on the day of upload. One of Matts stellar ideas, as he advertised the hell out of the new video during the week, using footage from the first video. It was a double win that always paid off. People would watch the first one if they hadn't already, subscribe, and then wait for the next. They were quickly getting a reputation for being authentic, and it was drawing them a lot of attention.

Tonight's hotel was like gold for the crew, such a famously haunted location was always a treat, but as Matt flicked the indicator and turned onto the car park Meredith wrinkled her nose. It didn't look imposing; it didn't even look as big as the photographs suggested. The building was square and grey. The windows symmetrical and long. A two-column porch stood over wooden doors at the top of the central steps. It was a little after 8pm, and the dull spring day was just starting to wane, the imposing building casting long shadows as little carriage lights flicked on at the entrance.

Even that didn't look eerie.

'What's with the look?' Matt said with a laugh.

'It doesn't look haunted.' she said, peering through the windscreen at the Georgian mansion.

Matt raised an eyebrow as he pulled into a space and turned off the engine.

'I remember you saying that about some castle up in Scotland once,' he said looking at her. 'Just days before you were possessed by a small girl.'

Meredith narrowed her eyes with a nod. 'Good point. Shouldn't judge a book by its cover.'

Matt laughed. 'You should know better by now.' He turned to look at her with a contented sigh and reached a hand to massage the back of her neck. 'God, it's so good to see you, Meredith, I've missed you.'

She grinned, placing her hand on his thigh with a squeeze. 'You've been away for two days.' She said, purposely omitting the intense feeling she'd had at home waiting for him to get there.

'Two days too long. Next time you're coming with me.'

'Uh oh, that means I'll have to meet the family.'

He smiled and leaned across the seat to kiss her. Electricity ran through her as his warm soft lips met hers, but they had barely begun when there was a banging on the car window. She broke away, rolling her eyes, and brought a finger up to his lips even as her own tingled with longing.

'Hold that thought, the cavalry's here.'

'Bad timing,' he said with a sigh.

Meredith grinned at Steve through the driver's side window. The black t-shirt he had chosen today simply stated 'my ghost is better than your ghost.'

'No time for that, lovebirds, we have a ghost to hunt,' he shouted tapping his finger on his watch. Helen gave a little wave just behind him and Meredith felt the familiar flutter of nerves and excitement that she always got before a shoot with these three, amazing people.

Matt stretched across to open her door before getting out of his own and moving to the boot. Between the four of them they began grabbing the equipment that had put them all out of pocket back when they first started up on their own, banter and laughs already in full flow. Meredith stood back as they crowded the boot space, listening to them with a surge of affection.

Nothing in the world could match the feeling she had right now. It was worlds apart from where she had been just two years ago. Back when she'd had a job in the local post office, no time for friends, an abusive alcoholic mother who was getting dry for the third time, a dead sister who was terrifying her each night, and certainly no time to think about earning a living pursuing something she loved.

Mainly because she hadn't known she loved this until she had done it, and for that chance she only had one person to thank.

Kevin Spalding. Asshole extraordinaire—who didn't turn out to be so bad in the end.

Meredith grinned as she watched her partners in crime, including a man she loved intensely with all her heart. She realised without Kevin Spalding and his taking a chance on her, she would have known none of them.

Double thanks, Kev. You were a complete pain in the ass, but you changed my life, for that I will be forever grateful.

'Meredith?'

Meredith blinked and looked to Matt. 'What?'

'The bag,' he said, holding it out to her with a laugh.

She rolled her eyes with a smile.

'Sorry,' she said, taking it from him.

He turned to shut the boot and lock the car as Steve adopted a low narrator drawl, dropping his head and looking up from under his eyebrows.

'It's 8pm, at the Manor Hotel, and already Meredith is

taken over by the menacing forces that inhabit these dark walls. What unearthly—'

'I was just daydreaming, chill out.' she said, raising an eyebrow as she hoisted the bag onto her back with a grin.

Steve immediately shook off the persona, lifting his head, and holding out a hand.

'False alarm, everyone, she's fine. Keep the water in the tap.'

Helen giggled and knocked him with her shoulder playfully as they all laughed.

'Thanks for that Steve,' Meredith said, 'I now have to go in there all serious and introduce us as professionals without cracking my face.'

'And explain to them that their building doesn't look haunted, even though it's had celebrity crews running for the hills,' Matt added.

'She didn't.' Steve said, his mouth dropping open.

'She did.' Matt nodded.

'Oh, my days, better fill that jug with water, looks like we may need it after all.'

'I kind of agree,' Helen said, looking to Meredith, 'I'd happily stay the night, so far.'

Meredith nodded. 'See?' she said, looking to the men.

'I'm getting déjà vu,' Matt said looking at his watch with a grin as Steve let out a groan and shook his head into his hands. 'Okay, guys, it's nearly ten past, we all ready to go?'

'Ready,' Steve and Helen said together.

'Yep,' Meredith said with a nod of her head.

'Then let's go catch us some ghosts.'

THE END.

If you enjoyed this book it would be fantastic if you could leave a review.

Reviews help to bring my books to the attention of other readers who may enjoy them too.
Help spread the joy… or indeed, the fear!

Thank you!

**Enjoyed this book? Check out the previous release by
Rebecca Guy available at all major retailers now!**

RUIN

She will have to enter the darkness to find the light.

Darkness. Paranoia. Isolation.

Determined to start a new life as far from her shattered marriage as
possible Emmie Landers purchases 'Bruadair' – an isolated ruin in
the highlands of Scotland. A place where children are safe and
angry fathers are absent.

But safe is not a word that applies to Bruadair. This is a place of
uneasy darkness, where a deep cold penetrates the walls, shadows
linger, and the intense feeling of being watched leaves Emmie
unnerved. To add to her unease, chilling photographs of the family,
her family, are appearing in odd places around the house, and three-
year-old Grace is talking to empty rooms.

Down in Surrey, Scott Harvington is whipping up a storm. Furious
that Emmie should get to start over so easily, he is determined to
hunt her down and force her to face the consequences of tearing
apart his family. She ruined his life, and now he will ruin hers. Hell
bent on revenge, he is resolute. He will reunite his family – at
whatever cost.

As events spiral out of control, Bruadair's secret is blown open
with devastating consequences. Mentally broken, Emmie must face
her worst fears as the full force of a terrifying past ensures the
family's future is destroyed beyond repair.

Ruin.

Visit www.rebeccaguy.co.uk for more information.

What readers are saying about Ruin

A story of love, loss and suspense that will give you chills. A fabulous spooky read that you will struggle to put down!

*****

My emotions were on a roll, scared, wanting more, anxious, frightened, CRYING, and happy. BRILLIANT story, great imagination.

*****

Sooo creepy, sad and happy. A real page turner, kept me guessing right up to the end.

*****

My heart jumped out of my chest so many times… really had me gripped

*****

Creepy, atmospheric, and fast paced. I would never have guessed the twist at the end!

What readers are saying about Shattered.

If you like a psychological thriller, I promise you will love Shattered!

*****

Had me captivated throughout, highly recommend this book to the readers, who like books with a twist.

*****

OMG another fantastic read. Keeps you gripped, on the edge of your seat, you feel like you're one of the characters. I could not put this book down.

*****

Shattered shows how life can pull the rug from underneath everything you know and plunge you into a world of distrust and confusion. Well worth a read!

*****

From the 1st page, I was hooked, and kept finding spare minutes so I could sit and read Shattered, I so wanted it to end, but I didn't want it to finish!!

CPSIA information can be obtained
at www.ICGtesting.com
Printed in the USA
LVHW052128210921
698349LV00007B/273